After the Roses

Shayne Parkinson

ISBN 978-1517375836

First print edition published 2015.

This paperback edition printed through Createspace.

Other titles by Shayne Parkinson:

Sentence of Marriage (*Promises to Keep*, Book 1)
Mud and Gold (*Promises to Keep*, Book 2)
Settling the Account (*Promises to Keep*, Book 3)
A Second Chance (the sequel to *Promises to Keep*)
Daisy's War (*Daisy*, Book 1)

Family trees and some extra background to the book's setting may be found at:
www.shayneparkinson.com

Chapter One

November 1918

Sunlight turned the valley green-gold on the day Daisy's father came home. Her room still held a trace of the sun's warmth when she slipped into bed that night, a freshly washed pillowcase smooth and crisp against her skin. She drifted off to the murmur of voices through the wall, her father's deep tones blending with her mother's higher pitch to make the loveliest of music. When the first daylight crept through a chink in her curtains, Daisy woke to the glorious knowledge that was better than any dream could be: her father was home, and the war was over.

The three of them did the morning milking together; breakfasted together; walked to the horse paddock and cart shed together. Daisy watched her father heft the load of milk onto the spring cart, each of the tall metal cans that she and her mother could barely shift between them lifted as easily as if it were empty. She stood at her mother's side as they waved him off down the farm track, reluctant to let him out of their sight even for his trip to the dairy factory.

The factory visit took less time than Daisy had expected. A batch of scones was still cooling on a rack when they heard the rattle of the cart again, its rhythm telling Daisy that the horse was going at a brisk trot. A few minutes later her father came into the kitchen, strode over to the bench, and kissed them both.

'Those smell good,' he said, reaching for a scone.

Daisy's mother slapped his hand away. 'Wait till I've finished buttering it, Davie! You can't be that hungry, not after what you ate at breakfast.'

'Well, I am a bit. And I've missed your scones.' He cast a longing look at the laden plate as he pulled out a chair.

Her mother slathered butter on the last few scones, and Daisy spooned jam onto the centre of each one. They joined him at the table, a cup of tea steaming in front of each place setting and the plate of scones in the middle. Her father took a scone, which disappeared in two bites. Daisy picked up one for herself and ate it more carefully, savouring the feel of warm butter and tart strawberry jam melting on her tongue, the scone base soft and fluffy. Fresh baking was one of the many tasks she and her mother had been forced to let slip while they were running the farm on their own.

'You weren't long at the factory,' her mother said. 'We didn't think you'd be back for a while yet.'

'I made sure I didn't get talking to anyone—just your pa, and he was keen to get home, too. Oh, that's right, he said to tell you your ma says we're to go down there for lunch.'

People generally did as Daisy's grandmother told them. They arrived at Grandma's well in time for the midday meal, and Grandma herself stood in the doorway to call them inside. She had left her stays off that day, Daisy noticed when she was enfolded in a soft, squishy hug.

Grandma held on to Papa for a little longer than she did Daisy and her mother. 'I'm glad you're home, Dave.' She stepped back from him and took a handkerchief from her sleeve to dab at her eyes. 'Now, sit down and we can get on with it before the potatoes get cold.'

Daisy sat between her parents on the bench that ran along one side of the table, with Benjy, Kate and Aunt Maisie opposite them. She looked up from her plate to see Grandpa and Grandma smiling around at them all.

'It's good to see a decent crowd at the table again, eh?' Grandpa said. His three grown-up sons were all still on the other side of the world, waiting for a ship home from Europe.

Grandma nodded. 'Yes, it doesn't seem right, just the five of us. The place feels empty without those boys—and I'm still cooking too much half the time.'

'Shouldn't be too long now till they're on their way back. There's that many chaps over there, though, I suppose they'll need a fair few boats back and forth.'

'Well, the sooner they're back the better,' Grandma said.

'I'll say,' Aunt Maisie agreed.

The conversation among the adults shifted to discussion of the dairy factory and the weather, and family news that Daisy had already heard. She gave her attention to the roast mutton and vegetables before her.

'Did you hear they've closed the school up for the year, Dave?' Grandpa said, startling Daisy. 'Mr Connor said something about it down at the factory this morning, but I think you'd got away by then. His boy told him when he came home yesterday.'

'No, I didn't hear anything about that,' Daisy's father said, frowning. Daisy saw her parents exchange a glance.

'Are you sure, Pa?' her mother asked. 'It's only November, school shouldn't be finishing for ages yet. Mr Connor might've got it muddled somehow.'

'No, it's closed all right,' Grandpa said. 'I sent Benjy down to the school when I got back from the factory, to see what was going on.'

'Yes, and Miss Cameron was there on her own, packing up all the stuff,' Benjy said. 'I stayed and helped her for a bit. She told me it's

4

because of the flu going around—she reckons it's bad in the big places like Auckland, so they're making all the schools close early.'

'Oh, that's a shame, when Daisy was all set to go back,' Daisy's mother said. 'I don't know what that's got to do with our school, though, just because of people being sick in Auckland.'

Benjy shrugged. 'Well, that's what Miss Cameron said. She got a letter from the people up in Auckland, and they told her she had to close it.'

'I don't think Aunt Amy's said much about the flu up there in her letters—she might have said something about making up baskets of food for people who were poorly, but I think that was about it. Daisy, has Eddie mentioned anything about it to you?'

Daisy shook her head. 'No, except he's been helping with taking food to people. He hasn't said if his school's been closed up, either.' Her cousin's last letter had been shorter than usual, barely covering one page, and mostly concerned with talk of the Armistice celebrations in Auckland as well as good wishes on her father's return.

'Well, it can't be too bad, then, or one of them would've said about it. Don't you think so, Davie?'

'That's probably right,' Daisy's father said, but she noticed a thoughtful expression pass over his face at all this talk of flu, as if he knew more about it than he was willing to say.

Grandma piled more potatoes onto Benjy's plate, which Aunt Maisie had already replenished. 'Well, I think it's a jolly good idea,' she said. 'We're all topsy-turvy with half the men still away and everyone busy on the farms. And it's not as if Benjy can go back to school, anyway, not until the other boys are home to help your father.'

'I think I've got enough, thanks, Ma,' Benjy said. He sent a grin in Daisy's direction; Grandma was inclined to worry that Benjy might somehow go hungry, despite there never being any shortage of good food at her table. 'As long as they're back by February, I'll be all right for when school starts up again.'

His older sister Kate reached over to help herself to the potatoes. 'Don't worry, Benjy, I don't mind doing your milking for a bit if the boys don't get back till after school starts. You can help with the dishes to pay me back.' She gave his shoulder a playful poke. 'Not to mention peeling some of the potatoes.'

Mama put her hand over Daisy's and squeezed. 'February will come round soon enough, love,' she said quietly.

'I know.' Daisy managed a smile. 'It's all right—it'll be good to have the time at home with Papa.' Which was true enough; though it did not quite soften the sharp reminder that even with her father home safe and sound the world could still deliver disappointments.

5

'I think I might go down to the school and see if Miss Cameron's there,' Daisy said next morning over breakfast. 'I'd like to hear it from her about the school closing and everything, just in case there's been a mix-up.'

'I'll give you a ride down on my way to the factory if you're ready quick enough,' her father said.

Daisy hurriedly changed into a clean dress and brushed her hair, and by the time her father brought the cart around she was waiting at the garden gate. He leaned over to give her a hand up to the cart's seat, and Daisy slid along to press against him, her arm linked though his.

'Looks like she's there,' her father said when they drew near the school and saw the teacher's gig; Miss Cameron's horse was grazing in the school's small paddock. Papa drew the cart to a halt, and Daisy climbed down from the seat. 'I'll pick you up on my way back if you're still here then.'

Daisy crossed the patch of rough grass to the schoolroom. Miss Cameron waved through the open window, and a moment later appeared in the doorway.

'Daisy, I'm so pleased to see you! You'd better not come in just yet, though, I seem to have stirred up the dust. Let's sit out here while it clears.'

She came down the few steps and sat beside Daisy on a low bench in front of the school. 'I'd been thinking of calling on your family this morning once I'd finished tidying up here, but it's taken rather longer than I expected—I must be slow today.' She slid her spectacles down her nose and pressed a finger to the corner of each eye for a few moments before pushing the spectacles back into place. Daisy noticed that her eyes were red, and the skin around them looked swollen. She leaned back against the wall, as if sitting upright was too much trouble.

'So school's really finished for the year?' Daisy asked.

'Yes, I've decided to follow the rules at last.' Miss Cameron smiled at what Daisy knew must be a look of confusion on her own face. 'I must confess that I've been something of a rebel, Daisy. The instructions came from Auckland earlier this month that all the schools were to close at once, but I took it upon myself to leave ours open.'

'Benjy said it's because of the flu, but there's flu most years, isn't there? I don't think they've ever closed the schools over it.'

'No, but it's not usually as severe as this one seems to be. I gather you haven't been following the news in the papers recently?'

'Only things about the war. We've been busy on the farm, Mama and I, and... well, the war was the only thing that seemed to matter.'

'Of course it was. The flu's really quite severe in the cities, but we've been lucky in Ruatane so far, it hasn't been as bad here yet. It's the war that's turned our lives upside-down—your family's as much as anyone's. That's why I made the decision to keep the school open for as long as possible, and just hope that the Education Board in Auckland wouldn't find out. I'm sure the Board has better things to do than to check up on every single school in the country. There was so little I could do to help while the war was on, but I thought perhaps I could give the children some stability—just a scrap of normalcy to hold on to. Does that make any sense?'

'Of course you make sense, Miss Cameron. Yes, I think I see what you mean. It was good you could do that.'

'I'm just sorry I couldn't keep it open long enough for you to come back to school. I hope you're not too disappointed, but I don't think I can risk my small act of defiance any longer, or the authorities really will catch up with me.' The corners of her mouth turned up as she said it, but even that small movement seemed to take an effort.

Daisy had never seen her teacher looking so tired, and she was careful to keep any trace of disappointment or complaint out of her own voice. 'No, it's all right—Papa's back, and that's the main thing. February's soon enough to start school again.'

'Yes, we'll all be settled and back to normal by then, I'm sure.' Miss Cameron pressed her hands against the wooden bench and got slowly to her feet. 'I'd really better get back to work or I'll never get this finished.'

'Can I help you with it?' Daisy asked.

Miss Cameron shook her head. 'It's good of you to offer, but you'd better not come inside. I've quite a sore throat—it must be from the dust, and I wouldn't want you to get one as well.' She paused at the foot of the steps; Daisy saw her hand tremble a little where she gripped the rail. 'In fact I'm not sure that I'll stay any longer myself. I might just gather up the most important of the paperwork and take it with me—it's mostly the logbooks and rolls, I need to finish writing up the final records for the year so I can send them off to the Board, and I can do that just as well at home.'

She accepted Daisy's offer to catch the horse for her, and Daisy had it harnessed to the gig by the time Miss Cameron came back outside with a bundle of folders and notebooks, which she was stuffing into her leather satchel.

'Please give my regards to your mother, and tell Mrs Stewart I hope to call on her later in the week,' Miss Cameron said, tucking the satchel under the gig's seat. She placed a foot on the step, but made no move to hoist herself any higher. 'It's rather fortunate, really, that school's finished

7

for the year, I feel ready for a rest. And I've a friend who's just come over from Tauranga to visit—I haven't been a very good hostess so far, but I'll be better company for her now.'

Daisy helped her up to the gig with a hand under one elbow, concerned that her teacher might be a little too unsteady to manage on her own. 'Have a nice holiday with your friend, Miss Cameron. I'm glad you're going to have a good, long break from school.'

'Thank you, dear.' Miss Cameron coughed, and grimaced. 'It's odd, I didn't notice so very much dust inside, but my throat feels quite raw. I'm looking forward to a nice hot cup of tea when I get home, and perhaps putting my feet up.'

Daisy waved her off, and watched the gig shrink into the distance.

There was no point waiting at the school for her father to collect her; she had spent such a brief time with Miss Cameron that he was probably still on his way to the factory. Daisy turned away from the small blur that was all she could now see of her teacher and set off in the opposite direction for home.

It was a pleasant morning for walking, a light breeze giving the air crispness. To her right the paddocks were lush with spring growth, and fantails flitted in and out of the trees on the other side of the track. Daisy's steps took up a steady rhythm, requiring only an occasional glance at her feet to avoid turning an ankle on a rough patch.

She would go back to school next year, and do her best to catch up on the work she had missed. The war was over; school would start again; everything would be just the same as it used to be. Daisy had the odd sensation that she was somehow arguing against herself. She ought to feel happy; yet the time spent with Miss Cameron had left her with a sense of unease.

On the day her father came home the world had seemed as unbreakable as if it were made of shining metal. It was still just as bright, but now Daisy was reminded of a glass ornament she had once seen at her Aunt Sarah's house in Auckland: clear and perfect in every line, but with an air of fragility, as if a touch might shatter it.

When she got back to the house she went into her room to get changed. Her gaze fell on the pile of textbooks Miss Cameron had lent her earlier in the year, when Daisy had had to leave school to help on the farm after her father was conscripted. It was too late to return them now; she would have to wait till school opened again next year.

Daisy picked up the topmost item, which happened to be a grammar text. There seemed little point now in struggling through the schoolwork on her own, as she had been doing over the last few months. Now that she could not finish up the school year properly, she would have to go back into Standard Five next year, and do the work all over again.

She replaced the book and snatched up her other dress, eager to get out on the farm and work off the restless, unsettled feeling that had taken hold of her. Influenza in the cities seemed an odd reason to have shut all the schools, even in their little valley. The thought nagged at her that perhaps this outbreak was more serious than everyone around her seemed to think.

Eddie tugged the handcart along a rough stretch of footpath, occasionally glancing over his shoulder to check that the tall pots of soup were steady. There was a knack to keeping up a reasonable speed so that he could get around his assigned area in good time without overturning the cart.

He pulled a sheet of paper from his pocket to check the list of street numbers where he was to make his deliveries. The influenza committee's soup kitchen organised its team of volunteers, assigning each one a section of the city to travel around, delivering food to those houses where people were known to be ill and unable to fend for themselves. With so much free time now that his school had closed, Eddie had needed no prompting to join in the relief effort.

The next house on his list was some way up the street. Eddie took a firmer hold on the cart's handle and lengthened his stride.

It was a part of Auckland unfamiliar to him. Houses nudged up together with only a narrow gap between each one and its neighbour. Their front doors opened directly onto the footpath, and a thin backyard stretched out of sight behind each building.

A small child sat on the front doorstep of one house. Eddie smiled and nodded at her, then something about the child made him slow his steps and halt. She sat hunched in on herself, brown curls framing a thin face, her hands knotted in her lap.

Eddie checked that the cart was resting firmly on a level part of the footpath, and lowered its handle to the ground.

'Hello. What's your name?' he asked.

'Eileen,' the little girl whispered.

'Where's your mum, Eileen?'

'She won't get up. I made a cup of tea, but she doesn't want it.' Huge blue eyes stared up at him, unblinking.

'Is she sick, then? Has she got the flu?'

'Don't know.'

Eddie thought he saw her lower lip quiver. 'What about your dad? Is he at work?'

She shook her head. 'He's gone to the war.'

Her father must be one of the thousands of men waiting to be sent home. Eddie gave silent thanks that his Uncle Dave was safely back on the farm with Daisy and Aunt Beth.

Eileen stood, and reached up for the handle to push the door open. 'Please, Mister, will you come and see why Mama won't wake up?'

She was wearing a dress that must have been meant for a much older child, with a loose neckline that revealed sharp collarbones. Thin arms emerged from overlarge sleeves. Eddie wondered how the child had even managed to lift a kettle to make a pot of tea. Two paces brought him to the doorstep; Eileen clutched at his trouser leg, and he found himself being led into the small parlour that opened straight off the front door.

Eddie had never seen a dead body before, but his first sight of the figure sprawled on a mattress, a thin blanket covering her below the shoulders, told him that this woman was beyond waking. Not just because she lay so still, her head at what looked an unnatural angle, but because of the color.

He had heard rumours of bodies turning black from Spanish Influenza; this woman's face was more of a dark, blotched purple. It was not the colour of living flesh.

A chipped cup half-full of watery-looking brown liquid had been placed on the floor close to the mattress. A fly crawled around its rim; as Eddie watched, the fly lifted itself and blundered over to settle on the still figure under the blanket.

'See, I made her some tea,' Eileen said, pointing to the cup.

The awareness of a small hand slipped into his shook Eddie into action.

'That's good, Eileen, but your mum's too tired just now. I'll cover her up so the light doesn't disturb her.' He batted the fly away and drew the blanket over the woman's face.

He needed to get back to the depot and let them know there was a body to be collected; more urgently, he needed to find someone to look after the little girl. Most urgently of all, he needed to fill his lungs with fresh air.

Eileen seemed content to leave her hand in his and be taken back out to the footpath.

'Have you got any family around here, Eileen? Your granny, maybe, or an aunt?'

She looked at him blankly, showing no sign of even knowing what the words meant.

Eddie forced himself to think calmly, doing his best to drive from his thoughts the image of that hideously discoloured face. He had a vague memory of seeing someone in a backyard a few doors down; yes, there had been a woman hanging out washing. He strode out in that direction, realised almost at once that Eileen was trotting to keep up with him, and scooped her up in his arms.

The woman was still at the washing line. The strip of ground between her house and the next was rough and unpaved, and obviously not meant as a path to the backyard, but Eddie was unwilling to waste time knocking at the front door and waiting for a response. She stood with her hands on her hips watching him plunge through to the yard. When she saw the child in his arms, her wary expression changed to concern.

'Eileen? What's the matter, dear?'

Eddie lowered the little girl to the ground. She ran over to the woman and buried her face in her skirts.

The woman wrapped an arm around her, and studied Eddie. She was grey-haired and had a wrinkled, weather-beaten face, but her gaze was keen.

'And who might you be, then?'

'Eddie Stewart, Ma'am. I'm taking food around to people. I saw Eileen outside her house, and she wanted me to come and look at her mother.'

'She's been taken bad, has she?'

'She's...' Eddie flicked a glance at Eileen, then met the woman's gaze again. He shook his head.

Her eyes showed that she had understood his unspoken message. 'I've been trying to keep an eye on her, but I didn't manage to get over there this morning. My husband's down with it, too, and he was bad in the night.'

'She wasn't on my list of people to visit. I wouldn't have known she was there if I hadn't seen Eileen.'

'Well, you must have seen those notices up at the Post Office and Lord knows where else—they say folk are to help themselves, and only ask the district committee for help if they're in dire straits.' She looked Eddie up and down. 'There's not enough of you fellows to go around. Anyway, we're used to looking after ourselves here. We keep an eye out for each other.'

A child even smaller than Eileen came out of the house and crawled backwards down the steps; a moment later Eddie realised that the fruit box by one of the clothes props held a sleeping baby.

The woman followed his glance. 'My daughter's children.' Her mouth seemed to wobble on the word "daughter". 'I'm looking after them now.'

'I have to get back to the depot and tell them to send someone out to... you know... pick her up,' Eddie said, jerking his head in the direction of the house where the dead woman lay. 'Can you look after Eileen till someone comes? I'd take her with me, but I want to get there pretty smartly.'

'No need to rush, lad, Mrs Wilson won't be going anywhere. You might as well finish taking that food to the needy folks first.' She patted Eileen on the shoulder. 'Yes, leave her with me. One more won't make much difference.'

'She said her father's at the war.'

'That he is. He's in the ground at the Somme.'

So he was not one of those soldiers waiting for a boat back to New Zealand. He was one of the men who would never be coming home at all. Eddie looked down at Eileen, who was sucking her thumb and staring from one to another of the people speaking over her head. The thumb emerged from her mouth as she broke into a smile. She reached out her hand toward him.

Eddie crouched to take the small hand, with its rather damp thumb, in his. 'Hooray then, Eileen. You'll be all right, this lady's going to look after you.'

'My name's Mrs Parkes, in case you want to make a note of it,' the woman said as Eddie was turning to leave.

'Oh, that's right, I think I'm supposed to do that. Thanks.' He found a stub of pencil in one pocket, and carefully noted Mrs Parkes' details, as well as Eileen's, on the back of his list of delivery addresses.

Eddie waved to Eileen until he gained the footpath and she disappeared from sight. He retrieved his abandoned cart and, taking Mrs Parkes' advice, finished his deliveries before returning to the depot.

He passed on the information about Eileen and her mother, then headed for home. He was doing a lot of walking lately; few of the trams were running these days, with so many of the drivers off work with the flu. Eddie strode along Queen Street, where what seemed like more than half the shops and offices had their doors boarded up, and only a handful of people were about. The greatest sign of activity was at the entrance to the inhalation chamber, where people were queuing to breathe in a zinc sulphate spray that was supposed to protect against influenza. Eddie had already experienced the spray; Aunt Sarah had insisted that the whole household go to the nearest chamber as soon as it opened.

He turned off Queen Street and walked past the Technical College, which had been turned into an influenza hospital, then picked up his speed for the short remaining distance to his home.

His grandmother and aunt were both in the kitchen when he got to the house. Granny and the maids were cutting up vegetables and the cook was rolling out a huge round of pastry, while Aunt Sarah wrote out labels and attached them to baskets. Against one wall was a pile of folded sheets, probably fresh off the washing line. They were regularly sending supplies to the hostel that had been set up for children whose parents had been taken ill and who had no one else to care for them; in addition, they had their own small round of households where people were not quite desperate enough to need the help of the influenza committee, but were still struggling to get meals on the table and clean linen on their beds.

'You've been a long time today, Eddie,' Granny said. 'Here, I've made you a few sandwiches to be going on with—you must be hungry after all that walking.'

She picked up a plate with several sandwiches piled onto it, then paused in the act of passing it across the table. Eddie was aware that she was studying him closely, and he did his best to look unconcerned.

'Let's take these outside,' she said. 'I've made them quite full, and you don't want to be dropping bits on Mrs Jenson's nice, clean floor. I'll come out with you, I wouldn't mind sitting down for a minute or so.'

They went out the kitchen door and sat at a small table in the garden. 'Is everything all right, dear?' Granny asked when the first bite of sandwich was safely down.

'Mm.' Eddie took another bite at once; partly as an excuse not to say more, and partly because he had realised he was actually quite hungry.

'It's just that… well, I know there are a lot of sad cases. It's fine work you're doing, Eddie. You just remember that.' She squeezed his hand.

He wondered if she might press him to say more, but Granny was good at letting people be quiet if they wanted to be. She got up and strolled around the nearer part of the garden while he ate his sandwiches, then sat beside him once more.

'I was just thinking…' Eddie took a last swallow, and tried again. 'I know you're mainly doing plain stuff just now, but I wondered if I could have some biscuits or cakes—something a little kid might like.'

'Of course you can. What about some nice fudge? No need to bother Mrs Jenson, I'll make it myself.'

'That'd be really good.' He fiddled with the empty plate, tilting it back and forth on the table. 'They still haven't got the flu bad in Ruatane.'

'No, thank goodness. Auckland seems to have it worse than anywhere.'

'Do you think maybe it won't get bad in Ruatane at all?'

Granny paused for so long that he was not sure if she was going to reply at all. 'I don't know, Eddie. I hope not.'

The strawberry crop was a fine one that year. A few days after their visit to Grandma's, Daisy gathered strawberries until she had filled a basket with the fruit that escaped going straight into her mouth. She added the haul to a pile of rhubarb stalks already in the jam pan, and her mother set it over the heat, where the three of them took turns stirring until the sugar dissolved.

The day was warm, and Daisy soon opened the back door to let in the breeze. The pot bubbled away on the range, the jam's sweet, rich scent filling the kitchen. Daisy's apron was spattered with sticky red blobs, as was her mother's, and she noticed a small chunk of strawberry in her father's hair.

Her mother had poured a little jam into a saucer and placed it on the windowsill to cool; now she tipped the saucer from side to side, and prodded at the skin that had formed on the jam.

'It's ready,' she announced. 'Davie, you can lick this off the saucer if you like—that should be safe enough.' She grinned at Daisy's father, who had already burned his tongue by sneaking a taste of jam off the wooden spoon when he thought she was not looking.

He swiped the saucer clean with two licks, then lifted the heavy pan over to a cooler part of the range, close to where empty jars were lined up on a wooden slab. He carefully tilted the pan to the right angle and Daisy held each jar steady, a thick cloth protecting her hands, as her mother ladled in jam. Sunlight from the window struck the jars, turning the light ruby-red and making patterns on the floor.

Grandpa's tap on the door was so quiet that Daisy only realised he was in the doorway when she saw him standing there, one hand still raised to knock again.

'Come in, Pa, and I'll put the jug on,' her mother said, glancing up and smiling; a smile that faded almost at once. 'Whatever's wrong? You look as if you'd seen a ghost.'

Daisy's grandfather gripped the doorway for a moment as if to steady himself, then came into the room clutching his hat against his chest. 'I went into town this morning to see Richard. He was out when I got there, Maudie said she's hardly seen him the last couple of days, there's that many people come down with the flu.'

'Sit down and tell us all about it,' Mama said. She took Grandpa's arm and led him over to the table, where she sat beside him while Daisy and her father pulled out chairs for themselves.

'Richard came in after a bit,' Grandpa said. 'He'd been around at the teacher's—a friend she had staying with her came to fetch him.'

'Miss Cameron?' Daisy said, startled. 'Has she got the flu? Is she all right?'

Her grandfather looked across the table at her and shook his head slowly. 'No, she's not, love. She died this morning.'

Daisy was dimly aware of her mother's hand stroking her arm. Shock had left her unable to move or speak.

'What a terrible thing to happen,' Mama said. 'That's so sad, a nice lady like Miss Cameron.'

Grandpa cleared his throat. 'I went to see Richard because I wanted to get him out here. He's over at our place now.' His hand rested on the table; Daisy saw it shaking. 'Benjy's sick. He's got the flu.'

Chapter Two

Daisy's mother drew in her breath, the noise sharp in a room that had fallen silent. 'Benjy? But he looked all right—it was just the other day we saw him.'

'Last night he said he had a bit of a headache, and he went off to bed early,' Grandpa said. 'I didn't think anything of it. But he was in a bad way this morning—fever and chills one after the other, and he said he's got pains all over. Your ma couldn't get any food into him, either.'

'But Richard's there with him, he'll know what to do. Perhaps Benjy hasn't got such a bad case after all.'

'I don't know, love. We'll have to wait and see.' Grandpa heaved himself to his feet, and Daisy and her parents stood, too. 'I'd better be getting back home, see how things are.'

'Yes, don't wait for us,' Daisy's mother said. 'Tell Ma we'll be over soon.' She led Grandpa to the door and kissed him goodbye.

'Poor Pa, he looks so worried,' she said when Grandpa was out of hearing. 'But Benjy's a healthy boy—I know Ma's always thinking he's frail, but he's hardly had a day's sickness in his life. I mean, it's very sad about Miss Cameron, but she might have had something else wrong with her as well. It's old people who get the flu bad, not boys like Benjy.'

Daisy's father tapped his fingers against the back of a chair. 'I don't know about that.'

'But I've heard Uncle Richard say the same thing,' Daisy said, finding her voice again at last. 'He says in the winter it's always old people he has to worry about with flu.' Which made it even more shocking that someone like Miss Cameron, who was not at all old, should have died of it.

'This Spanish flu's different.' He looked from Daisy to her mother. 'They had it in the army camp while I was there. A lot of the blokes caught it—I didn't, I was lucky—and a fair few of them died. They were all fit young chaps, too. I heard one of the doctors say stronger people get it the worst. They sort of fight against themselves.'

Mama was staring at him. 'You never said anything about that.'

'I didn't want to worry you while I was away. And afterwards… well, I just wanted to forget all that. And I thought maybe we wouldn't get the bad flu up here.'

'I wish you'd been right.' Her mother's words came out on a sigh. She crossed the few steps to the bench. 'You get the gig out, Davie, while Daisy and I finish up here.'

They left the remaining jam in its pot, where it would set and need to be boiled up again. Daisy placed a lid on the pot and a clean dishcloth over the open jam jars to keep out any insects, then gave the bench a hasty wipe, while her mother quickly packed a small basket. They pulled off their aprons and hung them behind the door, but did not bother changing into smarter dresses before going outside.

The two of them waited by the garden gate for Daisy's father to bring the gig around, her mother jiggling from foot to foot in her anxiousness to get going. She glanced down at the basket she had looped over one arm, as if noticing it for the first time, and lifted a cloth to reveal several little cakes and half a dozen currant buns.

'I don't know what I was thinking of, bringing that stuff,' she murmured. 'Benjy won't be wanting anything rich like that.'

It was a bumpy ride to Grandpa's, with Daisy's father driving the gig faster than usual. When they drew up to the house, Daisy and her mother left Papa to tether the horse while they hurried over to the open back door.

Grandma's kitchen was normally full of chatter and laughter and the noise of eating, but today it was almost silent. Kate was stirring a pot on the range, while Grandpa sat at the table fiddling distractedly with a pea pod from the pile in front of him.

Kate looked up when they came in, eyes red and swollen and her face streaked with tears. 'Benjy's really...' she began, but the words at once dissolved into sobs.

Daisy's mother put down the basket and enfolded her in a hug, pressing Kate's face against her shoulder while she made soothing noises and patted her sister's back.

No one was better at calming upset people or animals than Mama. Daisy sat down beside her grandfather and shelled a few peas; when her father came in a little later he sat on Grandpa's other side and joined in the task while they waited for Mama to settle Kate.

The sobs gradually subsided; Kate pulled away and rubbed her sleeve over her eyes. 'They're all in the parlour with Benjy—Richard and Ma and Maisie. Pa and Richard carried Benjy in there.'

'Richard said we don't want him getting cold at nights, so we put him by the fireplace,' Grandpa said. 'We can have a fire going all night for him if that's what he needs.' He snapped a pod in two between his fingers, and let both halves fall onto the table. Daisy retrieved them, scraped the peas into a saucepan, and added the empty pod to a growing heap. 'No use me hanging around getting under everyone's feet, I might as well see if I can be any use out here.'

'I'm making some broth, but it won't be ready for ages yet.' Kate dabbed at her eyes with a handkerchief Daisy's mother slipped into her hand, then took hold of the spoon and began stirring once more. 'Benjy can't have anything heavy, but we've got to get food into him. Richard said broth would be all right.'

'I'm sure it'll do him good,' Mama said. 'We'll go and see him, then, just for a bit.'

Daisy rose from the table, but her father did not move from his place next to Grandpa. 'No, I think I'll stay out here,' he said, taking up another handful of pods. 'Sounds like there's enough people up there already, I'd only get in the way.' He met Mama's eyes, and Daisy saw her nod of understanding: just now, Grandpa needed the company of someone as solid and calm as Daisy's own father.

On such a fine spring morning the parlour would have been flooded with light if the heavy drapes had not been drawn almost closed. The furniture had been pushed back against the walls, and when Daisy's eyes adjusted to the dimness she made out figures gathered around a mattress on the floor. Grandma and Aunt Maisie were kneeling either side of it, while Uncle Richard stood by the mantelpiece.

Benjy lay on the mattress, face flushed and contorted in a grimace as his head tossed from side to side. His pyjama jacket was open to reveal a chest shining with perspiration. Aunt Maisie mopped at his brow while Grandma sponged his chest, dipping their cloths in and out of the tin bath that had been carried into the room.

'You can open the windows for fresh air if it's a warm day, but keep the curtains closed,' Uncle Richard was saying. 'Bright light would only make the headaches worse. If he appears to be—' A creaking floorboard caught his attention. He glanced across the room and saw Daisy and her mother by the doorway. 'Daisy, I don't think you should be here.'

Grandma had shown no sign of having heard their arrival, but at Uncle Richard's words she looked up at once. 'No, you keep out, Daisy. I don't want you getting this, too.'

A deep line was etched between Grandma's eyebrows, and her mouth was oddly twisted, as if Benjy's pain was hurting her too. Daisy stared from Grandma to the wretched figure on the mattress until Mama gave her shoulder a nudge.

'Off you go, Daisy,' she said quietly. 'I'll stay in here for a bit.'

Her mother's voice wavered as she said it, and Daisy saw tears brimming in her eyes. She also saw a determined expression that meant, no matter what Uncle Richard or even Grandma might say, her mother was going to have a proper look at Benjy, who was, after all, her little brother.

Daisy did as she was told, and slipped back into the passage. No one

18

had actually said she had to leave the house, only the room, so she hovered just outside the parlour listening to the voices.

'His fever's high, but it could be a good deal worse,' Uncle Richard said. 'You've done well, but you must keep up the sponging to stop his temperature rising too much further. The morphia will help with the pain, but don't give it more often than four times a day, and be careful with the dose. Is all that quite clear? Lizzie, is that clear?' His voice grew sharper on the last few words.

The crack between the door and its frame gave narrow glimpses of the parlour. Daisy peered through, and saw her mother stroking Benjy's cheek while Aunt Maisie wrung out a cloth over a basin.

'Yes, yes, I'll give him another dose soon.' Grandma was still sponging Benjy's upper body, and it was clear even from Daisy's awkward viewpoint that all her attention was on him, not on Uncle Richard's instructions. 'Maisie, we'll need more of that water soon, get Kate to fetch some out of the rain barrel.'

Uncle Richard shook his head, though no one but Daisy was looking at him. 'No, there's no need for another so soon, that dose will last for several more hours yet.' He gathered up his stethoscope, and some other items that Daisy could not quite see, and put them into his black leather bag. 'Lizzie, I do have to visit other patients now, but I'll be back as soon as I can—tomorrow morning, if I can manage it.'

Daisy turned away from the door and quietly walked down the passage. Just in case her uncle really had meant her to go some distance from the parlour, she wanted to make sure she was back in the kitchen by the time he appeared there himself.

Her father was still sitting at the table with Grandpa, empty pea pods piled high in front of them. The pot of broth simmered on the range while Kate moved around the room, picking up the salt pot and putting it down again, rubbing at an invisible spot on the bench, folding and unfolding dishcloths. One cloth was resting dangerously close to the edge of the hot range; Daisy moved it aside, and gave the broth a stir.

When Uncle Richard came into the room all activity stopped at once. In the brighter light of the kitchen, Daisy saw that his eyes drooped with weariness, and lines were etched around his mouth.

'How is he?' Grandpa asked. His voice was hoarse, as if it took an effort to get the words out.

'He's in a degree of discomfort, but the morphia seems to be dulling that. The fever is my main concern at the moment, especially if it should lead to delirium. I'll leave you some morphia, and these tablets are for treating the fever.'

Uncle Richard placed a narrow glass tube and a rectangular bottle on the table. During school holidays Daisy had sometimes helped her uncle take stock of his medicines. She recognized the tube of morphine tablets, but the name on the bottle was new to her. 'Aspirin,' she read aloud from the label. 'Is it specially for the flu?'

'It's a fairly new drug, though I believe the Germans made use of it before the war,' Uncle Richard said. 'Coupled with regular sponging, it's the most effective means of bringing down fever that I've ever encountered, and it seems to be quite safe even at high doses.'

'Will it make Benjy well again?' Kate asked, pleading in her eyes.

Uncle Richard grimaced. 'If only it were that simple, Kate. But it helps with the fever, and that's the best I can do. Now, can I explain the doses of aspirin and morphia to you? I'm afraid your mother is in no state to take in the details—and I don't think Maisie's much better—and of course your father,' here he nodded at Grandpa, 'will have to be out on the farm for much of the day.'

'What will I have to do?' Kate asked, looking doubtful.

'The usual aspirin dose is one tablet every four hours, but it's perfectly all right to give him two at a time if the fever seems to be worsening. It's important not to give too much morphia, though—keep strictly to the stated dose.'

Kate's face was already streaked with tears; at Uncle Richard's words they welled up again. 'But what say I forget when he got the last lot? I might get it wrong and make Benjy even worse.'

'I'm sure you'll manage. It's not so very complicated, dear.'

'But I was never much good at sums and all that at school,' Kate said, looking even closer to tears.

'Shall I write it out for you?' Daisy asked. 'I could make a list of what times Benjy's supposed to have each medicine, and how much he gets when.'

'That's an excellent idea,' Uncle Richard said, and Kate smiled her thanks. 'I'll check it when you're done, but I know you'll make a thorough job of it.'

Kate fetched notepaper and a pencil from a drawer, and Daisy carefully copied out the details from the medicines' labels.

'Please accept my sympathies on the loss of your teacher, Daisy,' Uncle Richard said as he watched her work. 'Miss Cameron's illness became severe very rapidly, a good deal faster than any of my other patients.'

'She didn't look well when I saw her at the school, but I thought she was just tired.'

'Yes, I suspect she may have forced herself to keep working rather than take to her bed at once.' Uncle Richard frowned suddenly. 'You saw her recently, then? Did you have any close contact?'

'Not really—we didn't shake hands or anything. And I didn't go into the school, she said it was too dusty. We just sat outside and talked for a bit.'

'I'm glad to hear it. This seems to be a highly infectious disease, spread on the breath of the infected person. Which reminds me—Kate, perhaps you could make up some cloth masks when you have a moment. Something that can be tied over the face whenever one of you goes in to see Benjy. I know it seems a little late for such precautions, but it may still be useful. Goodness knows there's little enough we can do against the illness.'

'I could cut up some muslin and sew tape on the corners to tie them at the back,' Kate said. 'Muslin's thin enough to breathe through.'

'That's just the thing. Boil the cloths each morning, and then dip them into an antiseptic of some kind before using them.'

'Would carbolic do for antiseptic?' Daisy asked.

'Yes, that would do very well. Mix a teaspoonful into a pint of water, and make up a fresh batch each day. In fact it would be a good idea to keep a large bowl of the solution just outside the sickroom, so that people can wash their hands on leaving.'

Grandpa stirred on his bench. 'Benjy was good as gold yesterday. I don't know how he could get crook that fast. He's going to be all right, though, isn't he? A young fellow like him, he'll get over it, eh?'

'I really don't know, Frank. I've given up trying to predict anything about this disease.' The trace of a smile passed over Uncle Richard's face. 'Benjy does have at least one thing in his favour—he couldn't ask for more devoted nursing.'

Kate offered to make Uncle Richard a cup of tea before he left, and to Daisy's eyes he was in sore need of a short rest and something to eat, but her uncle said he really must be off at once, as he was in a hurry to see his next patient.

While the rest of them returned to their various tasks, Grandpa stood in the doorway, watching Uncle Richard's retreating figure and talking under his breath.

'He was all right just yesterday,' Daisy heard him murmur. 'It came on that sudden. I didn't think there was anything wrong with him. How could he get sick that fast?' It was the first time she had ever thought of her grandfather as an old man.

Frank Kelly had never felt more useless. While everyone else in the house threw themselves into caring for Benjy, the best he had to offer was to carry on with the farm work as well as he could, when he was not hovering about the kitchen trying not to get in anyone's way.

21

His son-in-law David arrived unasked at the cowshed on the first afternoon of Benjy's illness and quietly helped with the milking, but Frank dried off part of the herd as quickly as possible, getting the task down to one he could manage on his own. It meant long hours down at the shed, but he welcomed the weariness. At least he could tell himself he was still of some use.

Lizzie sat with Benjy day and night, leaving the parlour only to answer a call of nature, and reluctantly even then. Maisie would have stayed there with her the whole time had Lizzie not insisted every evening that she go off to the room she shared with Kate. If Frank got up in the night to check on Lizzie he would sometimes find her slumped in an armchair, snatching a brief, uneasy slumber. She would not allow Frank to sit up with her; he was busy with the farm and needed his sleep, she said whenever he offered to share her vigil, and she was perfectly all right there by herself. Frank's own sleep was a restless one, troubled as it was by his fears for Benjy and by the unfamiliar lack of Lizzie in his bed.

When he was not out on the farm he spent much of his time in the kitchen with Kate. Beth and Daisy brought fresh bread each day, but Kate was having to manage cooking the meals on her own just now. She was grateful for the small help he could offer with peeling potatoes or drying dishes, and Frank was grateful for her quiet company.

Kate had always been the most easily overlooked of his eight children, Frank mused as he watched her going about her work. As a little girl she had been constantly in the shadow of Rosie, several years her senior and possessed of a large share of self-confidence. Kate had lost even the small distinction of being the youngest in the family with Benjy's arrival.

After the initial shock of Benjy's illness, her steady nature had soon reasserted itself. Now she got on with her work quietly and without fuss, moving about a kitchen that smelt of those endless pots of broth, occasionally cut through with the scent of lemon drinks. Richard stressed that it was important for Benjy to drink plenty of fluids. Kate provided a constant supply, while Lizzie and Maisie took care of getting them into Benjy and out again.

The current batch of broth could apparently be safely left unattended for a time. Kate took a seat at the table and flicked through a small pile of papers. Frank recognized them as the most recent batch of sheet music she had asked him to order from Auckland.

The piano stood idle while Benjy lay tossing and turning in the parlour. Frank had bought the fine instrument while his oldest daughter Maudie was still at school, when Lizzie had got the idea in her head of turning Maudie into an accomplished young lady. That was years ago, before Kate had even been born, but Kate and Benjy were the only ones out of all the children who had ever shown any real interest in music. Kate claimed that Benjy was the better player, but he always insisted she was at least as good, and would sometimes persuade her into playing duets with him.

She slid a piece from the pile, one with a cover showing a young woman strolling through a rose garden; opened it to lie flat, and ran a finger along the rows of incomprehensible black marks that could somehow be turned into music. Frank heard Kate humming under her breath as she followed the notes, and recognized a pretty tune that she had been teaching herself in the days before Benjy fell ill.

Several strands of hair had escaped from their pins to lie against Kate's cheeks; she pushed one behind an ear, but it fell again almost at once. Frank had been vaguely aware of discussions in recent weeks about starting to put her hair up; unlike Rosie before her, Kate had been in no hurry to do so, and she still seemed to be struggling to manage the task. She looked very young under that unsteady pile of hair, tracing her way with a finger along the sheet of music like a child learning her letters.

'How old are you, love?' Frank asked.

Kate looked up from her music and gave him a tiny smile. 'Seventeen. I'll be eighteen in May.'

Just a few months younger than Lizzie had been when he married her; and Kate's three sisters had all been engaged or married by the same age. Perhaps he would finally manage to have a daughter turn eighteen before giving her to a husband. And perhaps Benjy would get well again, the flu would pass, and Frank would still have eight children.

The sickly-sweet taste of carbolic was strong on Daisy's tongue as she breathed through her muslin mask. It was not very pleasant, but it did mean that Grandma would let her into the parlour to see Benjy for a few minutes. Kate was conscientious about handing Daisy and her mother masks as soon as they arrived at the house, although Daisy noticed she herself often did not bother when she slipped into the room with a fresh lemon drink or bowl of broth. Grandma refused to use one, claiming that it would somehow get in her way.

Benjy had been ill for almost a week now. Every day Daisy studied him anxiously for any sign that he might be getting worse, but every day he seemed much the same. He tossed restlessly on his mattress, always slick with perspiration despite the constant sponging; occasionally drifting into what appeared to be an uneasy sleep when he had been given a dose of the pills Kate so carefully doled out according to the timetable Daisy had written for her. Despite all the medicine, Daisy always had a strong sense that he was in pain.

Her mother was allowed to stay on and take a turn in the sickroom with Grandma and Aunt Maisie, but Daisy soon found herself shooed out of the room to join Kate and Grandpa in the kitchen. She took off the muslin mask, and the carbolic smell was at once replaced by a mixture of broth and the more pleasant one of the fresh-baked bread Daisy and her mother had brought over with them.

Kate was cutting up mutton for a stew, while Grandpa peeled potatoes. Daisy put on a borrowed apron, and had set to work helping with the vegetables when Uncle Richard arrived for his daily visit. He stopped in the kitchen just long enough to let Kate take his hat before he hurried off up the passage in the direction of the parlour.

They had a saucepan full of peeled potatoes by the time Uncle Richard returned to the kitchen. Daisy had thought he looked tired when Benjy first fell ill; now she wondered if her uncle had slept at all in the days since.

'There doesn't seem to be any change in Benjy's condition since yesterday,' he said before anyone had the chance to ask. 'I've warned Lizzie to watch particularly for any signs of delirium—any hint of raving or delusions, or extreme agitation. That would indicate a dangerously high fever. Judging by the progress of some of my other patients, the illness is at the stage where that's a real possibility.'

'What can we do about it if he gets that high fever?' Grandpa asked.

'Bring it down by whatever means possible. Give him higher doses of aspirin, and if that does no good you may have to put him into a bath of cool water. Anything to get that fever down.'

'Would you like a cup of tea before you go, Richard?' Kate asked. 'I was going to make one anyway.' She always offered him one, and he was always in too much of a hurry to be able to accept.

'Thank you, dear, but I'd better be on my way. I'm running late as it is.' Uncle Richard dredged up something like a smile. 'I'm beginning to think one of those motor cars might be useful, as long as it could cope with the Ruatane roads.'

Grandpa shifted in his chair. 'I wish I could get Lizzie to take a rest and let the girls look after Benjy for a bit. I'm just about as worried for her as I am for him if this is going to keep up much longer.'

'I don't think it will, if that's any comfort. Cases don't seem to last much more than a week—two at most.'

'So we'll know pretty soon,' Grandpa said. 'One way or the other,' he added under his breath.

Frank woke to a cold bed, and out of long habit reached for the warm body that should have been close by. The realisation of Lizzie's absence brought him fully awake. He rolled on to his side and drew over himself the blankets that he had tossed off while asleep.

Rather than slipping back into sleep, he slowly became more alert as he grew aware of the sound coming from the parlour: a low moaning, mingled with small cries of distress that he recognized as Lizzie's. Frank got out of bed and pulled his dressing gown over his nightshirt.

The parlour lamp that was kept burning all night meant his bedroom was dim rather than in its usual full darkness. He found his way by its light, across the passage and into the parlour.

Lizzie was kneeling by the mattress, one arm curled around Benjy's head while she held a glass in her other hand. Sweat ran along his forehead and down his cheeks, small pools of it forming in the hollows of his collarbone. His head jerked from side to side, despite Lizzie's attempts to hold it steady, and all the while he kept up that moaning sound, like an animal in pain.

Frank saw the fear in Lizzie's face when she looked up at him. 'I think he's worse,' she said, her voice strained taut. 'I was going to come and get you, but I didn't want to leave him thrashing about like this. He seems hotter than he was, and I can't keep him still long enough to get the medicine into him.'

Was this the delirium Richard had warned of? Frank left the thought unspoken. He dropped to a crouch at Lizzie's side, placed a hand on Benjy's forehead, and felt heat searing his palm.

'We've got to get him cooled down.' He glanced behind him at the tin bath of water that Lizzie had been using to sponge Benjy. 'Let's get him in the bath.'

Lizzie undressed Benjy, and Frank gathered him in his arms. Benjy had lost so much weight that his body was no great burden. Frank lowered him carefully into the small bath, letting his arms and legs sprawl over the edge, until the water came halfway up Benjy's chest. He cupped Benjy's head in his hands, keeping it away from the hard metal ridge of the bath, while Lizzie scooped up cool water and poured it on Benjy's upper body, over and over again.

After what felt like hours, Benjy seemed a little easier. Frank held his head still while Lizzie put several of the aspirin tablets that Richard had said would help reduce fever into his mouth and poured in just enough water to make him swallow them. She held a water-wrinkled hand to his cheek. 'He's a lot cooler,' she said.

Frank lifted him from the bath, and noticed that Benjy was able to take a little of his own weight. They wrapped him in damp towels and laid him on the mattress with a sheet covering him.

Even by the low light of the lamp he could see that Benjy's face was a less angry shade of red. And he was breathing more easily, without the groaning effort at the top of each breath. His eyelids fluttered open, and Frank thought he saw the briefest hint of a smile as Benjy looked up at Lizzie.

'He knows me,' Lizzie murmured. 'For a while there I thought he didn't.'

Frank managed to persuade her to sit on the sofa rather than the floor, curled into the crook of his arm and with her head resting on his shoulder. After a time he knew from her breathing that she had actually nodded off to sleep, perhaps her first real sleep since Benjy's illness. He sat very still, careful not to disturb her.

Lizzie woke soon after the first daylight made its way through a gap in the curtains. Benjy was dozing, still breathing easily, and with his colour close to normal. She felt his forehead, then looked up at Frank and smiled, her eyes brimming with unshed tears.

Frank walked back and forth across the room, easing the stiffness in his legs, while Lizzie sat by Benjy. After a few minutes they heard the creak of a bedroom door, followed a moment later by footsteps coming up the passage.

Maisie entered the room, already dressed, with Kate in her wake, still in her nightgown. Maisie's face lit up at the sight of Benjy lying so comfortably. She hurried over to the mattress; Benjy, roused by the noise, smiled at them all; and for a few moments everything was a confused delight of tears and hugs.

Kate was hanging back, Frank realised from his vantage point by the piano. She stood close to the door with one hand on the back of a chair.

'Come over here, Kate,' Maisie said. 'Come and see how well he looks.'

'I think I might need to go back to bed.' Kate's voice was faint, as if coming from a long way off. 'I don't feel very…'

She swayed, and Frank, crossing the room at a dash, was there just in time to catch her as she fell.

Chapter Three

Even to Daisy, who was only allowed to see her for a few minutes at a time, it was obvious almost from the beginning that Kate was more seriously ill than Benjy had been. She was racked with coughing, and her throat was too raw for her to swallow more than a sip or two at a time, making it difficult to get any medicine into her to lower the fever or even ease her discomfort. She was barely able to keep water or an occasional lemon drink down, usually vomiting up anything more substantial with a violence that left her weak and sobbing, with her stabbing headache made even worse. On Uncle Richard's visits, when he looked grimmer and more tired than ever, he sometimes injected her with morphine, a more powerful treatment than the tablets that were no longer having much effect.

Benjy had been moved back to his own room, still weak but able to sit up against his pillows and to manage light food like junket, while Kate had taken his place in the parlour. During Daisy's daily visits she spent much of her time with Benjy, fetching him snacks and fresh drinks or simply keeping him company, while her mother stayed in the parlour doing what little she could to help Grandma and Aunt Maisie tend to Kate. Feeding the rest of the household was not a problem; the other families in the valley, various uncles and aunts and cousins to Daisy, were over the worst of their own share of flu cases, and they all took turns sending meals to Grandpa's house. It was Daisy's job now to make the lemon drinks, and to mix up the day's solution of carbolic.

One morning Benjy did not greet Daisy with his usual question as to how she thought Kate looked that day. Daisy would have struggled to answer; Grandma had sent her out of the parlour even more abruptly than usual.

'She was bad in the night,' Benjy said. 'Calling out like she was scared of something, and it sounded as if they were having to stop her trying to get out of bed.' He looked away from Daisy, as if his far wall had suddenly become of great interest. 'I think she might be getting worse.'

'Uncle Richard should be out soon,' Daisy said, grasping for any scrap of news to lift Benjy's mood. 'He can give her another injection for the pain, that might help her settle a bit.' She did not add that the injection of morphine wore off after a few hours, and her uncle could not manage to visit the valley more than once a day; she knew Benjy was just as aware of that as she was.

She fetched Benjy a bowl of junket, then sat watching him eat, grateful for the noise his spoon made against the bowl. It made it easier to pretend not to hear the sounds coming through the wall from the parlour.

Her mother's silence as the two of them rode home together told Daisy she shared her sense of foreboding. Their return to Grandpa's the following morning was another quiet ride. They entered the kitchen, found it empty, and went through the door to the passage.

Daisy had dreaded hearing Kate's cries and ravings, but all she heard from the direction of the parlour were muffled voices. Her mother's pace grew more rapid, and Daisy quickened her own to match. As they passed his room, Benjy called out, wanting to know what was happening, but they ignored him and pressed on.

Grandpa, Grandma and Aunt Maisie were all in the parlour. On the mattress Kate lay, still and silent and with her face turned blue-black.

Carrying his own child to the grave was not a burden Frank had ever thought he might be called upon to bear. His three grown sons had survived a war, but this illness had struck down his daughter in her own home, where he should have been able to keep her safe.

He shared the weight of the casket with his three sons-in-law. Its wood was plain and unadorned; the carpenter who made Ruatane's coffins had struggled to finish them quickly enough in recent weeks, and had no time for anything more elaborate. There was a whole row of fresh graves in a cemetery that in normal times might see only one or two burials in a month.

None of Kate's four brothers were there to see her buried. The three older boys were still in England, among the thousands waiting to come home from the war, and Benjy was not yet strong enough to leave the house. Daisy was looking after him while they were at the funeral; there were few people Lizzie would entrust Benjy to, but Daisy was a sensible girl.

They lowered the casket into the ground and joined the small knot of women. There were no children here, and few enough adults. New cases of influenza were slowing down, but large gatherings were still best avoided, especially by those most at risk. That included expectant mothers, Richard said. Rosie, who was carrying her third child, had reluctantly stayed away, even though her pregnancy was not yet showing, but her three sisters and Maisie were there, surrounding Lizzie.

The girls made a space for Frank to take his place by Lizzie's side. He slipped her arm through his, and felt her hand clutch at him so tightly that he wondered if she might have been about to fall. Her mouth wobbled, but for the moment she seemed drained of tears. She kept her hold on his arm, her gaze turned on that gaping hole in the ground.

A shuffling of feet told Frank that people were readying themselves to move away. The minister must have said the final prayers; Frank had been too concerned with Lizzie to do more than murmur an "Amen" along with everyone else. The women kissed; the men shook hands. Richard took Maudie away to rejoin their children, and Bernard set off towards his own home, where Rosie waited.

David and Beth rode with Lizzie, Frank and Maisie; there was ample room in a buggy that had often been crammed to overflowing when the family were all still at home. Back then it had meant smaller children sitting on the laps of the older ones to fit everyone in for outings noisy with the high-pitched laughter of little ones. Today's was a much quieter journey. The others kept their voices low, and Lizzie barely spoke at all.

Frank knew she blamed herself for not seeing Kate's illness earlier, even though Richard had done his best to assure her this was a disease that could come on with no warning. Kate herself might not have known she was unwell until the morning she had collapsed in the parlour.

Or perhaps Kate had not wanted to worry her family when they were so frantic over Benjy. The thought was one Frank was sure nagged even more sharply at Lizzie than it did at him.

When they got to the farm David offered to look after the horses and put the buggy away, allowing Frank to take Lizzie straight up to the house; a house that no longer held their youngest daughter.

'How's Benjy?' Lizzie asked when she saw Daisy in the kitchen doorway waiting to meet them.

'He's good—he had a little sleep, but he's mostly been sitting in the parlour. Uncle Richard said it was all right, as long as I made sure he was warm and didn't get overtired,' Daisy added in response to Lizzie's doubtful expression. 'Can you come up there now? He wants to show you something.'

The parlour had been aired, and its furniture moved back to the usual places. There was no mattress on the floor now. Frank had expected to see Benjy on the sofa, but instead he was on the piano stool, in his pyjamas and dressing-gown and with a blanket over his shoulders.

Frank and the other adults sat around the room, while Daisy went over to stand by Benjy, one hand ready to turn the pages of the music for him.

Benjy started picking out a melody, slowly but with each note clear and true. After a few moments Frank realised why it sounded familiar: it was the piece Kate had been practising so short a time ago. Benjy began singing very softly in a voice still to recover its strength, and Daisy joined in more hesitantly, her words coming a fraction after Benjy's.

With his eyes half closed, Frank could picture Kate sitting on that very same piano stool, Benjy at her side as they played a duet. Older memories surfaced, of back when Kate must have been seven or eight and just beginning piano lessons with her Aunt Lily. Benjy had been too young then for proper lessons, but Frank recalled Kate had sometimes lifted him onto the stool next to her when she was practising. She would guide his chubby little fingers to the proper keys, and join in his delighted giggles at the sounds he made.

Frank looked over at Lizzie, and saw the trace of a smile hovering on her lips. She remembered, too.

The two voices rose in the chorus:

> 'After the roses have faded away,
> After their splendour has gone,
> After a night filled with mocking joy,
> After the silent dawn.
>
> 'After the birds fly away to the south,
> With their song of a summer's day,
> Wherever you are, you're my guiding star,
> When the roses have faded away.'

The sickness that had come hard on the heels of four years of war lasted only a matter of weeks. Early December saw the final new cases in Ruatane, and by Christmas Daisy's Uncle Richard had no seriously ill patients, though many still had several weeks of recovery ahead of them.

Christmas of 1918 was the quietest Daisy had ever known, even more subdued than the wartime Christmases. No one felt like making a fuss or celebrating, and the season was made all the duller when, for the first time in Daisy's life, Granny and Eddie were unable to come. The coastal shipping was settling down at last, but Aunt Sarah had turned her drawing room into a small convalescent home, and Granny was busy helping look after their patients, while Eddie was needed for running messages and delivering food parcels to people recovering at home.

For a time Daisy thought she might not see Eddie at all that summer, but he and Granny managed a hurried visit in the new year, when all of the convalescents had gone home except a few family members of Aunt Sarah's staff who could easily be cared for by the maids. They could only stay for a week; the influenza outbreak had led to matriculation examinations being postponed till the third week of January, and Eddie would need to be back in Auckland in time for them. He grumbled over having to spend his summer holidays studying for exams, but only a very little. This was not a time for grumbling over small things.

Granny mostly wanted to spend time with Grandma, sitting quietly with her and letting her talk about Kate. Eddie and Daisy went down with her one morning so that Eddie could see Benjy, who was now able to sit out on the verandah and even take short walks, but for the rest of Eddie's visit they stayed close to the farm, making the most of their time together.

On a particularly warm afternoon they sat on the creek bank where it was shaded by manuka trees, dangling their feet in the cool water.

'Only a couple of days before we have to go home,' Eddie said. 'It feels like we just got here—mind you, we haven't had long this time.'

'It always goes fast in the holidays, even when you can stay the whole summer,' Daisy said. 'It's a shame Aunt Sarah couldn't come, though.'

'She said it wasn't worth sailing all this way just for a week. But Granny wanted to—I think she'd have come even if it was only for a day. She felt bad we couldn't be down here for Kate's funeral, but it wasn't safe to be travelling then.'

Daisy studied Eddie. His large hands rested on his thighs, the fingers of one toying with a twig, and his sleeves were rolled up above the elbows, revealing arms that pressed tightly against the shirt's seams. A stray gleam of sunlight through the leaves caught his hair, as if a flame had been set there. He was so full of life that the very air seemed warmer around him.

Just the sort of strong, healthy person the flu had attacked most viciously. Thankfulness for Eddie's safety made her reach out and brush against his arm for a moment, reassuring herself of his solid presence. Eddie looked up and gave her a startled smile.

'I wonder why some people caught it and not others,' Daisy said. 'There didn't seem any sense to it—I heard about families with everyone catching flu except one, but sometimes only one or two got it.'

'Maybe you can find out all that stuff when you're a doctor,' Eddie said, grinning at her. 'No, I mean it,' he added when she aimed a half-hearted slap at his shoulder. 'You're going to be a doctor, all right. You'll be a good one.'

Daisy turned the slap into a quick, grateful squeeze. Eddie was the only person in the world who knew her dream of becoming a doctor. She trusted him to keep the secret; and trusted him to make it feel possible that the dream could actually come true some day.

'I might ask Uncle Richard about it—later, I mean. It doesn't seem right asking a lot of questions just now, with Kate and everything.' A small shudder ran through her at the memories of that dreadful time. 'It was awful, seeing how bad she was with it. And when she died... did you know people sometimes turned black?'

Eddie was silent for a few moments. 'Yes, I did. I saw one once—when I was taking food around to people, there was a lady in one of the houses. There was a little kid, too—she didn't understand about her mother being dead. It was like you said, the lady had turned black. Hey, don't let on about that to anyone, eh? I didn't tell Granny about me seeing someone dead, I didn't want to go worrying her.'

'I won't,' Daisy said. Eddie could trust her with his secrets, too.

A few days after Eddie and Granny left, a telegram arrived from England, telling the family that Grandpa's big boys were on their way home at last. They had managed to get themselves all on the same ship; with two older brothers to help him get about on his wooden foot, Uncle Danny would not have to wait for one of the special sailings of men who had lost limbs. They would not be home before March, but Grandma seemed just a little brighter at the news.

When term began in February it would mean a new teacher for the valley school; an odd notion for Daisy, who had never known any teacher but Miss Cameron. The teacher was a man, making it all the stranger. Grandpa had been chairman of the school committee for many years, so he could tell Daisy and her parents something of Mr Fawcett before his arrival.

'He's getting on a bit, I think,' Grandpa said. 'He probably would've been thinking about retiring, but with a lot of the teachers going off to the war I expect they talked some of the older fellows into staying on.'

With the war over and the teachers returning home—those who had survived, at any rate—Mr Fawcett had apparently decided to settle in a quiet part of the country for his final year or so before retirement. He was a bachelor, and would be staying at a boarding house in the town.

Daisy was down at the school in plenty of time for the first day of term, not wanting to risk being late when meeting her new teacher. His gig was already there, and soon after Daisy had let her horse into the school's paddock Benjy arrived; not on horseback, but sitting beside Grandpa on the spring cart.

'Ma said Pa has to take me to school and fetch me home again—for the first week of term, anyway,' Benjy said when they had waved Grandpa off. 'I think she was worried I might be taken poorly and fall off the horse if I came on my own.'

He smiled it off; Daisy would have been self-conscious at the fuss, but Benjy never seemed to suffer from embarrassment.

There had been some doubt over whether he would be coming back to school at all, and not just because his brothers were yet to return. Grandma had not been easily convinced that he was strong enough. But as she was adamantly certain he would not be fit to work on the farm for some time, and in any case Grandpa was now used to managing on his own, Benjy had managed to persuade Grandma that no harm would come to him from sitting in class all day.

He did seem quite healthy again, but not quite the same old Benjy. His face had lost its softness, with his cheekbones noticeable despite Grandma's best attempts at feeding him up. His hair had come out in clumps after his illness; it had begun growing back, and Grandma had cut the remaining hair much shorter than usual, but in patches his scalp still showed through. And even when he smiled, there was something solemn about his eyes.

Mr Fawcett appeared in the doorway, swinging the school bell, and Daisy had her first sight of their new teacher. He was tall and thin, and somewhat stooped in the shoulders. His suit looked to be black where the dust of the road had not turned it as grey as his thinning hair.

The children lined up with the youngest in front; she and Benjy were now the two oldest, Daisy realised. There were no little ones coming to school for the first time, which struck her as a good thing; Mr Fawcett did not have the sort of face that would put a small child at ease.

The teacher looked over the dozen or so children waiting to be told what to do. 'Come up to my desk and I'll enter your names in the records,' he said, then turned and went back into the schoolroom. There was a stiffness about his movements that gave Daisy the feeling he might creak as he walked.

Mr Fawcett seemed to take a long time over adding each pupil to the book open before him. As she and Benjy shuffled their way closer, Daisy noticed him going back and forth between the roll book and a printed list that he flicked through.

'What's your name, boy?' he asked when their turn came at last.

'Benjamin Kelly, Sir.'

'Kelly,' Mr Fawcett muttered under his breath, running a finger down the printed list. 'You passed Standard Five the year before last, I see.'

'Yes, Sir. I started Standard Six last year, but I had to leave pretty early on, so I could work on the farm. My brothers were all at the war.'

'I've no records of last year.' Irritation was clear in Mr Fawcett's voice. 'Your late teacher had them all at her home, and a busybody of a doctor ordered all her papers to be burned when she died. Some notion about infection, I gather, and it's a great nuisance. With the examinations being cancelled, I was supposed to go by last year's records when deciding in what class to enter a child.'

The teacher turned to a fresh page of the roll book, dipped his pen in an inkwell, and wrote "Standard VI" in large letters at the top of the page before adding Benjy's name.

'And yours, girl?' he asked, looking up from the book.

'Margaret Stewart, Sir,' Daisy said, remembering in time to give her rarely-heard real name. 'I was in Standard Five last year—'

'So she'll be in Standard Six with me,' Benjy cut in. He caught Daisy's eye and gave a quick shake of his head.

Startled, Daisy shut her mouth on what she had been about to say: that she had missed several months of school while her father was away in the army camp, and fully expected that she would have to repeat her Standard Five year.

'Two of you in Standard Six, then,' Mr Fawcett said, writing Daisy's name under Benjy's. 'All right, go and sit down. I'll give the work out shortly.'

Daisy followed Benjy to the bench at the back of the room, which they had to themselves. 'I don't know if I'm meant to be in Standard Six,' she whispered.

'Of course you are.' Benjy's voice was low, but still well above a whisper. 'No, don't worry,' he said when Daisy cast a nervous glance towards the front of the room. 'I think he's a bit deaf, he won't hear us as long as we keep our voices down. You only missed a few months, and you did all that stuff at home to keep up. You'll be fine with the Standard Six work.'

'But what say they find out—the people at the Education Board, I mean—about me not finishing Standard Five?'

'No one finished it—not properly, not when the exams were cancelled. That just means the teacher can decide what class you should be in. And he's put you in Standard Six.'

Benjy flashed a grin that lit up his face; but only for a moment. 'If you did Standard Five again you'd have to wait another year before you could go to high school. It's no good wasting time like that. You never know what might happen.'

Chapter Four

Almost all the men of the valley found some excuse to be at Ruatane's wharf on the day Frank's sons came home. Various uncles and cousins stood around talking while they waited for the boat to arrive, then joined in the back-slapping and handshaking and general well-wishing that greeted the boys when they made their way off the gangplank. Noticeable by his absence was Lizzie's brother Alf; but Alf never did leave his own farm these days. Not since he had come home from the war a broken man.

Lizzie clung to each of the boys in turn, dabbing at her eyes with a handkerchief when she finally released Danny. There had been some talk of going to the cemetery to visit Kate's grave, but at the sight of their travel-weary sons Lizzie said they should go straight home.

Frank knew it was Danny she was most worried about. The boys were two years older than when he had seen them last, and those years showed on the faces of all three, but Danny was the one who had lost part of a limb.

The wooden foot was hidden by a boot, and while Danny walked stiffly, he seemed to get about fairly well. He had a pair of crutches, which he kept tucked under one arm when he was not using them to point out a missed piece of luggage still waiting on the wharf. Joe and Mick hoisted him up to the buggy while Frank was still dithering over whether to offer Danny a hand, and Danny stowed his crutches under the seat he shared with his brothers.

Danny seemed to have more to say for himself than the other two put together, but Frank soon realised that Joe was contributing an occasional remark that was all but lost in the rattling of the buggy.

'Speak up, Joey, I can hardly hear you over the noise,' Lizzie said.

'He was just saying Ruatane doesn't look much different since we've been gone,' Danny said. 'He can't talk too loud, Ma, his lungs aren't what they were. Not since the gas.'

Lizzie was taken aback; Frank saw it in her eyes when they met his. Lung damage from the gas was what had put Joe in hospital, and then a convalescent home, for the latter part of the war, but neither Frank nor Lizzie had considered that the damage might be permanent. The good, strong voice that Joe had had right from babyhood, when his was the lustiest cry of all their children, had been turned into a hoarse whisper; and who knew what other damage there might be to his lungs?

But their sons had all come home, which was more than many families could say. That was something to be thankful for.

'Well, you'd better rest your voice for now, while it's noisy,' Lizzie said, matter-of-fact once again. 'We can talk properly when we get home. And we'll take you to see Kate on Sunday after church, you'll be feeling more up to it by then.'

'That'd be good,' Danny said. 'We were all sorry to hear about her.'

Danny appeared to have become the voice for all three boys. Mick still had all his limbs, and had spent no time in hospital at all, but he was even more quiet than Joe. He was probably just tired after the long journey, Frank thought; tired and hungry, according to Lizzie.

'You all look as if you need a decent feed,' she said. 'Gee those horses up a bit, Frank, I want to get on. Maisie'll be doing a nice lot of scones for when we get home.'

Maisie had stayed behind, to leave more room in the buggy as well as to get dinner underway. At the sight of the boys she gave way to a bout of tears; Maisie had been with the family since Danny was little more than a baby, and she was something between big sister and fond aunt to all the children.

When the boys had been thoroughly fussed over they were sent off to their rooms to wash and change. By the time they reappeared Benjy had come home from school, and there was more handshaking to be done, along with remarks on how much Benjy had grown in the last two years.

Dinner was a reasonably noisy affair, with Danny again taking a large share of the conversation. Joe, too, often spoke up, and as the rest of the family gradually got into the way of falling silent whenever he opened his mouth, it grew easier to make out his words. From time to time even Mick's voice was heard, when he accepted an extra helping of food. Mick might not have much to say for himself, but he appeared to be enjoying his meal as much as even Lizzie could wish.

The parlour was busier than it had been in a long time when the family gathered there after dinner. Lizzie insisted that Danny sit in one of the more comfortable armchairs. He leaned his crutches against the wall and lowered himself onto the chair.

'Do you mind if I take this thing off?' Danny asked his mother, pointing at the artificial foot that was covered by a heavy woollen sock. 'I like to get rid of it of an evening.'

Lizzie assured him that she did not mind in the least. Benjy fetched Danny a footstool, stood there watching for a few moments, then asked the question Frank had been turning over in his own mind: 'Does it hurt?'

'Mm?' Danny paused in the task of pulling up his trouser leg. 'No, the stump's healed over pretty good now—it's going on for eighteen months since they chopped it off. It's a funny thing, though, the foot's gone but it still gets a bit of an ache once in a while. And you wouldn't believe how bad the bugger itches sometimes.'

'Hey, watch your language in front of the ladies, eh?' Frank said, and Danny had the grace to look awkward.

'Sorry, Ma. The nurses kept us in line when I was in the hospital, but once I was on the boat home I got back in the way of only having blokes around.'

An able-bodied Danny might have found himself threatened with not being allowed any pudding in the next few days for such a lapse, but Frank was not surprised when Lizzie waved it off, claiming she had not heard what he said.

Danny finished rolling up the trouser leg and peeled off his sock. The wooden foot was attached to a leather sheath wrapped around his calf, with metal struts to support the leather and buckled straps to tighten its fit. Danny undid the buckles and tugged at the leather, and the whole contraption came off, revealing the stockinette-covered stump. He placed the false foot beside his chair and heaved the stump onto the footstool. Danny then proceeded to ignore it, and Frank did his best to follow his lead.

Benjy played a few piano pieces; Maisie brought in supper; they talked of the boys' voyage home and the latest family news. The mantel clock chimed nine o'clock, and it was high time for bed. Their good-nights said, a whispered one in Joe's case, Danny reached for his crutches and hauled himself upright, while Mick got up from his chosen corner off to one side of the room where the light was dimmest, gathering up Danny's discarded foot on his way out of the parlour.

'Well, it could be a lot worse,' Lizzie said when she and Frank were alone in their room.

Frank had dried off much of the herd while Benjy was ill, and the remaining cows were down to once a day milking, so there was not a heavy burden of work to be shared among four grown men. He welcomed the absence of any urgent tasks; it meant he could take some pains over finding out just what Joe and Danny were capable of.

Doing the milking went reasonably smoothly. Danny could walk, albeit stiffly, without his crutches for much of the time, mostly using them when he had tired himself out by being on his feet too long. Getting up and down was hard on him, so Frank installed him on a milking stool and left him to get on with it while Joe and Mick brought in the cows and let them out again. Lung damage meant Joe tired more easily than he should, and Lizzie was careful to check that he wore a scarf if the day looked likely to be cold, but he managed well enough as long as they took regular breaks.

For many years Frank had taken pride in keeping his fences well-maintained. It was one of the things he had been forced to let slip with his sons away at the war, and something he soon began catching up on now that they were home.

One morning they were working on a fence not far from the cowshed. Frank reached for another nail, and noticed that only a few of the right size were left in the pouch.

'Pop up and fetch some more of those four-inch nails, Mick,' Frank said. It had taken an effort to get out of the habit of calling on Danny for such jobs; as the youngest of his sons working on the farm, he had always been the first chosen when there was a message to be run.

Mick set off, and Frank took the opportunity to stretch his back. He glanced at the stack of timber ready to be used next; they would be getting low on posts before long, he realised.

'I think we'll go over the back and split a couple of logs after lunch,' he said. 'That'll see us right for posts for a while. No need for you to come, Danny, you can make a start on cleaning the tack.'

He saw Joe and Danny exchange a glance. 'Splitting posts with gunpowder and all? How about I come with you and Joe, and Mick does the tack?' Danny said.

'I don't think that's such a good idea, boy. The ground's pretty rough over where we're going, you know, and there's a few drains on the way.' Not to mention at least half a dozen fences, which for Danny meant walking to a gate, however distant, rather than climbing over at the nearest point.

'You and I can do the posts on our own, Pa,' Joe said in his husky voice. 'Get Mick to help with the tack.'

Cleaning tack was a quiet job that could largely be done sitting down. It certainly did not need two men. With Joe liable to be racked by a hacking cough if he strained himself lifting anything heavy, splitting logs would not be an easy task even for three of them.

'No, he can do the posts with us,' Frank said. 'We'd take all day over it otherwise.'

Somewhat to his surprise, the boys looked as if they might want to argue the point. Then Joe gave a quick nod of his head, and Danny shrugged agreement.

Frank mentioned the log-splitting again when Mick returned with the nails. He saw his son's eyes widen in what looked like fear; Mick mumbled an 'all right' and turned away, and Frank decided he must have imagined it.

When they set out after lunch Frank found that the way to the bush clearing was just as rough as he had remembered, leaving him even more certain it would have been too much for Danny. His own breathing was more rapid than he would have preferred by the time they had reached it, and Joe was wheezing so heavily that Frank made him sit down for a few minutes before beginning the work.

They pulled back a canvas tarpaulin to uncover a stack of puriri logs, felled and cut to length in a previous season. Joe and Mick lifted a log from the stack and placed it to one side, while Frank set out the gear he had been carrying.

There was an art to splitting logs into useful posts rather than splinters, and Frank still preferred to do this part of the task himself. He drilled a hole about two feet from one end of the log, pushed in a wad of paper, and carefully poured in a small amount of gunpowder. He inserted a fuse, pushed in more paper, and filled what was left of the hole with brick dust tamped hard with a stick. Having glanced around the clearing to see that Joe and Mick were well out of the way, as well as to check that his own path was clear, he struck a match and lit the length of fuse hanging out of the hole, then stepped away smartly to get to cover behind a large tree.

He waited a safe time after the booming crash to be sure there were no stray chips of wood flying, then emerged to check his handiwork. To his satisfaction, the log had split cleanly into roughly equal sections that could be finished off with some axe work to make tidy posts.

'Let's get on with this lot, you fellows,' he called.

There was no response. Puzzled, Frank walked across the clearing to where he had last seen the boys.

Joe was crouched at Mick's side, one hand on his brother's shoulder. Mick cowered, hands clenched into fists that covered his ears, his whole body shuddering.

'It's the noise,' Joe said, looking up at Frank's approach. 'It's a bit like how it was over there, with the guns and all.' He glanced back at Mick and shook his head. 'How about I take him back to the house, get him to sit quiet on the verandah for a while? He's not going to be up to any more work just yet.'

Shock at Mick's state robbed Frank of speech. He nodded, and watched Joe persuade Mick upright then lead him away.

It was no use trying to carry on by himself, and whatever was wrong with Mick did not seem likely to come right in a hurry. It might be best to wait until David could spare the time to help; the two of them could split some posts for his son-in-law as well.

By the time Frank had gathered up the bits and pieces of gear and set out towards the shed where the tools were kept, Joe and Mick were some way ahead of him. He was still trailing behind, and still somewhat dazed by the whole episode, when he saw Danny making his way awkwardly down a slope towards them.

Joe and Danny looked to exchange a few words when the boys met up, then Joe carried on up the slope with Mick, while Danny stayed where he was and waited for Frank.

'Mick had a bit of a turn, did he?' he asked when Frank reached him and the two of them set off at a slow pace.

'He sure did. Joe said something about the noise worrying him, but it wasn't that bad.'

Danny stumbled on an uneven spot, and grasped at Frank's arm to steady himself. 'Should've brought those blasted crutches with me,' he muttered. 'Thanks, I'm right now,' he said, shaking his head when Frank offered a shoulder for support. 'Mick had it the worst of us, that's the trouble.'

'Eh?' Frank said, startled. He had become used to thinking of Mick as the lucky one; the only one of his boys who had come home unscathed. 'But what about that business of yours?'

'This thing?' Danny followed his father's pointing finger to glance down at his foot. 'It's not so bad. I wasn't too happy at first when they chopped it off, mind you, but when I saw some of the other blokes they brought in, both legs gone, or arms, or... well, I was pretty lucky. Especially with it happening that fast—I thought I'd had bad luck, getting shot up the first week I was in the fighting, but it was a lot worse for the fellows like Mick, never getting a blighty—that's when you're crook enough to get sent back to England. If they're out there for all that time like he was, some of them go a bit funny in the head. Mick's not that bad, but his nerves aren't what they were.'

'And that's why he doesn't like loud noises?'

'Noise, bright lights—even too many people talking at once. He got a bit better with all that time on the boat, but for a while there if anyone so much as dropped a plate we'd have to stop him trying to get under the table.'

A memory almost thirty years old surfaced in Frank's mind: Lizzie checking on Mick in his cradle after some accidental crash, only to find him sleeping soundly. 'You could set a gun off beside that child and not wake him up,' she had said with pride. Their unflappable boy had somehow been turned into that frightened creature Frank had seen huddled by the clearing.

'It's just nerves, Pa,' Danny said, cutting into his thoughts. 'He's not off his rocker or anything like that. He could be a lot worse, you know.'

'No, I suppose it's not so bad.' But Frank could not avoid

uncomfortable thoughts of Lizzie's brother Alf, grim and silent and hiding away from the world ever since he returned from the war.

Later that week Frank found an excuse to ride into town on his own, telling Lizzie that he wanted to check how Bernard was getting along with a new piece of harness Frank had ordered from him.

He did indeed call briefly at his son-in-law's saddlery, where he learned that Bernard still expected to have the harness ready by the end of the month, just as he had told Frank previously. He then dropped in to the attached house to see Rosie; she was confined to home now that she only had two months till her baby was due, and she welcomed the company, but Frank stayed just long enough to pass on a recipe Lizzie had sent, and to be relieved of some sweets by her small sons.

His next call was the real reason for his outing, and he was glad to find Richard at home. Maudie took one look at her father's serious expression and sent the two of them off to Richard's study to talk in private. Lucy, the only one of the children not at school, made something of a fuss over not being allowed to stay and talk to her grandfather, and raised voices were heard from the kitchen until Richard closed his study door.

'Lucy's been trying Maudie's patience recently,' Richard said as he took his seat. 'I had to send her to her room the other day, and from her reaction you'd have thought I'd ordered her to take poison. Now, what can I do for you, Frank? Danny's not having any trouble with that leg, is he?'

'No, he seems to be all right. He said he'll need some new leather bits for it in a few months, but Bernard should be able to sort that out for him. No, it's Mick I'm worried about.'

'Mick?' Richard frowned. 'He seemed in good health when I saw him on Sunday.'

'Yes, he looks fine—I thought he was the best of the three of them. But now… well, I'm not sure he's right in the head any more.'

Richard listened closely, occasionally jotting something down in a notebook, as Frank recounted the state he had found Mick in after the log-splitting incident.

'It's hardly surprising that something as dreadful as a war should leave its mark,' he said when Frank had come to a halt. 'And sometimes the wounds that can't be seen are the most serious of all. But I'm not sure you should be too concerned. Mick's not suffering from delusions, and he's not at all violent or aggressive to those around him.'

'I just don't want him turning out like Alf,' Frank said, voicing his greatest fear.

41

'Of course you don't. Alf's is a sad case indeed, but Mick does have a good deal in his favour. He's much younger, for one thing—there must be twenty years between them, at least. And I gather that Alf saw his brother killed before his own eyes, which would make it all the worse.'

'Yes, he took that pretty bad, all right. Ernie was younger than him, too, and Alf thought he should be keeping an eye on him.' Frank shook his head. 'No, Mick's nothing like as bad as that. Do you think he might come right yet?'

'Well, we understand far less than we should of such nervous complaints, I'm afraid. But yes, I do think there's reason to be cautiously optimistic—he may not ever be quite the Mick we used to know, but with peace and quiet, and plenty of Lizzie's good food, I think you'll find he's reasonably happy.'

"Reasonably happy" was a thin enough hope, but one Frank snatched at eagerly. It was a good deal better than what he had feared for his son.

Daisy finished checking a piece of long division and put down her pencil. Benjy was still working on his; while she waited for him to complete the work, Daisy sneaked a glance at her science textbook, which had an interesting section on animal physiology, with drawings of several skeletons.

Science was not a compulsory subject for the proficiency examinations she and Benjy would sit later that year, and Mr Fawcett did not feel the need to devote any class time to it. As there was no longer a woman teacher, Daisy was not obliged to do any needlework at school, which was something of a relief; there was always plenty of that to help with at home.

Most of their school day was taken up with composition, spelling lists, grammar exercises and arithmetic, which usually meant their teacher set them a chapter to read through and do the exercises that followed, although he did sometimes quiz them on their spelling, times tables or mental arithmetic. An occasional chapter from geography or history books gave only a slight variation to the routine.

The days would have been wretchedly boring without Benjy's company. Whenever Mr Fawcett was not actively taking notice of their bench at the back of the class, it was safe to risk whispered conversations. Sometimes they worked on the more difficult problems together; sometimes Benjy read out a passage from their grammar book in a silly voice, and Daisy would have to bite her fist to muffle her laughter. Benjy's lively recitations of passages from poems or plays had been one of the most enjoyable parts of school, both for Daisy as audience and for Benjy as performer; looking back, Daisy strongly suspected that Miss

Cameron had enjoyed it almost as much. They had quickly come to the realisation that their new teacher had no such interest.

Benjy had finished off his own list of sums by the time Mr Fawcett called for the work to be handed in. Their teacher placed all the workbooks in a neat pile on his desk, glanced at the clock which showed that it was still a few minutes till three o'clock, then looked at the lines of eager faces.

'You may go,' he said, his words followed at once by a rustling of papers and a scuffling of feet as all the pupils made sure of their escape before he could change his mind.

This particular day had seemed even longer than usual, with its end more eagerly awaited. It was the last day of term, and the May school holidays of 1919 were about to begin.

In the first year of the war, when it was still a distant threat that had yet to touch her own family, Daisy had gone to Auckland for the May holidays; a magical time that with each succeeding year seemed more dream than memory. The war was over, but there would be no travelling to Auckland that year. On the earlier journey her grandfather had taken her with him when he went up to Auckland for a special meeting of Dairy Co-operatives, but even with his big boys home Grandpa was far too busy trying to catch up with things that had been let go on his farm for any trips away.

Daisy went to stay with her Aunt Maudie and Uncle Richard for a few days during the holidays. The previous May her father had received his call-up from the army, and she had not wanted to waste a single day of his remaining time with them by being away from home, so this was her first stay with them in two years.

'It's nice to have you here again, Daisy,' her aunt said on Daisy's second evening there. 'Seven's a good number to have around the table. Especially when it was only me and the children during the flu.' Her smile faltered, and Daisy was sure Aunt Maudie was remembering her sister Kate.

'Father didn't eat with us or anything,' Lucy said. 'He had all his meals in his study.'

'Yes, I did what I could to reduce the risk of infection, however small,' Uncle Richard said. 'But that's all in the past now.'

'It could've been even worse,' Aunt Maudie murmured. 'Daisy, I think you're as tall as Lucy now,' she said after a moment, her voice determinedly bright as she looked at the two of them sitting side-by-side. 'We'll get your uncle to measure you later with that special ruler he's got in the consulting room, but you look about the same—and there's nearly two years between you. You're going to take after your father for being tall. Lucy's filled out more, though.'

Lucy now had the first hint of a bosom, as she had been eager to point out to Daisy when they had changed into their nightdresses the previous evening.

Uncle Richard helped himself to more roast beef. 'Daisy, your parents tell us you're thinking you might like to go to high school next year.'

'Oh, that's right, so they did. They mentioned it on Sunday.'

Daisy was keenly aware of six faces turned on her with varying degrees of interest. Aunt Maudie and Uncle Richard both seemed mildly amused. Flora gaped at Daisy, and Lucy dropped her fork with a clatter; even Nicky and Timmy had been briefly distracted from the food before them. She felt her own face grow warm at being the focus of such attention.

'Why on earth would you want to do that?' Lucy demanded. 'They'll make you do all sorts of boring arithmetic and things. It'd be even worse than ordinary school, and that was bad enough. I was *dying* to stop going.'

Lucy had finished Standard Six the previous December, and was now supposedly busy helping her mother around the house. Since Aunt Maudie had a lady in to do the heavy work anyway, and since making Lucy do anything that did not hold her interest was, her mother said, 'More trouble than it was worth,' Lucy appeared to be filling her days with drawing and painting; occasionally doing a little half-hearted dusting; and from time to time baking elaborate cakes and pastries.

'You don't have to go to high school, you know,' Lucy said. 'It's not like with primary school, there's no law says you must go.'

'I know.' Daisy was annoyed at how foolishly small her voice sounded. 'But I want to.'

'Why? That's just silly.'

'Lucy, don't tease Daisy,' Aunt Maudie cut in while Daisy was still gathering her thoughts. 'Everyone's different, you know—just because you didn't like school doesn't mean no one else does. It's very nice that Daisy's thinking she might want to be a teacher.'

'Ugh, I'd hate to be a teacher,' Lucy said, giving a dramatic shudder to emphasise her point.

'Well, it's a good thing not everyone thinks the same as you, or there wouldn't be any schools to go to. It can be a nice thing for a girl to do before she gets married—Aunt Lily used to be a teacher before she married Uncle Bill, you know.'

Her aunt probably thought Daisy was on the verge of tears, thanks to the redness of her face as well as her voice being so shaky. Daisy did not feel in the least like crying; it was an uncomfortable mixture of embarrassment at all the attention and now irritation at everyone's assumption that going to high school meant being a teacher that was narrowing her throat and making it hard to speak.

'I don't know if I do want to be a teacher, anyway,' she said, keeping her voice calm with an effort.

'No, I expect you thought you might like to because you had such a nice teacher yourself,' Aunt Maudie said. 'But there's plenty of time to decide, it's only May.'

'Yes, there's no need to make firm plans as yet,' Uncle Richard said.

Her aunt and uncle were both smiling kindly at her, and Daisy managed to produce a smile of her own as she murmured polite thanks. She *would* go to high school—if she managed to pass her proficiency examinations, at any rate. And she would most certainly keep quiet for as long as possible about her more distant ambitions. The very idea that she might go to high school caused enough fuss without people finding out that she wanted to be a doctor some day.

Chapter Five

Rangitoto Island dominated any view of Auckland Harbour, and Eddie had been familiar with the sight of its strikingly symmetrical cone spread along the horizon for as long as he could remember. He had always been fascinated by the idea of having an island volcano that had been active not many centuries ago almost on his doorstep, but he had never actually set foot there. When sailing with his aunt's friends he had often had a closer view of the island, and from time to time there had been talk of having a picnic there, but somehow one of the gentler islands with wider beaches and grass in place of sharp rocks had always been chosen instead.

So when his form master at school, Mr Wallace, announced in October that he was arranging a day's outing to the island later in the month, Eddie put his name down for it at once. He remembered somewhat belatedly to get permission from home, which his grandmother was happy to give. The only thing that might have stood in the way of the outing was bad weather, but the chosen day dawned as clear as he could have wished.

Eddie got to Queen's Wharf well in time for the morning's sailing, to find a few of his classmates already there. Mr Wallace arrived soon after, the others joining them in dribs and drabs. Several boys had been unable or unwilling to come, but about twenty of them had assembled by the time the boat's whistle sounded to urge them on board.

Mrs Wallace waved as the boat pulled away. The teacher's wife had come down to the wharf to see them off, and her presence was causing a certain amount of excitement among some of the boys. She looked to be quite a few years younger than her husband; small and plump, with fluffy blonde curls emerging from under a close-fitting hat, pink cheeks, and a bright smile.

'See the bosom on her?' one boy murmured. 'It's like she's got a couple of melons jiggling around under there.'

'Yeah, big ripe ones. It'd be good to have a squeeze of those, eh?' That was Stanley, a classmate whose company Eddie did not particularly enjoy. 'I reckon old Wallace is dying to get home and back between the sheets with her. She'd be well up for it, too—did you see her wink at me?'

'Don't talk rot,' Eddie said. Mrs Wallace was, he supposed, quite pretty for a lady old enough to be someone's mother; pretty or not, he was certain she would not give any of the boys a second glance. Not in that way, at any rate. Stanley was well-known for his exaggerations and outright lies, especially regarding his experience with girls. He claimed to be a regular at a high-class brothel, which Eddie gathered was a place where men paid for the attentions of women. Stanley even boasted, in the face of open disbelief from the other boys, that he was such a favourite with the ladies there that they did not charge him for their services. 'Anyway, shut up or Mr Wallace'll hear you.'

'I don't care if he does,' Stanley said. He did, however, have the sense to lower his voice for whatever he muttered next. Two or three boys standing close to him laughed, while Eddie and several friends moved across to the far side of the boat.

It was a fresh spring day, sunlight bright through clear air, and the harbour looking its finest. A stiff breeze whipped the sea into whitecaps, throwing up spray whenever the ferry broke through a wave. Some of the passengers seemed a little uncomfortable during the rougher moments, but Eddie always enjoyed a lively sailing.

Rangitoto loomed larger; gradually at first, then more rapidly. The boat entered calmer water in the lee of the island, then nudged against the jetty with a thud that Eddie felt through his feet. Lines were thrown over piles and a gangway run out. Eddie and his group held back politely as the other passengers pressed forward, then as soon as the gangway was clear they all crowded onto it, each of them eager to be the first one ashore.

'Steady there, boys,' Mr Wallace called, sounding more amused than annoyed. They were not actually in school, after all, or even wearing their uniforms. And it was not as if any of them was silly enough to fall into the water; not even Stanley.

The other passengers seemed content for the moment to find seats close to the shore, while Eddie and his classmates at once made for the track to the summit, which headed inland a short distance from the wharf. The boys set off in a close bunch, but soon divided into smaller groups determined by walking speed, preferred companions, and how interesting each walker found the various distractions along the way. When Mr Wallace was safely out of sight there was a fair amount of good-natured pushing and shoving, and at one point Eddie felt a foot hooked around his ankle and given a tug. He stumbled slightly, and pretended to be on the point of falling, flailing his arms theatrically, while regaining his balance almost at once. The culprit was a friend of his, Geoffrey. Eddie grinned and gave him a shove, but not hard enough to make him stumble in his turn. Eddie had long grown used to being the biggest and tallest in his class, and it was second nature for him to hold back in such contests.

The path would not be pleasant to go sprawling on. Lava rocks had been packed into a surface that was firm underfoot, but with jagged edges that would give nasty grazes. An occasional rock was loose enough to turn the ankle of an unwary walker, and Eddie was glad of his sturdy boots.

The rough ground did not look a welcoming place for plant life, but the island was surprisingly green. Bristly manuka and several broadleaf trees grew alongside the track for much of its length, their growth lower and more scrubby than that of similar varieties on the farm, where Eddie was used to exploring the forest with Daisy. The roots must have taken hold wherever they could make their way through narrow crevices in the rock, finding small pockets of soil and snatching at rainwater before it drained away to the sea. There were even small ferns, of an unusual species that coped with such harsh conditions.

From a distance Rangitoto looked no great height at all, but as the summit grew closer the climb felt steeper. Their path left the dark grey chunks of lava and crossed into the red-brown scoria of the volcanic cone, dry and crumbly underfoot and throwing up the heat more fiercely on the exposed sections. Eddie wiped his sleeve against his forehead and gave thanks that Mr Wallace had not chosen a day in high summer for the outing.

Despite the challenge of this final section, he increased his speed. The end of the climb was now in sight, and he wanted to be first to the top. So did most of his companions, of course. Those around him walked faster and faster, shouldering aside any unwary strollers in their way. Eddie's stride grew longer, and one or two boys broke into a trot.

He reached the flattened edge of the cone several paces ahead of the others. His friend Philip, who arrived barely a step in front of Geoffrey, showed his admiration of Eddie by landing a casual punch on his shoulder, but Eddie kept his small surge of triumph to himself and made sure he looked only mildly pleased as he flopped onto the ground. He would no more boast of such a thing than make a fuss over scoring a try in rugby. That would mean being a skite, and few things could be more loathsome.

The island had sheltered him from the wind for much of the way, but the breeze was welcome now. Eddie felt it cooling sweat on his forehead as he leaned back on his elbows and studied the view.

Seen from any part of the mainland Rangitoto spread low and wide, as if reaching out a long arm from either side of its cone, but from this vantage point its shape was revealed as the near-circle shown on maps. Pohutukawa trees dominated the vegetation; more of them than Eddie had ever seen in one place before. They were still a month or so from flowering. The sight must be stunning when the buds opened and the trees were smothered in red.

Eddie knew a little about volcanoes, from books and occasional references in newspaper articles. Auckland was largely built on ancient volcanoes, but Rangitoto was by far its youngest. He recalled reading somewhere that it had last erupted about five hundred years before, which he gathered was very recent in volcanic terms, and the reason soil was sparse here. It was also why the volcano was considered dormant rather than extinct.

He shifted position to gaze into the crater. There was no trace of steam or hot water to give any hint of its violent past; not like White Island, a most definitely active volcano that could be seen from a safe distance off the coast at Ruatane. Here was only scoria that had been colonised by tough vegetation, mostly manuka and bracken even more stunted than that on the lower slopes. He closed his eyes for a moment and tried to imagine Rangitoto turning the night sky red with an eruption, as he had seen in a painting of somewhere in Italy—Mount Vesuvius, that was it.

The rest of his party straggled onto the summit, with Mr Wallace bringing up the rear, and everyone found a more or less comfortable spot to sit. Eddie's rucksack had felt promisingly heavy on the steepest part of the track. He removed from it two tin lunchboxes that proved to be packed tightly with sandwiches, savoury pies, sausage rolls, small cakes and jam tarts. Their cook, Mrs Jenson, had put in food enough to share with Geoffrey and Philip, even with the appetite the walk had given him.

His companions had brought perfectly adequate lunches of their own, and it took some time to do justice to the contents of all the boxes. There was no hurry; they would not have to head back down to the wharf for at least an hour or so.

When the food was finished at last, Philip elected to stretch out just inside the crater rim, where he was sheltered from the breeze, using his rucksack as a pillow. Geoffrey and Andrew, another of their companions, set off to walk around the rim; Eddie joined them for part of the way, then decided to explore the crater a little further.

'Ed's off hunting bugs,' Geoffrey called to everyone; Eddie grinned back at him and did not bother protesting, though in fact he liked looking for all sorts of plants and animals, not just insects. When he was younger he had often come home with pockets full of interesting bits and pieces that caught his eye: pebbles, seashells, dried berries, bright-coloured feathers—and yes, an occasional dead insect. He was too old for such indiscriminate gathering now, of course; there was also not much space left in his room to display all his finds. Granny had occasionally persuaded him to cull his collection, pointing out that it was difficult for the maids to dust around.

He caught a glimpse of something shiny against the rough scoria. It was a lizard: a small skink, basking on the warm rocks. Eddie crouched down to get a better view, moving slowly so as not to startle it.

The lizard's smooth skin with its tiny scales was like burnished metal in the sunlight. It clung to a lump of scoria, front toes wrapped tightly around the rock, with its bright eyes fixed on Eddie. It was clearly aware of his presence, but for the moment comfortable enough not to move. Eddie held himself still, even making his breathing shallow.

Scoria crunched behind him, and the lizard darted out of sight. Eddie looked over his shoulder to see Mr Wallace approaching; he had been going from group to group, chatting with each of the boys.

'Finding much to catch your attention are you, Stewart?' Mr Wallace asked, smiling at him.

'Yes, Sir.' Eddie rose from his crouching position. 'It's interesting to see how the trees grow, with hardly any soil. I haven't seen any ponds or streams, either, so they must be good at making do without much water.'

'Hmm, I hadn't thought of that. Very interesting,' Mr Wallace said, though his tone suggested he was being more polite than strictly honest. 'Well, I'm glad you're enjoying the outing—it's perhaps the last chance you'll have before you'll need to knuckle down and study for the end-of-year examinations. Have you settled on what subjects you intend to take at university?'

'My aunt wants me to take a couple of law papers—company law, that sort of thing, just to do with business. But I mainly want to do zoology and botany. I'm thinking I might do some geology, too.'

'Not Latin, then?' Mr Wallace's smile had turned rueful; that was the subject he taught.

'I wouldn't mind taking that as well if I can fit it in—I like Latin, I'd like to study it a bit further.'

'I'm pleased to hear it. You realise you're very fortunate, choosing your subjects purely on the basis of what you enjoy,' he said, his expression becoming serious.

'Yes, Sir, I know I am.' Eddie turned aside a little to hide his awkwardness over the topic of money. He would be sitting the scholarship examination at the end of the year simply because everyone else did, while he knew that for some of his classmates the twenty pounds a year the scholarship offered might make the difference between attending university at all or going straight into a job in some office.

'If you were seeking a profession such as the law or medicine, Latin would be essential, of course.' Mr Wallace smiled once again. 'I must say it's rather pleasant to imagine studying purely for the love of the subject. Make the most of your opportunities, Ed.'

Eddie blinked, startled at the use of his first name; his teachers usually kept strictly to surnames. 'Thank you, Sir. I'll do my best.'

Mr Wallace nodded, then moved on to speak to another boy; one who would probably not be going to university.

Eddie's hands felt gritty from the scoria; he wiped them against his trouser legs before climbing to the crater rim and studying the view. This side of the island faced away from the city and out to sea. Neighbouring Motutapu was so close that it looked about to bump into Rangitoto, but the two islands could hardly be more different, with Motutapu all lush, green farmland.

He looked around him, storing away the details of his surroundings so that he could recall them for Daisy in his next letter. There were no pretty pebbles to collect as a keepsake for her; he would have to make do with telling her all about what he had seen and done. She would have enjoyed this outing.

Daisy had her own examinations at the end of the year to prepare for; examinations that were probably more important to her than his own upcoming ones seemed to him. And when she finally got to university she would be choosing subjects so that she could be a doctor, not just because they were fun. Continuing his Latin studies at university abruptly changed from a vague notion to a settled decision: perhaps he would be able to help Daisy in some small way if he kept his hand in with the subject.

Eddie recalled noticing a brooch in the window of a jeweller's store on his way to the wharves that morning, made of different-coloured enamels separated by fine wire. The small lizard catching the sun's light reminded him of it. The brooch would make a nice gift for Daisy; a better reminder of the outing than a lump of rock or an insect skin, and just the thing for a good-luck present before her exams. He smiled at the thought.

The proficiency examinations were held in early December, with pupils coming from all the schools in the area to take the test at Ruatane District High School. Grandpa and Grandma took Daisy and Benjy in the buggy; there had been talk of her grandparents waiting in town to take them home again, until the family learned that the examinations were to run from half-past nine till half-past three.

'What, the whole day just doing exams?' Grandma had said, shocked at the idea. Benjy needed to give her a good deal of reassurance that they would be allowed breaks between each examination, and would be in no danger of missing out on lunch or snacks.

Grandma said she was happy enough to spend the morning with Aunt Rosie, who now had a baby girl she had named Kate, and to visit Aunt Maudie in the afternoon, but six hours was longer than Grandpa wanted to stay in town. He dropped them off in the morning, and would collect them all again that afternoon.

The buggy ride into town gave ample time for Daisy's nerves to twist themselves as tightly as the handkerchief in her lap. Benjy seemed as calm as usual, which helped a little. They tried some last-minute preparation, asking each other grammar questions or words to spell, but it was difficult to concentrate with Grandma interrupting every few minutes to check that they had things like warm jackets, plenty of clean handkerchiefs, and their lunchboxes.

Grandpa dropped them off at the school gate. 'Good luck,' he said as they climbed down. 'I reckon you two will both do all right.'

'Of course they will,' Grandma said. 'Mind you don't sit in a draught, Benjy,' she called after them.

The last few days had seen a stream of well-wishes; at school where all the other pupils had said good luck, and Mr Fawcett had startled Daisy by adding his own good wishes and even smiling at them; from aunts and uncles and cousins on Sunday; and from her parents that morning when Grandpa came to collect her.

Daisy had never visited the district high school before. It had two steep, double-gabled buildings with asphalt between them and sports fields beyond, the school and its grounds taking up an entire block. Compared to their little one-roomed school it all looked enormous. She took a deep breath in an attempt to calm herself, and clutched surreptitiously at her new brooch. It was much too pretty to wear on an ordinary day at school, but today its reminder of Eddie was just what she needed for a burst of courage.

She and Benjy joined a line of pupils waiting to be allowed inside. There looked to be around thirty of them by the time the doors were opened and they were called in; Daisy recognized two or three from church, but most were unfamiliar to her. They filed into a huge classroom that must have been able to hold at least forty children, and when everyone was seated the first examination papers were given out.

It felt as long a day as Daisy had ever experienced, though punctuated with sections that went by in a rush as time ran out for a particular test. Often during the day she found herself touching Eddie's brooch for encouragement. She moved from paper to paper, grateful for the short breaks between each one. For her reading skills to be tested, she went to another, smaller room to read aloud to the headmaster, who was a stranger to her. It took an effort to make her voice come out clearly, and to remember to put some expression into the words.

She and Benjy sat on a wooden bench close to the asphalt tennis courts to eat their lunches, discussing the questions over sandwiches and biscuits. Benjy thought he might have made a spelling mistake in the composition test, but Daisy told him she was sure he would get a good enough mark in reading to make up for it.

The arithmetic tests seemed the longest of all. By the time Daisy had calculated how much it would cost to carpet a room of twenty feet by seventeen feet with carpet two feet and four inches wide at three shillings per yard, the numbers were blurring before her eyes. She blinked to clear them, checked her work, and moved on to a question about percentages and commission.

She did her best to keep her writing neat, particularly in the composition test. Her hand was cramped by the time the teacher supervising the room said it was time to put down their pens and sit with arms folded, waiting for the papers to be collected.

Grandpa and Grandma were there with the buggy when Daisy and Benjy joined the other pupils filing out of the room and down the steps.

'How did it go?' Grandpa asked.

'Not too bad, I think,' Benjy said. 'It's hard to tell, though.'

Daisy nodded her agreement; talking would have taken too much of an effort. She was so tired that on the way back to the valley she nodded off to sleep, head resting on Benjy's shoulder.

The results arrived a few weeks later, during which Daisy had wavered between cautious optimism and certainty of failure; just in time for the last week of school. Mr Fawcett positively beamed as he announced to the pupils that Daisy and Benjy had both passed the examinations, and called them to the front of the room to present their certificates.

Daisy gazed at the piece of card. Underneath the heading "Certificate of Proficiency", it stated that Margaret Amy Stewart, aged twelve years and nine months, had "fulfilled the requirements" of a certificate in December 1919. She clutched at it, and smiled across at Benjy. She had done it. She had the qualification to get into high school.

The certificate was made much of at home, first by Daisy's parents and soon after by Granny and Eddie when they arrived for the holidays. They all passed it from hand to hand, and while at first Daisy had to resist the urge to ask them to be careful with it, she could see there was no real need to be anxious: everyone treated her precious certificate with the proper respect.

Daisy's family went to her Uncle Richard's for lunch after church on the following Sunday. Granny went off with Uncle John instead, to spend the afternoon with her brothers and their families, but Eddie came along with Daisy and her parents.

Electricity had recently become available in the town of Ruatane, although there was no likelihood of it reaching the valley in the foreseeable future, and Uncle Richard was one of the first householders to adopt the convenience. The parlour and kitchen now each had a light bulb suspended from the ceiling, and Uncle Richard had sent away to Auckland for an electric iron, which was plugged into one of the light sockets when Aunt Maudie wanted to use it.

They all politely admired the electric light, even though there was not a great deal of effect in daylight. Granny and Eddie did not mention that they were quite familiar with electricity at home; even Daisy had become acquainted with its benefits on her own visit to Auckland years before.

After lunch, the adults settled into the parlour and Aunt Maudie sent the rest of them outside to enjoy the fine weather. Daisy saw a look of relief flit over Eddie's face; he found Lucy easier to cope with when they were not in a confined space. In some particularly strict families children were not allowed to play at all on a Sunday, but Aunt Maudie made do with telling them not to be too noisy about it.

Lucy strolled around the garden with a basket over one arm, gathering flowers to paint as well as to decorate the house. Flora settled onto a sofa on the verandah and flicked through the pages of a magazine belonging to her mother, full of illustrations of ladies in fancy clothes.

Lucy and Flora's little brothers, nine-year-old Nicky and Timmy who was almost seven, did not know Eddie well, and were uncharacteristically quiet around him at first. They joined Daisy and Eddie in a game of croquet, their shyness evaporating as Eddie got them talking about their friends and their favourite pastimes. When they learned that Eddie had played rugby for one of the best school teams in Auckland they could hardly get their questions out quickly enough, asking him about his best games, the biggest crowds and his most dramatic injuries.

'I don't suppose you play cricket, do you?' Nicky asked, looking hopeful. Both boys' faces lit up when Eddie said he had played it at school; Daisy added the information that he had been in the First Eleven. They at once abandoned their croquet mallets; Timmy ran and got bat and ball, and they insisted that Eddie show them his stance and grip.

The little boys were not at all ready to part with Eddie when Aunt Maudie came out to the verandah to tell them Daisy's parents were ready to go home. Only when Eddie promised that he would visit again over the summer and give them some proper coaching could Timmy be persuaded to let go of his sleeve.

Daisy went back into the house in time to catch the tail end of a conversation between the adults that had clearly been going on for some time.

'Oh, we wouldn't think of taking anything for her board,' Aunt Maudie said.

'Are you sure? We could manage a bit.' That was her father.

'No, Maudie's quite right, there's absolutely no need for that,' Uncle Richard said. 'She's our goddaughter, after all, and it'll be our pleasure to have her.'

'One more won't make much difference, anyway,' Aunt Maudie said. She turned to face Daisy. 'You're going to be boarding with us during the week when you go to the high school, dear.'

'And I'll look forward to having your help when I next have to do my stocktaking,' Uncle Richard added, smiling at her.

Aunt Sarah arrived just before Christmas, and Daisy's proficiency certificate was admired once again.

'And of course we've a longstanding agreement that I'm to have the privilege of paying any expenses,' she said to Daisy's parents; Daisy had been told that right back when she was a baby Aunt Sarah had announced she would insist on doing so.

'That's very good of you, Sarah,' Mama said. 'There won't be much to pay, though—Richard and Maudie won't take a penny for her keep.'

'Yes, how good of Doctor Townsend. I do recall a time when he wasn't quite such a supporter of higher education for girls.' Aunt Sarah's smile was a small one that seemed meant to be private. On the few occasions when Daisy had seen her aunt conversing with her Uncle Richard, she had had the sense that there was a certain prickliness between them, despite careful politeness on both sides. 'But I imagine there'll be a uniform to buy, and exercise books, that sort of thing. I'll write you a cheque before I leave to cover anything that might come up.'

No one was foolish enough to try arguing the point with Aunt Sarah. She brushed aside any attempt by Daisy and her parents to thank her, and changed the subject.

It was the first Christmas since Grandpa's big boys had come home, and Grandma wanted the whole family there for Christmas lunch. That meant six from Aunt Maudie's house, six from Daisy's, and five from Aunt Rosie's, along with the seven living at Grandpa's. They made such a crowd that Grandpa and the boys set up two trestle tables outdoors.

'It's nice to have us all together for a proper Christmas,' Grandma said when Grandpa had finished saying grace. 'All of us who've been spared, anyway.' She dabbed at her eyes, and everyone was silent for a few moments, remembering Kate; everyone except the youngest of the children, who soon began clamouring to be fed.

When they had all had as much as they could wish (or fit) of roast mutton and vegetables followed by Christmas pudding with cream, the women and girls did the dishes and joined the others on the verandah. The grown-ups chatted, and the older children played with the smaller ones, until the heat made the youngest children sleepy, along with more than one of the adults. Aunt Maudie and Aunt Rosie, who both had to get all the way into town, gathered up their children and husbands, said their goodbyes, and set off for home.

Daisy's family stayed on a little longer. She and Eddie followed Benjy to a far corner of the garden where a plum tree carried a small amount of fruit, which Eddie reached down for them from some of the higher branches.

'That's good about you being all set to go to high school,' Benjy said, wiping a trail of juice from his chin. 'I suppose I'd better get on and see if Ma will say I can.'

'Haven't you asked yet?' Daisy spoke around a mouthful of plum.

Benjy shook his head. 'I've been passing the odd remark about high school for a while now—you know, just saying how the work might be interesting, that sort of thing—but she hasn't taken the hint yet.'

'Why've you been putting it off so long?' Eddie asked. 'She won't mind, will she?'

'Well, it wasn't worth making a fuss about until I knew whether I'd passed the proficiency or not. And then with Christmas coming up I didn't want to upset her, not when I knew she was thinking about Kate a lot of the time.' Benjy glanced over his shoulder at the grown-ups still sitting on the verandah. 'And I'm not sure if she'll be as keen on the idea as all that, either.'

Haymaking finished on an afternoon in early January. This was always a time of satisfaction for Frank, when he could look at his tidy haystacks and know that feed was secure for the winter ahead. He glanced around the parlour that evening, and was not surprised to see that Joe and Mick had both nodded off, while the newspaper was wavering in Danny's hands. None of the older boys had quite the same endurance he had once been used to seeing in them, and Frank was feeling all of his own fifty-seven years. It was almost time to retire for the night; the thought of bed, and of resting his tired muscles, was an appealing one.

Benjy had worked as hard as any of them, though in his case it left fewer traces. He still looked wide-awake and alert as he closed the piano and studied his mother with what struck Frank as a somewhat wary expression.

'You did a good job today, boy,' Frank said. 'We can all take it a bit easier tomorrow, eh?'

'Thanks.' Benjy's gaze flicked to Frank, then rested somewhere in the space between his parents. 'It's not too long now till school starts up again—only about a month.'

'Mm? Yes, I suppose so.' Lizzie appeared to be only half-listening; she did not look up from her mending.

'Did you hear Daisy's going to board with Richard and Maudie when she goes to high school?'

'Yes, I did,' Lizzie said. 'It's good she can stay with them, that'll be a help.'

Her lips pursed in something like disapproval; Frank knew she had mixed feelings over Daisy going to high school. 'It's not a bad idea having her spend a bit of time in town,' she had said to Frank in the privacy of their room the previous evening. 'We've all got a bit too related to each other in the valley now, she'll need to get out and about more so she can meet other people. But I hope she won't go getting funny ideas at that school. Some of those women teachers end up as old maids.'

'I…' Benjy paused, cleared his throat, and tried again. 'I thought I might like to go to the high school, too.'

The mending dropped into Lizzie's lap. 'What would you want to do that for?'

'Well, they study interesting sorts of things—plays and poems and stuff, and learn French, and all that—much more than what we did at primary school.'

'That's all very well, but it hasn't got anything to do with farming, has it? Your father knows all there is to know about that, he can teach you better than some chaps at a school.'

'But I might want to find out about some other stuff.' Benjy spoke so quietly that Frank was not sure Lizzie had heard; she certainly showed no sign of it.

'Now, it's nice for Daisy, she might want to be a teacher for a little while before she gets married. And I suppose it's all right for boys like Eddie, if they want to get some flash job in the city and they're living handy to a school. But you don't want to be going all the way into Ruatane, not when we've finally got the other boys home again. You'll be able to help your father, and you and your brothers will all be working together. It'll be very nice.'

Lizzie had a look about her that Frank recognized from the time when Maudie had first grown old enough to argue; he had not seen that particular expression since Rosie married and left home. In those days

Lizzie had often ended the discussion by cutting off an argumentative daughter's protest with a firm, 'The subject's closed.'

There was no need for such a remark on this occasion. Although it was the first time Frank could ever recall Lizzie telling Benjy he could not have something he had asked for, his son did not make any fuss.

'All right. Never mind,' Benjy said, his voice low. He tidied away his music, and left the room with a murmured, 'Good night.'

Benjy's older brothers had taken no apparent notice of the conversation, but the noise and movement roused them sufficiently to stir in their places. Soon afterwards they took themselves off to bed, and Lizzie went down to the kitchen to help Maisie get ready for the morning.

Lizzie did not remark on Benjy's request when she joined Frank in their room a little later, and Frank himself said nothing on the subject. He lay awake in the darkness for a time, remembering the look of resigned disappointment he had seen on Benjy's face.

'How about you come down to the dairy factory with me?' Frank said to Benjy after the milking. 'I'm a bit weary this morning, I could do with a hand unloading the cans.'

Benjy jumped onto the cart seat beside him readily enough; he was always quick and obliging when given a task. While his brothers were away he had worked hard and without complaint, though Frank had never seen any actual enthusiasm from him, even when he had tried to engage Benjy in discussing milk yields or breeding lines.

They bounced along the track, the horses soon settling into a steady plod.

'So what's this about you wanting to go to high school?' Frank asked.

Benjy shot him a startled glance before his gaze flicked back to the road ahead. 'It doesn't matter. Ma said I couldn't.'

'Well, it won't do any harm to tell me about it. Come on, then, why do you want to go there? Not so keen on the farming, eh?'

'I don't mind helping with stuff, but I'm not much good at it, am I? Not like you and the others.'

'You're all right—I couldn't have managed without you while the other fellows were away, that's for sure.'

Benjy shrugged. 'I suppose so.'

Frank studied him, hunched in his seat and staring steadfastly ahead. He looked older since his illness, but it was still a boy's face under that mop of fair hair.

His older sons had all been so eager to go out with their papa that he had begun occasionally taking them about on the farm almost as soon as they were able to walk. Benjy was so much younger than the other boys that they had all left school to begin working with their father by the time it had struck Frank that he might be old enough to take out on the farm in his turn.

Benjy must have been around four years old then; somewhat small for his age, with hair so blond it was almost white, and bright blue eyes that studied the world with keen attention. He had held Frank's hand and trotted along at his side, staring around the milking shed, patting the new calves, and looking suitably awed when Frank lifted him onto a fence rail to see the bull. But for the entire time Frank had had the odd sensation that his small companion was humouring him; displaying an interest in whatever he was shown simply because it would please his father. It had been unsettling to feel himself indulged by a child who barely reached his elbow.

'So what do you reckon you'd like to do instead of farming?' Frank asked.

There was no immediate answer; he shifted the reins to a more comfortable grip, and glanced across to see Benjy picking at a callous on his palm.

'I don't exactly know,' Benjy admitted, not looking up. 'I'd like to find something I could be good at, but I don't know what it might be.'

'Well, maybe you should have a go at finding out. I don't see why you shouldn't go along to the high school for a bit, I think the rest of us can manage all right.'

Benjy's eyes met his; he saw a spark of hope that dimmed almost at once. 'But what about Ma?'

'I'll have a talk with her, see if I can get your ma to have another think about it. No promises, mind, but I'll see what I can do.'

Frank waited until he and Lizzie were alone that evening before raising the subject.

'Benjy's pretty keen on this high school business,' he said from his comfortable position propped against the pillows as he watched Lizzie brushing her hair.

The brush's strokes continued unabated. 'Oh, he's not really. It's just because of all this talk lately about Daisy going there—and then with Eddie down, too, talking about exams and the university and all. That's put the idea in his head.'

'No, I think there's more to it than that. I got him on his own today away from the boys and set him talking about it. I'd say he's had the high school in mind for a fair while now. I think we should let him do it.'

Lizzie lowered the brush and twisted on her chair to face him, her brow furrowed. 'Why would we want to do a thing like that? Boys don't go to high school to learn about farming—you certainly didn't.'

'Not everyone's cut out for the same thing, love. Benjy worked that hard helping me when the boys were away, I couldn't have asked for more. But his heart wasn't in it, not really.'

'But I don't want him going away like that.' There was a tremble in her voice; one that came all too readily ever since Kate's death.

'It's not so far, you know, it's not as if we'd never see him. He could stay with Maudie and Richard like Daisy's going to, they'd look after him all right, and he'd come home on the weekends.'

Lizzie looked on the verge of tears. Frank got out of bed and crossed the floor to her. He placed a hand on her shoulder and rubbed gently.

'There's been that much waste with the war and Kate and everything, love. Joe with his voice all but gone, and that cough of his never giving him a rest, and Mick just about jumping out of his skin if you so much as close a door too hard. And Danny with half his leg gone.' Not to mention Lizzie's youngest brother dead and buried in France, and Alf coming home a shell of a man. 'Benjy's got the idea he'd like to have a go at something different, and there's no harm in that. Let the boy do what he wants.'

'Letting another one go away when we've already lost Kate,' Lizzie said, her voice still quivery. 'I was looking forward to seeing her marry a nice chap and have little ones of her own.'

'And we could have lost Benjy with the flu as well. We could have lost any of the boys in the war—plenty of other families did. Benjy pulled through all right, and we should be grateful for that. And we should let him make the most of his life.'

'You really think he'd like going to that high school?'

'Well, he seemed to quite enjoy school here in the valley—more than any of the other kids did, anyway.'

Lizzie chewed at her lip, a habit that made her look much younger than she was. 'I want him to be happy, of course I do. But what's he going to do if it's not working on the farm?'

'I don't know, there's no hurry. He's a smart kid, getting the proficiency like that, maybe he might decide to be a teacher.'

Lizzie's eyes lit up. 'Yes, I've always said he was the cleverest of the lot of them, you know. He might end up being the teacher right here in the valley. That Mr Fawcett can't be far off retiring, Benjy could take over from him. He'd live at home and just go down to the school every day.'

Frank smiled at the ringing certainty in her voice. He had no idea whether Benjy wanted any such thing, let alone the likelihood that Mr

Fawcett might obligingly retire at just the right time for Benjy to take over from him. But it was good to see his confident Lizzie back again.

'Well, you never know how things might turn out.' He bent and kissed the top of her head.

Chapter Six

Daisy's Uncle Richard and Aunt Maudie were perhaps a little taken aback to learn that they would have two new members of the household rather than just Daisy. But they welcomed Benjy quite as warmly, and an extra bed was squeezed into Nicky and Timmy's room for him.

Lucy magnanimously cleared out one small drawer for Daisy, and perhaps an inch or two of wardrobe space. Aunt Maudie then did some tidying of the drawers and wardrobe, creating more than enough room for the few clothes Daisy would need during the week.

On the first day of term Daisy and Benjy set off with Flora and the two little boys. They all had the same destination; unlike the secondary schools in larger towns, where children went when they finished primary school around the age of thirteen, Ruatane had a district high school that covered both primary and secondary schooling on one site. Aunt Maudie and Lucy waved them off from the front gate, Lucy visibly aware of her status as the only one of them who had left school, and was therefore (in her own eyes, at least) a grown-up.

Nicky and Timmy soon crossed the road to walk with some boys they knew. A friend of Flora's came out of a gate, and Flora dropped back to dawdle along chatting with her, leaving Daisy and Benjy to themselves for the remainder of the walk. Benjy looked smart in his dark blue shorts and shirt, with a round cap on his head, while Daisy felt quietly proud of her own uniform: a navy serge tunic over a white blouse, and a straw hat trimmed with matching blue ribbon.

Two weeks earlier she and her mother had gone along to the town's dressmaker, Mrs Winder, who had measured Daisy and sent away for the uniform. There had been some discussion about underwear; in the last few months Daisy had developed enough of a bosom for Mrs Winder to suggest she needed support in that area.

'She's much too young for corsets and all that, though,' Mama said, much to Daisy's relief.

A brassiere would be quite sufficient, Mrs Winder said. Daisy's bosom was now firmly enclosed in a band of cotton brocade, hooked at the back and with tapes over the shoulders. As there was ample money left over from the cheque Aunt Sarah had written out, Daisy's mother had chosen one of the prettier brassieres, with lace edging and embroidery across the yoke, which cost three shillings more than the plainest one.

All her garments for the first day of school were new ones, right down to the pair of drawers fresh on that morning. Aunt Maudie had ironed the blouse for her the previous evening, using her smart new electric iron.

Grandma had expressed doubt that such a light piece of metal could be effective, but Daisy's blouse was beautifully pressed. The iron was much easier to use, her aunt told her, than the heavy ones Daisy was used to at home, which had to be lifted on and off the range as one cooled and the next was ready. The electric one only needed to be left plugged into the light socket till it heated up, although you did have to remember to unplug it, or it would just keep getting hotter and hotter. Aunt Maudie was yet to trust any of the girls with the new iron.

When they reached the school gates, Daisy checked that the pleats of her tunic were hanging straight and her stockings were unwrinkled before she entered the grounds at Benjy's side. A pleasant quiver of anticipation ran through her at the awareness that she and Benjy belonged here. They were high school pupils now.

They joined a trail of pupils to an open area behind the nearest building. A large number had already gathered; Daisy guessed there must be well over a hundred, almost all of them younger than her. A boy standing off to one side swung a noisy bell, and the children milling about formed into rows.

This must be an assembly, something that was never bothered with at the little valley school. Eddie had talked of such things at his school in Auckland, though those had taken place in a large hall, not out in the playground. Daisy and Benjy copied the others, joining a row near the back with what looked to be the other children of high school age.

Several grown-ups who must be the teachers came out of the building and lined up facing the pupils, followed by a dark-haired man with a large moustache; Daisy recognized him as the headmaster, Mr Harman. He gave a short address, welcoming them all to the school whether they were returning for the new year or arriving for the first time, and expressing a wish that they would work hard and do well in their exams.

Each teacher then stepped forward in turn, and called out the class that was to follow him or her; Daisy saw Flora, Nicky and Timmy going off with different teachers. A kind-looking lady gathered up the very smallest children, and the remaining two teachers called for the high school pupils to come with them.

Daisy and Benjy followed the others, most of whom looked quite at home; they were probably pupils who had been at the district high school right through their schooling, starting from five years old and now moving on to the secondary department.

This department had its own building, set off to one side of the main part of the school. There were two large classrooms, and one smaller room that seemed to be a mix of office and storeroom. One of the teachers went through the nearest door and called to the third-formers to follow him inside.

The first year of high school was called the third form; Daisy had gathered it was because some schools had Form One and Form Two instead of Standard Five and Six, and it all had to match up when people started high school. There was only one Form Three here; not like at Eddie's school, where each form was divided into half a dozen or more, graded by ability. Daisy counted seventeen in the room; that was fewer than the number who had passed the proficiency examinations, but several of those pupils would have gone straight into the sort of job that required a proficiency certificate; good jobs like working in a bank or delivering telegrams.

Tall windows lined two sides of the room. One wall had a door opening onto a corridor, and the remaining one was shared with the other classroom. The map of the Empire was a larger one than in their old school, and Daisy noticed a map of France next to it, along with some photographs of interesting-looking buildings that she would have liked to examine more closely.

Rather than the long, shared benches Daisy was used to, this room had a separate desk for each pupil, with a lid that flipped up and an inkwell set close to the top edge. She and Benjy chose neighbouring desks near the front of the room.

The teacher, Mr Grant, looked to be about Grandpa's age, Daisy thought. He had thin brown hair well on its way to turning grey, and creases around his mouth that suggested he often smiled. Mr Grant called out names in alphabetical order from his roll book; Daisy was relieved when she heard her own, last on the list. Mr Fawcett had assured Daisy and Benjy that he would send their details to the high school, and he had clearly kept to his word.

With the roll checked, Mr Grant wrote out a weekly timetable on the blackboard for the class to copy down in their exercise books. He explained that he would take them for English, French and history, while for mathematics and science they would go to Mr Ritchie's classroom next door.

The subjects all sounded interesting, though Daisy was quietly disappointed that there was no mention of Latin, which doctors all had to know. She clung to the thought that perhaps it might be offered after the third form.

'The girls will have domestic science lessons for two hours a week,' Mr Grant said. 'Mrs Dawson from the primary school will take you for that.'

Benjy met Daisy's eyes and sent a sympathetic look; he must know she would not be particularly happy at having to spend precious high school time on cooking and sewing. And what would the boys be doing that she would miss out on while she had to take domestic science? Daisy wondered. Probably something far more interesting, not to mention more useful to anyone wanting to become a doctor.

'And you boys will all be having lessons in agricultural science,' Mr Grant announced. 'That's considered an important subject in rural areas like this.'

Benjy's face was a picture. Daisy might have struggled not to laugh if amusement had not been driven out by a rush of sympathy.

'After Pa saying it was all right if I didn't want to go farming, and then him talking Ma around so I could come here,' he murmured to Daisy as soon as the teacher's attention was elsewhere. He grinned ruefully. 'I don't think I'll be in too much of a hurry to tell them about the school making me do this agriculture stuff!'

There was a good deal to get used to at the new school, and Daisy was glad of Benjy's company. To be surrounded by strangers all day would have been overwhelming without his familiar presence. Benjy himself did not appear to find it at all difficult to cope with their new surroundings; in fact he seemed to enjoy having so many new people to meet and make friends with. Everyone liked Benjy. It was just how he was made.

The appeal of being able to study a foreign language made up a little for Daisy's disappointment at the lack of Latin in her timetable. In their first French lesson later that week, Mr Grant went through the present tense conjugations of *être* and *avoir*, which meant "to be" and "to have", writing the various forms on the blackboard for them to copy down, and set a short list of vocabulary for them to practise at home. He also instructed them in how to introduce themselves; Daisy was quietly pleased at already knowing the words for this thanks to Eddie, who had taught her a few phrases of French soon after he began high school himself. The teacher even praised her pronunciation, to Daisy's mingled embarrassment and delight.

Mr Grant was a nice man, but Daisy did not yet feel confident enough to ask questions in class. Confidence was never a problem for Benjy, though. Towards the end of this first lesson, he raised his hand and waited to get the teacher's attention.

'Sir, why don't we have Latin as well as French?' Benjy asked when Mr Grant nodded in his direction. 'They do in the high schools in Auckland, don't they? Is it because we're just a district high school in the country?'

Daisy had admitted to Benjy on their first day of school that she was disappointed not to be learning Latin, although not the reason for her disappointment. For a moment she thought she might suffer the mortification of having him tell Mr Grant that it was Daisy who really wanted to know. But he merely flashed a small grin at her and turned back to the teacher.

'No, many of the other district high schools do offer Latin—the larger ones, at any rate,' Mr Grant said. 'But I'm afraid we're simply too small here in Ruatane. Our secondary department's roll is barely enough for us to be allowed two teachers, and we've all we can manage with the subjects we currently have—even if my Latin were strong enough to teach the subject, which I'll confess it's not. It does make passing the matriculation examination a little more complicated, of course, but it can be done even without Latin.' The corners of his mouth twitched, as if he were struggling not to smile. 'And matriculation is only strictly relevant if you're aiming to attend university. Is that what you're planning, Benjy? You'll be the first from Ruatane if you do reach such lofty heights.'

Benjy met his gaze without the least trace of embarrassment. 'I don't know what I'll do yet.' He turned his brightest smile on Mr Grant. 'But I might go to university. You never know, eh?'

Few people could resist that grin of Benjy's. Mr Grant allowed his mouth to curve into a smile of its own. 'No, you certainly don't.' He raised a piece of chalk to the blackboard. 'Now, shall we come back down to earth and on to the second person plural?'

Mr Ritchie's classroom, where they went for their mathematics and science lessons, was just along the corridor from Mr Grant's. The rooms were much the same size, but as well as its rows of desks Mr Ritchie's had a bench that ran the length of one wall, which they used in science classes. The bench had a sink at either end, with running water connected, and there were several spirit burners, which were like small lamps with glass bowls. The burners were filled with methylated spirits and their wicks lit, then used to heat the contents of glass beakers. Wooden racks of test tubes were stacked along the bench, ready to have various chemicals measured into them.

The room's back wall had a large chart on it, labelled "Periodic Table of Elements"; some of the elements were familiar substances like iron and sulphur, but many of the other names were new to Daisy. A glass cabinet under the chart held small balance scales and a set of weights, all made of brass, and on a shelf next to that stood a wooden case that Daisy thought might hold a microscope; her Uncle Richard had a similar case in his study.

The next year up from Daisy's, Form Four, generally swapped with her class from room to room for the different subjects. Form Four had fifteen pupils, two fewer than Daisy's year. Most pupils only spent two years in the high school classes; that was generally considered a sound secondary school education, and was enough for entry to quite a few office jobs. A few stayed on longer: as well as these two classes, the school had a Form Five which this year contained four pupils.

With only two classrooms in the secondary department, the fifth-formers could not have one to themselves; instead they sat at a small knot of desks at the back of the room during the younger pupils' lessons, and the teacher spent time with them when he had set the larger class some exercise to work on. When they were in the same room as Daisy she sometimes managed to overhear whatever they were discussing. The snippets she caught of their mathematics lessons made little sense, and she could translate only a very occasional word of what French she heard, but some of their science classes sounded quite interesting.

Unlike at much grander secondary schools like Eddie's old one, there was no sixth form at Ruatane District High School. Goodness only knew where they could sit if the school did have any sixth-formers, Daisy mused as she glanced around the crowded classroom.

At high school the other pupils all seemed to refer to their parents as "Mum" and "Dad", rather than Ma and Pa, as Daisy was used to hearing in the valley. Their schooldays would probably run more smoothly the better they fitted in, even in such small matters, so Daisy and Benjy soon took to imitating their classmates' use during school hours.

Daisy was at an age where she might have begun calling her parents Ma and Pa at home, as Benjy did with Grandma and Grandpa, but whenever there was no one outside the family to hear she clung to her old names for them: Mama and Papa. The familiar words had been a comfort during the dark days when the army had taken her father away and her mother had seemed worryingly fragile, and they were a comfort now, when so much was new and different. Perhaps it was babyish from a girl of nearly thirteen, but that did not matter.

The changes in Daisy's life went beyond a new school. She had stayed at her uncle and aunt's on several occasions in the past, but boarding with them demanded adjustments of its own.

The bustle and noise of a house shared with half a dozen others, especially when one of those was Lucy, could be an enjoyable change when it was only for a few days out of the year, always with the comforting thought that she would soon be back in the peace and quiet of her own home with her mother and father. But now the months stretched ahead, carrying the awareness that except during the school holidays she would be living here all the time, only going home on the weekends. Somehow that made the household seem even busier and more noisy.

At lunchtime one day she confided to Benjy that she was finding it a little difficult to get used to living at her uncle's.

'I never really thought about that,' Benjy said. 'I suppose it does get a bit noisy, especially round the table when everyone talks at once. I don't mind it, though, it's like being at home. Well, like it used to be at home, anyway, before the war and the flu and all.' His smile was rather wistful.

Learning to cope with a lively household was a small enough cost when it meant she was able to go to high school. And her uncle and aunt were very kind, never giving the slightest impression that it was any trouble to have two extra people in the house. Aunt Maudie always asked how their day had gone at school; if she sometimes gave the impression that she was not really listening to their answer, that was probably because she was thinking about the dinner cooking on the range, or whether Nicky and Timmy had washed their hands, or when Uncle Richard might be home from visiting a patient.

Uncle Richard often asked about their day, too, over the evening meal or later in the parlour, and in his case always seemed genuinely interested in the answer.

'We had French today,' Benjy said at the dinner table after their first lesson in the subject. 'Daisy's really good at it, Mr Grant said so.'

'He didn't really say that,' Daisy protested. 'It was just that I already knew a little bit of French from Eddie telling me.'

'Father can talk French, too,' Lucy said. 'We went to France when I was little—Father and Mother and Flora and me—and he talked to people there just as if he was French himself.'

'I don't remember that,' Flora said, looking up from her rice pudding.

'No, you were just a baby,' Aunt Maudie said. 'You were born while we were in England, just before we went over to the Continent.'

'That's right, Flora was too little to take any notice. I remember it, though, going to France and everywhere,' Lucy said.

'Of course you don't, Lucy, you were barely three. You've heard us talking about it, that's all. I suppose you might remember coming back on the boat, but not all the rest of it.'

Lucy insisted that she remembered every detail of their travels; Aunt Maudie insisted that she did not. Voices were raised, and no doubt would have been raised higher had Uncle Richard not cut in.

'I'm sure your mother is right, Lucy. No, that's enough,' he said; Lucy, who had opened her mouth to argue the point further, shut it again under her father's steady gaze and scowled down at her bowl.

Uncle Richard turned his attention to Benjy and Daisy. 'Yes, I do speak a little French—or at least I did at one time. It's thoroughly rusty these days. Hmm, let me see...' His forehead creased in concentration. *Je pense que le temps sera beau demain.* "I think the weather will be fine tomorrow"—at least I hope that's what I said,' he added, smiling.

'It sounded pretty good to me,' Benjy said. Daisy murmured agreement; she recognized the phrase from practising French with Eddie, but had no intention of boasting the fact.

'Thank you, Benjy, though I suspect you're being too generous. I'm pleased to hear that you and Daisy are off to a good start with your own studies.'

With the last of his pudding finished, Uncle Richard rose from the table and left for the parlour, while Aunt Maudie and the girls began clearing the table.

'I do so remember going to France,' Lucy muttered when her father was safely out of earshot. She snatched at the nearest plates and stacked them with a clatter, scowling at them as if they had offended her in some way.

'Careful with those dishes, Lucy, don't go chipping them,' Aunt Maudie said. 'Come on, you boys.' She left the girls and Benjy to do the dishes, and led Nicky and Timmy off to their room, where she would help them into their pyjamas and make sure they washed their feet before letting them sit in the parlour until their bedtime.

On their first day of school Aunt Maudie had told Daisy and Benjy not to bother helping with the dishes, since they had so much schoolwork to do; they had thanked her, then quietly got on with their share of washing and drying. They needed the table cleared of dishes and the room cleared of cousins before they could get on with their homework; almost as importantly, Lucy's temper would not be sweetened by the sight of them sitting at the table while she had to do the dishes.

Aunt Maudie was back in time to help them finish putting away the plates. When the kitchen was tidy, Lucy and Flora headed off to the parlour, Daisy and Benjy spread out their textbooks and exercise books on the table, and Aunt Maudie pulled the cord that made the electric light come on, turning the edges of their books sharp and clear.

'I don't want you straining your eyes with all that work,' she said. 'And don't keep at it too long, I'm sure the teachers don't mean you to sit up late working.'

Having Benjy to work with made the task much more pleasant. They puzzled their way through exercises from their textbooks, and practised speaking French to each other. It was a little like the times when Eddie had helped her with her schoolwork back on the farm; though Eddie, of course, had done similar work several years before, and generally knew the answers without having to try very hard.

Not only might it have been boring if Daisy had had to sit in the kitchen all by herself, it would probably have worried Aunt Maudie. Being alone was not something anyone in that busy house (except perhaps her uncle) was used to. Her aunt might even have told Lucy to stay out there with Daisy to keep her from being lonely, which would not have helped her concentrate.

But as it was, with Benjy's company it seemed hardly any time at all before they could pack up their books and join the others in the parlour for the nicest part of the evening.

The little boys lay sprawled on a large rug, playing a card game that involved matching up pictures of different animals. Uncle Richard sat in the largest armchair, reading what Daisy recognized as a medical journal that was sent to him from England. Aunt Maudie was mending a cuff on one of the boys' shirts, Flora had some knitting that looked like a doll's cardigan, and Lucy was stitching at a piece of fine linen held taut in a wooden hoop, doing the finishing touches on a bouquet of flowers embroidered in shades of blue and mauve, the colours blending subtly into each other. Lucy could make up her own patterns for quite complicated embroidery, rather than following a printed one.

Daisy paused to admire Lucy's work before settling onto one of the heavy, well-upholstered sofas. Domestic science had been one of her lessons that afternoon, and she had done what felt like quite enough sewing for one day. Instead, she took up the book she had left on a side table the previous evening, one belonging to Lucy, full of boarding school tales of midnight feasts and hockey matches.

The little boys looked up from their game as Benjy passed them on his way to the piano. Timmy nudged Nicky as if daring him to speak.

'Timmy wants to know why you do the dishes, Benjy,' Nicky said, only partially successful in suppressing a giggle. 'Boys don't have to do that.'

Benjy twisted on the piano stool to face them. He was actually their uncle, as Aunt Maudie was his big sister. But since he was even younger than Lucy, no one ever suggested that the boys should call him "Uncle".

'Dishes aren't that hard to do,' he said, flashing a grin at Aunt Maudie. 'Of course girls are better at it, but boys can manage, too.'

Nicky frowned, clearly disconcerted. 'But that's not... I didn't mean—'

'It's worth doing them, too,' Benjy cut in. 'Didn't you know your mother keeps the best biscuits for whoever does the dishes?'

Nicky's mouth dropped open, Timmy let out a startled squeak, and both boys turned indignant faces on their mother. 'That's not fair!' Timmy said.

'I think Benjy might just possibly be teasing you boys,' Uncle Richard said, a smile in his eyes. 'I don't believe your mother is in the habit of hiding food from you.'

Aunt Maudie was clearly struggling to hide her own amusement. 'As if you two don't get plenty of biscuits already! And I'm not likely to trust you with my good dishes, anyway.'

The boys looked less than convinced. They studied Benjy through narrowed eyes for a few moments, then returned to their game as Benjy took up the nearest piece of music.

From their first evening here, Daisy had noticed that the tunes Benjy chose seemed simpler than the ones she heard him play at home. She had soon realised why: Benjy was always careful to persuade Flora to perform as well. Flora's playing sounded nice enough to Daisy, but she could tell that it was not as accomplished as Benjy's. The complicated pieces he liked to try at home, when his fingers sometimes looked as if they were dancing over the keys, would have made Flora far too shy to play after him.

He played a few pieces, then called Flora over to the piano, claiming he was getting tired.

'We should try a duet some time,' Benjy said as he made way for Flora on the stool. 'I miss doing those.' Flora looked dubious at the suggestion, though Daisy expected Benjy would manage to persuade her before long.

Nicky and Timmy's game had involved a fair amount of laughing and occasional protests as each card was slapped down, but by the time Flora was on her second piece Timmy's head was drooping and the game seemed all but forgotten.

'Time for bed, you two,' Aunt Maudie said. Nicky's half-hearted protest, insisting that he was not tired, was interrupted by a huge yawn. After goodnights and kisses, Aunt Maudie carried Timmy from the room with Nicky trailing behind.

'They sleep like rocks, those two,' Benjy remarked. 'Last night I tripped over a toy train or something when I was going to bed, and I let out a bit of a yell before I could help it, but I didn't hear a peep out of them.'

Aunt Maudie returned from tucking in the boys. She tidied away their game and took up her sewing once again. Flora played a little more, Daisy got to the end of a story about a horse that had been saved from some vague but ominous fate, and had gone on to be a champion show jumper. Her eyelids were feeling heavy, so rather than start the next story she closed the book and replaced it on the side table.

Later hours were kept in her uncle's house than Daisy was used to at home, and she would not have felt any particular resentment if she had been sent to bed when the little boys were. But it was pleasant enough to sink back into the sofa, listening to the music and to the quiet voices around her, letting her eyelids droop until the room's light turned dull red.

'You'd better be going off to bed, you've got school tomorrow,' Aunt Maudie said after what felt like quite some time. 'I think Daisy's just about asleep already.'

Lucy was always careful to claim her right to sit up a little later than the others. She bestowed a warm smile on the younger three as she wished them goodnight, looking very like her mother.

Daisy took a candlestick and followed Benjy and Flora out into the passage, cupping one hand around the flame to shield it from draughts. The glow of electric light spilled from the parlour, bleaching her candle's flame until Aunt Maudie closed the door in their wake.

The girls undressed by candlelight. Daisy hung up her clothes and shrugged on her nightdress, then blew out the candle and joined Flora in the bed.

By the end of the first week of term, crammed as it had been with strange faces and unfamiliar experiences, Daisy was more than ready to see home and her parents again. On Friday afternoon she and Benjy walked back from school more briskly than usual, soon leaving the younger children, who were ambling along with friends, in their wake.

Grandpa's buggy was on the road outside Uncle Richard's, the horses tethered to the fence, and Grandpa himself appeared on the verandah with Aunt Maudie and Lucy a few moments after Benjy pushed the gate open.

'You two just about ready to go, then?' he asked. 'I'd like to get on.'

'They need to get changed out of their uniforms first, Pa,' Aunt Maudie said. 'It'll only take a minute or so.'

She hurried them inside and down the passage to their rooms; she and Lucy followed Daisy into hers. 'Your grandpa's keen to get back to the farm,' Aunt Maudie said, taking hold of one of Daisy's cuffs to undo its buttons. 'It's not a good time of day for him to go out, with milking and all.'

Daisy pulled the tunic over her head and undid her blouse. Lucy held out her ordinary dress, and hung the uniform in the wardrobe while Daisy scrambled into the frock.

'I've packed yours and Benjy's bags—I left most of your things in the drawers, you shouldn't need to take much home just for a couple of days.' Aunt Maudie placed Daisy's small suitcase by the door. 'I should've told you to do it last night, I just didn't think of it then. You're just about ready? Good. I'll go and see if Benjy needs a hurry-up.'

She darted from the room, with Lucy in her wake. Daisy, caught up in her aunt's haste, hurriedly fastened her last few buttons, checked that nothing vital had been left in the chest of drawers, and took her suitcase out to the passage.

Benjy was already there with his own case. Aunt Maudie had disappeared, but she returned a moment later, carrying a plate wrapped in a clean tea towel.

'There's no time to make you a proper afternoon tea, but take these biscuits with you,' she said, handing the plate to Daisy. 'You've got your case too, Benjy? Come on, then.'

Grandpa was already in the buggy. Daisy and Benjy clambered in, Grandpa flicked the reins, and they were off, Aunt Maudie and Lucy waving to them from the gate.

'It's just about four o'clock,' Grandpa said. 'I didn't think of it being that sort of time before you got back from the school. Ah well, never mind about that. It can't be helped.'

'We'll be pretty late with the milking, eh?' Benjy said.

'I told the other fellows to just get on with it, not wait for me. They'll still be at it by the time we get back, though.'

'I'll give you a hand,' Benjy said. 'I've had the whole week off milking, time I got back into a bit of farming.' He shot a grin in Daisy's direction; she was sure he was thinking of his agricultural science classes.

'As long as I can talk your ma into sparing you. She's been just about beside herself all day, looking forward to getting you home again.' Grandpa smiled as he spoke, but it was a tired sort of smile.

When the horses had been walked long enough to get rid of any stiffness, Grandpa urged them from a walk into a trot.

'How are you getting on at the school, then?' he asked.

'Pretty good so far,' Benjy said. 'The other kids seem all right, and the teachers are good, aren't they, Daisy?'

'Yes, they are. We've mostly had Mr Grant so far—he's our form master.'

'He takes us for English and French. We're going to learn about Shakespeare this year. And we've done quite a bit of French already.'

Benjy launched into a detailed description of their various subjects, though Daisy noticed he made no mention of agricultural science. Grandpa nodded and smiled, and added an occasional 'Is that right?', or 'That sounds pretty good,' when Benjy seemed to be expecting a comment.

'Your Ma would've liked to come in with me to fetch you this afternoon,' Grandpa said when Benjy's recital came to an end at last. 'But she said she'd stay home so she could make you a special dinner. I don't think she trusted Maisie to get the pudding right on her own.'

Grandpa let the horses ease back to a walk on the rougher sections of the road; eager as he obviously was to get back to the farm, it was not right to treat animals harshly just because you were in a hurry. It was almost an hour after they had left Aunt Maudie's when they reached the track that led up to Grandpa's house.

The buggy was halted just long enough for Benjy to jump down. He headed off towards the house, and Grandpa flicked the reins to get the horses started again for the last part of the journey to Daisy's home.

'Sorry to be such a bother, Grandpa,' Daisy said.

'That's all right, love, don't you worry. It won't be dark for a fair while yet, and your grandma won't mind waiting dinner for us.'

Grandpa was never one to complain or growl about things, but Daisy knew perfectly well that it was a nuisance for him to have to come and fetch Benjy and her. And while the evenings were still long, by the end of term dusk would be falling not much past five o'clock.

'This is close enough, I can walk from here,' she said when they got to her father's farm. But Grandpa smiled and shook his head, and insisted on taking her right to the house.

Daisy felt a twinge of guilt as the buggy carried her up the hill, remembering the sight of Benjy trudging along the steep track to his own home. But a glimpse of her mother and father waving at her from the yard in front of the cowshed drove out all thoughts beyond her eagerness to join them and share her news.

Grandpa dropped her off at the garden gate. Daisy raced up to the house, pausing there only long enough to drop her suitcase in her room and fling a pinafore over her dress to protect it from dirt. In the porch she removed her shoes and pulled on a pair of boots, then ran down to join her parents at the cowshed.

It was hard to get the words out quickly enough to match the speed of her thoughts. Daisy was quite hoarse by the time she had told her parents all that had happened during the week, and more than ready to hear their talk of small events at home.

She sat on a milking stool and closed her eyes, content to listen to their voices against the background of milk swishing into buckets, an occasional quiet snort or the stamp of a hoof. The shed smelt of milk and the grassy breath of cows. It was warm and familiar, and she had almost two whole days ahead of her before she would have to say goodbye to her parents for another week.

Chapter Seven

Eddie loved university at once. High school had been enjoyable enough for the most part, but now he had said goodbye to irritations such as his mathematics teacher, while finding whole new opportunities to explore the subjects he liked best.

He had heard from some of Aunt Sarah's acquaintances that the university colleges in the South Island, established earlier than Auckland's and with more solid funding from the government, were grand affairs, with imposing stone buildings spread over large sites. Auckland University College, by comparison, was a jumble of old buildings that had been designed for other uses but now did service as lecture rooms and offices. Until a few years ago, lectures had been held in the shed-like building that had been Parliament way back in the 1850s. The old building had finally been demolished the previous year, to no one's regret as far as Eddie could tell.

His college might not look particularly impressive, but it was wonderfully convenient. Eddie only had to cross the street from home and he was there. It was so close that he could have slept in every morning and still easily arrive at his lectures on time, as he pointed out in the drawing room one evening, but Aunt Sarah said it would not be fair to upset the routine of the kitchen staff just for him to lie in bed of a morning.

Though there was no longer anything quite as shabby as the old Parliament House, most of the facilities were showing their age. The shining exception was the brand new science building, which had had its official opening just a few months earlier. It dominated one corner of the University's site, its plaster and red brick standing out against the old wooden buildings, with a grand frontage complete with arches and pillars.

Two of Eddie's classmates from high school had also enrolled at the university, though he shared only one course with each of them. Geoffrey planned to become a teacher; among his other subjects, he took Latin with Eddie. Philip had found a position as a law clerk, and could only attend classes part-time. While Aunt Sarah had stood firm on her decision that Eddie should study a certain amount of law, he had managed to negotiate this down to a single course in property law, which happened to be one of Philip's subjects.

Latin and law were among the two-thirds or so of university lectures still held in the old grammar school buildings, which had been abandoned when the school moved to its current site; much as Eddie enjoyed having his friends' company, the cramped and dingy rooms made him appreciate science lectures all the more.

The science building held lecture theatres, laboratories, and miscellaneous rooms with a variety of uses, including several dark-rooms and one set aside for grinding rocks. The biology department occupied most of the building's upper storey, and its lecture theatre was the largest in the whole college, with room for two hundred students on tiered seating, and projection lanterns for the slides that illustrated lecture topics. There were rooms with charts and photographs, and the laboratories had been set up with the latest equipment; one laboratory was an open-air one, with concrete tanks for live specimens.

Eddie started the year knowing none of his fellow science students. He was soon on a friendly basis with them all, but was happy enough to work on his own much of the time.

With such interesting subjects and fine equipment, it was easy to become engrossed in the work. A few weeks into the first term, Eddie was in one of the biology laboratories, studying a set of microscope slides that showed the cell structure of various plants. From time to time he glanced up from the microscope to note his observations, drawing an occasional rough diagram to remind himself of what he had seen.

It was fascinating to observe the subtle details of various species, several of which he was familiar with in their full-grown form. Eddie was so caught up in his task that he was startled when the supervising lecturer called out that it was time to pack up their work.

Eddie put away the slides and bundled his notes into a satchel before making his way into the corridor. He had enough time before his next lecture to go home for a snack, as he quite often did during the day. But Philip would be arriving from work before long, so Eddie decided to go to the Common Room instead, hoping to meet up with his friend there.

His route took him past the biology department's museum, with its cases of mounted insects and fine collection of New Zealand plants. He had explored the museum twice already, but he paused at the doorway, wondering if he had time for a brief visit. Probably not, he reluctantly decided. But he was familiar enough with the museum's contents to describe them in the next letter he would send to Daisy, one he had begun the previous evening. Not that he was having any difficulty finding things to write about lately; with so many new experiences and discoveries, his letters were sometimes so thick that it was a struggle to fit them in an envelope.

At the head of the stairs Eddie stood to one side to let two girls whom he vaguely recognized from botany lectures go down ahead of him. After having spent his entire high school years at a boys-only school, sharing lectures with girls had taken a little getting used to, but he no longer found their presence overly distracting. There were several in his Latin classes, too, and Geoffrey said girls outnumbered boys in French. This was something Geoffrey seemed more than happy about; one girl in particular he mentioned quite often, and Eddie gathered he had gone as far as actually having a brief conversation with her.

He exited the science building and ambled over to the Common Room. There were no girls here, of course; they had their own separate one. He exchanged nods and hellos with the half-dozen or so fellow students already there as he crossed the room and claimed a chair at a table near the windows.

Eddie opened his satchel and pulled out his notes from the laboratory session, glanced at the clock, and shoved the notes away again. It would be better to leave re-drawing his illustrations and writing up his notes until he was home, with space to spread his textbooks around the room.

Instead, he took out the unfinished letter to Daisy, which he had slipped into his satchel that morning. It already ran to several pages, but he added a few lines about his work in the laboratory while the details were fresh in his mind.

He had just begun telling her about the biology museum when Philip dropped into a chair on the opposite side of the table, grinning broadly.

'I saw Geoff over by the library,' Philip said, tilting his chair until its back rested against the wall. 'I don't think he noticed me, though. He was talking to a girl—must be that one he's been going on about—so I thought I'd better not butt in.'

Eddie grinned back. 'Good thing you didn't. He wouldn't have thanked you for it.'

'I'll say. She's not bad-looking, either. Tidy pair of legs on her, from what I could see.' Philip glanced down at Eddie's letter, and his grin widened. 'What are you up to, anyway? Writing to your girl, eh?'

Eddie snorted at the suggestion, although Philip was clearly joking. 'Of course not—it's just to my cousin, telling her about this place. I think she might be going to university in a few years. Hey, did you finish that law essay?' he asked, for some reason struck by the urge to change the subject. 'What did you put about leases?'

'Oh, yes, I asked one of the older chaps at work about that.' Philip readily launched into the topic, going into rather more detail than Eddie had expected. It was something of a relief when Geoffrey joined them, looking decidedly pleased with himself.

'I asked Dora if she'd like to go down to a tearoom some time for afternoon tea,' he announced, taking a chair by Philip.

'So she's real after all, eh?' Eddie said. 'I was starting to think you'd made her up.'

'And she said yes?' Philip affected a look of mock concern. 'Are you sure she's not soft in the head?'

If they had still been at school, the conversation might have degenerated into a wrestling match at this point, but university demanded a certain decorum. Geoffrey made do with digging his elbow into Philip's arm and muttering 'Idiots' at them both, grinning foolishly all the while.

'Well, I'm just about ready to give up on the pair of you,' Philip said, sliding his chair out of easy reach. 'You sitting there like a pup with its tongue hanging out, and Ed's got nothing better to do than write love letters to his girl.'

'She's not my girl!' Eddie protested. 'Well, she's a girl, but she's just my cousin. I told you, it's just a letter to Daisy.'

The ink was dry on his last few words. He folded the page, slid it closer to the edge of the table, and rested one hand on the paper, shielding it from sight.

Daisy soon became used to moving from room to room for their different subjects. Benjy's favourite was English, especially when they began studying a play by Shakespeare called *The Merchant of Venice*. Daisy enjoyed lessons with Mr Grant, but chemistry classes next door with Mr Ritchie were the ones she most looked forward to each week. Chemistry was the only subject on offer that seemed to have any clear connection with learning to be a doctor; it must surely be useful to know the chemical properties of the various substances that went into medicines, and how they reacted when combined.

Even more useful would be to learn just how these chemicals worked on people, but their science lessons were divided between chemistry and physics, and did not seem to include anything at all about living things.

Daisy decided to ask about this when the bell rang at the end of a physics lesson one day, marking time for morning interval. She finished jotting down her notes on the lesson, which had been about light and its different wavelengths, then stood back as the other pupils made their way out of the room.

Benjy glanced back inquiringly from the doorway. It was tempting to ask him to put the question for her, but she brushed that thought aside; she could not go all through high school hiding behind Benjy. Instead she mouthed, 'In a minute' at him, and watched him disappear into the corridor.

She waited for Mr Ritchie to finish putting away the lenses in a drawer under his desk, not wanting to startle him while he was handling the delicate equipment. When the drawer was safely closed, she cleared her throat and spoke.

'Excuse me, Sir, I was—'

'Eh?' Mr Ritchie jerked his head upright. He was stockier than Mr Grant, and probably several years younger, with sandy hair on his head and over much of his face. Sunlight from the windows reflected off his spectacle lenses; despite looking almost as thick as the ones from their wavelength experiment, they did not always seem to be of much use. If someone asked a question during class he was inclined to stare about on all sides for a while before identifying the speaker; at present, with no one there but Daisy, it took him only a few moments to peer in her direction. 'Yes, ah...' He squinted more narrowly at her. 'Daisy. Yes, what is it?'

'I just wondered why we don't have any lessons about plants or animals—it's very interesting to learn about chemistry and light and everything,' she added quickly. 'But are we going to study those other things later?'

Mr Ritchie had a face that was less likely to fall into a smile than Mr Grant's, but now that she was used to him Daisy did not find him at all frightening. He seemed mildly amused by her question.

'It's simple enough,' he said, gathering up papers as he spoke. 'There isn't time for all the sciences, so we cover the most important ones. That obviously means chemistry and physics.'

'I see,' Daisy said, though she was not at all sure that she did.

Fortunately Mr Ritchie appeared ready enough to elaborate. 'Chemistry is, of course, the foundation on which all other branches of science stand—it even forms a large part of the so-called agricultural science. And physics is a good, solid subject, where you can take accurate measurements without worrying about things changing on you.'

'Like animals and people?' Daisy asked. She did not bother mentioning domestic science; she doubted if Mr Ritchie considered it to be science at all.

'Exactly. Once you get into zoology and physiology and the like, it all gets terribly vague. They have their place, naturally, but the syllabus gives priority to the more serious branches of science, ones with a proper mathematical basis.'

Mr Ritchie's eyes glinted behind their lenses. He sometimes became quite animated during mathematics lessons, a subject which he appeared to find even more interesting than science.

'I see,' Daisy repeated. 'Thank you, Sir.'

She had no intention of arguing with her teacher, so fought down the urge to suggest that perhaps studying how human beings worked might be the most serious subject of all. Daisy smiled politely and slipped out to the corridor to join Benjy, who was waiting patiently for her.

Twice each week, Daisy and Benjy parted company for their separate lessons in domestic and agricultural skills.

Domestic science, a fancy name for cooking and sewing, had turned out to be somewhat less boring than Daisy had feared. One of the teachers from the school's primary department, Mrs Dawson, took their lessons, which were held in the staff-room and the small kitchen attached. She was a cheerful lady who when she was not actually giving them instructions was quite happy to let the girls chat away as they worked.

Cooking lessons usually seemed to mean making a tasty lunch for the teachers to enjoy, but Mrs Dawson always let them prepare more pudding than necessary, and then eat it together just before the class ended. During their sewing lessons they took turns on the school's sewing machine which, unlike the ancient machine at home that had once been Granny's, was worked by a foot treadle rather than a hand-wheel. While she waited for her time on the sewing machine, Daisy gathered frills on an elaborate new petticoat that seemed likely to take her the whole term to finish, and practised fine embroidery stitches on squares of linen.

They were also meant to study laundry-work, though Mrs Dawson made do with having them iron their sewing projects. The school was connected to the town's electricity supply, which meant that as well as having proper light to stitch by even on dull days Daisy at last had the chance to try out an electric iron.

Along with their practical tasks, Mrs Dawson gave them talks about such topics as which foods were good for growing children and how to make suitable meals for invalids, and the importance of washing one's hands. They were generally things Daisy was familiar with from home, but it was interesting to hear a little of the theory behind such matters as building strong bones, which apparently required calcium. She copied down Mrs Dawson's notes under the headings of "Nutrition" and "Hygiene", resolving to see if she could learn more on these subjects from some of the books in her Uncle Richard's study.

Poor Benjy, on the other hand, was finding agricultural science just as unrewarding as expected. Their lessons, he told Daisy, largely consisted of studying the mineral contents of different soil types, or copying out tables of such dry facts as crop yields, meat production per acre, and fertilizer use. It was no real surprise to hear that Mr Ritchie managed to turn the subject into a list of sums. His practical lessons provided no relief when they turned out to be spending an hour or so a week with the school's groundsman, digging over the garden beds.

Benjy grumbled half-heartedly to Daisy, but gave no hint of his dissatisfaction to anyone else. No wonder: Daisy could picture Grandma descending on the school in wrath, telling the authorities in no uncertain terms that they were not to make Benjy dig gardens, an event that would shake even his self-assurance.

In any case, neither of them had any desire to let slip a word of complaint about school. They were lucky to be able to go to high school at all, rather than straight to work or helping at home the way most people did. And they were both well aware that various family members were going to a good deal of trouble to get them to and from the farm each week.

There was some talk of getting Daisy and Benjy to ride to and from town on their own, but the idea was soon dismissed; horses were too necessary on the farms for two of them to be spared all week to stand around cropping Uncle Richard's lawn. After that first Friday when Grandpa had collected them, he and one of Daisy's parents generally took turns to make the trip into town; usually her mother, as her father was better able to manage the milking on his own. Those trips home were rushed affairs, with everyone eager to get back to the farm work while daylight lasted.

'Do you think you could get Ma to come and pick us up sometimes?' Benjy asked his father one afternoon.

It seemed a reasonable suggestion to Daisy, as Grandma was not involved in milking, but Grandpa shook his head.

'No, I wouldn't want to worry her like that. Your ma hasn't driven the buggy in years, she's got out of the way of it. Mind you, she used to be pretty good at the driving in the old days. Back when we'd first got married.' He smiled; the small, private sort of smile a person wore when thinking of something not to be shared aloud.

Aunt Maudie generally looked anxious when Grandpa had to fetch them, and one Friday she surprised Daisy and Benjy by announcing that she would be taking them home that afternoon.

'I saw Aunt Lily in town yesterday, and I sent a message with her to tell Ma and Pa I'd bring you. I was thinking of going out to the valley and visiting Ma this week anyway, so it'll suit me nicely,' Aunt Maudie claimed, though Daisy was sure it could not have suited her to go out so late in the day.

Lucy and Flora were left to get the dinner on, which perhaps did not bode well for the meal, and to watch their young brothers until their mother came home.

It was close to five o'clock when they pulled up to Grandpa's house. Benjy doubled Daisy home on one of the farm horses to save her aunt

81

the extra journey; when they met again on the following Sunday he told her that Aunt Maudie had already left when he arrived back home, having stayed barely a quarter of an hour according to Grandma. Even so, the sun must have been getting low in the sky by the time her aunt got back to town.

Aunt Maudie did take them home on a few more occasions until the days grew too short for it to be at all sensible; she certainly could not drive her buggy home by herself in the dark. Fortunately by then they were beginning to dry the cows off, and milking was taking less time, so it was easier for Grandpa or Daisy's parents to manage the special trip into town.

There was no escaping the fact that they were being a nuisance, but somehow or other it worked out each week, and none of the grown-ups grumbled; at least not in Daisy's or Benjy's hearing.

By the time their first term was drawing to a close in May, milking had finished for the season and Daisy had grown used to arriving home after dusk each Friday. They had their term examinations that month; both passed easily, with Benjy topping the class in English and Daisy well ahead of her classmates in chemistry.

The May holidays meant two lovely weeks at home; to make the break even more delightful, Eddie came down with Granny and stayed for a few days. It was his first May visit in years; while he was attending high school, this time of year had been devoted to rugby. Now that he was at university, he told her, he might be too busy in August studying for the end-of-year examinations, but he did not want to wait until December to visit the farm.

'And I can try out for the university rugby team when I get back to Auckland,' Eddie said, his smile making it clear how confident he was of being selected.

Daisy had already learned about Eddie's university in some detail from his letters, but she was more than happy to hear it all again in his own voice. In his turn, Eddie wanted to hear about her own new school, asking her what she was covering in the different subjects and getting her to describe her classrooms.

During much of Eddie's stay the weather kept them indoors, but on his last afternoon the sky settled to a steel grey that looked reliable enough for the two of them to risk a stroll in the bush.

The morning's rain weighed down each leaf, fat drops occasionally sliding off, and the branches poised to deliver a small cascade if Daisy or Eddie brushed against them as they passed. Somewhere out of sight a bellbird was caroling, while a fantail flitted about in their wake, darting at the insects their steps were disturbing.

'Totara—that's called "Podocarpus totara" in Latin.' Eddie slapped the rough, flaking bark of a tree trunk towering over their path. 'I can't remember what rimu is, though. Something-or-other cupressinum, I think.' He pulled a length of supplejack vine aside for Daisy to pass. 'That's good you're getting on all right in science—I expect you need chemistry to be a doctor.'

They had both been careful not to let slip a word of Daisy's secret when in the hearing of others, and this was the first chance they had had to broach the subject.

'I suppose so, with all those medicines. But...' Daisy trailed off, chewing at her lip.

'What?' Eddie prompted. 'You're not worried about it, are you? You're really good at it. Heck, you came top of your class!'

Daisy smiled at his praise. 'No, chemistry's all right. It's Latin—I thought we'd do it at high school.'

'I thought you would, too. I'd never heard of a high school not doing Latin. But it mightn't even matter—maybe you won't need it.'

'I think I will, though. Uncle Richard said one time that doctors all do. His books use Latin for the names of diseases and parts of the body and everything.'

'Do they? Hmm, that's a bit of a nuisance, then.' Eddie frowned in thought, but moments later his brow cleared. 'No, it'll turn out all right— the roll might go up next year, and then they'd probably get a Latin teacher. It wouldn't matter that you'd missed a year, you'd catch up no trouble.'

Eddie had a way of making the world seem brighter, though Daisy found it a good deal harder to believe that her school's roll would magically increase for no particular reason. But she answered Eddie's smile with one of her own. It was a relief to have shared her worries, even if it made no real difference.

Chapter Eight

All through Daisy's years at primary school the winter term had felt longer than the others. This year those months seemed to drag even more.

It was the wettest time of year, and the drive home to the valley every Friday afternoon frequently meant a lowering grey sky and sheets of rain drumming against the buggy's top, mud splashing up from the track to spatter their clothes. Walking to school on days when it was windy as well as rainy often left them damp despite their coats, and the fire in each classroom struggled to heat the draughty building.

Her uncle's house was warm and comfortable, and a good deal larger than Daisy's home in the valley, but it could feel crowded on those winter days when they had all been trapped indoors, first at school then at home; especially when it came to the little boys. Nicky and Timmy seemed to put the energy that would have gone on kicking a ball around the playground or climbing trees in their own backyard into making noise. Sometimes they ran around the house, banging against walls and furniture in spite of their mother's urging to be careful. When Aunt Maudie persuaded them to play one of their board games instead, their voices tended to rise in both pitch and volume until they were all but shouting.

Daisy was relieved if her uncle happened to be at home when the boys got particularly noisy, as he was more likely to insist that they settle down. It was a relief tinged with guilt: being glad that Uncle Richard had been disturbed did not seem right. In any case, even a scolding from their father did not have a long-lasting effect on the noise.

The August holidays came at last, allowing Daisy to go home to the valley in time to teach that season's batch of calves to drink from a bucket. Milking had started again, and she helped her parents with the twice-daily task. Granny came for a week; she spent much of her time in the kitchen, filling the cake tins with half a dozen different sorts of biscuits.

'No, I enjoy it. It's the only chance I get to do any baking these days,' Granny always said if Daisy's mother told her not to go to any bother.

As he had warned in May, Eddie did not come down for the holidays. There was talk of his being busy with study, though Granny said he also planned to go out on the train one day with friends from university to do some walking in the Waitakere range to the west of Auckland.

'It's still a bit wet for wandering around up there, he'll probably come home covered in mud. Not that he'll mind.' Granny smiled as she spoke.

She was used to boys, she often said, with four brothers, then two sons, and now Eddie.

The new term began, and now the end of the year, with its all-important examinations that would allow them to go on to Form Four, seemed to be drawing close at an alarming rate.

Daisy and Benjy were getting more homework these days, which meant spending longer working in the kitchen each evening. On some nights they were still hard at it when Aunt Maudie sent the little boys off to bed; she would then insist that Daisy and Benjy come through to the parlour for a while before their own bedtime.

They could not spread out their exercise books until the kitchen was free, which was not till dinner was finished and the dishes done, but they sometimes used the parlour for a while when they came home from school, doing the reading set for them, testing each other on questions from their textbooks, or practising their French vocabulary. Making such use of the parlour was only possible when the weather was fine enough for Nicky and Timmy to be playing outside, Flora was not at the piano, and Lucy was not in the mood to demand Daisy's attention for whatever project had currently captured her interest.

A few days before the examinations were due to start, Mr Grant had Daisy gather up the class's French homework and bring it to his desk. She placed the exercise books before him, then took the opportunity to put the question that had been preying on her mind.

'Sir, do you think we might start doing Latin next year?' she asked, keeping her voice low so as not to attract attention from her classmates. 'If the roll goes up, I mean—then we might get an extra teacher so we could have Latin.'

Mr Grant shook his head. 'I shouldn't think so, Daisy. If anything, the roll might be down a little next year. Though I'm fairly confident my own position and Mr Ritchie's are safe enough, I don't think there's any danger of my being required to start teaching Latin to the children of Ruatane.'

He smiled as he spoke, but Daisy did not find it easy to muster an answering one.

Benjy gave her a quizzical look when they were outside eating their sandwiches at lunchtime.

'Are you all right?' he asked between bites. 'You're pretty quiet today.'

The half-hearted effort she had been making to hide her disappointment had clearly not been enough to fool Benjy. 'I'm just thinking about exams and next year and all that,' she said vaguely. 'I hope we can use the parlour today, I want to write up those chemistry notes straight away.'

'I expect we'll be able to.' Benjy studied Daisy's lunch packet more closely. 'I'll have that biscuit if you don't want it,' he added.

Benjy's optimism was not rewarded. When they got back to Uncle Richard's after school, the sound of voices from the parlour told them the room was fully occupied, though not by small boys. Aunt Maudie was entertaining a guest.

'Blast—it's Aunt Susannah,' Benjy whispered to Daisy after risking a glance around the edge of the door.

They all called the rather grand lady "Aunt"; she was, in fact, Granny's stepmother. In fairy tales the word always seemed to have "wicked" attached to it; while Daisy had never actually heard anyone describe Aunt Susannah as wicked, she was fairly sure that Granny did not like her stepmother very much.

He had not pulled back out of sight quickly enough. 'Is that you, Benjy?' Aunt Maudie called. 'Come in here a minute, you two. Say hello to Aunt Susannah.'

Benjy pulled a face at Daisy, but it was too late to make their escape. They dutifully filed into the parlour, where the guest had established herself in the best armchair. Lucy sat to one side, fingering a pile of fabric swatches that had no doubt been brought by Aunt Susannah, who was considered an expert on matters of style, despite still choosing to wear the more fortified fashions of earlier years rather than the looser, more comfortable-looking dresses generally preferred by younger women like Aunt Maudie. Uncle Richard was on the other side of the fireplace, his face set in the sort of expression people wore when trying to seem a good deal more interested than they actually were.

Aunt Susannah must be quite old, as she had two grown-up sons as well as step-children, but she still held herself erect, and her gaze was sharply alert. She always gave Daisy the impression of being encased in particularly rigid underwear; it was difficult to imagine her ever bending in the middle. Perhaps she still wore the older style of corset, which Daisy's mother recalled with something of a shudder: heavily boned and designed to be tightly laced, with not a hint of the elastic panels found in more modern garments.

Daisy and Benjy each murmured a polite, 'How do you do'. Aunt Susannah inclined her head, with its crown of firmly pinned grey hair, and bestowed a smile on them before returning to what she had been holding forth on before the interruption: how busy her son Thomas was with his job, and how well he was doing.

Daisy saw her Uncle Thomas occasionally at church, and sometimes in the Bank of New Zealand where he worked. He was a nice man, always ready with a smile and a kind word. 'Tom must have the patience of a saint, putting up with his mother all these years,' she had once overheard Grandma remark. 'He's just like Amy,' Grandma had added; Amy was what she called Granny. Aunt Susannah had another son, Daisy's Uncle George, a large, cheerful man. Daisy met him less often, as Uncle George was usually off on his sailing ship or at his home somewhere to the east of Ruatane.

She and Benjy made their escape from the room without even pausing to take one of the biscuits arranged on a dainty tiered china plate. Uncle Richard was getting up from his chair as they left, and when they set off down the passage Daisy heard him making his apologies to Aunt Susannah, saying that he had work in his study that he needed to get back to.

The kitchen table was as cluttered as it always was at this time of day, so they went out to the verandah. There was no chance of spreading out any exercise books, as the only table at hand was barely large enough to hold a cup of tea, but they settled themselves into two cane chairs overlooking the lawn and picked up a textbook each, piling the others at their feet.

They worked their way through a list of important dates in the Wars of the Roses from their history book, then moved on to French, taking turns to recite the conjugations of several irregular verbs. It was not the most exciting of work, and Daisy was ready enough to let Benjy persuade her to practise some French conversation every now and again, even though that would not be part of their examinations.

The younger children, who had lingered behind with friends on the way home, got back soon after Daisy and Benjy had settled down to work. Flora slipped off to join the others in the parlour, while Nicky and Timmy set up their wicket and began a game of two-man cricket, accompanied by much whooping and shouting.

From time to time the boys called out to Benjy to come and play; he managed to resist until he and Daisy had got all the way to the end of their list of verbs at *venir*.

'Let's leave the rest of this lot till after dinner when we can use the kitchen table,' he said to Daisy. 'We've done pretty well for now.' He closed his French book with a slap, placed it on top of the pile, and rose to his feet. 'All right, you've talked me into it,' he called over the verandah rail to Nicky and Timmy.

Writing up her chemistry notes was still on Daisy's mind, but Benjy was right: there was a limit to what they could manage without a proper table to use. She frowned in thought, then gathered up her books and made her way through the house to the one room where it might be possible for her to work.

The door to her uncle's study stood just sufficiently ajar for Daisy to see Uncle Richard behind his desk, reading something. She knocked, pushed the door further open, and took a step inside.

There was a rustling of paper as Uncle Richard looked up; Daisy might have thought he looked a little embarrassed, if the idea had not been so unlikely.

'What can I do for you, Daisy?' He glanced at her pile of books. 'Ah, you're wanting somewhere to study, are you?'

'Only if I won't be a nuisance.'

'Not in the least, dear.' He raised his hands from behind the desk to reveal a rather crumpled newspaper held between them. 'As you can see, I'm not so very busy at the moment, despite the impression I may have given in the parlour.' He smiled at Daisy, folded the newspaper and put it to one side. 'I do feel rather superfluous when the conversation turns to the latest fashions, so I decided to make my escape while I could.'

Her uncle's desk was a large one, and the corner nearest Daisy held only a few medical journals, which he retrieved and placed on the nearest shelf. 'Will this do? Have you room enough?'

'Yes, this is really good, thank you.'

Daisy spread out her books and writing materials and set to work, while her uncle returned to his newspaper. She was soon engrossed in the details of that day's chemistry experiment, which had involved adding sulphuric acid to zinc, then dripping copper sulphate into the test tube. There were tables of results to set out on carefully ruled lines, along with a diagram of the apparatus used. Mr Ritchie had hinted that a description of just such an experiment might be included in their upcoming examination, so it was worth making an effort to record the details properly.

Some time later Daisy became aware that she was being observed. She glanced up from the page to see that Uncle Richard was now standing by his bookshelves and looking over at her work.

'That looks rather impressive, Daisy. Ah, chemistry, I see.'

'We've been studying catalysts.' Daisy moved her arm to one side to give him a better view of the page. 'We did an experiment today, with zinc and copper and acid, and we made some hydrogen gas.'

Uncle Richard appeared genuinely interested. He pulled his chair around the table and sat beside her. Prompted by his questions, Daisy explained her diagram and the results.

'I used to enjoy this sort of thing myself, back in my student days,' her uncle remarked. 'Chemistry took up a good deal of the first year of study, I seem to recall. Oh, and when we moved on to studying pharmacology, great store was set on shaping the various materials so that they created perfectly round tablets,' he adding, smiling. 'Nowadays I can buy most of them ready-made, so I'm sure my skills in that area have lapsed.'

It was good to have someone to discuss chemistry with, though a glance at the shelves beyond him reminded Daisy of the treasures they held: books on anatomy and medicines, with wondrous illustrations of the body both inside and out, and ways to treat disease and injuries. For all Mr Ritchie's talk of chemistry as the most important of the sciences, she could not help but feel disappointed at not being able to study biology at school. It was even more disappointing not to study Latin, and have the hope of being able to understand the descriptions within those books for herself.

'Speaking of tablets, that reminds me—I should get on and check whether I need to add anything to my order before I send it off tomorrow,' Uncle Richard said, rising from his chair.

'Can I help you?' Daisy asked. While she was at primary school she had sometimes assisted her uncle with similar tasks when staying with Lucy during the school holidays.

'No, there's no need for that, you're quite busy enough with your own work.'

'It's been good doing it in here. Thank you for letting me use your desk, Uncle Richard.'

'You're most welcome, dear. Please feel free to ask whenever you've the need. I'm more than happy to share my sanctuary with a fellow devotee of peace and quiet.'

Daisy watched him gaze around the room, his smile turning pensive. 'There's such a thing as too much quiet, of course,' he said. 'During the influenza epidemic I spent my entire time right here in this room when I wasn't out seeing patients.'

'Lucy told me you slept in here back then.'

'Yes, I did. I set up a camp stretcher for sleeping, and your aunt would bring my meals around to the outer door and leave them on the verandah for me to collect. I barely saw the children that entire time, and your Aunt Maudie and I could only converse through the door, or with the length of the verandah between us.'

Daisy heard the remembered loneliness in his voice. 'You helped a lot of people get well again,' she said, her own voice made quiet by the solemness of the subject.

'Perhaps in some cases. I did my best, at any rate. But I don't think I've ever felt more helpless, Daisy.'

He was staring at the length of wall where his camp stretcher must have been during that lonely time. As Daisy watched, he gave his head a quick shake, as if recalling himself to his present surroundings.

'I'm sorry, dear, don't let me keep you from your work,' he said.

Uncle Richard began sorting through his medicines, and Daisy returned to her study. She had finished off the chemistry notes and was well into her mathematics homework when the scraping of chairs made itself heard from the direction of the parlour, followed by what seemed to be a drawn-out farewell at the front door. Footsteps approached her uncle's study, and a moment later Aunt Maudie appeared in the doorway.

'Was that your Aunt Susannah going?' Uncle Richard asked.

'Yes, at last! I thought she'd never leave. I mean, I like talking about the fashions and all, and she brought around some nice magazines she gets sent down from Auckland, but she always stays so long. It's all very well for her, but I've got to get dinner on. Oh, you're hiding away in here too, Daisy?' Aunt Maudie said, smiling at her. 'Look at you with all those books of yours! You're always working, aren't you, dear? I'm sure you'll do very well with the teaching business, being so keen on books and all.'

Aunt Maudie disappeared before Daisy had the chance to think of a suitable reply. She fiddled with her pencil and stared at the row of equations before her, but now the figures refused to make sense, her concentration broken. How was she supposed to answer when people kept talking about being a teacher? By smiling and nodding and saying nothing at all? It felt like putting on an act, and she was tired of it.

'Your aunt's quite right, you've an excellent attitude to your work,' Uncle Richard said, sliding a drawer closed. 'That will serve you well as you go on with your studies. I expect you're very much looking forward to becoming a teacher.'

Saying yes would have been an outright lie. Daisy gazed fixedly down at the page, with its rows of meaningless figures, and heard the silence grow loud as Uncle Richard waited for her answer.

'Daisy? Are you all right, dear?'

Daisy lifted her gaze to meet her uncle's quizzical expression. 'I don't want to be a teacher. I want to be a doctor.'

She spoke quietly, but her words broke the calmness of the room like a stone dropped into a still pool. Her uncle looked startled, then she saw a flicker of amusement cross his face until he schooled his expression into a more sober one.

'Daisy, if I've influenced you in some way while you've been living under my roof—I know at times I've allowed you to look at books that perhaps weren't always quite appropriate—or simply by talking too much about medical matters without considering my audience... I'd hate to think I've put such an... unexpected idea into your head.'

'No, it's not from books or anything. I've wanted to for years and years, ever since I was quite little. I think it might have started when I first heard about you saving Mama's life when I was born,' she added shyly, and saw the trace of a smile curve her uncle's lips.

'That's why I wanted to go to high school,' Daisy went on, her voice gaining strength now that the confession was out. 'I knew I'd need to do that before I could go to the university and learn to be a doctor. I want to help people, like Mama when she was sick, or all those people who had the flu. I think I could do it, too—I like finding out how hearts and livers and everything work, and I could learn about the different medicines and things...' She trailed off. It sounded like boasting. Said out loud in this room, surrounded by medical books and in front of a real doctor, it sounded like nonsense. 'I didn't ever want to be a teacher, people just thought I must do,' she finished in a smaller voice.

'And you chose not to correct them, because of the reaction you expected to get. Including from me.' Uncle Richard was smiling more openly, but not as if he thought it was silly, or a joke. He put down his notebook and sat on the edge of the desk close to Daisy.

'At first I didn't know if I could even try doing it,' Daisy said. 'I wasn't sure if they'd let girls be doctors, but then I heard there're some lady ones.'

'There are indeed—I was reading just this week of a lady doctor who did heroic service for her community during the epidemic. I imagine women who succeed in medicine tend to be quite exceptional people.'

Exceptional. Not ordinary like her. Not just a girl from a farm who went to Ruatane District High School. 'I thought I could be one, too. But I suppose I'll have to think of something else to do now. I probably can't be a doctor.'

'Why do you say that, dear? You sounded so full of enthusiasm a moment ago.'

'I think those girls who get to be doctors must go to bigger schools than ours, so they can study the right things. We don't even have Latin at our school, and you have to know Latin to be a doctor, don't you?'

'Oh, certainly. That's essential.'

'I thought so. Because you need to know Latin to understand the names of the bones and veins and things, and all those different medicines.'

'Well, yes, that does help, but that's not what I meant. Latin is the foundation of a true education—an education for one of the professions, that is. One can't have a proper grounding in reasoning—in the ability to think logically—without at least a basic training in Latin.'

Either the room had somehow grown larger, or Daisy herself had become smaller. 'Oh. I didn't know that,' she said, slumping a little lower in the chair.

Her uncle was staring thoughtfully at her, while Daisy wondered if she could manage to leave the room without making things even more embarrassing by crying.

'You've truly set your heart on this, haven't you?'

Daisy nodded, not trusting her voice.

'You must realise that it's not an easy path, least of all for a woman. Still, I don't see that it would do any harm to set you a little further along the way.' He reached across and patted Daisy's hand. 'Perhaps you'll prove to be exceptional, Daisy. I rather think you might.'

Daisy sat taller, warmed by her uncle's praise. 'But what about the Latin?'

'Well, we may be able to do something about that. I'll need to begin tutoring the boys before too much longer—they'll be off to boarding school in a few years' time.'

'Won't they be going to high school here?'

Uncle Richard shook his head. 'I expect Nicky and Timmy to enter one of the professions—not necessarily medicine, of course, unless they're drawn in that direction. I'm sure that your teachers do their best, but, as you've already realised for yourself, your school doesn't provide an ideal foundation for a higher education. So we'll need to send them to school in Auckland before their high school years begin. Ideally, they'd already be attending what's known as a prep school, but your aunt and I don't wish to send them away from home so young. I plan to give them what preparation I can for grammar school myself, and of course that means a basic grounding in Latin. Would you like me to tutor you at the same time?'

Would she like it? The mingled relief and gratitude made Daisy feel as if her chest might burst. If she had been just a little younger she might have skipped around the room. Instead she made do with giving him her brightest smile and saying, 'Yes, thank you, Uncle Richard. I'd like that very much.'

'We can begin lessons when you're not quite so busy with your examinations.' Her uncle got up and slid his chair around to its usual position on the far side of the desk. 'What do your parents think of this ambition of yours, Daisy?'

'I haven't told them yet. You're the first person I've told ex—' *Except Eddie*, she had been about to say, but the hint of a frown she saw on her uncle's face made her bite back the words.

'In that case, I suggest you do so at the earliest opportunity. I'll need to hear that you have their permission before we do anything about your Latin—I couldn't possibly encourage such an ambition behind their backs.'

'I'll ask them when I go home this weekend. Will that be all right?'

'Yes, that's an excellent idea.' His frown had disappeared now. 'Assuming they're happy with it, I'll very much look forward to making a start on this, Daisy.'

'I will, too,' Daisy said, returning his smile.

Chapter Nine

It felt like far too serious a discussion to squeeze into a quiet moment during milking, or while helping get dinner on. Daisy waited until she was settled comfortably in the parlour with her parents that Friday evening, nibbling at an almond-topped biscuit while her mother told her about a horse she had been treating for a nasty abscess.

'Mr Gibson was going on about it down at the factory, singing your Ma's praises,' Daisy's father put in when her mother had finished the tale. 'He said he thought he might have to shoot that horse, it was in such a bad state. "Stewart's wife's a wonder, the way she's got with animals," he was telling all the other blokes.'

'Oh, such a fuss some of those men make,' her mother said, smiling and shaking her head at the same time. 'He gave me two and sixpence, so I suppose he must've been pleased. I think it was a rough bit of harness that started the trouble—it looked just about worn out, so I told him he should get a new lot from your Uncle Bernard.'

Daisy took a sip of warm milk to wash down the last of the biscuit, then placed the cup on the arm of her chair.

'I've got some news, too,' she announced.

Both faces turned to her, probably expecting something about her examinations or a lesson at school, and managing to look more interested than they might actually have been.

'Have you, love? What's your news, then?' her father asked.

How did you announce something so momentous? It was probably best to be straightforward. 'I've decided what I'm going to do when I finish school.'

They both looked mildly puzzled. Daisy was sure the word "teacher" was hovering on one or both pairs of lips; she spoke quickly to forestall it.

'I want to be a doctor.'

Puzzlement turned to confusion, bordering on astonishment. They glanced at each other, then turned back to Daisy. Her father's mouth fell open; her mother was the first to recover the power of speech.

'A... doctor?' she echoed, as if unsure she had heard properly. 'I never thought of you doing something like that, Daisy.'

'Is that the right sort of thing for a girl to do?' her father asked. He winced a little at the look her mother shot him. 'I mean, it could be a pretty rough sort of job, couldn't it?'

'Well, I suppose if a girl really wanted to...' Mama said, though she looked uncertain as she turned back to Daisy. '*Can* girls be doctors, though?'

'Yes, they can—I heard about some lady doctors, and then Uncle Richard told me just the other day about one.' It would be as well not to mention that the lady doctor in question had died in the course of her work during the influenza epidemic. 'I'm sorry, I know I should have told you first, but we were talking about school and it just came out. He didn't give me the idea or anything, I thought of it for myself.'

Only for the briefest of moments had she considered keeping her uncle's role quiet; conscience got the better of her almost at once. Fortunately her parents did not seem bothered over not being the first to hear; they were more concerned with other matters.

'I don't know about the idea of a girl doing some of the jobs doctors have to,' her father said. 'I mean, looking after men and all. I suppose nurses do that stuff, too, but I don't know if I'd be too keen on you being a nurse, come to that.'

Her mother's quick grimace suggested she was equally unconvinced, but Daisy snatched at her father's words.

'But don't you think it would be good for women to be able to have a lady doctor if they wanted one? It must be hard for them sometimes, having to let a man doctor look after them.'

Her parents' eyes met. 'Yes, it is,' her mother said quietly. 'It's very hard.'

'Wouldn't you have rather had a lady doctor when… you know, when I was little?' Daisy asked, pressing her point as firmly as she dared; having babies was not a subject grown-ups liked to talk about in front of girls her age.

'I'd never heard of such a thing then. But yes, I would. It would've been much better.'

'It sure would,' Daisy's father said. 'I'd have far rather you could have just had women looking after you.' He covered Mama's hand with his own much larger one, and for a few moments they almost seemed to forget Daisy's presence.

Mama retrieved her hand, and they both turned to face Daisy again.

'Of course they didn't have lady doctors back then,' her mother said; Daisy was fairly sure that was wrong, but now was not the time to argue over something so unimportant. 'But in the olden days they didn't even let women vote. Times have changed, and a jolly good thing, too. Anyway, I've always said people should do the things they're best at.'

'Like getting Papa to knead the bread?' Daisy asked.

'That's right,' her mother said, smiling at Papa. 'You're much better at kneading bread than I am, with those great big hands of yours.'

'And then there's the way you've got with animals,' Papa said to her. 'They just about talk to you, like your pa's always said. Some chaps say men are the only ones who know anything about farm work, but that's a lot of rot.'

'So it is. I don't see why a girl couldn't be just as good as a boy at doctoring, either. But how do you learn to do it, Daisy?' her mother asked. 'They don't teach that at the school, do they?'

'No, you go to university to learn those things. I'll have to do the matriculation exam while I'm at high school, you need that to get into university. Then I'd have lots more exams to pass before I could be a doctor. I think they're really hard ones, too.'

'But you've always done so well with the schoolwork, I shouldn't think you'll have much bother passing the exams.'

'Of course you won't,' Daisy's father agreed.

Daisy was quite sure it would not be as simple as that, but her parents' easy confidence set a warm feeling in her chest.

'We can go over to your grandpa's tomorrow,' Mama said. 'We should get on and tell everyone over there that you're going to be a doctor.'

'Yes, we'd better,' Daisy's father said. 'We'd never hear the end of it if your grandmother got wind of the news from someone else first.'

Daisy and her parents arrived at Grandpa's next day in time for afternoon tea, to find the whole household gathered around the kitchen table. Uncle Mick half-rose when they came in, and Daisy noticed him flick a glance at the far door as if planning an escape; Benjy had mentioned to Daisy that Uncle Mick generally left the room if visitors seemed likely to be noisy. But when Uncle Danny saw that it was only Daisy and her parents, he took hold of his brother's arm and pulled him back down to his seat.

Her mother added a plate of ginger biscuits to the food already set out. She and Daisy's father took the chairs Grandma directed them to, while Benjy slid along his bench to make room for Daisy.

She left it to her parents to raise the subject of medicine, and her mother wisely waited until Grandma had loaded up their plates with the biscuits she thought they should have and had told Aunt Maisie to put on a fresh pot of tea. It was always best to let Grandma organise everyone first; otherwise she would only interrupt whoever tried to talk until she had finished having her say.

Mama poured tea for herself and Papa, stirred sugar into her cup, and waited till Grandma paused for breath.

'We've got some news about Daisy,' she said into the sudden peace. 'She's going to be a doctor.'

Daisy stared down at her lap, aware of all eyes in the room turned on her. She made herself look up to meet those gazes.

Aunt Maisie showed blank astonishment, while Grandpa's big boys appeared only mildly interested. Grandpa himself was looking surprised and perhaps a little bit proud at the same time. Benjy's mouth hung slightly open; Daisy felt a pang of guilt at not having shared her secret with him before the rest of the family learned it.

Grandma's reaction was the one Daisy awaited most apprehensively. Her expression gave nothing away, and Daisy's mother spoke again before Grandma had the chance to say anything.

'They have lady doctors nowadays, you know, and I think it's a jolly good idea—Davie and I both do. It'd be much better for women to be able to have another woman look after them. I wish there'd been lady doctors when Daisy was born.'

Mama was looking at Grandma as she spoke; it was clear that, like Daisy, hers was the opinion she was particularly anxious to hear.

Grandma nodded slowly, her expression thoughtful. 'Lady doctors, eh? Well, they didn't have such notions in my day. But yes, you're quite right. That'd be a fine thing when there's any sort of trouble like that.'

She was taking the news so calmly that for a moment Daisy doubted the evidence of her own ears. But Grandma had, after all, had eight babies. Though Daisy had no idea if her grandmother had ever let a doctor near her at such a time (and it was not easy to imagine that she might), Grandma must know a lot about the things that could go wrong.

'I've always had a feeling you might go off and do something a bit odd, ever since you got the idea in your head of going to high school,' Grandma remarked.

Grandpa reached across the corner of the table and squeezed Grandma's hand. 'It's good to have a few people getting funny ideas sometimes,' he said, smiling at Daisy. 'We'd never get anywhere if we all just went on the same way forever.'

Uncle Danny took the largest of the biscuits. 'There's nothing wrong with women doing that stuff,' he said between bites. 'Those nurses were pretty good in the hospitals, eh, Joe?'

'They sure were,' Uncle Joe said. 'Really kept your spirits up, too.'

'She's not going to be a nurse, she's going to be a doctor,' Mama said while Daisy was still wondering if it would be considered cheeky to argue with her uncles. 'It's not the same at all.'

'No, no, of course not,' Uncle Danny said, picking up a few crumbs. 'They were just about as good as doctors, anyway, some of them.'

Benjy got up from the table. 'I'd like to look at a bit of homework with Daisy while she's here,' he said, catching Daisy's eye and indicating with a tilt of his head that she should come with him. She murmured an 'excuse me' and followed him from the room then up the passage, leaving her mother still fruitlessly trying to convince the uncles that a lady doctor was quite different from a nurse.

Benjy had shared his bedroom with Uncle Danny until his big brothers all went off to the war, but now that they were home again he still had the room to himself. The older boys had decided they would rather bunk in together, even though it made for a crush. Sometimes, Benjy had told her, they sat in their room after dinner instead of joining the rest of the family in the parlour. On warm evenings they would leave the door open; with smoke billowing out from the three of them all puffing away, Aunt Maisie had once rushed in thinking the room was on fire.

Benjy pulled the door closed so that they would not be overheard. 'You kept that pretty quiet,' he remarked.

'I didn't want to say anything until I knew I could really have a go at it—I thought it was better not to in case it all came to nothing. Sorry, Benjy, I wish I could have told you before.'

'No, that's all right, don't worry about it. You don't always want to be telling other people all your business.' Benjy flopped onto the bed, and Daisy sat down next to him. 'Looks like I'll be doing this teaching business on my own, eh?' he said, grinning at her. 'That's if I turn out to do it after all.'

'I don't suppose you're interested in being a doctor, are you?' Daisy said, returning his grin.

Benjy pulled a face. 'I think that'd be worse than being a farmer. I bet you'll be good at it, though. So how do you get to be a doctor, anyway?'

Daisy shared the scraps of information about examinations and Latin and university study that she had managed to gather so far. Benjy pulled out an exercise book; though only, as he frankly admitted to Daisy, so they could honestly tell their parents they had looked at their homework. They spent the next few minutes glancing at a mathematics problem and then flicking through a history textbook.

'Daisy?' That was her mother's voice, calling up the passage. 'Don't be too much longer, love, we're going home in a minute.'

Benjy closed his books, and the two of them went back out to the kitchen. Daisy's father was talking of bringing the gig around, but Grandma insisted that they all have another cup of tea and a few more biscuits before she would let Daisy and her parents leave.

'So you'd have to go away to Auckland or somewhere to learn about this doctoring business, would you?' Grandma asked.

Daisy had just taken a bite of a jam-filled biscuit. While she was swallowing it down, Benjy spoke for her.

'Yes, she'll need to go to university after high school,' he said. 'Probably the one in Auckland, it's the closest. It's good Daisy'll be going up there the same time as I will, isn't it, Ma? When I go to university to learn how to be a high school teacher, I mean.'

Benjy managed to make it sound as if the idea that he would be going off to university was something that had been talked about for years, although Daisy strongly suspected it was the first his mother had heard of it. But Grandma barely had time to look puzzled before Benjy moved the conversation back to Daisy, talking about Latin and chemistry and the other subjects she might have to study, and then asking Daisy's mother for the details of how she had treated Mr Gibson's horse, until Papa said they really should be going now.

Grandma and Grandpa walked down the path from the back door with Daisy and her parents. When they were saying their farewells at the garden gate, Grandma kissed them all and enfolded Daisy in a hug against her soft bosom; Daisy had grown so much in the last few months that she could almost see over the top of her grandmother's head.

'You're just like your Granny Stewart, coming up with such an idea,' Grandma said, smiling fondly at her. 'She was a great one for books and that sort of thing when she was your age, and for a lot of talk about Auckland and all.'

She released Daisy, and planted an extra kiss on her cheek. 'Mind you, I don't think even your Granny ever got an idea like *that* in her head.'

The little that remained of the school year went by in something of a blur. Amid the relief of knowing that she would have the support of her parents and her uncle's help with Latin in pursuing her dream, Daisy found herself not at all nervous during the end-of-year examinations, and both she and Benjy passed comfortably.

A few days before term ended, Uncle Richard brought two dog-eared books into the parlour one evening and handed them to Daisy.

'I managed to find these when I was excavating a trunk of books I haven't looked at in years,' he said. 'They're old Latin schoolbooks of mine. You're welcome to take them home for the holidays if you'd like to make a small start on the subject before we begin properly in the new year.'

Daisy thanked him, and at once began looking through one of them, turning each page with care out of respect for the book's worn state. Only the parts written in English made any sense at all, but it was the Latin words that she concentrated her attention on, trying to imagine being able to unlock their meaning.

Some pages had what Daisy at first took to be notes written in the margins. A small drawing on one page caught her eye, and she paused to examine it more closely. It appeared to be a stick figure of a man waving his hands in the air, unruly hair standing out all around his head. A few words were written underneath the drawing, but as they appeared to be in Latin Daisy could only guess at their meaning.

Her uncle leaned over from his armchair to follow her gaze. 'Oh. I'd forgotten how I used to mistreat some of my books—not to mention treating some of my schoolmasters with less than the respect they deserved. Just ignore my nonsense, Daisy.'

It was not easy to imagine Uncle Richard scribbling in books at all, let alone writing rude words about teachers. Daisy assured him that she would do her best, but she could not resist sneaking glances at the scattered pencil marks. The few written in English seemed to be comments on grumpy teachers or particularly boring lessons, so she suspected that the Latin ones might be much the same.

Lucy was sitting next to her on the sofa, stitching at some embroidery. Daisy noticed her sneaking glances at Daisy's reading matter, lips firmly pursed in obvious disapproval.

As soon as Daisy had gained her parents' permission to become a doctor, Uncle Richard had told Aunt Maudie and the others. While Aunt Maudie gave the impression of being determinedly cheerful about a notion that she was not sure she quite approved of, Lucy had been so shocked that she had not spoken a word to Daisy for two whole days. Even now, she was still rather cool in her manner.

Daisy turned away slightly, but she was all too aware of Lucy's stare boring into her. She closed the Latin book and placed it to one side, instead taking up a magazine she had been flicking through earlier. Life in Uncle Richard's house was a good deal more comfortable when you managed to get on with Lucy.

Lucy kept up her distant manner right until the last day of term. But that afternoon, when the time came for Aunt Maudie to take Daisy and Benjy home to the valley, Lucy wrapped her arms around Daisy's neck and kissed her, saying that she would miss her dreadfully, and even crying over the thought of having to do without Daisy for the whole of the holidays.

The long summer holidays had always been Daisy's favourite time of the year, and after spending so much of the school year away from home and her parents she looked forward to the season even more than usual.

Granny, Eddie and Aunt Sarah came down from Auckland the following week, and they were barely inside the house before Mama told them the news about Daisy deciding to be a doctor.

There was no need to be nervous about any reactions this time. Granny's smile lit up her whole face, Aunt Sarah said it was a wonderful idea, and Eddie made a fair attempt at pretending surprise.

'And what does Doctor Townsend think of your chosen profession, Daisy?' Aunt Sarah asked when the flurry of questions had settled.

'He's going to help me—we don't do Latin at my school, and I have to learn it to be a doctor, so he'll teach it to me.'

Aunt Sarah's eyebrows travelled some distance up her forehead. 'My goodness, how modern your uncle has become.' She gave a little laugh. 'I think you must be a good influence on him.'

The days were full of farm work and walks and paddling in the creek, but almost every evening Daisy pulled out Uncle Richard's Latin books and Eddie spent some time helping her decipher their contents. They slowly worked their way through the grammar book until the unfamiliar terms made sense to Daisy. She was used to parsing sentences in English, and to conjugating in French, but words like "declension" and "dative case" were new to her. Eddie was good at explaining things, and generous with his praise whenever Daisy gave a correct answer.

They did not spend long on the other book, Caesar's account of the Gallic Wars, which Eddie had studied so thoroughly at school that he could recite whole passages from memory, both in Latin and translated into English.

'You'll have plenty of time to look at those things next year, it's best to get the grammar sorted out first,' Eddie said; although he did teach Daisy to say aloud the first few sentences, and guided her through translating them.

Eddie also deciphered Uncle Richard's scribblings for Daisy, most of which were along the lines of how long the lesson had dragged on, or complaints about it being too wet for cricket. He paused over the final one, and grinned. ' "Mad Old Henshaw", more or less. Sounds like he didn't like that teacher.'

Aunt Sarah went back to Auckland in January, just a few days into the new year of 1921. Eddie made himself useful up and down the valley with the annual haymaking, then he and Granny left towards the end of the month, in time for Eddie to crew on a yacht in Auckland's annual regatta.

The weeks he had spent on the farm seemed to Daisy to have flown by. For the entire drive into town she and Eddie sat in the back of the cart exchanging words back and forth as rapidly as they could manage, neither of them wanting to waste a moment of what would be the last time they would see each other for months.

The *Ngatiawa* was tied up at Ruatane's wharf, waiting for her passengers to board. Eddie carried the bags aboard, and Granny kissed Daisy and Papa goodbye.

'I wish you were coming with us,' she said, hugging Daisy tightly. 'It'd be lovely to have you stay again. I know you're too busy with your schoolwork these days, though—I'm so proud of you, darling, wanting to go to university and be a doctor and everything.'

Eddie returned from stowing their bags just as the whistle sounded to hurry along the last few passengers. 'Better get a move on, Granny, we don't want them going without us.'

He shook hands with Daisy's father, and planted a kiss on Daisy's cheek. 'You'll do really well with the Latin and everything,' he said. 'Make sure you tell me how you're getting on, I want to hear all about it.'

A second whistle blast sent Eddie and Granny scuttling for the gangplank. They stood on the deck waving goodbye, and as the boat pulled away Eddie leaned over the rail.

'Vale, mea cognata,' he called to Daisy.

It took her a moment to recognize the Latin as 'Farewell, my cousin'. She had just enough time to call a 'Vale' back. The exchange earned her quizzical stares and grins from some of the people milling about on the wharf, but Daisy took no notice. All her attention was fixed on the boat shrinking away into the distance.

Chapter Ten

February saw the beginning of the school year, and Daisy's return with Benjy to her uncle's house. She started her Latin lessons that very first week.

'You've made good progress,' Uncle Richard said when he found that Daisy was already familiar with the early part of the grammar book. 'I really didn't expect you to spend your entire holidays studying, dear.'

'I didn't do it all the time, just a little bit most days. Eddie helped me, so it wasn't hard.'

'Ah, yes, you had the aid of a true Latin scholar.' Her uncle smiled. 'I suspect that Eddie's knowledge is rather more up-to-date than mine. But I'll do my best.'

Lessons twice a week would be enough to be going on with, Uncle Richard said. Judging from their grumbling, Nicky and Timmy considered that to be twice a week too often, but their father held firm.

'You need a proper grounding in Latin, or you'll find yourselves lagging behind your classmates when you go to grammar school. I'm sure neither of you wants to be dunce of the class.'

The boys admitted that they wanted no such thing. As a matter of form, they still grumbled under their breaths when Uncle Richard called them into his study for a Latin lesson, but Daisy could see that their mutterings about there being plenty of work at school without having to do more of it afterwards were half-hearted. They could complain as much as they liked, but they knew perfectly well that they had to do what their father said.

In any case, it was obvious that Nicky and Timmy were actually quite keen on going to school in Auckland, though perhaps not because of its academic advantages. The boys had taken the opportunity over the summer holidays to ask Eddie about his old school, their interest confined solely to the rugby and cricket played there, and were now more enthusiastic than ever. Aunt Maudie was inclined to look sad whenever the subject came up, but her careful attempts to assure them that they would enjoy the big school, and would hardly get homesick at all, were clearly a wasted effort.

Timmy was only eight, while Nicky had turned ten just a few months before; Daisy was four years older than Nicky, though the age gap felt greater. Uncle Richard was realistic about how much sustained concentration he could expect from the boys. He limited their lessons to half an hour at most, while spending a good hour with Daisy.

After her work with Eddie over the summer, Daisy was well ahead of the boys from the very beginning, and the lessons soon fell into a pattern where she would work on a grammar exercise or a piece of translation while Uncle Richard went through a simpler exercise with Nicky and Timmy. He would then release the boys, go over Daisy's work with her, explaining whatever she might have found puzzling, and set her fresh tasks.

'You're coming along very well,' he assured Daisy more than once, his praise encouraging her to try all the harder.

Daisy turned fourteen a few weeks into the new term. Ruatane District High School felt quite familiar now, its buildings and all those people crammed into them no longer daunting. They had the same teachers, the same subjects, and most of the same classmates; only two or three of last year's pupils had left school to take up work or help at home. Flora no longer joined them on their walks to and from school; she had managed to pass her Standard Six examination the previous year, and had made it clear that she had no desire to go to high school before anyone had even had the chance to ask.

Daisy's Latin lessons with her uncle were generally on Tuesdays and Thursdays, and it was not far into the term before Benjy pointed out that she always walked a little faster on the way back from school on those days.

'You must be the only person in the whole school who'd be in a mad rush to get home just so you can do more schoolwork,' Benjy said, grinning at her.

Daisy grinned back, not at all put out by his gentle teasing. When Uncle Richard had asked if he would like to learn Latin as well, Benjy had let out an emphatic 'No fear!' He did sometimes join Daisy in her uncle's study during the lessons, but only because he was steadily working his way through Uncle Richard's collection of plays and poetry.

Among these books was a large volume containing the works of Shakespeare. Mr Grant had said they would be studying another Shakespeare play that year; Benjy's eyes had lit up at the news, and when their teacher told them the play would be *Macbeth*, he at once set to reading it from Uncle Richard's volume, not wanting to wait until Mr Grant issued the school's battered old set to the class.

Macbeth, Benjy announced when he finished reading the play, was a fine piece of work.

'There's witches and kings and a ghost, and just about everyone's dead by the end,' he told Daisy. 'I don't know how you'd get some of the stuff to work in a real theatre, smoke and fog and all. There's a bit with a dagger, too—"Is this a dagger that I see before me?",' he said in a tone much deeper than his natural one. 'Macbeth sees it sort of floating in the air in front of him, but no one else can because it's magic by the witches, or maybe a ghost is doing it. It'd all be too scary for little kids, that's for sure. No wonder we didn't do anything like that at primary school.'

Mr Grant handed out printed copies of the play the following Monday, each one to be shared between two or three pupils, as there were not enough to go around.

'Sir, do you think we could put this play on in front of everyone?' Benjy asked. 'We could have the whole class in it, and put it on for the secondary school.'

Benjy managed to sound full of confident assurance, but Daisy knew him well enough to be sure that was faint hope rather than any real expectation she was hearing. She was not at all surprised when Mr Grant smiled and shook his head.

'I'm afraid that would be far too ambitious, Benjy—much as I admire the reach of your imagination.'

The last copy of the play hung loosely from Mr Grant's hand, apparently forgotten for the moment. 'I once saw *Macbeth* performed on the London stage,' he said, his gaze now turned on some unseen distance beyond the room's windows. 'Henry Irving and Ellen Terry at the Lyceum Theatre. That must have been a good thirty years ago, but I'll never forget it.'

Benjy at once pressed Mr Grant for details of what he had seen, and their teacher was quite happy to oblige. He perched on the edge of his desk and launched into descriptions of the actors and actresses, names that he seemed to think the class might recognize, praising their performances. Prompted by Benjy, he described the costumes and sets; the fog, he said, had been particularly effective, and the entry of the witches had been marked by a very realistic flash of lightning.

'As for those witches,' Mr Grant said, 'I don't mind telling you that they gave me bad dreams afterwards, they had such an air of malevolence.'

But when Benjy asked just how the fog had been produced, and how they had managed to have a fire on the stage for the witches' cauldron without setting the theatre alight, Mr Grant spread his arms wide in a gesture of helplessness.

'I'm afraid I've really no idea. I was so caught up in the performance that it didn't occur to me to wonder at the time—in any case, it was all done so deftly that I don't think the mechanics of the process would have been at all obvious. I imagine they had some sort of stage machinery, and probably a small army of stagehands moving pieces about whenever the lights were down. I can only tell you that however they managed it, the results were thoroughly convincing.'

He smiled at what were clearly pleasant memories, and Benjy left him to his reminiscences. A few moments later Mr Grant shook his head again, still smiling.

'I think you'll agree, Benjy, that such a production would be well beyond any resources we could muster.'

'I suppose that's right,' Benjy said with only a trace of reluctance; Daisy had half expected him to argue that they could indeed put on the play complete with fire, fog, and floating daggers.

The glint in Benjy's eye told Daisy he was not quite ready to admit defeat. 'It's a really good play, though. Do you think… Sir, what say we put it on just here in the classroom? We wouldn't need fancy sets or costumes—well, we could have cloaks or something, and maybe rig up spears or swords out of wood.'

'I'm not sure how much class time I could devote to that,' Mr Grant said, though his expression showed that he was intrigued by the idea. 'We certainly couldn't do anything elaborate. Still, I wonder, since we're to study the play anyway… yes, I think perhaps we could do a play reading as part of our class work.'

This meant, Mr Grant explained, that he would assign parts to everyone and they would read the play aloud, with no need to memorise the words. 'Delivering the lines with a suitably dramatic interpretation, to the best of everyone's ability,' he said. 'All going well, it might give you a better understanding of Shakespeare's masterful way with language.'

If nothing else, it would keep Benjy happy. He talked of little else in the days following, reciting aloud passages he especially liked during Daisy's walks with him to and from school, speculating on which of their classmates might be best suited for a particular part, or musing on what they might be able to do in the way of costumes.

Mr Grant told the class to read the play as homework, which Daisy did over the next few days. It was something of a relief to get the details of the plot straight at last, after trying to make sense of the various snippets Benjy had come out with during his own reading.

'I'll tell him you should be Lady Macbeth, because that's the most important part for a girl,' Benjy said to Daisy one afternoon. 'I bet he'll say that's a good idea—it's got to be someone who can say the lines properly.'

Mr Grant had had ample time to note which of his pupils were the most fluent at reading aloud, and which ones were likely to become tongue-tied. Several were given the role of messenger, with perhaps a line or two, while others were various soldiers or spear-carriers, with no words at all to stumble over.

There were fewer parts for girls, which did not work out too badly, as there were more boys than girls in the class. And some of the smaller roles described only as "attendant" or "messenger" could, their teacher said, be played perfectly well by girls.

Benjy proved to be quite correct in his prediction when Mr Grant told Daisy she was to be Lady Macbeth.

'It's by far the largest of the female roles, but I'm sure you're up to it, Daisy. And of course there's the matter of the three witches. Do we have any volunteers for those roles?'

Every female hand remained firmly pressed on its owner's lap. A few of the boys appeared to be whispering among themselves; no doubt swapping suggestions for likely witches. A pointed stare from Mr Grant silenced the sniggering.

'Of course in Shakespeare's day women weren't permitted to act on the stage, so the female roles were all performed by boys,' he said. 'Perhaps I should revive the practice.'

Daisy saw several of her male classmates exchange horrified looks. She smiled at the thought, although she was fairly sure Mr Grant would not carry out his threat; most of the boys would probably consider leaving school altogether rather than pretend to be a girl in front of all the others.

'All right, I'll choose the witches myself.' Mr Grant flicked a glance over the boys, allowing himself a small smile, then settled his attention on the girls. 'Elsie and Phyllis,' he said, naming two of the prettiest girls in the class. 'As a small consolation for taking on such loathsome roles, you can be Lady Macduff as well, Phyllis. And Elsie, you'll be a lady-in-waiting. Daisy, you'd better be First Witch—she's never on stage at the same time as Lady Macbeth, so it shouldn't be a problem.'

It would probably be much easier than when Benjy had persuaded Daisy to be both the fairies in the play he had written some years before; though this time she would have the roles of two somewhat unpleasant characters, rather than a good one and a wicked. The witches were far more scary than the wicked fairy had been; fortunately there would be no small children to frighten.

Benjy met her eyes. 'Told you he'd pick you,' he murmured, grinning broadly.

'I expect you'll want to take the title role yourself, Benjy,' Mr Grant said. 'Seeing as you are, after all, the main driving force behind the whole production.'

'Thank you, Sir, but I'd just as soon not,' Benjy said, clearly startling Mr Grant. 'I don't want to be too busy with the acting—that way I can keep an eye on things, make sure everyone comes on at the right time and all that.'

Mr Grant's eyebrows rose even higher when Benjy added, 'I think you should be Macbeth, Mr Grant.'

'Really? Why is that, then?'

'Well, it needs to be someone tall and grand-looking, doesn't it? So it stands to reason you should do it, Sir.'

Benjy bestowed one of his brightest smiles on their teacher, who looked amused and perhaps just a little puffed up. 'I could do Banquo and Macduff if that's all right, Mr Grant? That shouldn't keep me too busy.'

'Oh, I'm sure you're more than capable, Benjy,' Mr Grant said.

In the days following, whenever a fresh idea regarding the play struck Benjy during class he could not resist whispering it to Daisy, which did not help her concentrate on whatever she was supposed to be studying at the time. It was worst of all during mathematics lessons, when Benjy's mind was inclined to wander even when he did not have an upcoming play to distract him.

After being interrupted yet again while she was in the midst of attempting to calculate the volume of a cylinder, Daisy resorted to warning Benjy that if Mr Ritchie caught him talking while they were supposed to be working silently, he might tell Mr Grant, who might just decide to cancel the play. As she pointed out to Benjy, it was not as if Mr Ritchie would be at all interested in their play, unrelated as it was to science or mathematics. To her relief, her warning worked far better than any threat of being caned might have.

It was easy to be caught up in Benjy's enthusiasm. Back at primary school, English had been almost entirely grammar, especially under Mr Fawcett. Now they regularly studied poems, with Mr Grant showing them just how clever the words often were, and their teacher appeared to love plays almost as much as Benjy did.

On several occasions Benjy rushed back into their form master's classroom after the class had been released, so that he could discuss his latest idea with Mr Grant.

'He says he'll have a word with Mrs Dawson and see if she can figure out anything about costumes,' Benjy reported to Daisy after one such conversation. 'Domestic science is about sewing and all that, so I thought she might have some ideas. I know we can't do anything fancy, just stuff people can put on over their uniforms, but I want to have something that looks old-fashioned, anyway.'

Mr Grant must have been as persuasive as Benjy himself would have been. At the end of Daisy's domestic science class that day, Mrs Dawson told the girls that if they brought along to their next lesson any old skirts their mothers might have put into the rag bag, or large scraps of whatever fabric might be around the house, they could spend the class making up cloaks for the play.

Aunt Maudie's discarded clothing was usually far too good for a rag bag, consisting as it did of smart garments with only small signs of wear, and was instead given to poor families in town. But she offered Daisy a skirt that had a rip near the hem, where she had caught it on a rosebush, as well as a worn old blanket. The skirt was in dark blue wool, which Mrs Dawson pronounced just the thing as a cloak for one of the noblemen, and had a satin lining that she suggested Daisy should unpick and then hem the raw edges, so that she could wrap it around herself as a makeshift skirt for Lady Macbeth. The old blanket, Daisy decided, would do as a witch's cloak.

The other girls had brought quite a range of fabrics, many in cheerful colours, including a length of cotton patterned with pink rosebuds.

'I can't really imagine a soldier wearing that, Doris,' Mrs Dawson remarked, smiling. 'Never mind, at least it's a nice, big piece.'

They set to work, cutting and pinning, then taking turns at the sewing machine, Mrs Dawson helping. Two busy classes later, the cloaks were ready.

Although Mr Grant had said they could simply read aloud from the printed text, Benjy managed to persuade Daisy to learn some of her lines off by heart. Her delivery would be much better that way, he insisted, and she did not really mind making the effort; not when the play meant so much to Benjy. Most afternoons they practised together in the study; Uncle Richard had been a little startled when he walked in on one of Lady Macbeth's more fervent speeches.

The performance took place just after lunch one Wednesday. Benjy supervised as the desks were pushed against the back and side walls, then in a flurry of activity costumes were handed out and extra scripts found for the pupils who had mislaid theirs.

Daisy took her place at the front of the room with the two other girls who were being witches. One of them was wearing the pink flowered cloak that had been roundly rejected by all the boys; it seemed to Daisy just as unsuitable for a witch as it would have been for a soldier, especially since Elsie had insisted (against Benjy's objections) on wearing a matching hair ribbon.

Mr Grant shushed everyone else. Daisy took a deep breath, hunched a little in her blanket cloak, and said her first lines:

' "When shall we three meet again
In thunder, lightning, or in rain?" '

Elsie smiled brightly at the audience, then looked down to read the next lines from the book in her hands:

' "When the hurlyburly's done,

When the battle's lost and won." '

After that, the play seemed to go by in a rush. With only a few actors at the front of the room at any one time there was always an audience, albeit a constantly changing one. Fortunately for Daisy, there were gaps between the scenes where Lady Macbeth or the witches appeared, giving her time to shrug off the witch's cloak and pin Lady Macbeth's satin skirt on over her gym slip.

When she was not busy performing or changing her costume, Daisy watched the action at the front of the room. In between his acting roles, Benjy darted around organising entrances and costume changes. He was excellent, of course, as Banquo and later Macduff, along with an occasional small role with a line or two. He wore the cloak made from Aunt Maudie's old skirt, and hanging from his belt was a sword that looked surprisingly real from a distance. He had made it from scraps of wood Grandpa gave him, and Lucy had painted it so that it looked like metal.

A few of the other boys also had homemade swords, though theirs were all of plain, unpainted wood. One had brought along a garden trowel that he appeared to think made a serviceable dagger; fortunately his cloak hid it most of the time.

Mr Grant had politely declined the offer of a cloak, but even without any sort of costume he looked quite impressive, standing a head taller than any of his pupils as he delivered his lines in a deep voice that seemed to fill the room. Most of Daisy's scenes as Lady Macbeth were performed with him. Once she got past the awkwardness of scolding her teacher, telling him to stop dithering and be brave, she enjoyed acting opposite him. She was glad that Benjy had convinced her to learn the more important passages by heart.

Lady Macbeth made her final appearance, wandering back and forth while she rubbed at her hands, fretting over the imaginary blood they bore. Daisy glided offstage, leaving the doctor (Benjy) and a lady-in-waiting (Elsie) discussing her words. She made her way quietly to the back of the room, unpinned the satin skirt and put it to one side, then sat on a desk to enjoy the rest of the play.

Mr Grant and Benjy as Macbeth and Macduff met onstage in the final scene, their duel confined to words flung at each other. They went off to one side, still shouting, and Macduff returned in triumph, announcing that he had killed Macbeth. The play's directions said that Macduff should be holding Macbeth's head aloft at this point, and Benjy had suggested using a papier mâché one, which he was sure he could persuade Lucy to make, but Mr Grant had not been keen on the idea of elaborate props. Benjy's other thought, that he might bring in a sheep's head from the farm, he had only got as far as sharing with Daisy, and had reluctantly agreed with her that the smell would probably annoy people.

The final speech was from the boy playing King Malcolm, who read the words clearly enough but in a disappointingly flat tone. The last words were uttered, and there was a moment's silence, broken by Mr Grant.

'Congratulations, everyone. I think we've all earned a round of applause.' He began clapping, and Daisy joined in with the others, odd though it seemed to be applauding themselves. 'And I think Benjy deserves a round of his own,' Mr Grant said when the clapping died down. 'Well done, Benjy—you've been the driving force. One might say an irresistible force,' he added, smiling.

Benjy beamed at him. 'Thank you, Sir. Do you think we could do another one next term?'

'Oh, I think one performance is excitement enough to last quite some time. Now, shall we return to the real world? Chairs and desks back in their proper places, please, and open your French books to Chapter Two, the section on conjugating verbs ending in "re".'

The next few minutes were full of the sound of desks being dragged across the wooden floor. Daisy took her seat, and looked over at Benjy. The play had been fun, and she had enjoyed taking part in it, but "enjoyed" was not a strong enough word for what she saw shining out of his face.

Benjy grinned at her. 'That was pretty good,' he said, keeping his voice low. 'Some of the stuff didn't work too well, but that's all right. I'll do a much better one next time.'

The May holidays brought Eddie and Granny to the farm. As usual when they had been apart for any length of time, there hardly seemed to be enough hours in the first few days for Daisy and Eddie to discuss all that had happened since they had last seen each other.

It seemed that everything was going on much as usual at the big house in Auckland. Walter, who looked after the grounds and the carriage, had been more fortunate than many, having returned from the war with nothing worse than permanent stiffness in one leg and a weakness in his chest that made him prone to bronchitis in the winter. A boy came in regularly to do the heavy digging, and Walter insisted that he could still manage everything else.

Eddie was taking Latin again at university that year, along with a course in contract law to please Aunt Sarah, but his favourite subjects were still botany and zoology. Now that he was eighteen, he was attached to a local unit of the Territorial Force and had to attend occasional military drills. He was in a university rugby club, and occasionally went on outings with a tramping group. There was talk that he might go on an excursion to the volcanoes of the central North Island later in the year, and perhaps even see some snow.

Daisy's own news felt much smaller in comparison, but Eddie was interested in it all, especially her Latin sessions with Uncle Richard and her science lessons at school.

When they went down to Grandpa's one afternoon, Benjy made it quite clear that he considered their play reading the most important event of the year at Ruatane District High School. He launched into a detailed explanation of the plot, halted only when Eddie said that he had studied *Macbeth* himself while at school. Eddie then listened patiently as Benjy described how they had gone about sharing roles, managing entrances and exits, and what they had done for costumes.

'Daisy was really good in it,' Benjy added. 'She was the best by miles out of all the girls.'

Eddie smiled. 'Of course she was,' he said.

Chapter Eleven

The winter of 1921 saw its share of colds and chest complaints, and Daisy was sure that Uncle Richard was watching carefully for any sign of an epidemic like the terrifying influenza that had followed the war. Nothing so dreadful marked the season, but it was still a busy time of year for her uncle.

On Tuesdays after lunch Daisy had mathematics followed by chemistry. Mathematics lessons sometimes seemed particularly long, and it was a relief one afternoon to put away her protractor and compass and move on to the last class of the day.

They were currently studying the properties of various metals in chemistry, and today they were actually going to experiment with electricity.

Several of Ruatane's businesses now had telephones; Uncle Richard was among the handful of householders with one, although people still usually sent a boy with a message when they wanted to contact him, as so few other people in the town were connected. A wooden box was mounted on a wall in the passage, with bells on the front that sounded when a call was made. The telephone receiver hung from a hook on one side of the box, connected by a thick, plaited cord. When her uncle wished to make a call, he turned a handle on the other side of the box, which operated a dynamo that notified the telephone operator.

The telephones were powered by dry-cell batteries, which took up much of the space inside the wooden box. The Post and Telegraph kept stocks of replacement batteries, and would send a boy around to a subscriber to replace them as necessary. Mr Ritchie had managed to acquire half a dozen of these batteries from the Post and Telegraph, which would supply the power source for today's experiment.

The class formed pairs for practical experiments, with Daisy and Benjy always choosing to work together. Benjy regarded their mathematics and science classes as something of a necessary evil, but ever since he had singed a sleeve over the spirit burner one day he had been particularly careful during experiments, and made a good lab partner.

They first set a beaker of water heating over their burner, and when it was hot stirred in crystals of copper sulphate, enough to turn the water a deep blue rather like the pockets of coloured clay they sometimes found along the creek bank. While the solution was cooling, they set to work gathering their remaining equipment and materials.

The battery was a tall cylinder, with its solid case wrapped in heavy paper. On top of each battery were two metal projections called terminals, one positive and the other negative, each terminal having a short lead trailing from it. Daisy attached a coil of copper to the positive terminal, which was called the anode, while Benjy clipped a brass key onto the lead hanging from the negative terminal, or cathode. They lowered both key and copper wire into the blue liquid, taking care not to let them touch.

The theory, Mr Ritchie explained, was that their copper sulphate solution would conduct electricity from the wire to the key. The electrical current now flowing from the battery made the wire lose electrons, adding copper ions to the solution. These ions then travelled to the key, and if all went well it would end up coated with copper; a process called electroplating.

While they waited for the proper chemical reactions to take place, Daisy jotted down Mr Ritchie's notes from the blackboard, to be written up neatly later along with diagrams illustrating the process. She sneaked an occasional glance at their experiment, hoping to see some sign of a coppery colour on the key.

When all the beakers had been left for half an hour, and the keys removed from the solution, Daisy and Benjy's experiment turned out to have worked beautifully, with the key now quite neatly plated with copper. This was not the case with some of their classmates, whose keys had acquired a soot-like substance; a sign, Mr Ritchie said, that their solution had not been strong enough.

Afterwards came clearing up; Daisy fully agreed with Benjy that this was the least enjoyable part of the lesson. They rinsed out the beakers and put away all the equipment, with Benjy taking special care to check that the spirit burner had been completely extinguished before moving it aside.

While she and Benjy waited for the last of their classmates to finish tidying up, and for Mr Ritchie to set their homework, Daisy studied the large Periodic Table pinned to the wall. Many of the symbols had seemed odd to her when she first encountered them; however had iron become Fe, or gold Au? She had the answer now, thanks to her lessons with Uncle Richard: the names came from Latin, where iron was ferrum and gold aurum. She mentally ran through all the ones she could remember as she scanned each line. Na for sodium; that was from natrium. Pb was lead; that was how plumbing got its name, because of lead pipes. Now, what was tin again?

Mr Ritchie's voice cut into her thoughts. Daisy noted down the homework exercise, packed away her notebook, and filed outside with the others when Mr Ritchie released them for home-time.

Tuesday was one of her days for Latin, and Daisy looked forward to asking her uncle about the word for tin before going on to the next section of Cicero. But when she and Benjy got back to the house, Lucy greeted them with the news that Uncle Richard was out.

'He's had to go and see a patient,' Lucy announced when they stepped into the kitchen.

'Yes, it's Mr Gilbert.' Aunt Maudie was up to her elbows in flour as she rolled out the top layer of pastry for a large apple pie. 'That oldest boy of theirs came over with a message from his mother, saying he'd been taken bad.'

Uncle Richard was always careful to say little about his patients, but it was difficult to keep secrets in a place like Ruatane. Daisy had already heard from Lucy that Mr Gilbert had kidney trouble of some sort, and she knew it had been going on for some time.

Aunt Maudie carefully laid the pastry over the slices of apple. 'Poor Mrs Gilbert. All those children to look after, and now her husband not well enough to work. I don't know how she manages.'

Mr Gilbert had been a roadman before being taken ill, looking after the stretch of road to the west of town, spreading new gravel and keeping the worst of the potholes under control. It was not work that paid highly, and while such matters were not openly discussed in her uncle's household, Daisy had picked up enough remarks to know that the Gilberts were the sort of family Uncle Richard would not accept payment from. It was not uncommon for Aunt Maudie to find a box of vegetables or some fruit left at the back door by such grateful patients, but the Gilberts could probably not spare so much as a potato these days.

'Oh, Daisy, your uncle said to tell you he might be a bit late for your lesson,' Aunt Maudie said.

Nicky and Timmy, who had arrived home soon after Daisy and Benjy, looked up from helping themselves to scraps of pastry.

'So we won't have to do any Latin today?' Timmy said. He and Nicky whooped in unison.

'I don't know about that, you two,' Aunt Maudie said, frowning. 'Your father said you should make a start on your own if he's late. He doesn't want you getting too behind with all that Latin business.'

The boys insisted that they could not possibly do the work on their own; that it was much too hard; that they would not know what to do.

'And we might go learning it wrong,' Nicky said, his expression earnest. 'Then Papa would have to go to all the bother of getting it straight again for us. That'd be a lot of trouble for him.'

'Well, I'm sure he wouldn't want you to learn it wrong, but he did say you were to do some work. Oh, I don't know.'

'I could help Nicky and Timmy,' Daisy offered; she did not like to see her aunt looking so anxious. 'We'd only have to do a little bit, just some of your verbs, maybe,' she said to the boys.

Aunt Maudie's face cleared. 'Yes, that's a very good idea. Thank you, Daisy.'

'But only if Uncle Richard's really late.' Daisy ignored the scowls the boys had turned on her.

'Yes, he might be back any time now,' Aunt Maudie said.

But by dinner time Uncle Richard had still not returned. Aunt Maudie put his meal by the range to keep warm while everyone else tucked into theirs.

'Let's get on with your Latin, then,' Daisy said to the boys when the dishes were done. 'Come on, it'll only be a few minutes.'

'Yes, off you go,' Aunt Maudie said. 'Daisy will tell you what to do.'

Nicky and Timmy grumbled half-heartedly, and dragged their feet all the way to their father's study, but once there they settled in willingly enough. Daisy went through half a page of *De Bello Gallico* with them, prompting for the translation of each line as they took turns reading aloud, then had them recite the conjugations of the verbs they had learned most recently, correcting their efforts as necessary.

That was as far as she felt comfortable relying on the boys' good nature. Daisy released them to the parlour and their games, then took up her own study.

She was well into translating a passage from Cicero's letters when Benjy came in.

'Don't mind me,' he said. 'I just felt like a bit of peace and quiet.' He helped himself to a book from Uncle Richard's shelves and settled into a chair.

Daisy was happy enough to work on her own, but it was nice to have a friendly presence in the room. She worked away at her translation, a small part of her attention given to listening for any sound of her uncle's return, for an hour or so until Aunt Maudie came to fetch her and Benjy into the parlour.

'I'm sure you must have done enough studying for one day, Daisy,' her aunt said. 'Anyway, you'll give yourself eyestrain looking at that tiny print for too long.'

The study had a small fire, but it was much cozier in the parlour. Benjy played the piano, and Daisy flicked through some of her aunt's magazines. Lucy had positioned herself to make the most of the electric light, and was engrossed in a charcoal sketch, while Flora stitched the hem of a skirt. Aunt Maudie kept the fire burning brightly; when the wood basket was empty, Benjy went outside to refill it.

The mantel clock chimed the half-hour, and Aunt Maudie set her sewing to one side.

'Time you were in bed, you two,' she told Nicky and Timmy. 'No, you can't wait for your father—goodness knows when he'll be back now, Mr Gilbert must be in a bad way. Papa will look in on you to say goodnight if you're still awake.'

She ushered the boys off to their room, and was back a few minutes later. 'I hope your father's had something to eat,' she fretted. 'Of course he wouldn't want to bother Mrs Gilbert and go asking, but I suppose she'll have had to get a meal on for her little ones. Here, have another biscuit, Benjy,' she said, pushing the plate in his direction.

By the time another half hour had passed, Flora was nodding off in her chair. Aunt Maudie gently patted her arm to rouse her, and sent her to bed.

'You two shouldn't sit up too late, either,' she said to Daisy and Benjy. 'Not when you've got school tomorrow.'

'We'll be all right for a bit longer, won't we, Daisy?' Benjy said. He met Daisy's eyes, and she gave a small nod to tell him she had caught his unspoken message: they would stay up and keep Aunt Maudie company. There was Lucy, of course, but at the moment Lucy was so caught up in her sketch that she appeared unaware that anyone else was in the room. At least that kept things peaceful; if Lucy were to become fretful for some reason, she would not be a soothing companion.

Daisy put the magazines aside. Aunt Maudie was used to having Uncle Richard to talk to by this time of day, and Daisy was keen to do her best to help Benjy fill the gap. They told Aunt Maudie about their schoolwork, with their aunt showing a polite interest. They discussed the weather, and the latest comings and goings in the town. The most recent issue of the *Ruatane Herald* had included speculation that a motor car service might be starting up between Ruatane and the large inland town of Rotorua to the south, a snippet of news Aunt Maudie was particularly taken with, as she and Uncle Richard had spent their honeymoon in Rotorua.

'Back then you had to take the boat to Tauranga first and stay the night there, then go on the mail service to Rotorua,' she reminisced. 'It took ever so long to get there, but it was a lovely place to visit.'

Every so often Aunt Maudie would suggest that perhaps Daisy and the others should go to bed, but she did not press the point. Benjy returned to the piano and played quietly, and Daisy felt her eyelids growing heavy.

'Goodness me, it's ten o'clock,' Aunt Maudie said, startling Daisy into alertness. 'I really can't keep you children up any longer.'

'That's all right,' Benjy said. 'Another five minutes won't hurt.'

Lucy put her drawing aside. 'I'm sure Father will be home quite soon,' she said, adding her own voice to the discussion as if she had been part of their conversation all evening.

It was closer to half an hour than five minutes before they heard the crunch of footsteps on the gravel path. Aunt Maudie hurried out into the passage, closely followed by the others, in time to see Uncle Richard come in through the back door.

'Here you are at last!' Aunt Maudie said. 'You must be worn out—I hope you didn't take a chill—is it raining? Here, let's get these damp things off, and you can come into the warm.' She helped him out of his coat and hat, which Benjy took away to hang up.

Uncle Richard washed his hands in the scullery, and wiped them on a towel that hung by the doorway into the kitchen. 'You didn't need to sit up so late, darling—my goodness, have you all been waiting up for me?' he asked, looking around at Daisy and the others, who had all crowded into the kitchen.

'Yes, they've been very good, keeping me company. Is Mr Gilbert all right?'

Uncle Richard shook his head. 'No, I'm afraid he passed away. Mrs Gilbert is in quite a state, poor creature, but an aunt of hers was there, she seems a capable sort.'

'Oh, the poor thing. I'll make up a basket with some pies and things and take it around tomorrow—she can have that leg of ham Ma brought in the other day, too. And a few clothes for the children, Timmy's got a lot of things he's just about grown out of, they'll fit one of her boys.'

'Yes, I'm sure that would be very welcome. They certainly don't have much in the way of comfort.'

He sat down at the table, and Aunt Maudie placed his dinner before him.

'I don't think the meat's dried out, I had another plate on top of this one,' she said. 'I'm afraid it's not very hot, though.'

Uncle Richard took a few bites, then put down his knife and fork. 'It's very nice, dear, but I'm afraid I don't quite feel up to a large meal. I'm sorry to waste it.'

'Don't worry, I'll make rissoles tomorrow and mince it all up. Just have some tea and a bit of apple pie, then. We might as well finish this up.'

Aunt Maudie sliced up the remaining pie, Lucy made a fresh pot of tea, and they all sat around the table tucking into the pie.

'I hope you haven't gone hungry all this time,' Aunt Maudie said. 'You've been out for hours.'

'No, Mrs Gilbert insisted on offering food—mostly in the form of bread and dripping, I'm afraid. Of course I couldn't insult her by refusing it, but I must say it's sitting rather heavily now.'

Uncle Richard had eaten a fair portion of the large slice of pie Aunt Maudie served him; now he was pushing the remainder around his bowl somewhat distractedly. He met Daisy's gaze across the table, and the corners of his mouth turned up in an attempt at a smile.

'I'm sorry you had to miss your Latin today, Daisy. Perhaps we can do a little extra on Thursday.'

'That'd be good, if you have the time,' Daisy said. 'I did some on my own, though, so I didn't really miss out.'

'Daisy made sure the boys did theirs, too,' Aunt Maudie put in. 'She got them working away nicely.'

'That was very good of you, Daisy,' Uncle Richard said. 'I don't want them to fall behind in their studies, so that's a weight off my mind.'

His praise made the small effort of persuading her young cousins to work on their Latin feel all the more worthwhile. 'That's all right, it was no trouble, really.'

She hesitated before voicing the question on the tip of her tongue, torn between curiosity and the desire not to speak out of turn. Her uncle liked to keep people's medical problems private, but surely it was all right to talk about it when a person was dead.

'Was it Mr Gilbert's kidneys that went wrong?' Daisy asked.

Her uncle put down his spoon. 'Yes, it was. He had chronic renal disease that was gradually worsening, and ultimately his kidneys broke down completely.'

"Renal" meant relating to the kidneys, Daisy remembered from perusing one of Uncle Richard's anatomy books. It was from Latin, of course, as all the important medical terms seemed to be.

'Renal disease is a debilitating condition, leaving the patient increasingly helpless, and with poor prospects.' His mouth twisted in a grimace. 'It's the worst part of this profession, Daisy—our failures are inevitable, and they're inclined to involve real human tragedy.'

Aunt Maudie reached across the table and patted his hand. 'I'm sure you did your best for him, Richard.'

'Well, I may have extended his life slightly, with appropriate treatment and medications. And I was able to ease his passing, at any rate, thanks to generous doses of morphia. That's a small achievement to take some comfort in.'

'I don't think it's a small achievement,' Daisy said, although she felt shy at the thought of contradicting her uncle. 'I think helping people like that's a big thing—a fine thing.'

'It certainly is,' Aunt Maudie said. 'You're quite right, Daisy.'

Uncle Richard managed a real smile, one that made him look a little less weary.

'Perhaps that's as useful a reminder as the salutary lesson in the limitations of medicine.' His gaze took in both Daisy and her aunt. 'Thank you, my dears.'

Chapter Twelve

Occasional discussion of a trip to the mountains of the central North Island, usually in the form of a vague mention that such a trip would be great fun, had dragged on for so long that Eddie had resigned himself to the thought that it would never go beyond talk. But late in the winter term it abruptly became a real possibility.

'Would you be on for going down to Mount Ruapehu next month?' Geoffrey asked Eddie when he joined him in the Common Room one afternoon in July.

'I'll say!' Eddie answered at once, then belatedly asked the details.

It turned out that Geoffrey's brother-in-law was the main instigator of the excursion. Ronald Gillan was married to Geoffrey's older sister, Kathleen, and had a senior position of some sort in the Railways Department. While on one of his frequent rail journeys up and down the North Island, Ronald had made a brief side-trip to the Ruapehu area, and had come home full of its praises.

'He wants to take Kath for a look around, and he said we might as well make an outing of it and all go,' Geoffrey said. 'It'll be in the first week of the holidays. Dora's keen, too, and her mum said it's all right as long as Kath's there.'

Geoffrey seemed to be spending a good deal of time these days with his classmate Dora, much of it supposedly working together on their French essays. Nothing in the nature of a formal engagement had been announced, but they had what Eddie's grandmother called an understanding.

'There's a place you can stay, partway up the mountain,' Geoffrey said. 'Just some sort of hut, but that'd be all right for a few days—we'd probably be gone for a week all up. And if we can organise a few other chaps, we could hire the whole hut—that'd save a bit of money. Ronald can probably get us cheaper fares on the train if there's more of us, too. I think the hut can fit a dozen at a pinch.'

They discussed the idea of putting up a notice in the Common Room, but soon decided it would be better to ask around among those of their acquaintance who seemed likely to make good travelling companions.

'Phil's sure to want to,' Eddie said. 'So that's one more for a start.'

But when Philip dropped in briefly before hurrying off to a lecture, he shook his head at the suggestion.

'I wouldn't be able to get the time off work,' he said gloomily. 'I won't get any holidays till Christmas, except for a couple of days around exam time. It's all right, I'm not all that keen on going, anyway,' he added unconvincingly.

Eddie and Geoffrey both made an effort not to spend all the time discussing their plans when Philip was there, but it was impossible to avoid the subject altogether. Eddie's enthusiasm grew even stronger when Geoffrey announced that Ronald had said there might be a chance to try skiing while they were at the mountain.

'I expect you'll both come back on crutches, then,' Philip said. 'You're sure to break a leg—unless you're lucky and land on your head.'

It was easy enough to find several of their fellow students who were eager to be part of the excursion, though when it came to the point of committing to paying for it, the number shrank. But between them Eddie and Geoffrey came up with three more definite travellers.

'So that's eight of us altogether,' Geoffrey said. 'A couple more wouldn't have hurt, but that'll do.'

Aunt Sarah had invited the Wells family for afternoon tea the following Sunday.

Mrs Wells was an old friend of Aunt Sarah's, and the whole family sometimes came to visit on a weekend. Eddie always enjoyed talking to Mr Wells, and it would be impossible not to like Mrs Wells, but their daughters could be overwhelming, especially when all four of them were present; so many high-pitched voices at once took some enduring. Fortunately Granny was keeping the two youngest, whose names Eddie always struggled to get straight, busy and fairly quiet, admiring some sort of embroidery and looking through a pile of illustrated magazines, while the older two took turns at the piano, one playing as the other turned pages for her.

Savouries and small cakes were brought in, and there was a brief pause in the various conversations as people loaded up their plates.

'Did Eddie tell you he's going to Mount Ruapehu?' Granny asked.

'Are you indeed?' Mr Wells said. 'I've heard that's a fine spot to visit. I'm not sure Emily's very keen on the idea, though,' he added, smiling at his wife.

'Oh, I'd be delighted to visit the area,' Mrs Wells said. 'You may book the journey whenever you like, Martin—just as soon as they've built a proper hotel, that is.'

'Well, there's talk of such a thing, I believe, so I may yet hold you to that, though I imagine it's still years away. But young chaps never worry about that sort of thing. What do you intend to do on your visit, Ed?'

Eddie explained that they were planning some hiking and general exploring. 'And we might have a go at skiing if we can get hold of some skis,' he added.

'Really? I believe that's quite exhilarating. I've never tried it myself, of course—we'd barely heard of such a thing when I was your age. Some fellow imported the first pair of skis into the country just before the war, I recall. Ah well, I expect I'm too old to take up such an activity these days. What was that, Emily?'

Mrs Wells, who had murmured something that sounded very like 'I should say so,' smiled sweetly at her husband. 'Nothing, darling. Just thinking aloud.'

The Wells' oldest daughter, Beatrice, came over to sit beside her mother. 'I've seen pictures of mountains,' she said. 'In Switzerland, I think they were. It looked so pretty—meadows full of flowers and snowy peaks behind. I'd love to go down there.'

'You could hardly go with a group of boys, dear,' Mrs Wells said, amusement in her eyes along with just a hint of a frown.

'But Eddie, didn't you say there were some girls going as well?' Granny said. 'There's a married couple going with them,' she added, turning to Mrs Wells. 'So they'll keep an eye on the younger ones. Mr and Mrs Gillan, isn't it?'

'Oh, Kathleen and Ronald Gillan?' Mrs Wells said. 'We know them, don't we, Martin? Kathleen's a lovely girl, very sensible.'

'Yes, and Gillan's a steady fellow. I know he's well thought of in his position.'

'They've been to your garden parties once or twice, Sarah, haven't they?' Mrs Wells said. 'Yes, I like them both.'

'So I *can* go.' Beatrice beamed at her parents.

Eddie's heart sank. He was not overly fond of Beatrice Wells, whom he found at best boring and at worst irritating. Her parents had held quite a grand party for her eighteenth birthday that winter, and he had somehow found himself expected to spend much of the evening in her company, sitting by her at dinner and then having to dance with her several times. His utter inability to find a subject that held any interest for Beatrice while at the same time being something he could bear to talk about had made the hours stretch very long.

'I don't know if you'd like it much,' he said, putting all the doubt he could muster into his tone. 'There's just a hut where we're going to stay, nothing very smart or anything. And there might be a fair bit of walking to do.'

Beatrice gave a small toss of the head, setting the ruffles of white lace around her neck fluttering. 'Well, if the other girls don't mind about it, I'm sure I won't.'

'I wouldn't be quite so confident about that, my dear,' Mr Wells remarked.

'And you really shouldn't go inviting yourself like that, Beatrice,' Mrs Wells said. 'They might be full up already. Is there even room for anyone else, Eddie?'

All faces turned to Eddie, and the temptation to lie was a strong one. He slumped in his chair. 'Yes, there's room for one more,' he admitted.

'Oh, good,' Beatrice said, smiling triumphantly. 'I'm sure it'll all be just lovely.'

Catching the train meant an early start, with the morning sky still dim. Kathleen and Ronald Gillan were already there when Eddie arrived at the station, with Ronald showing the group where to stow their baggage and directing them to their carriage, and Kathleen checking that they all had warm coats.

They were all seated by the time the train gave a large hiss and jerked into motion, soon settling into a steady rhythm as it clattered along the track. The carriage gradually warmed up, from the train's heaters and from the well-clothed bodies in such close proximity.

'That's better,' Stephen, one of Geoffrey's classmates from English, said, shuffling his boots against the footrest. 'I couldn't feel my feet for a while there.'

'Well, we could all smell them,' someone muttered, to general laughter.

There were nine of them in the party; looking about him, Eddie realised that he was probably the only one in the group who had met all the others before today. Even Geoffrey's classmates, Stephen and Anthony, he knew from the Common Room, and Geoffrey had made a point of introducing Dora to all his friends earlier in the year.

The train made its way out of the city, giving occasional glimpses into backyards that must get regular dustings of soot from their closeness to the track. The built-up area gave way to farmland, well-tended and dotted with houses, and with no hint of the wilderness Eddie looked forward to seeing as they drew near the mountains.

Their first stop, and the chance for a cup of tea at the station tearoom, would not be until Frankton, still several hours journey, but they were barely out of the city before Kathleen had Ronald retrieve a huge hamper that proved to be crammed full of tasty-looking food. She handed out sandwiches to the whole party, pressing a second one on Eddie as soon as he had finished the first.

'You need to keep your strength up,' Kathleen said. 'We'll expect you young fellows to carry everything inside when we get to the hut—not to mention chopping all the firewood.'

Eddie grinned back at her around a mouthful of cheese sandwich. He had met Kathleen Gillan several times over the years, at Geoffrey's home and at his Aunt Sarah's annual garden parties, and she invariably seemed to be smiling. She was six or seven years older than Geoffrey; 'She used to boss me around like nobody's business when she was still at home,' Geoffrey had once claimed in front of Kathleen in a futile attempt to annoy her. Kathleen had simply laughed and said that was the job of a big sister.

During the boys' years at high school Kathleen had often helped Geoffrey with his homework, and she had always been ready to make up the numbers for a game of backyard cricket. When she married, Geoffrey had pretended relief that Ronald was taking her off his hands, but it was obvious to Eddie that he got on well with his sister.

Kathleen was a useful person to have around, and not just for the food she had brought. She soon took Beatrice Wells under her wing, relieving Eddie from a vague sense of obligation that he should, as the inadvertent cause of Beatrice's joining the party, be keeping an eye on her.

Eddie had gathered from Geoffrey that Ronald was a good ten years older than Kathleen, putting him somewhere in his late thirties. The two of them did not have any children, which Eddie's grandmother considered very sad, though she did admit that they seemed quite happy as they were.

Ronald was the sort of man who always knew what was going on to do with the government, if there might be workers' strikes looming, or what exports were currently the most valuable. Rather more usefully for the moment, he also knew all about railway timetables and which stations had the best tearooms.

They stopped at several as the hours passed, piling onto the platform at each one for a leg-stretch, as well as a cup of tea for those willing to brave the crush at the counter. Fortunately there was no need to chance the food on offer, as Kathleen's hamper was something of a bottomless pit when it came to the sandwiches, pies and cakes that emerged from it to be passed around the carriage.

Geoffrey and Dora had contrived to find a seat to themselves somewhat apart from the rest of the party, and were generally engrossed in a private conversation. Eddie and the others spent much of the time gazing at the passing scenery, with Ronald drawing their attention to various points of note along the way. He had a map showing their destination, with its three volcanoes close together: Ruapehu, the highest and much the largest; Ngauruhoe, with its cone drawn as a near-perfect circle; and the heavily weathered, spread-out slopes of Tongariro.

The land grew wilder as they left the farmed plains behind and entered an area of hills, cross-crossed with gullies carved by myriad streams. Ronald pulled out another map, this one showing the railway's route, with all the bridges and viaducts marked. They travelled over one just south of the town of Te Kuiti, a tall structure of wrought iron soaring high above a river. There were far more dramatic viaducts further along the line, Ronald said, bridging the deep-cut gullies of that even wilder land, and constructed only with great difficulty. His regret was obvious as he reported that their route would not take them far enough south to see the most impressive of these works.

Great achievements as the tall viaducts that bridged ravines undoubtedly were, Ronald's description of the engineering behind them went into a level of detail slightly beyond Eddie's ability to show polite interest; he was relieved when Ronald paused for breath and Kathleen nudged him with her elbow.

'It's really not fair to take advantage of a captive audience, darling,' she said, handing her husband a small cake.

Ronald took the cake and grinned, which suddenly made him look much younger. 'You're quite right, of course. I'm sure they get enough of lectures in term time.'

But the section of track known as the Raurimu Spiral, shortly before their destination at Waimarino, was undeniably interesting. Eddie was glad to learn more about it, and Ronald was only too happy to oblige.

Waimarino was more than seven hundred feet higher than Raurimu, though only four and a half miles from it in a direct line. Covering this journey, particularly the short section just south of the Raurimu township, in anything like a straight line would have meant a gradient of one in fifteen, which was far steeper than the trains were capable of negotiating.

The solution, Ronald explained, had been to turn that mile or so at Raurimu into more than four miles, thus creating a gradient of one in fifty. The short stretch of track made a great spiral, curving and turning across the hillside, diving through tunnels, and looping back on itself in a complete circle.

Eddie stared out the window, craning his neck to see as much as possible. It was a pity there was no way to view the area from above, but he did his best to envisage the whole as they travelled through the spiral, and to imagine the work of building this marvel of engineering. It had been a vast undertaking, Ronald said, with the early engineers having to slash their way through dense bush, sometimes scrambling up trees in an attempt to get a better idea of their surroundings.

The last sharp bend was negotiated, and a short time later they were pulling into Waimarino station, where a man with a horse and cart was waiting to meet the train.

Eddie and the others spilled out onto the platform to begin the task of retrieving their baggage and loading up the cart. Rucksacks and blankets were piled in, along with crates of food. Eddie noticed loaves of bread, a sack of potatoes, and what looked to be a large ham wrapped in brown paper. They had all put in money towards these supplies, and Kathleen had organised the purchase of everything.

He hefted in the last crate, then clambered onto the cart and perched on his rucksack, just in time for the cart to take off with a lurch.

The first few miles out of Waimarino were along quite a decent road, although exposed to a chilly wind. A lowering grey sky currently hid the mountains from view, but Ronald pointed out the direction of their destination on the slopes of Mount Ruapehu.

There was a brief, animated burst of voices as several people claimed to be able to see the mountain through a break in the clouds, but conversation halted abruptly when they turned off the road and the cart plunged onto the rutted track that was to be the remainder of their route.

'Bloody hell, that's rough!' one of the boys said. 'Sorry,' he added, grinning shamefacedly. 'It's jolly bumpy, though.'

Eddie saw several blanched faces in the group. He was used to rough tracks from his regular visits to the farm, but he readily admitted that this one was particularly bad. The light pumice soil had been scoured by recent rains into deep ruts and frequent potholes. He steadied himself on the cart's side when they hit the largest of the bumps and forded streams, and did his best to distract himself by identifying as many species as he could among the scrub and tussock they were passing through.

It took at least an hour, and felt somewhat longer, but at last the cart pulled up in front of a low building.

'Here you are,' their driver announced. 'This is your hut.'

'Oh, my goodness,' Beatrice said. 'Is this where we have to sleep?'

It would not have been fair to think too badly of Beatrice for her reaction, as the modest hut was certainly not the sort of dwelling she was used to. The walls and roof were all built of corrugated iron, so battered that it might have been salvaged from an older building. Off to one side was a much smaller shed that probably held a long drop toilet; it was fairly close to the hut, but would no doubt seem a long way on a cold night.

And it was certain to be a cold night. Low clouds hid the summit of the mountain, but snow was visible on the lower slopes, their bulk imposing through thin grey mist. A gusty wind nipped at Eddie's cheeks, making his eyes water.

One or two of the boys looked equally unimpressed by the hut as they all scrambled out of the cart, and Eddie heard mumbling along the lines of "What a dump". Kathleen declared the building to be magnificently rustic, though even her determined cheerfulness was briefly dented when an exploration of the hut revealed that there was no fireplace on the girls' side.

'Well, I call that the limit,' Kathleen said, hands planted on her hips as she stared around the hearthless room. Even if the boys had offered to be gallant, swapping sides was not an option, as the six of them would not have fitted in the much smaller space set aside for girls. 'Ah, well, I suppose we'll just have to press up close and make the best of it, girls. I don't expect we're in any real danger of dying from the cold.'

The days were still short at this time of year, and twilight was drawing on by the time their baggage was all stowed away. Most of the food was stored outside, where the cold would keep it reasonably fresh for a few days. There was a flurry of activity as the fire was lit and dinner prepared, with Kathleen finding tasks for them all. They ate off tin plates by the light of kerosene lamps, and Ronald declared he had never enjoyed sausages and mashed potatoes so much.

They all sat on around the rough wooden table after dinner, the fire crackling and sparking whenever a fresh log was flung on. Dora made hot cocoa for them all, and Kathleen suggested a sing-along. Eddie cupped a mug of cocoa in his hands, and occasionally joined in the chorus when the song was one he recognized. One of the boys had brought a mouth organ, which helped with keeping in time.

Beatrice sang a song unaccompanied; apparently it was in Italian. Kathleen made much of saying what a lovely voice she had, and Beatrice pretended to be shy of the attention, which Eddie knew was perfect rot. Beatrice was used to having a fuss made over her. Eddie had gathered that she was considered very pretty, though he had never seen it himself. Some people seemed to like dimples and fluffy blonde hair. Beatrice always struck him as somehow fluffy in general, all soft edges, even now without her usual lace and frills.

No one was in any great hurry to go to bed, and Kathleen said she wanted the door between the boys' room and the girls' left open as long as possible to take the chill off for the girls. But after a second round of cocoa, with the wood basket almost empty and no one keen to go outside and refill it, Ronald piled the last of the logs onto the fire and said they had better turn in for the night.

Eddie woke next morning to awareness of a hard bunk and a full bladder. The others all seemed to be still sleeping as he pulled on his trousers over his long woollen underwear and slipped outside as quietly as he could manage.

He crunched through frosted grass to an out-of-the-way corner, relieved himself, did up his buttons and headed back around the hut. As he neared the doorway he glanced up, and stopped in his tracks.

The cloud had lifted during the night, and the mountain reared before him, sharp-edged against a sky pale with the first light of morning, sun sparkling against the snow-blanketed peak.

It was breathtaking, and not just because the air was so very chilly as Eddie stood gazing at the sight through the thin mist of his own exhalation. The wind had died away since yesterday, and in the stillness it felt as if he had the whole mountain to himself.

He rubbed his hands up and down his arms and stamped his feet against the cold, reluctant to lose this moment. Then he heard Kathleen calling from the girls' side:

'Get dressed, you fellows, and fetch a load of wood in. We'll make you some porridge as soon as you're decent.'

He realised how hungry he was, as well as how cold, grabbed an armful of wood and went into the hut.

The view was loudly admired when everyone spilled outside after breakfast, the girls looking rather odd but very warm in riding breeches with short skirts worn over the top. More of the mountain was in sunlight now, and the snow looked tantalizingly close.

Climbing up to the snow-line would be for another day; Ronald planned to talk to a guide that morning, and arrange an outing later in the week. For today, they were to hike to the Tama Lakes, a walk that was expected to take the whole day.

The early section of the walk was mostly through beech forest. It was the first time Eddie had encountered New Zealand beech trees, which looked quite different from the pictures he had seen of European beeches. They were evergreen, of course, as almost all native trees were, with thick, furrowed bark and small leaves that grew in clusters, giving each tree a soft, pillowed appearance. Eddie knew there were several species of beech, though the differences between them were subtle. He snapped twigs from a few low branches and slipped them into a pocket, with the idea of checking the leaves against a reference book when he was back at home.

After an hour or so of following the course of a stream that rushed along a rocky bed carved through the forest, Eddie realised that the low rumbling he had been vaguely aware of for some time was growing louder. The group rounded a corner in the track, and the rumble became a roar as a large waterfall loomed into view, plunging down a cliff face to tumble into a deep pool.

Ronald said the waterfall was eighty feet in height; it was certainly impressive. They dropped their rucksacks and sat munching sandwiches on the edge of the pool furthest from the falls, though even at this distance Eddie felt a mist of spray gathering on his face; he had grown warm enough for the cool mist to feel pleasant against his skin.

He filled a drinking bottle from the pool, the chill of the water making him gasp. This would be a fine swimming spot on a hot day; he studied the waterfall speculatively, and wondered if it would be possible to slip in between the water and the rock wall, to experience the full thunder of the cascade at close range.

They set off again, and a quick scramble up a steep path revealed a narrow plain, with Mount Ruapehu visible again for the first time since they had entered the forest. A quiet stream meandered through tussock and low scrub, until it came to what Eddie recognized from his geology studies as the edge of an old lava flow.

While he waited for the tardiest of the group to make the climb, Eddie picked his way over broken rock to get a better view of where the stream leapt over the cliff edge and into empty space. He planted his feet on a flat boulder and leaned a little further to watch the water crash into the roiling pool below.

'Do be careful, Eddie,' Kathleen called. 'I'd hate to have to tell your aunt that we'd lost you.'

'And what a waste of your return ticket,' Ronald added.

If it had been one of his friends passing the remark, Eddie might have made a rude response; as it was, he ambled back to the group, smiling. 'Nothing to it,' he said with exaggerated nonchalance. 'I thought of having a dive from up here, but I suppose it's a bit cold for that.' Kathleen shuddered at the unlikely suggestion.

The early part of the walk, with the rocky stream bed overhung by pillowy beech trees, had been declared very pretty by the girls, and the boys had allowed that it was a fine sight, but several in the group appeared less impressed by the next section.

'I thought there'd be flowery meadows and things.' Beatrice studied her surroundings disapprovingly. 'It's all just ugly little shrubs and that dead-looking grass.' She flicked a hand in the direction of a patch of golden tussock, a tough native grass that grew in tight clumps. 'Is it going to be boring like this all the rest of the way? We've got *hours* to go yet.'

Eddie did not bother dignifying her comments with a response, although Kathleen remarked that there was 'something of a stark beauty to it all.' He considered this area quite as interesting as the beech forest, if one only bothered to look properly.

The vegetation might be sparse, with its stunted shrubs and occasional mounds of tussock, but the very fact that anything could grow at all in this thin, pumicey soil that was icy in winter and must get baked in summer, not to mention being subjected to harsh winds all year around, spoke to the toughness of these plants and their superb adaptation to their setting. Even the bare banks of earth exposed where water had carved out channels were fascinating, with each clearly delineated layer of ash and fine pumice telling a narrative of old eruptions.

The Tama Lakes were set in ancient explosion craters on the saddle that ran between Mounts Ruapehu and Ngauruhoe. It was past midday by the time they reached a point overlooking the first, and more accessible, of the two lakes, where they paused to admire the view over the turquoise water. The flat area here was declared an ideal spot for lunch.

'Let's take a run up to the other lake first,' Eddie suggested, eyeing the clouds scudding overhead. 'It looks like the wind might be getting lively, and we'll be right in the way of it up there.'

Beatrice gave the route to the other lake, a rocky slope that rose two hundred yards or more overhead, a scathing stare. She dropped to the ground, where she sat with arms firmly folded.

'I'm not going up there,' she announced. 'It looks horrible.'

'Oh, I don't think it's as bad as all that,' Kathleen said. 'It's a stiff climb, but it's not far. And I've heard the view's lovely.'

Eddie saw her exchange a glance with Ronald. She let out a barely perceptible sigh and gave a quick nod. 'But there's no need to make yourself go if you're frightened, dear,' Kathleen said. 'We'll wait here, and you can help me set lunch out.'

Ronald offered to stay with them, but Kathleen insisted that he go with the others. A rather weedy-looking boy named Neville said he would be glad to stay behind and 'look after the ladies', and made a great show of placing a rug for Beatrice and Kathleen to sit on. Since Neville had been noticeably out of breath after climbing up from the waterfall, Eddie suspected gallantry was not the main reason behind his offer.

'What I wouldn't give for a nice, hot cup of tea,' Kathleen said, slapping at her arms to warm them. 'Lugging thermos flasks all this way would be such a bother, though.'

'It really should be billy tea made over a campfire for the full outdoor experience,' Ronald said, handing her a wrapped sweet before taking one for himself.

'The full outdoor experience can haul its own billy—not to mention the wood to burn under it. Off you go, we'll have the lunch ready by the time you get back. You might as well leave the rucksacks here, there's no sense carrying them all that way.'

Eddie snapped a large chunk from a slab of chocolate and popped it into his mouth, then added his rucksack to the pile and headed off up the slope.

The climb was a steep one, through loose pebbles of scoria that rolled and slipped underfoot, making it a challenge to get proper purchase, but it took no great time. Eddie was at the top first, his long stride a real advantage in this terrain, but Stephen and Anthony were not far behind. Dora had decided to come along with the boys, and was managing perfectly well, although Geoffrey appeared to find it necessary to hold her hand much of the time, and to slip an arm around her on particularly challenging patches. Ronald brought up the rear, keeping up a fair pace as he trudged along stolidly with the assistance of a walking pole.

A narrow ridge followed by another climb, this one much shorter, led to a vantage point over the lower lake where they had left Kathleen and the others, and their first view of the upper lake, which stretched out below them with the snow-covered cone of Mount Ngauruhoe as a dramatic backdrop.

Eddie stared down at the lake, its water pale blue through a thin layer of ice. Sometimes in winter the ice was thick enough to make skating possible here; though it would be quite a scramble to get down the steep sides of the crater, and a harder one to climb back up.

The wind was too bitterly cold at this height for anyone to want to stand about in it for long. Eddie took one last look around him to fix the place in his memory, then set out to race his companions back to their picnic spot and the lunch that awaited.

Next morning dawned fine and clear. Eddie stood in the hut doorway sipping at a mug of tea, and gazed across at the perfect cone of Mount Ngauruhoe, the sunlight reflecting off its coating of snow so bright that it made his eyes water. In the clear air it looked no great distance. He pictured Ronald's map in his head and did some rough mental calculations. Yes, it ought to be possible, if they set out promptly and kept up a good pace all day.

'How about we have a go at climbing Ngauruhoe today?' he asked. 'There'd be a great view from up there.'

Eddie had known full well that not everyone would be keen on the idea; what he had not expected was the chorus of groans that greeted his suggestion. There was much grumbling about stiffness after the previous day's walk from those less used to vigorous activity, and several complaints of sore feet; he could not help thinking that it served the latter group right for not bothering to bring proper walking boots. The two or three others who were still hale and hearty frankly stated that they couldn't be bothered. Geoffrey was among these latter, which was something of a disappointment.

'Eddie, you're not thinking of going up there on your own, are you?' Kathleen asked, brow furrowed in concern. 'I'd really rather you didn't.'

Eddie was indeed considering just that. A vague sense of having been let down by Geoffrey warred with an awareness that going climbing in unfamiliar territory on his own was perhaps not the wisest of ideas. But what a fine thing it would be to climb so far above the snow-line, and look down on a sea of white on one hand and into a volcanic crater on the other. Then the descent: the final section would be a run-jump-slide down the scree slopes, a mass of loose stones and pebbles on the skirts of the mountain, going as fast as he possibly could, with the knowledge that a tumble might be a messy business adding to the thrill of it all. How could anyone with an ounce of sense want to miss such an opportunity?

Ronald settled the matter for him. 'I don't think it can be done, old chap,' he said. 'Not with this much snow on it—not unless you had the right gear. A while ago I spoke to a fellow who'd climbed Ngauruhoe with a couple of friends, around this time of the year. He said the snow was frozen hard when they got up higher, and they had to cut steps in it for the last two thousand feet or so. You'd need an ice-axe at the very least.'

The adventure's allure dimmed abruptly. The thought of cutting all those steps was not an appealing one, even if he had had the equipment. Considered sensibly, such an excursion would be better suited to a summer visit.

'All right, never mind about the mountain,' Eddie said. 'What shall we do instead, then?'

The overall feeling was that a gentler day would be in order: a slow start after a second cup of tea, and shorter strolls near the hut. Someone remarked that another bite to eat before setting out would be a fine thing, and Dora, who had turned out to be a dab hand at cooking under makeshift conditions, made a batch of griddle scones. She baked them on a sheet of metal over the fire, and they turned out quite tasty when topped with generous slabs of butter, rock-hard from being stored outside the hut with the other perishables but melting deliciously through the hot scones.

Ronald consulted his map, and after a much-delayed setting out they spent what remained of the morning in search of what he referred to as "silica rapids", although he was vague on the details. They followed one of the many streams in the area up its course, fording it several times. There was no real track here, and at times they had to clamber over tumbled rocks, narrowly avoiding a ducking in the icy-cold water.

They rounded a bend and came across a section of stream bed that was a rich, golden yellow, giving the illusion that the water itself was tinted gold.

'Oh, isn't that pretty,' Dora said. She listened quite attentively when Eddie explained that the golden colour came from dissolved minerals in the water that had been deposited on the rock; probably some sort of iron oxide. 'How interesting. Thank you, Ed.' She smiled at him, then she and Geoffrey exchanged a soppy look, as if she had said something terribly clever.

The trees gave way to a boggy area of wiry rushes and stunted ferns, plants tough enough to survive in this thin, acidic soil. Eddie and his companions threaded their way through the swamp, picking out the driest patches as best they could, until they came to firmer ground. Here the stream bed widened, and the rapids were revealed: water rushing and tumbling over a series of broad, shallow terraces coated in creamy white silicate deposits. The sun emerged from behind thin clouds, and the light pierced through clear water to strike against the smooth, white rock of the terraces.

It was a fine sight, everyone agreed, and well worth the scramble it had cost them. There was no shortage of flat, dry boulders to sprawl upon, the glistening rocks seen through constantly shifting waters a beguiling vision while they ate lunch.

'Those terraces really are quite lovely,' Kathleen said.

'Mm.' Ronald shaded his eyes as he studied the view. 'It reminds me a little of old pictures I've seen of the Pink and White Terraces—my mother and father went there on their honeymoon. These are far smaller, of course, but they seem much the same.'

Kathleen gave a shudder. 'I certainly hope they don't meet the same fate—particularly not while anyone's present to witness it.'

Eddie had been thinking much the same thing. The Pink and White Terraces near Rotorua had been destroyed by the eruption of Mount Tarawera many years ago, long before he was born; an eruption that had killed more than one hundred people. He studied the summit of Ruapehu, imagining wisps of smoke swelling into a huge, billowing black cloud of hot ash, with a river of molten lava flowing beneath, obliterating everything in its path. Even if the crater lake were to burst its walls, it could do a good deal of damage on its way down the slope.

But it was not worth worrying about such things, and surely the people in charge of the area kept an eye on the mountain. Eddie returned his attention to his sandwiches.

After lunch they retraced their steps through the swamp and back into the beech forest. The line of walkers stretched out, with some wanting a more leisurely pace than others. For much of the walk Eddie stayed near the front, talking with Ronald and Stephen.

Sunlight striking the red-tinged foliage of a sapling beech caught Eddie's eye. He left Ronald and Stephen deep in a discussion about railway engines, and took a few steps into the forest for a closer look.

Near the sapling was an old beech tree; perhaps even its parent. Patches on the trunk showed signs of decay, the rotten wood pock-marked with small holes.

One hole stood out from the others by virtue of its neat edges, which had obviously been nibbled away quite recently. Eddie peered more closely, and thought he caught a glimpse of its inhabitant.

He snapped off a dead twig and carefully inserted it into the hole. When there was no immediate response, he poked it in a little further. A moment later, a large, well-armoured insect crawled backwards out of the hole, its barbed back legs raised ready to strike.

Eddie held his breath in admiration of the magnificent creature. It was a weta, an insect native to New Zealand. In appearance it was rather like a giant brown cricket, but with the addition of impressive defences. The jaw was powerful, and a bite would no doubt be unpleasant, but its long back legs were more effective weapons. Those barbs could inflict painful scratches, as Eddie had found out when he was much younger. On the farm he and Daisy often spent long hours exploring under the trees, and he had once made the mistake of poking a finger into a pile of leaf litter occupied by a weta.

The creatures were nocturnal, and not usually seen in daylight unless disturbed. This one might still be quite sleepy, and less inclined to sudden movement, but Eddie knew better than to risk another scratch. He reached out gingerly with the twig, intending to brush one of the weta's back legs as gently as possible.

'What are you looking at, Eddie? Is it a flower or something?'

Beatrice's voice from immediately behind his shoulder startled Eddie, making the twig in his hand jerk. The weta thrust itself further outwards, flicking its back legs upright in an attempt to rake their barbs over the attacker, and Beatrice let out a piercing shriek, her mouth painfully close to Eddie's ear as she did so.

She ran to Kathleen, who was a few steps behind, and pressed against her.

'There's a horrid big thing—it's got claws and fangs—tried to bite me—'

The rest of her words came out muffled through perfectly ridiculous coughing sobs, but from Kathleen's assurances and the quick smoothing she gave Beatrice's curls, Eddie gathered that there was some nonsense being talked about the insect leaping at Beatrice and getting caught in her hair. As if the weta wanted anything to with her!

Kathleen managed to calm her down, and when the sobs eased she offered Beatrice a tasty-looking bar of chocolate.

'You're all right, dear, I don't think it was trying to jump at you. It's probably more frightened of you than you are of it.'

This was the first sensible thing Eddie had heard for some minutes. He turned his back on them both, steadfastly ignoring Beatrice's reproachful looks, and renewed his study of the far more interesting weta.

It was standing its ground, legs still held aloft; probably waiting until it was safe to lower its defences and crawl back under cover. While it was a fine specimen, it was not a particularly large one; perhaps two inches long, not counting the legs. Given Beatrice's reaction to this creature, he would certainly not mention that in some weta species the body might grow to more than twice that size.

Kathleen came to take a closer look, leaving Beatrice at a safe distance. 'My goodness, what a hideous creature,' she said, peering at the weta. 'I wouldn't like to find one indoors, though I'm not sure it was worth quite such a fuss.'

She glanced over at Beatrice, who had now gone on ahead to catch up with Ronald and Stephen. 'You really shouldn't have called her over to see it, Eddie. You can't expect young ladies to be interested in bugs and beetles,' she said, smiling.

Eddie's ears were still ringing from Beatrice's shriek, but he managed to grin back at Kathleen, fighting down his indignation at the very suggestion that he might have invited Beatrice to see the weta. He would not have dreamed of doing any such thing.

Of course girls could be interested in bugs and beetles. Just as long as they were sensible ones, anyway. Girls like Daisy.

The following day saw one of the highlights of the visit: a chance to try out skiing. Ronald had arranged the hiring of a pair of skis, along with a guide to accompany the group.

The guide, Mr Garner, was a man of few words, probably aged somewhere in his thirties, with a wiry build and a weather-beaten face. He set a good pace on their walk up to the ski area; as the path grew steeper, Eddie heard a certain amount of puffing and gasping from some in the party. The boys took turns to carry the skis, which were lengths of wood almost eight feet long, balancing them on their shoulders. Eddie had been briefly disappointed when he learned that only one pair of skis had been hired, but from the grumbling he heard from time to time he soon decided that carrying a pair each would not have been a popular idea.

They trudged along a path through the forest, emerging more than an hour later above the tree line to see a wide expanse of snow, with occasional jagged boulders jutting through the white blanket.

It was Eddie's first sight of snow. He at once kicked a small furrow around himself, then plunged his gloved hands into an undisturbed patch, scooping up a fistful to examine more closely. It looked like finely crushed, powdery ice, its surface softening and beginning to melt as soon as his breath touched it.

The slopes were gentle here, in stark contrast to the mountain peak rearing behind. 'Here's the ski field,' Mr Garner announced. 'Let's get on with it, then.'

There was general agreement that Ronald should have first go; he had, after all, paid for the skis and for the guide's time. Mr Garner attached the skis to Ronald's boots, a long-winded process involving straps and buckles. When that was done, he demonstrated with body movements and arm-waving, accompanied by a few terse phrases, how to use them, then gave the nod and Ronald pushed off.

He looked quite impressive as he glided down the gentle slope, the effect marred slightly when he tipped over into a snowbank. He clambered out and brushed himself off, grinning broadly and not the least abashed by his tumble, then picked his way clumsily back up the slope and set off again.

Ronald was preparing for his third run when Mr Garner remarked that it was possible for a skier to take a second person along, as long as the passenger was not too heavy.

'Want to give it a try, Kath?' Ronald asked.

Kathleen had climbed on almost before he finished speaking. She placed her feet behind Ronald's and clutched him firmly around the waist.

The two of them charted a somewhat wobbly course, Kathleen whooping with delight as they slid along. A tumble into thick snow, sending her woolly hat flying, just made her laugh all the more merrily.

Ronald retrieved her hat and helped her up. 'That'll do me for now,' he said. 'Time for a bit of a sit-down, I think.'

Geoffrey wasted no time in claiming his turn. As soon as he had attached the skis to his boots, Dora followed Kathleen's example and climbed on behind him. Once again, there was a good deal of laughter and shouts, punctuated by tumbles into the snow.

Eddie had waited with all the patience he could muster for his own chance. The moment Geoffrey set the skis to one side, Eddie strode over to him as quickly as the snow allowed.

He was about to pick up the nearer of the skis when he noticed Beatrice making her approach. Realisation struck: she intended to ride behind him, copying Kathleen and Dora.

His mind raced as he clutched desperately at a means of escape. He stared around wildly until his gaze lit on Stephen Hunter.

'Oops, my boot lace has come undone.' Eddie dropped to a crouch, and made a show of fiddling with a boot that was still quite securely fastened. 'Blast the thing, it's got into a knot,' he said over one shoulder. 'Stephen, you might as well go before me.'

Stephen took his place readily enough. Eddie risked a glance in Beatrice's direction, and saw her studying him through narrowed eyes. A moment later she turned a smile on Stephen and asked in that silly, high-pitched voice of hers if she could ride along with him. To Eddie's huge relief, Stephen agreed at once; he even looked pleased at the suggestion.

While waiting a turn with the skis, the others played about in the snow, exploring its possibilities for entertainment. Their best efforts at making a snowman, which turned out to be more difficult than Eddie's childhood reading had made it appear, resulted in a lop-sided blob topped with a smaller, equally irregular one. The snowman was then pulled apart to make snowballs, which they threw at each other until everyone's hair was damp with the stuff.

Beatrice shrieked and squealed as she rode along behind, probably distracting Stephen, and the two of them fell over even more than the earlier skiers had, but Stephen seemed pleased with himself when he handed the skis over to Eddie.

His turn had come at last. When not trying out snowball throwing, Eddie had taken every opportunity to observe what the others were doing on the skis. Now he attached them to his boots, did a quick mental run-through of what Mr Garner had told them, and pushed off, using the pole that had been supplied with the skis.

It would all have been far more exciting if the slope had been steep enough to get up any real speed, though Eddie had to admit that he would also have been far more likely to take a real tumble. He crouched, holding the pole horizontally across his thighs and leaning from one side to the other when he felt his balance shifting. As he approached the end of the run, he tried Mr Garner's suggestion of using the pole as a sort of rudder, dragging it along behind him. This had mixed success, though he did manage to veer slightly in the chosen direction before falling.

Mr Garner had said that the easiest way to do a sharp turn was to fall over deliberately, then get up again facing the chosen direction. There was apparently some technique that people in countries like Switzerland knew about, which meant they could turn at quite a speed without falling, but according to Mr Garner even the most experienced of the local skiers had yet to figure it out.

Eddie knew that he was certainly not going to discover the secret himself on his first ever day, but he cheerfully accepted falling over as part of the fun. Each run down the slope was better than the last, with the only real annoyance being the skis' tendency to come adrift from their bindings, which meant stopping and going through the whole rigmarole of re-attaching them.

The others were still playing about in the snow, piling it into small heaps and throwing snowballs. Geoffrey had spread out his jacket, and Dora was using it as a makeshift sled. It was not working particularly well, and she seemed to be having a jolting sort of ride, but they were clearly enjoying themselves. Dora was tossing her head, laughing all the louder whenever she hit a bump.

Barely an inch or so of her hair was visible under her knitted hat. Dora had taken up the current fashion of having her hair cut short; "bobbed", they called it. It was not a fashion Eddie was at all keen on. He much preferred long hair on girls; preferably red.

A memory from summers gone by slipped into his awareness. His Uncle Dave had made a wooden swing many years before, back when Eddie first came to the farm. He had used it until he got too old for such play, and sometimes Daisy still did. He could see her quite clearly, head tilted back, and hair flying free.

Beatrice was still hovering around Stephen, squealing as she flung snowballs at him, her aim wildly astray, while he carefully missed her in his turn. It was a relief for Eddie to know that he was no longer in any danger of having Beatrice demand to ride the skis with him, but he could not help thinking that it would be nice to have a pair of arms wrapped around him, and to catch a glimpse of long, red hair flying out behind.

The last day of their visit came all too quickly. They would have to leave soon after midday to catch the train, so there would be no chance to venture far afield.

'Let's go back to that waterfall,' Stephen suggested, and the idea was readily taken up.

Kathleen insisted that they do a thorough clean-up before setting out, unmoved by assertions that there would be plenty of time after the walk. While she stacked the dishes and others went to work on stripping the bunks, Eddie was dispatched to the nearby stream with two empty kerosene tins to fetch water for the washing-up.

It had snowed in the night, with a light fall right down to the hut. The edges of the stream had frozen over; Eddie was careful to keep his fingers clear of the water as he lowered the tins, splintering the crust of ice.

When the dishes were done and their baggage piled up ready for the cart, they set out. There was no need to go at any pace above an amble; even with the vast amount of cleaning and tidying up that Kathleen had felt was essential, they had plenty of time to get to the waterfall and back before the cart was expected.

The snow was not thick enough to make walking difficult, but it was sufficient to have changed the appearance of their surroundings. The rough wood of the footbridge was blurred by a soft layer of it; spiky grasses pierced through a light, fluffy blanket of white; and every tree branch looked as if it had been dusted with sugar. The girls kept exclaiming over how pretty it was, and Beatrice talked some nonsense about fairyland; rather to Eddie's disgust, he heard Stephen agreeing with her.

He only knew Stephen Hunter from occasional rugby games, but had regarded him as a sensible enough chap before this outing. Now he was hovering over Beatrice, holding her hand when they crossed streams, and generally hanging on her every word. Eddie had privately considered Geoffrey to be just a little bit silly over Dora, but that was nothing in comparison to how Stephen was carrying on; especially since Dora actually seemed capable of intelligent discourse.

Geoffrey and Dora had taken to speaking French to each other from time to time. Eddie had at first assumed they were practising for their upcoming examinations, but he had since realised they were probably hoping it would keep their conversations more private. Eddie had not taken French since high school, and he was sure those lessons had not included what were quite obviously soppy expressions, given the meaningful looks and smothered giggles that accompanied them.

'You know, Geoff, I think you must have forgotten that my French is actually rather good,' Kathleen remarked when they had all paused to admire a view towards Ngauruhoe, with its fresh coating of snow. Dora blushed, while Geoffrey grinned, quite unabashed.

The waterfall, framed by snow-clad trees, looked even more impressive than on their previous visit, but it was too cold to linger by the pool, where the spray felt as if it were made of ice crystals. There was a general consensus that heading straight back to the hut would be a good idea.

'We'd have time for a hot drink, too,' Geoffrey said. 'A shame you made us pack up the tea and all that, Kath.'

'Oh, I think you're rather underestimating your sister's foresight,' Ronald said, exchanging a smile with Kathleen.

'Of course he is,' Kathleen said briskly. 'I left the tea caddy and some sugar out, and I made sure the mugs are in the top of one of the hampers. There's still some milk around the back, and we'll be throwing out any that's left. Then just a quick rinse of everything, and we'll be all set.'

The promise of a hot mug of tea spurred the others to set off at some speed. Eddie found the thought appealing, but he was reluctant to say goodbye to the forest any earlier than he had to. He slowed his pace, letting his companions go on ahead until they were out of sight, leaving him surrounded by snow-coated trees in the silent woods.

Moss was thick under the beech trees, softening the lumpy ground, its green patched with white where the fall of a large tree had opened up a slice of forest to let snow creep through. Silvery-grey lichen trailed from tree branches, forming nets for snowflakes.

Eddie ambled on, noting the varying textures of tree bark and the patterns made by branches. A low bank ran alongside his path, an occasional small fern or knot of grass emerging from the damp soil.

A small plant near the base of the bank caught his eye. At a brief glance it appeared to be stems of grass, but a second look showed something quite different: it was a tiny native orchid.

Orchids sometimes appeared in floral arrangements at home in Auckland, where Aunt Sarah's gardener, Mr Jenson, raised several varieties in the greenhouses. Those were large plants with thick, fleshy leaves and long sprays of showy flowers in various shades of yellow, pink and mauve, barely recognizable as any relation of this shy little thing.

Eddie dropped to a crouch to examine the plant more closely. There were several related species, but going by illustrations he had seen this one was probably a Greenhood orchid, with a scientific name based on the Greek for "winged".

The orchid was just a few inches high, its leaves pale green with a darker strip along the spine of each one. Within the leaves was a tightly furled bud, striped green and white with a hint of pink around its edges. That bud would open in a month or so into the hooded flower that gave the plant its common name.

Greenhood orchids had a clever way of getting themselves pollinated. When an insect landed on the lip of the flower, it would find itself tipped inside, and would then have to crawl back out, in the process covering itself in pollen. It seemed a wonderfully intricate system to be contained in a modest little plant, so insignificant that he might easily have stridden past without noticing it, or even accidentally crushed it underfoot.

Eddie lifted the flap on his jacket pocket and pulled out a notebook and pencil. Using his thigh to rest the book on, he noted down the date and place of his orchid sighting, along with details of its size and colouring, then sketched it as neatly as his awkward position allowed.

He closed the notebook and considered what he should do next. There was probably little point in taking the orchid home with any idea of replanting it; a plant that was suited to this alpine area was unlikely to thrive in Auckland. He could try pressing it between the pages of a book, but picked so early in the season, before it had properly flowered, it would probably end up looking like an undistinguished grass-like weed, all its subtle beauty lost. In any case, Eddie was not entirely sure that digging up plants was allowed in a national park.

Best leave it to flower in peace. He checked that he had not disturbed the plant, then rose to his feet, dusting the leaf litter from his palms, and put away the notebook. No doubt he could easily catch up with the others if he broke into a run; perhaps he might even be able to point out more orchids closer to where they were walking. None of his companions had any particular interest in botany, though; certainly not enough to make them take note of the orchid's subtle beauty.

He gave the orchid one last glance before setting off at a brisk walk. While Kathleen might be right in saying that most girls were not interested in bugs and beetles, he was fairly certain that even the silliest of them liked flowers, as long as they were fancy enough. But he had no intention of wasting this orchid on someone like Beatrice Wells.

Chapter Thirteen

In the warmth of December it was not easy for Daisy to envisage snowy mountains. But Eddie's descriptions were so vivid that she managed to form as clear a picture as she possibly could without ever having actually seen either snow or real mountains.

She had seen illustrations of such things, of course, in books and magazines. Being able to imagine Eddie striding about on the mountains added sharpness to her mental images; better yet, he brought her some drawings. He had originally done them in pencil, then copied a few in pen and ink, and the two he considered his best were among his Christmas gifts to her, each in a neat wooden frame.

One showed the mountain called Ngauruhoe, snow halfway down its flanks and a thin curl of smoke emerging from its crown. The other was a plant that Eddie told her was a tiny native orchid. He had drawn one he found while walking, and alongside had added an illustration copied from a book, showing the species in bloom. His drawing was done with a fine-nibbed pen, the outline in black ink and details added in green and a soft pink.

Daisy propped them on her dressing table, so that she would see them morning and evening whenever she was home; a reminder of Eddie, and of what sounded a wonderful adventure. Perhaps one day she would see mountains for herself.

But for now, it was enough to be back home on the farm, with Eddie for company. She seemed to have spent so much of the year indoors, whether at school, doing homework at the kitchen table, or working on her Latin, so it was a delight to be outside and active.

'It doesn't look like there are as many calves this year,' Eddie remarked one day as they were admiring that spring's new arrivals. He grinned as he added, 'Maybe it just seemed like there were more of them back when I used to help you with the hand-feeding.'

Daisy shook her head. 'No, we're not keeping as many these days. Papa sold a fair few of last year's, too, so they'd have less milking to do. It's because I'm not here to help with it any more.'

She picked at a loose bit of wood on the nearest fence post. 'They haven't said anything about it, but I know it must mean the cream cheque's down. Aunt Sarah gives them money for my uniform and books and everything, but I wish they didn't have to let the herd get smaller just so I can go to high school. I'm very lucky to have everyone helping me so much.'

'Well, that's because we all want to show off about having a lady doctor in the family,' Eddie said, rousing Daisy to a smile.

The new year of 1922 came in, and what remained of the summer holidays rushed by as they always did. Eddie left, February arrived, and it was time for Daisy to return to school.

She and Benjy were in the group of four pupils who made up Ruatane District High School's fifth form. On the first day of term, when Mr Grant had set his third form class to work on writing their names and subject headings in their new exercise books, he gathered his small group of fifth-formers in front of his desk to discuss the year ahead.

Daisy and Benjy's classmates, two boys named Gregory and Albert, both intended to sit the public service examination at the end of fifth form and then begin earning a living. Gregory hoped to work at the Government Printing Office in Wellington, while Albert's uncle, who was a manager at a large insurance company, had promised to recommend him for a position there as long as he passed the examination.

'And what about you, Benjy?' Mr Grant asked. 'Have you decided what you want to do when you've finished school?'

'Yes, Sir, I have,' Benjy answered smartly. 'I'll do matric, then I'm going to university. As long as I pass it, anyway,' he added, that smile of his making it seem as if failure was the most unlikely thing in the world.

'Are you indeed? Yes, I rather thought you might do something out of the ordinary.'

Mr Grant turned his attention on Daisy. 'Well, Daisy, what are your plans? Are you hoping to match Benjy's lofty aspirations?'

Benjy's eyes were sending her an encouraging message; in any case, it was high time she told Mr Grant of her own ambitions. She would need any support he could offer.

'I want to be a doctor, Sir.' Rather than the firm announcement she had attempted, her words came out in a decidedly quavery tone.

Gregory stared at her, open-mouthed, while Albert whistled through his teeth. Mr Grant blinked hard, and gave his head a small shake. 'My goodness, Daisy, and I thought Benjy's aims were lofty! A doctor, eh? A worthy goal indeed.'

Their teacher folded his arms and leaned back in his chair. 'You'll all need to work hard this year—perhaps you most of all, Daisy. And in every subject, including the ones you don't particularly enjoy,' he added, with a pointed look in Benjy's direction. 'In fact, Daisy and Benjy, you have two busy years ahead of you if you've any hope of passing matriculation.'

Eddie had taken his own matriculation examinations in the fifth form, but Daisy had fully expected to have to wait till the sixth form for her own. Only the better schools managed to prepare their pupils for matriculation in three years.

'I'll have to go through the various memoranda that arrive in the office and refresh my memory on the requirements for entrance to university,' Mr Grant said. 'It's not something I've needed to take any note of, but I seem to recall a host of rules around the different subjects for matriculation.' He smiled at Daisy and Benjy. 'Well, you two have certainly given me quite a surprise to start the year!'

According to Mr Grant, the subjects that were compulsory for matriculation were inclined to vary from year to year. Because this was the entrance examination for going to university, the rules were set by the University Senate rather than by the people in the Education Department who ran the schools.

'And I'm afraid that the august members of the Senate don't have the teachers of small rural schools in mind when they put together their requirements,' Mr Grant said. 'We don't have the same flexibility in our timetables that a school with half a dozen secondary teachers would have.

'But Mr Ritchie and I will do our best to get you two prepared,' he went on. 'For now, we've decided it's best if you carry on with much the same subjects as before. Although there's one change for this year—now that you've done two years of it, you're no longer required to take agricultural or domestic science.'

Benjy whooped at the news, and only managed to look mildly abashed at Mr Grant's frown. While Daisy had not had an equal loathing for her own classes in domestic science, she was quietly relieved at being able to leave them behind. The hours would no doubt be short enough to fit in all her study and homework in the coming year, without having to fill notebooks with careful drawings of dress patterns, or detailed lists of nutritious menus.

The four of them were allocated a corner in each of the two classrooms, where they were left to their own devices much of the time, as their teachers were usually busy with the younger pupils. For French, Mr Grant might give them a passage to translate; in English there were pages of text with grammatical errors to identify and correct, and essays to write about whatever poem or novel they had recently been set to study. History mainly meant working through the textbook, reading a section then answering the questions that came at the end of each one. There was a good deal on the British Empire, and a smaller amount on New Zealand's place within it.

Mr Grant came and sat with them for a few minutes at a time, to discuss their work and give extra help where needed, casting frequent glances over his shoulder at the other pupils all the while, to check that they were working in an orderly fashion. For the rest of the time Daisy's group had to work quietly so as not to disturb the others.

During mathematics lessons with Mr Ritchie, he wrote up their exercises over to one side of the blackboard, marked off with a thick chalk line from the problems set for his other class. He would briefly talk through the work before leaving them to get on with it; Daisy suspected that Mr Ritchie sometimes completely forgot about the four of them for the remainder of each lesson. They soon learned that if one of them had a question, the most reliable way to get their teacher's attention was to call out an "Excuse me, Sir"; with Mr Ritchie's weak eyes, waving a hand from so far back in the room had little chance of being noticed.

Doing experiments in science classes was more difficult; the bench that ran along under the window was usually fully taken up by third- or fourth-formers working with racks of test tubes, or beakers set above spirit burners. Occasionally Mr Ritchie remembered to set up an exercise for the four of them to do clustered around the end of the bench, but disappointingly often they had to make do with writing up an experiment from the textbook.

Twice a week, Daisy continued to have Latin lessons with her uncle. Uncle Richard appeared to have had a fond hope that Nicky, who would be going off to a prep school in Auckland the following year, would start taking his own work in Latin rather more seriously, but he and Timmy still seemed to need just as much cajoling (and occasional scolding) to pay any real attention to the subject. They both had brief bursts of interest, followed by a dragging of pencils accompanied by much sighing, and Uncle Richard continued to keep their lessons shorter than Daisy's.

The days settled into their usual routine of school and Uncle Richard's house, and every Friday being taken home to the farm by whichever family member could best manage the inconvenient trip. From week to week each day seemed much like the last, until the afternoon when Daisy and Benjy got back to the house to be greeted by an excited Lucy.

'You'll never guess.' She took a quick breath before rushing on so swiftly that getting a word in would not have been possible even if Daisy had had the least idea what the news might be. 'Grandpa and Grandma came in this morning and told us—they'd got a real surprise, too. It's about Uncle Danny.'

Breakfast in Frank's house was generally one of the quieter times of day, with the loudest sound the scraping of cutlery against plates. On this particular morning he was feeling the effects of having been down at the milking shed well before sunrise, the pre-dawn chill cutting through his thick woollen jacket.

He moved on his chair, rubbing his back against the bent wood of its frame to ease cramped muscles, and stifled a yawn against one fist. It seemed harder to get up these days, especially on the coldest mornings when he would much sooner have stayed in bed pressed close to Lizzie.

A sudden clatter made him glance down the table. It was Danny, dropping his knife and fork onto a plate he had polished clean. Danny looked far more alert than Frank felt; almost jaunty, in fact, considering how little sleep he must be managing on. There had been a dance in the church hall the night before, and for a chap with only one foot Danny had, since coming home from the war, shown himself surprisingly keen on going to dances. Sometimes Joe went with him, but on the previous evening he had followed his mother's admonition to stay indoors out of the wind; Lizzie considered that Joe's weak chest was not up to riding at night in any but the warmest months of the year.

After the dance Danny had ridden back by moonlight, arriving home well after midnight. He could have spent no more than two or three hours in bed before getting up again for the milking, yet there he sat, beaming at them all. Perhaps when Frank had been Danny's age instead of on the point of turning sixty, he might have been as full of bounce after so little sleep, but just now being twenty-eight felt too many years ago to remember.

'I've got a bit of news,' Danny said. He glanced around the table to check that he had everyone's attention before announcing, 'I'm engaged. I'm going to get married.'

There was a moment of silence before Maisie blurted out, 'To a girl?'

Danny snorted. 'Well, I wouldn't be getting engaged to a cow, would I?'

'She can't figure out how you managed to find a girl you could talk into it.' Joe's grin suggested that the news came as no great surprise to him; Mick, too, was smiling.

'No, it's not… it's just… well, I didn't know you were thinking about anything like that.' Maisie was visibly flustered, which Frank did not find at all surprising.

'You've kept that under your hat, boy,' Frank said.

Danny's smile broadened. 'I wanted to find out if she'd have me first, before I let on to anyone.'

Even Lizzie had been briefly lost for words. 'Well, who is this girl, then?' she asked, finding her voice at last.

147

Danny was more than willing to talk about his chosen bride. Her name was Bella Crawford, and she came from a farming family on the other side of town. The surname was vaguely familiar to Frank; Ruatane was a small enough place for him to be more or less aware of most of its inhabitants, and he was fairly sure he had come across Mr Crawford at a dairy factory meeting.

Danny had met Bella at a dance some months before. 'We've been getting on pretty well ever since,' Danny said with a self-satisfied smile. 'You'll like Bella. She's a great girl.'

'We'll see about that,' Lizzie said. 'You'd better get on and bring her out here, so we can meet her.'

Fortunately for all concerned, when Danny brought Bella to the farm for lunch with the family Lizzie did like her at once. It would be difficult not to like such a cheerful girl, Lizzie said afterwards, and Frank agreed.

Bella had a round face framed by brown curls, with pink cheeks that dimpled when she smiled, which was most of the time. Frank would have guessed her age to be in the early twenties; Lizzie did not bother guessing, instead quizzing Bella thoroughly both during the meal and afterwards on all the details she considered relevant.

She was twenty-two, Lizzie reported to Frank, the third child and oldest girl in a family of six. Lizzie cautiously allowed that Bella appeared to have been properly trained in household arts, and approved her quickness in taking up a tea towel to dry the dishes; she was equally approving when Bella asked if she could have Lizzie's scone recipe.

After that first visit, secure in the knowledge that Lizzie was pleased with the match, Frank took Danny aside for a serious talk.

'You'll be able to take on running the other farm now that you're going to have a wife to keep house for you,' Frank said. 'Once the lease is up in December, we'll get you set up there.'

'That'd be good. Do you reckon you can manage this place if I take off, though? Especially if Mick comes as well. I mean, I know you had a beggar of a job keeping it going when we were off at the war.'

'I'll manage, don't you worry. I've always said that other farm would be for you and Mick one day. Well, now's the time.'

Although back when he had bought that farm, he had still had four healthy sons, each with a full set of limbs, and there had been no thought of a war that might injure all three of the older boys in some way. But Frank said nothing of that.

'I think Bella might want to put off having the wedding till the other place is ready,' Danny said.

'Well, it'd be a bit of a squash to give you a room of your own here, and I don't see that it'd be worth building an extra house when you'd only be here for a few months.'

'I suppose so.' Danny grinned ruefully. 'It seems a long time to wait, though.'

'I had to wait longer than that for your ma. She was worth it—Bella will be, too.'

Danny was still dropping occasional remarks about December seeming a long way off when Benjy came home for the weekend.

'You and Bella could have my room if you like,' Benjy said. 'I could sleep in the parlour when I'm here, it's only a couple of nights a week and the holidays.'

It was a testament to how well Lizzie already thought of Bella that she said the idea might be worth considering, rather than rejecting outright any suggestion that Benjy should have to give up some of his comfort.

But Bella herself shook her head firmly when the offer was made to her.

'I wouldn't want to put you all out like that,' she said over lunch that Saturday. 'Benjy's got exams and study and all that business, I expect he needs a decent sleep when he's home of a weekend. It's very good of you to offer, Benjy,' she added, with a smile and a flash of dimples.

Lizzie nodded approvingly. She had already remarked to Frank more than once that Bella was a sensible girl; no doubt this would only strengthen her opinion on the subject.

'I'd rather leave getting married till the summer, anyway,' Bella said. 'It'd be better to have nice weather for the wedding—it'll give me plenty of time to get my dress made, too.'

Danny made a poor attempt at looking solemn. 'I don't know, Bell, it might give me time to change my mind about the whole business.'

'The other way around's more likely,' Mick said. 'Bella might come to her senses and send you packing.' He slid along the bench just in time to avoid the mock-serious punch Danny aimed at his shoulder.

'Behave yourselves at the table, you boys,' Lizzie scolded, but Frank could see that she was hiding a smile.

The wedding would not be until the summer, but in the meantime frequent outings to dances in town continued.

'I don't know how you can manage it, staying on your feet all that time,' Lizzie remarked to Danny one day. 'I hope you don't go doing yourself an injury, dancing all evening like that.'

'Well, we don't spend the whole time dancing. Sometimes we sit down for a bit.' Danny's grin told Frank that the evenings might well include slipping out of the hall for some private courting; he was fondly reminded of doing just that with Lizzie at a dance in the schoolroom years before.

Bella was quite tolerant of Danny's failings on the dance floor.

'You don't want him planting that on you,' she said, pointing at Danny's wooden foot. 'He just about wrecked my good dancing shoes one time. He's not much of a dancer these days, but he manages pretty well, considering.'

'I wasn't much of a dancer before,' Danny said cheerfully. 'At least I've got a good excuse for it now.'

Bella had become a regular visitor to the farm, often coming out for the weekend with whoever was bringing Daisy and Benjy home that Friday. Maisie was happy to share her room, which she had had to herself ever since they had lost Kate. She got on well with Bella; they all did.

It certainly did no harm that Bella had the sense to treat Lizzie as a sort of oracle when it came to household matters, taking careful note of her remarks on laundry and cleaning, and scribbling down several recipes. But Maisie enjoyed her company, and Danny's brothers soon treated Bella as another sister.

While that meant Joe, and occasionally even Mick, felt free to tease Bella, perhaps claiming to have broken a tooth on her latest batch of biscuits, or trying to make her blush by remarking on how long she and Danny had taken to come back from some household errand that had provided useful privacy, Bella was used to brothers, and never rose to the bait, always maintaining the same steady cheerfulness. Often she would have them all in fits of laughter, recounting some tale about her family's pig escaping and leading them a merry dance down the muddy track, or a pet goat snatching her father's trousers off the washing line and eating a hole through the seat.

It was good to hear the kitchen or parlour full of laughter. That was not as common a sound as it had been back before the war and the influenza.

Bella would be a welcome addition to the family, and Frank was glad for Danny, but there was no denying that it would make running the main farm more of a challenge. As well as giving some cows to Danny and Mick to found their own herd, he would probably sell off more calves than usual that spring; thank goodness there was wider interest in pedigree cows once again, after the disruption of the war years. But even with a somewhat smaller herd, in the peak of the season it would still be too much for Joe and him to manage on their own.

He would have to find some way around that, and it would not involve telling Benjy he could no longer go to high school. That would be breaking faith with the boy, when Frank had told him he could follow his own path in life, even if that took him away from home and the farm.

Well, he had confronted hard challenges in the past, and come through somehow. He would cope with this one, and would not mar Danny's happiness by troubling him with his father's cares.

Back in what now seemed that long-distant time before war had damaged his three older sons in its various ways, if Frank had allowed himself to look forward this far he had vaguely assumed that Joe would be married by now, perhaps with a small son or two of his own, and Frank himself might be taking life just a little easier.

But things didn't always work out how you expected them to. You just had to get on and make the best of it.

Daisy and Benjy agreed that the journey home each Friday went more quickly when Bella came along for the ride. From the beginning she was just "Bella", insisting that she did not want to be called aunt, as she was not so very many years older than Daisy. Bella never seemed to run out of things to chatter about, asking them how school was going just often enough to be polite, but more commonly showing them swatches of fabric she was thinking about for a new dress, or revealing some piece of needlework she was doing for her future home. Sometimes she would try plaiting Daisy's hair in a new way, her fingers darting in and out around the strands of hair, moving in time with her lively speech.

Every time they saw her, Bella would remark on how many months or weeks were left till the wedding, and perhaps pretend to be worried that she would not have everything ready in time.

'I mightn't have done all the fancywork on the tablecloths by December,' she said one day. 'I don't know what we'd do then—I mean, you can't get married if you don't have enough cloths for the table, can you?'

Bella pulled such an outrageously frightened face that Benjy and Daisy both burst out laughing; Bella soon dropped her pretense and joined in.

Grandpa was the one taking them home that day. 'Well, summer's still a fair way off,' he said, smiling. 'And there's no need to go fretting over that sort of thing—I'm pretty sure Danny's not going to be worrying about tablecloths.'

Chapter Fourteen

Summer still seemed a long way off when the spring term began, with the end-of-year examinations months away. Soon after school started, Daisy's Uncle Richard told her that he had written to one of his medical acquaintances in Auckland on her behalf, and was waiting for a reply.

'Of course I know very little about the process of gaining a medical qualification in New Zealand,' Uncle Richard said. 'I imagine it's similar enough to my experience at Home, but we'd best be as well-informed as possible—especially as it may have some impact on your school studies next year.'

A few days into the spring term Mr Grant announced that the school inspector would be coming the following week. In earlier years these visits had involved the inspector sitting at the back of the room to observe a few lessons, and gathering up exercise books from several of the pupils, presumably to check the quality of their work. He would make a speech (hopefully short), exhorting them to work hard at their schoolwork, then disappear off for meetings with the teachers and the headmaster.

This year the inspector, Mr Thornton, was a stranger to them all, and paying his first visit to Ruatane. He took particular interest in the school's Form Five; even more so when Mr Grant told him that two pupils were planning to try for matriculation. Mr Thornton took the four of them aside, and had a few encouraging words for each one. He nodded approvingly when Benjy managed to suggest, without giving an outright commitment, that he was planning to be a teacher.

Daisy was not sure what response to expect when Mr Thornton turned to her; not everyone thought girls should be allowed to become doctors. But when she shyly announced her own intention, the inspector gave her a warm smile.

'A doctor, indeed? It certainly won't be the easiest of paths to follow, but that's a most creditable ambition, my dear. I expect you're interested in the sciences, then?'

'Yes, Sir, science is my favourite subject. I like finding out how things work. We mostly do chemistry, but we have a little bit of physics as well.' She could have said more on the topic, but that would have meant admitting she wished their lessons at school covered a wider range of scientific material, rather than concentrating almost entirely on the chemistry Mr Ritchie considered so vital. And she could hardly tell a school inspector that what she had gained from conversations with her uncle and looking through some of his books felt a good deal more useful than anything she learned at school.

'It's always pleasant to meet a fellow science enthusiast.' Mr Thornton glanced up at the wall clock. 'Yes, I think there'll be time for a short lesson this afternoon, if your science teacher will allow me to take over his classroom.'

During previous visits, Mr Grant had mentioned that the inspector might wish to conduct a lesson, but this was the first time it had actually come to pass. Mr Thornton's particular interest being in science was a stroke of luck, as far as Daisy was concerned.

After lunch, her fifth form class joined the fourth-formers in Mr Ritchie's classroom for Mr Thornton's lesson. Mr Ritchie sat off to one side, while the inspector took his place at the teacher's desk. Mr Thornton placed a leather case on the desk, opened it, and with a broad smile and something of a flourish removed a bundle of mysterious apparatus, which landed on the desk with a metallic clank.

It would have been too much to expect a class in anything specifically to do with being a doctor, but the lesson turned out to be in physics, which made a welcome change from the usual chemistry.

Mr Thornton's apparatus included a pendulum on a long chain. He had one of the taller boys, Trevor, climb onto a stool and attach the chain to a nail on an overhead beam. Trevor held one end of a measuring tape for Mr Thornton to check the chain's length; that done, he jumped down from the stool and moved it aside. The inspector noted the measured length on the blackboard, removed a stopwatch from his case, and called Benjy over to stand by the pendulum and take hold of its metal bob.

'Not too high—yes, that's a good angle. We don't want too large an arc. Now, on my mark I want you to set it swinging,' Mr Thornton said. 'Ready? *Go.*'

He barked the command so vigorously that Daisy jumped; she suspected that Mr Ritchie had come close to slipping off his chair. The pendulum swung, Mr Thornton clicked the stopwatch again, and wrote the time in seconds on the board alongside the chain's measurement.

'Let's see how the outcome is affected when we vary the length,' Mr Thornton said. He measured out and attached an extra section of chain, then had them repeat the experiment, this time letting Daisy use the stopwatch. It was an impressive piece of equipment that actually measured time in fractions of a second, and she handled it with due respect.

As she had expected, the pendulum took a little longer to complete its swing; a difference of around half a second. Mr Thornton wrote the time and the pendulum's new length on the blackboard.

'Now, what do you think might happen if we were to attach a heavier weight?' he asked.

'It'll go slower!' Albert, one of Daisy's fellow fifth-formers, shouted out, clearly too interested in the experiment to remember to raise his hand and wait to be called on. 'Sorry, Sir,' he added, an embarrassed grin creeping over his face.

Mr Thornton waved his apology aside. 'Slower, eh? Does everyone concur?'

There was a general murmur of agreement, which appeared to delight Mr Thornton. 'Yes, you might well think so. And you'd be wrong. Ah, I see you doubt my claim,' he said, smiling around the room at them all. 'Well, that's no bad thing—scepticism is a healthy quality when it comes to scientific inquiry. Let's test the assertion, then.'

He removed the shiny metal pendulum bob, and handed it to Benjy along with a larger one of dull grey. 'This one is lead. You'd agree that it's heavier than the brass one?'

'Yes, much heavier,' Benjy said, hefting a weight in each hand. Under Mr Thornton's instruction, he attached the lead bob and they ran the experiment once again.

To Daisy's surprise, and the inspector's obvious delight, the pendulum completed its swing just as quickly with the heavy lead weight as it had with the much lighter one. When she called out the result, several mouths hung open in disbelief, and one boy had the cheek to ask if Daisy had used the stopwatch properly.

'I'm sure our timekeeper took great care with the measurement,' Mr Thornton said. He gave Daisy an encouraging smile as he took the stopwatch from her. 'Yes, you've called the time quite correctly.'

'So it really doesn't matter about the weight of whatever's hanging off it?' Albert, who clearly still had his doubts, asked.

' "Weight" is for a sack of potatoes, boy. Please remember that when doing physics we use mass.'

He turned to the blackboard and took up a piece of chalk. 'Now, let us examine the formula that describes the behaviour we've observed.'

Mr Thornton wrote out a series of numbers and letters, including what Daisy recognized as the symbol for pi, and explained how the length could be calculated if the time of the swing was known, or by turning the formula around the time could be derived from the length.

'From this we can see that the period of time a pendulum takes to complete its swing is determined by its length, and is unaffected by either its mass or its amplitude—in this context, that's the angle of the pendulum's swing. The fact that the period is able to be reliably calculated is what makes pendulums so useful in timekeeping.'

Mr Thornton paused to give them time to copy down the notes from the board. 'Although as is often the case in science,' he said when the scratching of nibs against paper had ceased, 'things are just a little more complicated than that. This formula is perfectly serviceable for a small arc, but to be strictly accurate beyond that we need to account for the amplitude.'

He wrote out a new formula, this one including a symbol he called "theta". It looked like a zero with a wavy line through it and was, Mr Thornton said, a Greek letter, just as pi was.

'There's no need to copy this formula down, I'm including it merely for your own interest,' Mr Thornton said.

Judging from the pens left undisturbed on the desks around Daisy, and a certain rustling of books that usually accompanied the time when a lesson neared its end, that interest was limited. But she carefully noted down the formula in her exercise book, just in case it might somehow be useful to her in later studies. Any scrap of advanced scientific knowledge that came her way felt too valuable to be lightly discarded. Although she fervently hoped she would not find herself having to learn Greek; Latin was quite enough of a challenge.

'That wasn't bad,' Benjy remarked in the corridor after class. 'It was a lot better than usual, anyway—Mr Thornton was that excited about it all, you couldn't help but get a bit interested, too. I wouldn't mind having to take chemistry and physics if we had a teacher like that all the time.'

'So you're getting keen on science now, are you?' Daisy asked, doing her best to sound serious. 'Next thing you'll decide you want to be a doctor, too.'

Benjy snorted. 'No, I'll stick to plays and poems and all that, even if it means I have to be a teacher. You can have the doctor business to yourself, thanks very much.'

On their return from school one afternoon a few days later, Lucy opened the back door just as Benjy was reaching for the handle. 'Father had a letter about you,' she told Daisy, self-satisfaction at having news to deliver and curiosity as to its importance warring in her voice.

'Yes, it came in the mail this morning, before he went out,' Aunt Maudie said, appearing in the kitchen doorway. 'I think it's to do with the university or something. He said he'd talk to you about it tonight.'

It seemed a long two hours before Uncle Richard returned, just in time for dinner. He had barely taken his seat at the table and said grace, and Daisy was doing her best to wait patiently for him to start his meal rather than bombarding him with questions at once, when Lucy saved her the trouble.

'I told Daisy about that letter, Father,' she said. 'It's about being a doctor, isn't it?'

Uncle Richard put down his knife and fork. 'Yes, I've had a reply from my colleague regarding the medical school.' He directed what seemed meant to be an encouraging smile down the table towards Daisy. 'We'll discuss it later, dear.'

He remained impervious to Lucy's subtle and not-so-subtle attempts to get him to say more on the subject, leaving Daisy grateful at not having the business discussed in front of everyone, but all the more anxious to hear what it was her uncle had found out.

After the meal Uncle Richard went off to his study, and Daisy helped clear the table while Aunt Maudie filled the washing-up basin. A few minutes later, she glanced up from scrubbing a plate and tutted at Daisy.

'Look at you, frowning as if you had all the cares of the world on your shoulders! I'm sure you've no need to be worrying about that letter, Daisy. Here, give me that,' she said, taking the dish towel from Daisy's unresisting hand. 'You don't need to bother helping tonight. Off you go and see your uncle.'

'Thank you, Aunt Maudie.' Daisy ignored Lucy's pained sigh and pointed look at the pile of dishes to be dried, and slipped quickly from the room.

Her uncle looked up from his desk when Daisy entered the study.

'Ah, Daisy, there you are. Come and sit down, dear.'

Daisy took the indicated chair across the desk from him. A letter lay open close to her uncle's hand.

'Yes, Doctor Alderson has been most helpful in clarifying the situation. The main issue is that only one part of the University of New Zealand offers medical studies. And that is the college in Dunedin.'

'Dunedin?' Daisy echoed, her voice tight with the shock of his news. 'But that's way down in the South Island!'

'I believe it has a solid academic reputation—you'd come out of university with a very respectable degree.'

'I've never heard of anyone going to Dunedin. I don't even know how you'd get there.'

For a dreadful moment, Daisy felt her dream slipping away into the dark, unknowable distance that contained such places as Dunedin. She heard the catch in her own voice, and was sure her uncle must have noticed it, too. She shook her head, irritated at herself for sounding so foolish. She was not a whiny little child; she was fifteen, and she was going to be a doctor.

'Sorry, Uncle Richard, that was a silly thing to say. People must go to Dunedin all the time. There's boats and trains and all. It's just that... well,

I thought I'd be able to go to the university in Auckland. I got a bit of a surprise, that's all.'

'Of course you did, dear. I expect that the idea of going so far away from home must be daunting at your age.' Her uncle looked away as he spoke, making a show of shuffling the pages of the letter; he must have noticed the tears Daisy had felt brimming in her eyes before she regained her self-control.

'However, you won't need to make that particular journey for quite some time,' Uncle Richard went on. 'You've another year after this one at high school, to begin with. And my colleague informs me that the studies for your medical preliminary examination don't have to be taken in Dunedin—you'd be able to spend that year in Auckland.'

Daisy's spirits soared. 'Could I? Oh, that sounds much better. Thank you, Uncle Richard.' Two whole years stretched ahead before she would have to face Dunedin in all its brooding unfamiliarity, and one of those years could be spent in Auckland. 'What's the medical preliminary, though?'

'From what I understand, it's more or less a matter of demonstrating that you've reached a high enough standard of education to commence a medical degree. I believe that some of the better-resourced high schools allow their more advanced pupils to attempt the medical preliminary examination while still at school, but of course that won't be possible in your case.'

'No, it won't,' Daisy agreed. No one would call Ruatane District High School better-anything, never mind resourced.

'We've always known you'd face challenges beyond those of some more fortunate pupils. Gaining your matriculation will allow you to enter university, but for medicine a little more is required—above all, it's compulsory to pass the Latin section of the examination. I don't deceive myself that I'm capable of giving an education in Latin to a sufficiently advanced level, even with so diligent a pupil as you, Daisy,' he said, smiling across the desk at her.

'There's no rush—we still have over a year to decide such things—but nearer the time I'll help you choose exactly what courses to take during your year in Auckland. I'll do my best to help you make as much progress as possible with your Latin in the year ahead, so that you won't find yourself too far behind your classmates. Beyond that, I expect science studies will be the most useful. But let's not concern ourselves with the details just yet.'

Uncle Richard removed one sheet of paper from his letter, and slipped the other pages back into the envelope. 'There are a few more details here regarding the medical course that you may find of interest,' he said, passing the sheet across the desk. 'Feel free to look this over before joining us in the parlour.'

He rose and went out to the passage, pulling the door closed behind him, which left Daisy alone in the quiet room. She perused the letter, which said little more than her uncle had already told her, then folded it neatly and placed it on his side of the desk.

She leaned back in her chair, gazing around at the shelves laden with books. It was kind of her uncle to give her a moment alone, just in case she had still needed time to compose herself; but, at least for the moment, she felt calm and even confident. One day those books would unfold their contents to her, and she would understand them all.

Daisy sat on for some minutes, luxuriating in the awareness of a wealth of knowledge surrounding her, and making the most of the silence. This would be the last spell of peace all evening; in a moment, it would be time to make her way out to the bustling parlour and face Lucy's pressing inquiries.

Eddie and Granny arrived just before Daisy's school term ended in December; Eddie had already been on holiday for some time, as university finished much earlier than the schools did. He had now finished all the courses required for his Bachelor's degree, and expected to graduate the following winter.

His casual mention of such matters at first took Daisy by surprise, but he pointed out that acquiring a degree would make little difference to his day-to-day life. Aunt Sarah had made it clear that she intended him to gain some experience working (albeit unpaid) at the firm that handled her legal affairs, but he did not expect that to take up much of his time. He might well look into studying for a Master's degree, he said, concentrating on zoology or botany.

Uncle Danny and Bella were to have their wedding just before Christmas. Bella had apparently been busy with her wedding dress and with assembling a chest of household linens, while Uncle Danny had been doing his own preparations.

'He's got Bernard to make him new leather bits for his leg,' Benjy reported to Daisy and Eddie. 'The big flap at the top where the wooden part joins onto his real leg, and all the straps and buckles. It's quite flash leather, and the metal bits are all polished and shiny.'

'But no one will see it at the wedding,' Daisy said, frowning. 'That seems a lot of bother to go to.'

Benjy shrugged. 'Bella will, I suppose. Danny said he's going to make sure it looks pretty smart—he says he doesn't want to give her too much of a shock.'

He flashed a grin; the three of them glanced at each other, then looked studiously in different directions, but not before Daisy had seen an answering grin from Eddie and felt the corners of her own mouth tilting upwards as her face grew warm. Although it was not, of course, something to be discussed in any detail, she was quite sure they were all thinking about what would happen *after* the wedding, when Bella and Uncle Danny went off to their new home.

A few days before the wedding, Daisy and Eddie rode down the valley and several miles towards town, to join a small group of family members about to set to work on getting Grandpa's second farm ready for Uncle Danny and Bella to move in. Granny came along in the spring cart with Daisy's parents, while Grandpa had driven Grandma, Aunt Maisie, and Benjy in his buggy, with his big boys riding on ahead.

A man called Bradshaw had leased this farm from Grandpa for several years, making use of the house and the land immediately around it while Grandpa had the rest of the farm as extra grazing. Mr Bradshaw was a bachelor, probably aged somewhere in his fifties, and walked with a pronounced limp. This was, according to Grandpa, the result of an injury he had suffered years before, while working on the railways. When Daisy was still going to the valley school, one of the older boys had claimed that a train had gone right over Mr Bradshaw's leg; she and Benjy had believed the tale until Eddie, who knew more about trains, had told them this was highly unlikely; that in such a case the leg would have been sliced right off, not just left stiff and awkward.

Whatever the details of Mr Bradshaw's long-ago accident, it had been considered serious enough for him to be paid some sort of pension as compensation. He had kept a house cow and a flock of hens on the leased farm, and supplemented his modest pension by selling milk and eggs in the town.

According to Benjy, Mr Bradshaw had not grumbled or made any particular fuss when Grandpa told him he would not be renewing the lease.

'He said it was about time he moved on, he's had enough of having to load up his cart with the milk and all so he can take it to the store,' Benjy said. 'He's got relations in town—a nephew or something, I think—and he's going to live with them.'

The farmhouse had three bedrooms and a parlour, but Mr Bradshaw appeared to have left most of the house untouched. The parlour and two of the bedrooms were clearly unused; even their door handles turned stiffly, and the door into the parlour opened with a small "click" as the paint that had adhered between door and surround gave way.

Grandma stepped purposefully through the doorway Grandpa held open for her. 'Goodness me, it's stale in here. Not to mention dusty,' she added, dragging one finger along a windowsill. 'Still, it could be a lot worse—I thought it might smell of rats or something. And you can't expect a man living on his own to keep a place decent.'

Granny pushed back one of the faded curtains to peer through the grime-smeared window, a tiny figure beside Grandma's substantial presence. Daisy's two grandmothers were first cousins as well as being dear friends, but they did not look in the least alike.

'You sound as if you've been reading my books, Lizzie,' Granny said, smiling at her. 'There's a bit just like that in one of Miss Austen's stories—"A house is never taken good care of without a lady". I think that's how it goes.'

Grandma sniffed. 'I'm sure I didn't need a *book* to tell me that. You and your books,' she said, her expression softening. 'You've always been just the same.'

'So have you.' Granny pressed her cheek against Grandma's sleeve for a moment or two.

'Let's get on with it, then,' Grandma said briskly. 'Dave, you open these windows and we'll give the place a good airing—they'll need a jolly good shove, I expect.'

Grandma proceeded to assign tasks to everyone, including two of Bella's brothers, who had arrived a little after Daisy's family. Bella herself was nowhere to be seen. She had stayed home with the full approval of Grandma, who said she was sure to have more important things to do there, including putting the final touches to her wedding dress. It was the first time her brothers had met Grandma, but they took their orders good-humouredly, which was perhaps why Daisy later heard Grandma remark that they seemed sensible boys.

Two old chairs and a heavy table in the kitchen, with a fair share of gouges and small dents but still quite serviceable, had been in the house since before Grandpa bought this farm, but the rest of its furniture had belonged to Mr Bradshaw. Along with his cow and all his hens, Mr Bradshaw had taken most of the contents of the house with him, and the bits and pieces he had left behind were fit only for the rubbish heap, which was where Grandma set the boys hauling it.

When the old furniture and general debris had been cleared away, Grandma sent the men and boys off with Grandpa, saying they would only be in the way inside.

Under her instructions, Daisy and the others set to work, although Grandma would not allow Granny to do any but the lightest of the tasks. They scrubbed and dusted, swept and polished. Windows were thrust open in the neglected rooms, airing them for what was probably the first time in years. All the drapes were taken down and given a good shaking over the verandah rails.

As the youngest (and tallest) of the group, Daisy was given a large share of the tasks that required scrambling onto chairs to reach down drapes or dust high surfaces. The women chatted back and forth as they worked, their voices a cheerful backdrop to her own wandering thoughts whenever Daisy happened to be in a room with them. In quieter moments she found herself dwelling on schoolwork and matriculation, and a constant feeling that perhaps she should be studying.

The verandah provided a good vantage point over the farm. Daisy paused from knocking a cloud of dust out of the front bedroom's heavy drapes to catch her breath, and to see what the boys were up to. Her father and Grandpa looked to be propping up one side of the fowl house's roof, while Uncle Mick carried a load of timber in their direction. She leaned over the verandah rail, giving her a view a little further around the corner of the house, and saw Eddie in the vegetable garden with one of Bella's brothers, digging away vigorously. As if he had sensed her attention, he looked up and waved in her direction. Daisy waved back, and briefly considered running down to see him. A moment later Grandma's voice, loudly wondering why Daisy was taking so long with those curtains, recalled her to the task at hand.

The kitchen, as the room that would take the heaviest cleaning effort, was left till last. Fortunately Mr Bradshaw did not seem to have done much in the way of cooking; judging from the crumbs on every surface, he appeared to have made do largely on bread. Grandma said that Grandpa had told her Mr Bradshaw usually had lunch at his nephew's house on the days he went in to town. 'No wonder he never looked a very sturdy chap,' she remarked. 'I suppose he'll be able to have a decent feed every day now, anyway.'

When every surface was clean and the range shone with fresh blacking, Daisy and the others went outside to scrub their hands under the pump close to the back door, passing around slabs of Grandma's homemade soap that soon changed from yellow to a dull grey.

'You can bring those fellows up soon, Frank,' Grandma called in Grandpa's direction. 'We'll get the tea on now.'

There was enough wood stacked in the back porch to get a kettle of water heating; while they waited for it to boil, they unpacked the hampers. Even after the men had washed their hands, Grandma considered them and their muddy trousers unfit for the clean kitchen, so cups and plates were carried out to the verandah, along with the two chairs, which were set out for Grandma and Granny.

The other adults made do with boxes or the verandah steps, or just leaned against the railing, balancing plates and cups of tea. Daisy, Eddie and Benjy helped themselves to sandwiches and small cakes, along with a large jug of lemonade, then settled onto a blanket that Eddie spread for them in the shade of trees close to the house.

Daisy took a gulp of lemonade, enjoying the sensation of cool liquid sliding down her throat and washing away the irritation of having breathed in so much dust.

'You've made a good job of digging over that garden,' she said, admiring the bed of freshly turned dark earth.

'I've got the blisters to show for it, anyway.' Eddie held out his hands palm up, revealing several red welts. 'It's not too bad, though—not like when you and I did the potatoes, eh?'

Daisy recalled the hours she and Eddie had spent struggling to plough the potato paddock at home while her father had been away at the army camp during the war. Eddie had only been persuaded to stop when his hands were raw and bleeding. She brushed a finger over the nearer of his palms, the raised bumps warmer than their surrounding flesh but their edges already callousing. 'No, not a bit like back then. These should heal up just fine.'

Eddie gave her hand a squeeze before retrieving his own so that he could take an iced biscuit. 'We managed to leave those runner beans growing against the trellis when we dug over the beds. It should be quite a good veggie garden, anyway—the weeds were growing pretty well, so the soil must be all right. There were a few cabbages, too, but they were all going to seed.'

'They'll do for the chooks,' Benjy said. 'Ma's going to give Bella a rooster and a couple of broody hens to start her off, now that we've done the chook-house up a bit.' He nodded in the direction of the verandah. 'Pa said it was a wonder the whole thing hadn't fallen down on Mr Bradshaw's chooks some stormy night.'

Daisy followed his gaze to see her grandfather leaning over the verandah rail, pointing out where the men had been working.

'These nearer paddocks aren't too bad,' Grandpa said. 'A couple of them are a bit weedy, but we should be able to take a load of hay off them next month. Then we'll plough them in autumn and get some better pasture going. You boys can get on with sorting out the fences over winter.'

'I don't know, Pa, Mick and I'll have enough to do over winter with doing up that cowshed,' Uncle Danny said. 'I thought the fences looked all right.'

'Well, I'd say they'll hold up for a while yet,' Grandpa allowed. 'But you don't want to go waiting for something to go wrong before you fix them up. Best to make a decent job of it in the first place.'

Behind Grandpa's back Uncle Danny rolled his eyes, while Daisy and her companions shared a grin. Grandpa was known to be very particular when it came to fences.

The grown-ups appeared to have settled in for a while, but by the time the food had all been eaten Daisy had had enough of sitting down, so she readily agreed when Eddie suggested the three of them go for a stroll.

'Sounds like your dad thinks there's still a fair bit to be done around here,' Eddie remarked as they ambled along the nearest fence line.

Benjy never showed an interest in farming beyond what politeness demanded, but no one could grow up in Grandpa's house without picking up a certain amount of knowledge on the subject. He pointed out which areas of pasture his father had said needed special attention to their drainage and with removing weeds. The neglected potato paddock, with its weed-covered ridges, would be ploughed the following autumn, and would probably give a good crop in time for next Christmas.

Since he only had one cow, Mr Bradshaw had found it simpler to milk in the paddock, and the cowshed had not been used in many years. It was little more than a roof propped up on heavy poles, with a thick crust of well-trodden mud and ancient manure as floor. Pinpricks of sunlight pock-marked the mud, marking the sections where the roofing iron had rusted through, and ropes of abandoned spider webs swung from the rough wooden beams. Daisy noticed one trail of cobweb too late to stop herself from blundering through it; Eddie helped her pick the insect-coated thread out of her hair.

'Pa's not too impressed about the state of this shed,' Benjy said.

Daisy considered this must be understating the case. Grandpa's cowshed was a solidly built structure, with a concrete floor and a red-painted roof kept in good repair. Even their shed at home, which her father had rebuilt when she was a baby, was a tidy little building of neatly sawn timber. 'I suppose at least there's plenty of fresh air,' she said, turning on the spot as she gazed around.

Benjy snorted. 'That's just what Pa said.' He gave the nearest pole a nudge with his boot, setting a few of the cobwebs shivering. 'He reckons if it's stood here this long it should hold up for a few more months yet. Mick's going to patch up the worst bits of the roof, then they'll build a whole new shed over the winter, when they're not milking.'

'That'll be a big job,' Daisy said.

'I'll say—Pa said it has to be a decent one, with a concrete floor and all. Danny's talking about him and Mick doing it on their own, but I know Pa thinks it'd be too hard for them—I heard him say as much to Ma. It's not as if Danny can get up and down ladders or anything like that.'

They walked on, leaving the shed behind them. 'So they'll all work together on building it, come winter,' Benjy said. 'As long as they stick to school days I might get out of it myself.' Benjy met Daisy's sceptical expression and grinned. 'No, I wouldn't really mind helping. It'd make a change from all that maths and chemistry, anyway. And Pa won't be happy till they've got a proper shed for the cows.'

'Grandpa's going to give Uncle Danny and Uncle Mick some of his cows for them to start out with,' Daisy told Eddie. 'A good mix of heifers and a few older ones.'

'Daisy's mother helped him pick which ones,' Benjy said. 'She reckoned it was just so she could stop him from giving all his best ones away, but I think she was joking about that. Her and Pa had the pedigree charts spread all over the kitchen table, figuring it out.'

'That's because they wanted to make sure they're not all from the same bloodlines,' Daisy said. 'All Grandpa's cows have got good breeding, but when you're starting out with a small herd like that you have to make sure there's not too much inbreeding.'

'Mm, we did a bit on that in zoology last year,' Eddie said. 'Limited genetic variation, undesirable characteristics and all that. Hey, Benjy, it's going to be a bit hard on your dad, isn't it? Managing the farm without those two, I mean. You might have to give up the university business and go milking for your father after all,' he said, his tone making it clear that he was only half-serious.

Benjy gave an exaggerated shudder. 'Don't make jokes about it.' He paused to brush some dried mud from his sleeve, then quickened his pace to keep up with his companions. 'No, it'll all work out somehow. Pa said not to worry, he didn't mind me going back to school and then off to university.' He flashed his infectious grin. 'I've gone on about it that much, now even Ma talks about me being a high school teacher, and university and everything—you'd just about think it was all her idea.'

'Anyway, Pa's had a talk with Uncle John and Uncle Harry,' Benjy went on. 'He's sorted it out with them—one or two of their boys will come down every day and help Pa and Joe during the milking season. They said it'd be no trouble to spare them.'

Uncle John and Uncle Harry were Granny's older brothers. They lived on the next farm up the valley from Daisy's home, and between them they had five grown-up sons. 'More boys than they know what to do with,' Daisy had sometimes heard her mother remark. All the usable land on their farm had long since been put into production; there were more than enough men to milk all the cows the farm could support, and unlike

Grandpa the uncles had not managed to buy a second farm for any of their sons. It was no wonder that they had accepted Grandpa's offer so readily; not when he was insisting on paying proper wages for the boys, just as if they had not been part of the family.

They walked on a little further, following the line of a dried-up creek bed, until they heard Grandma's voice in the distance, calling them back to the house.

'They're probably thinking about heading off home,' Daisy said. 'We'll have to get on with milking as soon as we get back.'

A drain barred the fastest way back. Benjy jumped over it, stumbling just a little as he gained the far edge. Eddie stepped across easily, then caught Daisy when she made her own leap.

'This time next year you'll be just about set to come up to Auckland with us,' Eddie remarked, giving Daisy's shoulders a small squeeze before releasing her.

'I suppose we will.' Benjy beamed at the notion, his steps abruptly more lively.

Benjy sounded his usual buoyant self, cheerfully assuming that nothing would stand in the way of their ambitions, but Daisy's own feelings were more mixed. She wavered between an excited anticipation that had her feet wanting to skip, and anxious awareness of the stumbling blocks that still stood in her way. Next December she would have to face the matriculation examinations, with all the looming dread the very name held. Even if she conquered that obstacle and was accepted into university, after the limitations of their little school she was far from confident in her ability to become proficient in Latin, let alone the other subjects she knew only from exploring Uncle Richard's books.

Daisy felt Eddie's hand brush against hers. She looked up to meet that steady gaze on a face as familiar to her as her own, speaking to her of strength, and of a settled confidence that Daisy could do anything that she set her mind to, and the balance of her mood abruptly tipped over into excitement. She gave a small bounce on the spot, and Eddie's smile broadened.

Chapter Fifteen

Aunt Sarah arrived the day before the wedding. She at once told Daisy that she would be delighted to have her to stay during her year in Auckland.

'I only wish it could be for the whole of your medical studies,' she said. 'But I'm sure you'll manage nicely in Dunedin, and we'll make the most of the year we're to have the pleasure of your company.'

The wedding was held at Bella's family home, late on a sunny afternoon. Bella looked like an illustration from a fashionable magazine, in a white silk gown that hung straight from the shoulders and was gathered loosely over her hips, its hem a few inches above her ankles. The gown's long train was edged with lace and with rosebuds made of silk, and Bella's brown curls had been tamed to lie flat beneath a veil that covered her head cloche-style, then fell almost to the ground.

'I like to see a bride in a dress that shows off her figure properly,' Daisy overheard Grandma remark to Grandpa after the service. 'Still, that's the fashion these days. At least she'll be able to wear it later, even if she puts on a bit of weight. And she looks very pretty, I must say.'

Bella's eyes sparkled, and her cheeks were pink with the excitement of the day. Uncle Danny had a new suit for the wedding, and he looked quite handsome as he stood with Bella's arm tucked through his, the pair of them smiling for the photographer.

After the ceremony and the photographs, the guests piled into the large marquee that Bella's father had hired for the occasion. Food was brought out from the house and set on long trestle tables for the guests to help themselves to. A mismatched assortment of chairs and benches lined the walls of the marquee; the people who managed to find seats balanced plates (and occasionally small children) on their laps.

The bridal party had a table and chairs to themselves. Grandma and Grandpa were there, along with Bella's parents, Mr and Mrs Crawford. Between the two sets of parents were Bella and Uncle Danny, Bella's bridesmaid (her younger sister) on one side and Uncle Joe on the other.

There were speeches from the fathers, from the best man, and from the groom; all of them mercifully short, and in Uncle Joe's case almost inaudible from where Daisy sat. She could tell that her uncle was doing his best to make himself heard, but the gas that had damaged his throat and chest during the war had left his voice incapable of much more than a grating whisper. But the adults listened in polite silence, shushed any children too young to know any better, and clapped loudly when Uncle Joe finished his speech and sat down, clearly relieved.

Uncle Mick's voice would have been more easily heard, but Daisy was not at all surprised that he had been unwilling to act as best man. Her uncle had chosen a corner of the marquee away from most of the other guests, but even from its relative quiet she noticed him slipping outside from time to time, whenever the guests became at all noisy.

One of Uncle Richard's anatomy books had diagrams of the throat and of the vocal chords within it, which Daisy had studied one afternoon, picturing for herself just how the damage to Uncle Joe's throat might appear if she were able to examine it closely. But the books held no illustrations of what might be going on inside Uncle Mick's head. How could you draw a diagram of being frightened? Or of perhaps hearing noises much louder than other people did?

The speeches were over, and cutlery rattled against plates as the guests gave their full attention to what remained of the meal. Daisy's mother murmured something to Papa, then rose and went over to Uncle Mick's corner. She had already slipped over to sit beside him for a few minutes earlier during the meal, supposedly to make sure he had enough to eat, but more likely to check that he was not becoming overly troubled by the unaccustomed crowd and bustle.

'He seems all right,' Mama said when she returned to Daisy and her father, speaking quietly so that no one else would hear. 'He said he might go and sit in the garden when he's had his pudding and the music starts up—he won't want to dance, anyway. Poor Mick,' she murmured, looking over at her younger brother.

Daisy followed her gaze, but her attention was caught by the small group further along that side of the marquee. Grandma's older brother, Daisy's Uncle Bill, and his wife Aunt Lily sat with their daughter Emma and her little boy Dougie, who was currently munching on a slab of wedding cake. Emma's brothers were just outside, talking to a few other young men and fiddling about rolling paper around tobacco from tins to make cigarettes.

One person was missing from that family group: Uncle Alf. He never left the farm, and must be sitting there now, all alone in the parlour, or perhaps in his own small room attached to one side of the house. She had heard Grandma tell Mama that sometimes he didn't even bother to light his lamp, just sat there in the dark.

At least Uncle Mick had managed to sit through the service and much of the reception. Daisy had even noticed him smiling during one of the speeches, when Uncle Danny recounted a tale of the two of them as small boys, sneaking off to the creek for a swim instead of cleaning the harness, and Grandpa had pretended to look shocked.

The plates were cleared away, and two of the men opened the cases they had stowed behind their chairs, revealing a violin and an accordion. It was time for some dancing.

'But where's the dance floor?' Aunt Sarah asked, staring about as if an area of smooth wooden planks was hidden there somewhere.

Granny waved a hand at the grassy area before them. 'Here,' she said, smiling at Aunt Sarah's look of astonishment.

'My goodness,' Daisy's aunt murmured. 'Perhaps it's just as well that I didn't bring proper dancing shoes.'

The makeshift dancing space might not be wood, but the earth was dry and fairly level, and would probably do; at least for anyone determined to have a dance. Mr Crawford, Benjy had told Daisy earlier that evening, had gone to some trouble over it, choosing a spot where the ground had been rolled flat at some time in the past, then penning a few sheep there for several days to crop the grass neatly. Daisy glanced at her own good shoes, and studied the ground more closely. The area had obviously been raked carefully afterwards, leaving no visible trace of the animals' presence, but you could never be quite sure when it came to sheep.

The sun was low now, the sky fading from red-gold to a dim purple, and the worst of the heat had gone out of the day. Kerosene lamps had been hung around the marquee, casting pools of warm yellow light that merged into one another. The musicians finished their tuning-up and broke into a waltz, and Uncle Danny and Bella led off the dancing.

They had the floor to themselves for the first minute or so, which gave Daisy time to notice how nimbly Bella managed to move her feet out of danger whenever one of Uncle Danny's came close to landing on them. Then the music paused, the bridal couple gestured an invitation, and a large number of their guests stood up or shuffled about, preparing to join in.

'May I have the honour of this dance?' Eddie gave a slight bow, and managed to put an unfamiliarly formal note in his voice, but the smile in his eyes was one Daisy knew well. She took the offered arm and let Eddie lead her over to the other dancers, resolutely setting aside all thought of sheep marbles.

The accordion was rather wheezy, but the violinist made up for it with his lively, running notes. Even given the limitations of a grass dance floor, Daisy was sure it must be clear to everyone present that Eddie was a wonderful dancer. Aunt Sarah had made him take lessons some years earlier, which he had grumbled about at the time, but which Daisy was now happily reaping the benefits of. At her little primary school they had done a small amount of dancing, just enough to teach her the basic steps, but as Eddie led her around the floor she felt as if they were gliding a few inches above the ground.

The crowd thinned out after a few dances, as people wandered off in search of refreshments or to sit and talk. That meant more room for the remaining dancers, and the chance for Daisy to find herself being led in fancier steps and twirled around at some speed. When one particularly lively tune ended, she was grateful for Eddie's steadying hand against her back as they finished the dance with a final spin.

'I wouldn't mind a cold drink myself,' Eddie said, indicating with a lift of his chin the musicians, who had put down their instruments and gone over to a table laden with glasses and pitchers. 'Sit down if you like, I'll get you one, too.'

Daisy took a seat next to Granny, remembering just in time to lower herself gracefully onto the chair rather than flopping down any old how. Eddie was soon back with glasses of lemonade. She took a gulp, enjoying the delicious coolness.

'I've been enjoying watching you two,' Granny said. 'You and Eddie look so nice together.'

'Do you want to have a dance next, Granny?' Eddie asked, a gentle teasing in his eyes. 'If you stand on tiptoe I think I could just about reach down far enough to get an arm around your waist.'

Granny smiled and shook her head. 'I'll leave the dancing to you young ones, thank you. Sarah, you haven't had a dance yet,' she said, turning away from Daisy.

'No, I think I'll sit this evening out,' Aunt Sarah said, flicking a glance at the grass.

'But it's a shame not to dance at a wedding,' Granny said. 'And you dance so beautifully, too.'

'Well, fortunately no one's actually asked me, so I haven't had to risk causing offence by refusing.'

Eddie met Daisy's eyes and sent her a quick smile. 'Dance with me, then, Aunt Sarah. No, go on, or I'll be offended.'

Aunt Sarah gave a laugh. 'I hardly think you're so easily upset, Eddie! No, I'm quite content to sit here with your grandmother.'

But Eddie insisted; cajoled; pulled a mournful face that had the three of them laughing; and eventually got his own way. When the musicians started up again, Aunt Sarah allowed him to lead her onto the dance floor.

She danced well, in a stately way; like Eddie, Daisy's aunt had probably had lessons when she was younger. Eddie made a good partner for her, the two of them standing out from everyone else for their height as well as their proficiency. He and Daisy's father were the only men present who were substantially taller than Aunt Sarah, and she suspected that her father, who danced carefully rather than skillfully, would be a little nervous of taking on Aunt Sarah as a partner.

Aunt Sarah could only be persuaded into one dance. When that was over, Eddie escorted her back to her seat and once again held out his hand to Daisy.

Sitting with Granny had been pleasant enough, but dancing with Eddie was a good deal better. They glided and twirled their way through several more dances before again pausing for refreshments.

'Do you think there's anyone else I should dance with?' Eddie asked, glancing around the marquee.

Daisy did her best to ignore a pang of disappointment. 'Oh. Do you want to dance with some other people?'

'No, I was wondering if I should, just to be polite—' Eddie stopped abruptly and gave a snort. 'Actually I'm being an idiot, now I come to think about it. It's just that when we go to parties and receptions and all that with people Aunt Sarah knows, there always seems to be some girl I'm supposed to dance with, to show proper notice, or regard, or something.'

'What, because you're so important in Auckland?'

'Well, it's because Aunt Sarah is, really, with all the buildings she owns, and her committees and things. It can be a jolly nuisance sometimes.' He pulled a face. 'At the party for Beatrice Wells when she turned eighteen, I seemed to have to dance just about all the dances with her—it felt like that, anyway. Thank goodness she's got engaged, Stephen Hunter can be stuck with having every dance with her now. And thank goodness there's none of that nonsense here,' he added, smiling again. 'No one here cares twopence who I am, so I can dance with whoever I like.'

That meant her. The warm glow that rushed through Daisy made her feel suddenly magnanimous. 'Well, there don't seem to be as many boys as girls—not ones who'll dance, anyway. It might be nice if you had a dance with Lucy, or maybe Flora.'

Eddie glanced over at the girls who, no doubt because of the shortage of partners, were currently dancing with each other. Eddie and Lucy were generally on terms of cool politeness, but he gave a resigned sort of shrug.

'I suppose it wouldn't hurt. She's not as bad as Beatrice Wells, anyway.'

Perhaps Eddie was feeling as magnanimous as Daisy was herself; rather than choose one of her cousins, he ended up having a dance with each of them in turn.

Daisy had resigned herself to sitting out both dances, but Benjy, who had been moving around chatting with different knots of guests, managing to appear interested in whatever the topic of conversation was in each group, wandered over to her part of the marquee.

'Do you want to dance?' He cast a glance over his shoulder to where Eddie was steering Lucy around the floor, and grinned. 'It won't be as flash as with Eddie, but I promise to try not to stand on your feet.'

Daisy thought it unlikely that anyone in Ruatane was as good a dancer as Eddie, but Benjy was a perfectly adequate partner, light on his feet and with a good sense of timing.

'Look at Danny, checking out his new bits and pieces,' Benjy said as they neared the bridal table, having just managed quite a creditable twirl.

Daisy followed the direction he indicated by a tilt of his head. Uncle Danny sat with one leg resting on a spare chair. He had rolled that trouser leg up to the knee, revealing his sock-covered wooden foot and the upper part where it attached to the stump of his leg, which he was rubbing as if to ease a cramp. Light from a nearby lamp glinted against the shiny new metal buckles, and raised a glow on polished leather.

Uncle Danny glanced up, and caught them looking. Daisy felt a flush mounting over her face, but Uncle Danny grinned and gave them a wave. He nudged Bella and murmured something to her; whatever it was made Bella giggle.

The piece of music came to an end. Benjy went off to talk to some of Bella's cousins, while Daisy sat down by her parents.

'You've hardly missed a single dance,' her mother said, sliding along the bench to make more room. 'Aren't you tired yet?'

'No, not a bit.' What flowed through her must be the opposite of tiredness; every sound seemed brighter than ordinary noise, and it was difficult to keep still on the hard bench, when her feet wanted to be dancing again. She was astonished to see that her father was yawning openly.

'Well, it's good you're enjoying yourself,' Mama said. 'That was nice, you having a dance with Benjy for a change. You don't want to dance with the same person all the time.'

'But I like dancing with Eddie,' Daisy said, startled.

'Yes, I know you do, but... well, it's just better if you don't. Never mind about that, I think they might be finishing up soon, anyway. Danny's looking as if he'd like to get away—I'll just go and say goodbye to him and Bella before there's a crush.'

Daisy was still puzzling over her mother's remark about dancing too much with the same person when Eddie returned from escorting Flora back to her chair.

'I heard the chap on the violin say they'd just have one more dance and then the last waltz. Better make sure we don't miss out, eh?'

Daisy glanced at the distant figure of her mother, then took the offered arm. She was soon gliding around the floor, Eddie's hand a gentle pressure on her back.

Well, she had not danced every single dance with him, so it must be all right to have him as her partner for the last two of the evening. Anyway, Eddie had said something about a couple in Auckland having every dance together—those people were engaged to each other, though, which might make it different.

It was impossible to imagine there could be any harm in dancing with Eddie; although as they completed a circuit of the marquee and whirled past their seats again, Daisy almost thought she saw a frown on her mother's face. But soon afterwards, when her parents had taken the floor for the last waltz, she saw that they were both smiling as they picked their way carefully through the steps. It must have been just a trick of the light that had made her mother's expression appear so serious earlier.

After the waltz came a flurry of activity as the guests followed Uncle Danny and Bella outside and saw them into the gig loaned to them by one of Bella's brothers. Well-wishes were called after the bride and groom, along with a mock-serious warning to Uncle Danny that he should take care not to tip the gig into a ditch in his haste to get home, as they were waved away.

The guests milled about, and some sat down again, showing every sign of having settled back in until the last of the refreshments had been drunk, but Daisy's family were more than ready to make their own departure. They piled into a collection of buggies and gigs, along with a few riding horses for some of the younger men.

Daisy sat between her parents in their gig, while Granny and Aunt Sarah were in Uncle John's buggy. As the gig pulled away Daisy saw Uncle Mick climbing onto the back seat of Grandpa's buggy; Benjy had mentioned earlier that evening that Grandpa had said he should come home with them for a day or two rather than going straight to the new farm. Eddie rode alongside the gig, mounted on a sturdy farm hack that must be quite a contrast with Baron, his fine bay thoroughbred back home in Auckland.

Daisy's group had got away more promptly than the other valley families, and they soon had the track to themselves. The rattle of the gig and the thud of hooves against hard-packed earth beat out a rhythm, softened by the swish of waves against the beach on their left hand. The moon lit their way, its glow a long, milky trail over the water. The night was mild, with just a fitful breeze that picked up loose strands of Daisy's hair to brush against her face. After the sensation of being acutely wide-awake all evening, she was beginning to feel drowsy after all, in a warm, comfortable sort of way.

'Mind you don't go to sleep and fall off,' her father joked to Eddie, who had brought his mount to a walk to match the gig's pace as they came to a particularly rough section of road.

'No, I'm not that tired,' Eddie said, though his last word ended on what sounded suspiciously like a yawn. 'I'll just go faster for a bit if I think I might nod off—this fellow's got one heck of a bouncy trot, that'd wake anyone up.'

'Well, as long as you manage to hang on you'll be all right even if you do doze off,' Papa said. 'The horses know their way home.' He yawned, only remembering to put his hand over his mouth when Daisy's mother leaned across to poke him in the ribs. 'It's going to be a bit of a beggar getting up for milking tomorrow.'

'It was worth it, though,' Eddie said, and Daisy murmured an agreement that might have been inaudible to anyone else.

'You might not think so in the morning when you have to wake up. You too, Daisy.'

Daisy could hear the smile in her mother's voice. She was quite certain that no matter how sleepy she might be next morning, this evening would still have been worthwhile. But just then answering out loud felt too much of a bother.

The last haymaking of that summer was at Uncle Danny and Uncle Mick's farm. By then January of 1923 was almost at an end; it would soon be time for Eddie to go back to Auckland, and for Daisy to go back to school.

Daisy rode down with Eddie on the day the men expected to finish making the haystacks. They took a generous load of food to contribute to the workers' refreshments; 'It might be a bit much for Bella to manage on her own, when she's had to get her kitchen set up and everything,' Daisy's mother said.

Bella accepted the food gratefully, making room for it on a kitchen table already laden with sandwiches, cold meats, and slices of pie. Eddie went off to join the other men, while Daisy helped make even more sandwiches and placed small cakes onto plates. There was clearly more than enough, and with Bella's encouragement Daisy sampled several of the tastier-looking items.

'There, that should keep even that greedy lot happy,' Bella said when every plate had been crammed with food. 'Would you like to have a look around the house, Daisy? I like showing it off to visitors.'

The house looked a good deal more cozy and welcoming than when Daisy had last seen it, well-furnished with a mix of unwanted items given by various family members and some new pieces bought specially, including a solid-looking wooden bedstead in the main bedroom. Lacy doilies and crocheted runners covered side tables and mantelpieces in the bedroom and parlour, and the windows were draped in heavy cream cotton patterned with flowers, the upper edges concealed beneath freshly painted pelmets.

They passed the open door to Uncle Mick's room, but Bella made no move to enter it. 'It looks a bit bare, doesn't it?' she said. 'No doilies on the chest of drawers or anything like that, and just those plain curtains. Still, it's up to him how he wants his own room. Men aren't keen on a lot of lacy stuff and flowers, are they? Danny only puts up with it in the rest of the house for my sake,' she said, dimpling.

She crossed the passage, and pushed open the door to the house's remaining bedroom. 'This one gets the afternoon sun better than Mick's, but he said he'd rather have that one for his. It's good, really, this one's handier to ours, and it's just through the wall.'

'It's nice,' Daisy said, turning in place to look around the room. The only furniture was a wooden chest pushed into one corner, but the walls had been papered a cheerful yellow, and curtains in a pretty primrose shade fluttered in the breeze. 'You could put a dressing table or a set of drawers by the window, and there'd still be room for a bed.'

'Yes, I suppose we could. Not that we'll need a proper big bed in here for a while.'

'Only if you had someone to stay, I suppose.'

Somewhat to Daisy's surprise, Bella seemed to find the casual remark amusing, judging by the quick smile that flitted across her face. 'Oh, I shouldn't think we'll be having anyone to stay. Not someone who'll need a proper bed, anyway.'

When they had finished their tour of the house, Bella took Daisy outside to see the garden. The vegetable beds, which Daisy had last seen when freshly dug over by Eddie, now had rows of carrots and lettuces, onions and beetroot, with peas and runner beans scrambling up the trellis. The flower beds under the front windows were full of seedlings and cuttings coming along nicely, and would no doubt look lovely by spring.

Daisy had brought a bunch of delphiniums from their own garden, which Bella had put straight into water in the kitchen. When the two of them went back into the house, Bella arranged the flowers in a pretty glass vase and took them through to the parlour to place on the mantelpiece.

'There, that looks nice,' Bella said, admiring the effect. She gave a glance at the mantel clock. 'Time to take the food down to the men, I think. I'm ready for a feed myself, come to that!'

They loaded up several large baskets and walked down to the paddock that now had an impressive haystack at its centre. The men were more than ready to stop work; they saw Daisy and Bella coming, and hastened to relieve them of their burdens. Rugs were spread and food and drink laid out, and everyone set about doing justice to the refreshments.

Daisy sat by Eddie on one of the rugs, taking an occasional morsel from their shared plate but leaving the bulk of it for him. Bella was sitting with Uncle Danny, by the looks of them sharing some joke that had Uncle Danny grinning and Bella laughing out loud.

Uncle Mick sat off to one side, a little apart from the others, absently fingering the remains of a sandwich. Uncle Danny glanced over at him, then nudged Bella and indicated his brother with a tilt of his head. She nodded, loaded up a plate and took it over to Uncle Mick.

Daisy noticed how Bella's manner changed as she approached him, moving in a slow, deliberate way, her lively laughter replaced with a soft smile. She crouched down in front of Uncle Mick and touched his shoulder gently. He gave a start, focused on her, and met her smile with one of his own as he took the plate.

Eddie was watching, too.

'I think he sometimes forgets where he is, just for a minute,' he murmured to Daisy. 'I noticed it when we were stacking—once or twice he'd just stand there staring at nothing, then Danny'd give him a pat on the shoulder and he'd come right. Then someone dumped a hay fork on the back of the wagon and made a bit of a crash—he just about jumped out of his skin, poor chap.'

'Yes, poor Uncle Mick,' Daisy answered, her voice low. 'Uncle Richard says the shell shock never really gets better, you just have to help the person cope with it. Uncle Danny and Bella are very good with him, though. It's probably a bit quieter than it was at Grandpa's, too.'

'Seems to suit them all, anyway.' The remains of a slab of meat pie disappeared into Eddie's mouth. He slapped his hands against his knees to knock off the crumbs, then leaned back, propping himself on his elbows. 'Hope I haven't put you off your lunch—I must be pretty smelly by now, after tossing hay around all morning.'

'I hadn't really noticed. It's no worse than usual, anyway.' Daisy crouched down as Eddie snatched up a hardboiled egg and pretended he was about to throw it at her.

Instead of throwing the egg, he popped it into his mouth and chewed it down. 'At least it's not so hot when you're not working. A couple of the other fellows said they might have a quick splash around in the creek before we go, I think I'll hop in with them.'

Even after her own comparatively gentle morning, Daisy was aware of the fierce sun beating down on her straw hat. She peeled off a strand of hair that perspiration had stuck to her neck. 'I wish I could go swimming, too—not with all the men, though.'

'No, I don't think you'd like that too much,' Eddie said. 'I wouldn't like you to, either. Not with a whole bunch of chaps, anyway. Maybe just— no, sorry. I'm talking rot now.' He smiled at her, then looked away, almost as if he were a little embarrassed. For no reason that she could fathom, Daisy felt a fleeting awkwardness of her own.

'Only two more days and you'll be on your way back to Auckland, Eddie,' Granny remarked over dinner that evening. She would be staying on with them till early February, but Eddie planned to sail in Auckland's annual regatta at the end of January. 'The time seems to have gone so fast this summer.'

'It always does go fast when I'm here,' Eddie said. 'Probably because I work harder than I do the rest of the time,' he added, grinning at his own expense.

'How was Bella, Daisy?' Mama asked. 'Did she seem well?'

'Yes, she did,' Daisy said, puzzled as to why her mother would be asking after Bella in particular. 'She showed me the house and the garden and everything. Her and Uncle Danny and Uncle Mick all looked well.'

'That's good. She must be keeping all right, then.' Mama and Granny exchanged quick nods.

Daisy's father went off to fetch a piece of harness he wanted to take into town for repair, while the others took their cups of tea out to the verandah, taking advantage of the warm evening. Daisy and Eddie finished theirs quickly, then took a stroll around the front garden while her mother and Granny lingered over their own cups.

'Of course it's too early to know for sure,' Daisy heard her mother say as she and Eddie walked past the verandah. 'She shouldn't really get her hopes up, but it's good she's keeping well, anyway.'

'She does seem very happy whenever I've seen her,' Granny said. 'She'll know one way or the other before too much longer.' She glanced down at Daisy and Eddie, and abruptly seemed more interested in talking about the garden.

Daisy stirred from a light slumber when her grandmother slipped quietly into the bedroom that night. She pretended sleep so that Granny would not worry over having woken her, and lay still, mulling over the snatches of conversation she had heard earlier.

She had acquired a fair number of little cousins over the last few years; she had also helped with the calving every spring as far back as she could remember, and in more recent years had realised the connection between putting the bull in with the cows around nine months before that calving took place. Babies seemed to follow fairly close on the heels of weddings, so it did not take any great effort of thought to deduce the meaning behind the comments on Bella's health and what she might have her hopes up over.

It was probably also what had been behind Bella's remarks on the use she expected to make of her spare bedroom, now Daisy came to think about it; there would certainly be no need for a full-sized bed in that room for a good while yet.

From what her mother and grandmother had said, there must still be some doubt over whether there really was a baby on the way. Bella was certainly showing no sign of the swelling Daisy had noted when taken to visit her Aunt Rosie shortly before the arrival of a new baby, but then just as with cows and sheep that would only happen when the baby had grown enough to be taking up a lot of room inside.

There must be other, less visible, ways to know that a woman was having a baby. Daisy could not recall having come across any information on such matters when looking through various books of Uncle Richard's; perhaps that sort of thing was in the ones he tended to keep on shelves less easily accessed.

She would certainly keep her eyes and ears open for such signs in the future; she would also be careful not to let slip any remarks that could make her mother realise that Daisy had unraveled the hints about Bella. The grown-ups obviously wanted to keep such matters secret from girls of her age, so it might discomfit her mother if she found out that Daisy had worked it out for herself.

Lucy was quite good at finding out various things people might want to keep quiet. If Daisy had discussed the matter with her, she would probably find that Lucy had already heard about Bella; at the very least, Lucy would claim to have known all about it. But at the moment Lucy's attention was thoroughly caught up in the excitement of a trip that Daisy secretly wished she could be part of herself: soon after Eddie left for home, Daisy learned that Uncle Richard was about to take his entire family to Auckland.

Nicky was to start at boarding school this year, which Aunt Maudie saw as something of a necessary evil. She was determined to see the school for herself before entrusting her son to it; Uncle Richard was almost equally keen to meet the headmaster and inspect the facilities. Rather than leave the other children at home, they were to make a holiday of it, and spend a week in Auckland before Nicky's school term began.

Quite apart from inflicting Daisy with a resolutely hidden envy at not being able to join in the holiday, Uncle Richard and Aunt Maudie's absence led to a small difficulty as to where Daisy and Benjy would stay during the early part of the term. Nicky's school year would not begin till the middle of February, one week later than the district high school, and by the time the family had sailed back to Ruatane it would be a week and a half into Daisy and Benjy's term. A brief discussion within the family soon led to an arrangement for them to spend this time with Aunt Rosie and Uncle Bernard.

The adults all considered this a perfectly adequate solution, with the only minor drawback being that they would have a longer walk to and from school.

'It's good of your Aunt Rosie to have you and Benjy, when she's busy with the children,' Daisy's mother said. 'I suppose you might find it's a bit of a crush, their place is smaller than Uncle Richard's, but I expect you'll get on all right. It'll be nice and lively for you, anyway.'

Daisy kept her own doubts to herself as she set about packing her school uniform and other clothes along with all her books and writing materials. Just after lunch the following Monday afternoon, Daisy's father took her and Benjy in to town and dropped them off at Aunt Rosie's.

The house was indeed smaller than Uncle Richard's, and a good deal noisier. Aunt Rosie's older boys, Sammy and Brian, were aged seven and five, little Katie was three, and the current baby was almost one year old. The children who were old enough to walk appeared to prefer running, in the boys' case preferably climbing over any furniture in the way, and all four of them had inherited Uncle Bernard's loud voice, though at a much higher pitch. It all made the house seem even smaller than it was.

Aunt Rosie seemed quite untroubled by how often she had to shout to make herself heard. When Uncle Bernard came home of an evening, things would briefly get even louder. He always greeted Aunt Rosie with a big, sloppy kiss that left her hair awry and her cheeks pink; then after a hasty wash in the scullery he might hoist Katie aloft when she tugged at his trouser leg and shrieked for his attention, and toss the baby in the air, making it roar with delight. With Katie and baby Ian safely back on the floor, Uncle Bernard generally had a noisy romp with Sammy and Brian, before things at last settled down somewhat as everyone was mustered to the table.

When they all sat in the parlour after dinner, much of the time everyone seemed to talk at once, which made it difficult to concentrate on reading anything for school. Even when her aunt's children had been put to bed, reading something would have meant rudely ignoring the questions and remarks Aunt Rosie and Uncle Bernard posed every few moments.

'How old are you now, Benjy?' Uncle Bernard asked on their second evening.

'Seventeen—I'll be eighteen in September.'

Uncle Bernard whistled through his teeth. 'And still going to school? You know, boy, I was earning good money by the time I was your age. I expect you could be, too, a smart lad like you. I could probably find you something to do myself if you're not keen on farming.'

'Thanks, Bernard, that's really good of you.' Benjy managed to sound genuinely grateful for the offer, betraying no hint of what his real thoughts might be. 'I think I'll carry on as I am for now, though, and see how it all turns out.'

'Fancy wanting to stay on at school when you don't have to,' Aunt Rosie said, clucking her tongue in disapproval of the notion. 'I couldn't get away from the place quick enough. I wasn't all that much older than you are now when I got married, Daisy.' She and Uncle Bernard exchanged a look that Daisy would have preferred not to have seen; it felt a little too private to be shared with others. 'You don't need all this business with schoolwork and going away from Ruatane and all that.'

Baby Ian was sitting by her feet, sucking on a crust of bread. While Daisy was still trying to find a polite response, Aunt Rosie picked him up and plumped him on Daisy's lap, crust and all. 'Have a cuddle of the little fellow. There, that's nice, isn't it?'

Ian was quite a sweet baby when in a cheerful mood, but he was clearly unimpressed by his new perch. He screwed up his face, whimpered in a half-hearted way, and wriggled to be released.

'Jiggle him up and down a bit, he'll soon settle,' Aunt Rosie said.

Daisy jiggled as instructed, but Ian continued to show his dissatisfaction. His whimpering grew more insistent, and Daisy became aware of an unpleasant smell.

'I think he might have—' she began; to her relief, Aunt Rosie retrieved the baby and patted his back.

'He's usually so good about going to anyone, it's funny him getting upset with you.' She bent her head closer to Ian's napkin and sniffed. 'Oh, now he's gone and pooed, I only changed his nappy half an hour ago. I'll have to put another fresh one on him.' The frown she directed at Daisy made her feel vaguely guilty, as if she were somehow responsible.

Her aunt took a few steps towards the door, then paused and turned back. 'They can tell when you're not used to babies, of course. It's such a

179

shame, you not having any little ones at home so you can get in the way of looking after them. I used to help with Benjy—even with Kate a little bit when I was old enough.' She of course meant her sister, not her own daughter. Still,' she added, brightening, 'you're getting a bit of a chance with the little ones while you're here. I'll make sure you have plenty of time with Ian, he'll get used to you soon enough.'

Daisy murmured something like agreement, and looked over at Benjy, who was currently getting more of Uncle Bernard's wisdom regarding his future. Benjy must have realised her eyes were on him; he flashed her the briefest of grins, then turned back to Uncle Bernard, all polite attention.

Chapter Sixteen

Daisy was sure her uncle and aunt meant well with their comments and advice, but as the days passed she became increasingly uncomfortable about the impossibility of getting any schoolwork done.

She and Benjy were yet to be set any formal homework, as their teachers did not seem to know quite what should be expected of the two of them who now made up the first Form Six the school had ever had.

'Make a start on reading through your textbooks,' a rather distracted Mr Grant had said when snatching a few moments from his new Form Three class. 'Review last year's work, then you'll be better prepared for the new material we're to cover,' had been Mr Ritchie's suggestion.

But other than during a few snatched moments of comparative peace in the parlour of an evening, the books remained unopened. As soon as they got back from school each afternoon Daisy was busy helping her aunt in the kitchen; Benjy good-naturedly insisted on doing a share of the work, even though Aunt Rosie told him not to bother.

'I'm eating a fair few of these spuds, it won't hurt me to peel some of them,' he said, rolling up his sleeves and pulling potatoes from a large sack of them.

Aunt Rosie did have a lot to do, with so many little ones to look after and all the meals to get on, so it was only fair that they should do something to help, Daisy and Benjy agreed. But after the evening meal, when the dishes were done and the kitchen tidied, rather than allowing the two of them to settle in at the dining table with their books Aunt Rosie turned off the lamp and shooed them through to the parlour.

'You don't want to be sitting in there looking at a lot of silly books— you're stuck at school all day, you need a bit of fun in the evening,' she insisted.

Benjy was sleeping on a camp stretcher in Sammy and Brian's room, while Daisy shared with little Katie, so reading in bed would have risked disturbing a sleeping child. Other than during her grandmother's visits, Daisy was not used to sharing a bed, and Katie was not the easiest of bedmates. No matter how quietly Daisy tried to slip in alongside her, Katie always stirred and pressed up close for a cuddle. At a cooler time of year it might have been welcome, but on a hot February night her habit was more sweaty than endearing. Pushing her away would probably have woken her completely, and perhaps led to tears, so Daisy made do with carefully slipping the covers down and trying to think of cold things.

'It's only for a week and a bit,' Benjy said as they walked to school that Thursday. 'Just a few more days of it now.'

'Yes, this time next week we'll be back at Uncle Richard's,' Daisy said, clinging to that comforting thought.

But when Grandpa came to collect them the following afternoon, he brought with him a letter that had just arrived from Aunt Maudie.

'Turns out they've decided to stay on in Auckland for another week,' Grandpa said. 'There's a big cricket match on, Richard's taking the boys to it. All right if these two stay on with you a bit longer, Rosie?'

'Oh, yes, they're no bother—they're quite a help, actually, even Benjy. And Daisy's enjoying the little ones, she doesn't usually get the chance.'

Aunt Rosie looked so cheerful about the whole business that for a dreadful few moments Daisy thought she might suggest they stay there for the whole year. But Grandpa said Aunt Maudie's letter particularly mentioned that they were looking forward to having Daisy and Benjy back with them; she had even passed on a message from Uncle Richard saying that he would enjoy taking up Daisy's Latin studies once again.

'So you're sure Richard and Maudie are coming back the week after next?' Benjy asked Grandpa on the way home. 'They won't go staying on after that?'

'No, Maudie sounded pretty definite about it—that retired doctor chap Richard's got looking after his patients is going off on holiday himself any time now, he can't help out for much longer.' Grandpa directed a quizzical look at Benjy. 'Had enough of being at Rosie's, eh? You haven't fallen out with her, have you?'

'Oh, no, nothing like that. Her and Bernard have been really good. I just think Daisy's missing her Latin lessons with Richard,' Benjy said, grinning.

Daisy gave up trying to snatch even a moment with her textbooks during the remaining week and a half they spent at Aunt Rosie's. Her aunt had decided that Daisy should take the opportunity to learn how to bathe baby Ian, change his napkins, and settle him down to sleep; she and Uncle Bernard also spent much of each evening pressing advice on Benjy and Daisy.

Their teachers had now begun setting them homework. Daisy and Benjy left as much of it as possible to be done in a rush on the weekend; the exercises that had to be handed in earlier meant devoting a large part of their lunch hours to the task. One of Daisy's notebooks had a small calendar for the year inside the front cover; she had circled the date they were to return to Uncle Richard's, and every morning she took out a pencil and crossed off another day.

When they got back to the house on the third Wednesday of term, Aunt Rosie told them Aunt Maudie had sent Timmy around with a message to say that they were all back home in Ruatane, and Daisy and Benjy would be expected there after school the following day. They packed their suitcases that evening, leaving only their nightclothes to be added next morning.

Over breakfast Uncle Bernard offered to drop the cases at Uncle Richard's during the day, so that they would be able to go there straight from school. They snatched gratefully at the offer; thanked Aunt Rosie, with a heartiness that Daisy hoped sounded completely sincere, for having them to stay; and kissed her and Katie goodbye.

'I just hope Richard doesn't get it in his head to go off on holiday again this year,' Benjy said as they made their way towards the school. 'I mean, I don't begrudge them having one, but I'd just as soon it wasn't in term time.'

Daisy fervently agreed.

Returning to Uncle Richard's was almost like coming home. Aunt Maudie greeted them both with hugs, Uncle Richard smiled warmly at them, and even Lucy's rapturous greeting seemed quite sedate in comparison with Uncle Bernard's boisterous household.

The family's weeks in Auckland had been full ones. As well as visiting Nicky's new school, they had gone to the museum, the zoo, and one afternoon to a moving picture (though not to any plays, rather to Benjy's disappointment).

They had also clearly made the most of the chance to go shopping. The new clothes Lucy and Flora had come home with were spread over their beds to be shown to Daisy before she had even had the chance to unpack her own clothes and change out of her school uniform. She admired the dresses, skirts, blouses and coats, then managed to claim a small section of wardrobe so she could hang up her uniform before Lucy and Flora crammed their new garments into it.

But the most significant outing as far as Lucy was concerned had been a visit to Auckland's art gallery. The family had spent a whole morning there, and in the afternoon Lucy had persuaded her father to take her back to the gallery while Aunt Maudie took the other children to an ice-cream parlour.

Lucy, it was clear, had been entranced by the paintings. She described them with such eloquence that Daisy almost wished she could see them for herself, though by the time dinner was over and she had heard about what felt like hundreds of paintings her interest was waning. Lucy spoke of line and colour; treatment of light and perspective; different schools of artists and the styles associated with each. Daisy had never before seen her quite so animated.

She called on her father's opinion several times, wanting to check what school a particular artist was associated with, or whether she was using the correct name for a particular technique.

'Tissot counts as an Impressionist, doesn't he, Father?'

'I believe he may do, though I'm not sure. I seem to recall reading that he worked in Italy with Manet, at any rate.'

'And how do you say that word—you know, the one you said means light-and-dark.'

'Actually I don't think my Italian is up to saying it at all, Lucy,' Uncle Richard said, smiling at her. 'Any knowledge I have of art is strictly that of a keen amateur, dear—and even the snippets I might have acquired are well and truly rusty now. You'd be better-advised to look in one of your new books rather than rely on my limited information.'

Lucy's eyes lit with excitement. 'Oh, yes! Father bought me some lovely books about art,' she told Daisy. 'They're on the bed somewhere—I'll go and fetch them.'

She darted out, ignoring Aunt Maudie's plea to finish her pudding first. Lucy's apple pie would probably have cooled down quite a lot by the time she had found the books, Daisy reflected, if they were indeed under all those clothes strewn on the bed.

With Lucy out of the room, Daisy could pay more attention to what her aunt had to say. Aunt Maudie and the girls had visited Granny and Aunt Sarah for afternoon tea one day; they had been made very welcome, and Aunt Maudie was full of admiration for Aunt Sarah's beautiful home.

'She said we could have stayed with her if we'd liked,' Aunt Maudie said. 'It was very nice of her, but I think we'd be a bit much of a crowd, even in that lovely big house. Anyway, we wanted to be a bit closer to Nicky's school, so we could be sure he was settling in properly.' Daisy heard a catch in her aunt's voice as she spoke of Nicky. 'I'm glad we had that extra weekend with him, anyway. We were even able to all go to church in the cathedral with Eddie and your aunt and grandmother, Daisy.'

'And Eddie came to the cricket with us,' Timmy put in. Even through Lucy's fervent descriptions of the art gallery's contents, Daisy had been vaguely aware of earnest talk of wickets and innings from Timmy's end of the table, where he had made Benjy the main target of his enthusiasm.

'Did he, Timmy? That was good he could do that. Eddie knows a lot about cricket, he's even been on a team at the university.'

'Yes, Eddie was most helpful,' Uncle Richard said. 'He met the boys and I at our accommodation, and shepherded us on the trams to and from Eden Park. He took great care that we should be in no danger of getting lost,' he added, smiling. 'And he's quite familiar with the form and history of many of the Auckland players, so he could give us a useful commentary on the match.'

'The Auckland team wasn't much good, though,' Timmy said. 'England were much better—the Aucklanders probably felt silly.'

'Well, that's not entirely fair, Timmy,' Uncle Richard said. 'With New Zealand being so far from the rest of the world, the local teams simply don't get many opportunities to play against genuinely first-rate teams. But yes, the English team won handily, with an innings to spare—the match finished a day earlier than expected, in fact.'

'And a good thing, too, or you'd have wanted to stay on for another day,' Aunt Maudie put in, though she smiled as she said it.

Daisy and Benjy exchanged a glance expressing silent agreement. Even at the cost of a small pang of disloyalty to Eddie, who probably supported the Auckland team, she was fervently glad not to have had to spend another day in Aunt Rosie's household.

'Hmm, perhaps I might have been tempted for that last day,' Uncle Richard said, looking amused in his turn. 'Although we'd already kept Timmy away from school for a week longer than I'd originally arranged with his headmaster, so it was high time we came home. But it certainly was enjoyable. It rather took me back to my student days, when I used to attend a good many matches—I even played occasionally, though never with any sort of distinction.'

'That's when Papa was at Cambridge,' Timmy said to Benjy and Daisy, a touch of self-importance in his voice at being able to impart such knowledge. 'One of the men on the England team—Chapman, that's the one—played for Cambridge. It's the best university in the world, Cambridge is.'

'Some people might dispute that assertion, Timmy—including a good many Oxford men. But yes, it was good to see a Cambridge man making such a fine contribution to the outcome. I did experience a very small hint of reflected glory, however unmerited.'

Lucy returned from her search rather more quickly than Daisy had expected. She appeared in the doorway bearing an armload of books, an open one perched somewhat precariously on top.

'I found that word, the one that means light-and-dark—chi-something, it says. And look, here's a picture one of the artists who's in the gallery did,' she said, advancing on Daisy.

'Not at the table, Lucy,' Aunt Maudie said. 'Put your books in the parlour, you can show Daisy later. Come and finish your dinner now, I want to clear these things away in a minute.'

'I just have to check this first.' Lucy stood by Daisy's shoulder and flicked over to the next page, ignoring her mother's exasperated frown.

'Lucy, do as your mother tells you,' Uncle Richard said, raising his voice a little to get her attention.

She gave him a wounded look, then darted through to the parlour; Daisy thought she heard a thud as the books were dropped onto a side table there. A moment later Lucy returned, ready to give proper attention to her pudding.

After dinner, when the dishes were done and Daisy and Benjy had finished their homework, Lucy sat beside Daisy on one of the parlour's sofas and spent some time showing her pictures from the books and reading out information about the artists. Some of the paintings did look quite interesting, even in the small black-and-white photographs the books contained. Perhaps Daisy would be able to visit the art gallery herself when she went to Auckland next year; Eddie would be sure to take her if she asked. Although before she let her imagination run away with taking her on future outings, there was the not-so-small matter of the current year and its all-important examinations to get through.

'Do you learn about art at school?' Lucy asked, looking up from the book in her lap.

'No, nothing like that,' Daisy said. 'I think they might have it in the big schools—I remember Eddie did drawing when he was in third form, anyway. But we don't have it here.'

'Oh, well, it doesn't matter,' Lucy said. 'I just wondered if it might have been worth going to high school after all. But I'm glad I didn't if it's only boring things like arithmetic.'

Even without art, there were quite enough subjects to fit into this matriculation year. They had classes in English, French, history, mathematics and science, and two nights a week Daisy studied Latin with her uncle.

She had her first Latin lesson of the year on her very first evening back at Aunt Maudie's, leaving Lucy in the parlour curled up contentedly with her art books. Much to Daisy's surprise and pleasure, Uncle Richard had brought home two books for her as well: a new copy of a Latin grammar book in place of the much-battered one that had been her uncle's in his own schooldays, and a set of poems by Virgil.

'Timmy made it quite clear that a Latin textbook was not what he had in mind when it came to choosing souvenirs of our holiday,' Uncle Richard said as he presented the books to Daisy. 'I believe he'll be happy enough to make do with my old books until he follows in Nicky's steps and goes off to boarding school, but I thought you might like a copy of your own to annotate as you wish. And the Virgil will provide some fresh material for you to polish your translation skills on.'

186

Daisy readily took up his suggestion that they try a passage from the new book at once. The hour they spent on the work flew by, with Daisy relieved at how much she remembered, thanks to occasional Latin sessions with Eddie over the summer holidays. Her uncle was generous with his praise at how well she had kept up with her studies.

Timmy managed to get out of that first Latin lesson. When Uncle Richard said it was time to get out the books, Timmy said he was too sleepy, letting out a series of enormous (and quite obviously feigned) yawns in support of his claim. Aunt Maudie said he was probably still getting over the long trip home, and Uncle Richard said it would do no harm for him to miss a lesson.

In those first few weeks of term Aunt Maudie sometimes appeared on the verge of tears when Nicky came up in conversation. She had already marked the dates of the school holidays on the kitchen calendar, and Daisy sometimes saw her counting off the weeks under her breath.

'He's being so good about writing home every week,' she said one evening, her hand resting on Nicky's latest letter.

'Yes, he's a very reliable correspondent.' Uncle Richard's voice sounded serious, although Daisy saw a hint of amusement in his eyes; Nicky's first letter had stated quite frankly that all the boarders had to write home once a week. But he patted Aunt Maudie's hand, and when she said she would make up a hamper of nice food to send Nicky he said that was a very good idea.

Daisy was aware from snatches of conversation overheard at the weekends that Grandma did not quite approve of Nicky's being sent away to boarding school.

'He's only twelve, that's very young to be up there with people they don't know,' she heard Grandma say one afternoon. 'Daisy and Benjy going off to the university, that's not the same thing at all. Benjy'll be eighteen by then, and Daisy will be nigh on seventeen, and they'll have Amy to keep an eye on them. I wouldn't be letting him go otherwise.'

'Well, I expect they look after the kids all right at that flash school Nicky's gone to,' Grandpa said. 'And it's better than what Richard had when he was a boy, you know—he was only seven when his ma and pa sent him off to boarding school.'

'Yes, that sort of thing's dreadful,' Grandma said, pursing her lips. 'I'm sure Maudie would have put her foot down over that, even if Richard had been silly enough to want to do it. It still seems an odd business to me— there's nothing wrong with the school in Ruatane, look at how well Benjy's doing.'

At that point she noticed that Daisy and Benjy were listening, and changed the subject; Grandma did not like to be overheard criticizing adults in front of children.

On weekdays Daisy and Benjy sometimes sat out on the verandah after school with their homework, making the most of the shade and occasional breezes on warm summer afternoons. Lucy said the light was good there for sketching, and when Flora was not in the mood for playing the piano she would sometimes bring out a piece of embroidery to work on.

Timmy was out in the garden with his cricket bat one afternoon, hitting a ball against the base of the verandah, which was doing Aunt Maudie's flower bed no good at all.

'Stupid bloody thing,' he muttered as the bat struck the ball at an awkward angle, flinging it into the soft earth. He glanced up at the window, relief flitting over his face when he made sure that his mother was not within earshot before his expression settled back into a half-hearted scowl. Poor Timmy was clearly missing his brother, and from time to time seemed quite out of sorts rather than his usual cheerful self.

'Do you want to have a turn, Benjy?' he asked, looking up as he retrieved his ball from a patch of violas.

'I'm a bit busy just now,' Benjy said, pointing to the physics textbook on his lap.

'Come on, just for a couple of minutes. You can bowl or bat, whatever you like.'

Timmy looked so wistful that Daisy was not overly surprised when Benjy sent her a rueful look and joined him on the lawn. A little later she even allowed herself to be drawn in for a few minutes, when she felt the need to stretch her legs as well as fingers that were cramped from writing. Timmy did not bother asking his sisters, whose expressions made it clear what the answer would be.

According to Timmy, the ball they were using was much softer than it should have been; Uncle Richard had apparently said he did not think the windows would be safe if he allowed the boys to have a real cricket ball. It should, Timmy said, make a loud thwack when it hit the bat, rather than a dull thud. Daisy found it quite hard enough as it was, but when she caught a ball that he sent off the bat at a tricky angle he told her that she was not bad for a girl. Timmy obviously thought this was a compliment; Daisy exchanged grins with Benjy and said nothing.

'He's mad on cricket,' Benjy murmured to Daisy when the two of them had returned to the verandah and their books, impervious to pleas of "just for a bit longer". 'The other night I thought he'd never shut up about it, he went on that long after I'd put the light out. In the end I had to pretend I'd gone to sleep.'

'He'll probably be just as bad over rugby come winter,' Daisy said.

Benjy rolled his eyes. 'Yes, he'll have us kicking a rugby ball around the backyard then if we're not careful.' He turned the page of his chemistry textbook. 'Want me to hear you on the properties of metals again? Then I'll have a go at Boyle's law, see if I can get it right this time.'

It was good to pass questions back and forth as a change from working alone. At school, too, Daisy was grateful for Benjy's company, which saved her from being the only pupil in Form Six.

The headmaster was so pleased at having a sixth form that he actually came over from his office in the main part of the school and spoke to Daisy and Benjy; a rare occurrence. But deciding just what to do with the two of them was something of a challenge for their teachers.

The school's roll had risen somewhat, with several more third-formers than in previous years, and for a time there had been talk of setting up desks for Daisy and Benjy in the corridor. But in the end they managed to squeeze into a back corner of each classroom, even during the busiest English classes.

In between teaching his younger pupils, Mr Grant did his best to spend some time with Daisy and Benjy when they were working on English, French or history, setting exercises and answering questions, but they were generally left to their own devices during his classes. It was much the same in mathematics lessons, where Mr Ritchie would set them problems from the textbooks and then leave them to get on with it. If they struck a particular difficulty it could take some effort to attract his attention and ask for assistance.

Mr Ritchie, it appeared, considered that it would be too much bother to set up separate science experiments just for the two of them. It would be sufficient, he told Daisy and Benjy, for them to join in with Form Five for the practical part of the course, even though this meant repeating much of what they had already done the previous year.

There certainly seemed to be a good deal of material to cover when it came to theory. Daisy and Benjy filled their exercise books with carefully copied notes on the properties of various elements and compounds; lists of formulae; laws named for long-ago scientists. For homework they worked through the questions at the end of each chapter, neatly writing out their answers along with carefully drawn diagrams. Unlike Mr Grant, who often added useful comments when marking their homework, Mr Ritchie generally made do with a tick or cross against each answer; if he added a "Good", Daisy knew she had done particularly well.

Summer turned into autumn as the school term drew on towards the May holidays. Busy as she was, Daisy made time every week to write to Eddie. It was no hardship to devote an hour or so to filling the pages; not when Eddie was the one person she felt able to pour out her feelings to, sharing her small successes and admitting her fears.

It would not be right to worry her parents, or even Uncle Richard, about such matters; they had their own important responsibilities to concern themselves with. Benjy was a fine companion, but it did not seem fair to risk making him anxious about his own prospects; although Benjy's determined optimism might well have been proof against such anxiety.

'You can only do your best—that's what Pa always says,' Benjy remarked one day when the two of them had struggled through a particularly nasty geometry exercise, and were unsure of the accuracy of their answer. Daisy left unasked the question that hovered on her lips: what if your best wasn't good enough?

But with Eddie she was always sure of being understood without upsetting. He knew how much this dream of being a doctor meant to her; knew how frightened she sometimes was of failing, and of letting so many people down; knew just what to say in his replies to lift her spirits. She was careful to talk about cheerful things as well, but just to be able to admit those fears gave a large measure of relief.

Chapter Seventeen

Eddie's aunt and grandmother seemed to be more excited about his upcoming graduation ceremony than Eddie was himself. It was to be held in the Town Hall in the middle of May, with an array of distinguished guests and no doubt a great many speeches. Afterwards a grand ball would take place in honour of the new graduates, with academic dress to be worn for the first two dances.

His own academic gown, with a hood lined in dark blue silk bordered with white fur, had arrived well in time, and after being duly admired by everyone in the house, including the staff, now hung in his wardrobe, the trencher above it on a shelf. Aunt Sarah and Granny seemed particularly concerned with the dresses they might wear to the ball; the subject had certainly dominated several mealtimes.

The ceremony might be interesting, he supposed, and the ball would almost certainly have a good supper, but Eddie was currently far more absorbed with his studies.

He strolled across the road to the university most days, even when he did not have formal classes, to visit the library or talk with the lecturers. The direction his further studies might take, and what might be the subject of an eventual thesis, was gradually becoming clearer, shaped by his enthusiasm for hiking and exploring as well as his interest in the creatures found in remote or harsh environments. He had learned that there were parts of the country where the invertebrates had barely been studied, and there might even be new species to discover.

Aunt Sarah had always treated Eddie's interest in "bugs and beetles" with tolerant amusement, but she had made it clear that as long as he fulfilled his duties in learning more about business, and in sharing her involvement with various charitable foundations, she was perfectly content to continue supporting his studies.

The possibilities of such exploration in future years stretched before him, boundless and fascinating, and overshadowing any thought of ceremonies and balls. But Granny and Aunt Sarah were enjoying the thought of his graduation, and he was enjoying watching their excitement.

As May grew closer, Eddie realised that Aunt Sarah appeared to be planning an excursion that had nothing to do with graduation. The mother of his aunt's friend Mrs Wells had visited the spa town of Rotorua earlier in the year, and according to Mrs Wells it had done wonders for her health and general well-being.

'I'm sure it would do you good, too, Amy,' Aunt Sarah said to Granny after the two of them had paid a visit to Mrs Wells one afternoon. 'You might even put on a little weight—Emily said the hot baths gave her mother a hearty appetite.'

Eddie had once met Mrs Wells' mother, a substantial lady whose appetite seemed in no need of improvement. He was not surprised when Granny smiled and said she did not think hot baths would do much to change her build.

'Well, it would set you up nicely for winter, anyway—the cold weather doesn't agree with you, I've often thought.'

'There's really no need, Sarah. But if you think you'd like us to go to Rotorua, I'm sure it would be very nice.'

When Aunt Sarah set her mind to something, it usually came to pass. Casual discussion of such a visit soon grew into a settled plan of spending several days in Rotorua before the worst of the winter weather, taking in the various spa treatments.

'Do you think you'd like to come too, Eddie?' Granny said over breakfast one morning. 'It might be a bit dull for you, though, wandering around the town on your own while Aunt Sarah and I are having the mud baths and all that business.'

'Yes, you don't need to drag yourself away from your beetles if you'd sooner stay home,' Aunt Sarah said.

Until this point Eddie had not given any serious consideration to the notion, as a town full of people Granny's or Aunt Sarah's age intent on mysterious spa treatments did indeed sound dull. But in his geology courses he had heard Rotorua spoken of in a more interesting context, and the idea of visiting it did hold a certain appeal.

'No, I think I'd like to see Rotorua,' he said. 'It's got lots of thermal activity—geysers and mud pools, that sort of thing.' A thought struck him, giving the trip even greater appeal. 'Hey, if you could leave it till the school holidays, what about bringing Daisy along, too? She'd like seeing the geysers and all that.'

It was clear to him from the tone of Daisy's letters that she would also benefit from a brief change of scene; a rest from her diligent studying and a distraction from her worries. But he was quite sure she would not want him to let slip to anyone else just how anxious she sometimes became.

Granny and Aunt Sarah at once agreed that taking Daisy would be a fine idea, though there was some doubt over how they would go about getting her to the inland town. There was a good train service from Auckland, but travel from Ruatane had long been dominated by the coastal steamers, which would be no use for travel to Rotorua.

'Hang on, I think I saw something in the paper that might be to do with all that,' Eddie said. He took that morning's newspaper from a sideboard and scanned through its contents, searching for an advertisement he vaguely remembered seeing.

'Yes, here it is—there's a motor car service now, it goes every day. We could book it for Daisy, it says where to send a telegram.'

'My goodness, are the roads good enough for motor cars now?' Granny said, raising her eyebrows. 'They must have got a lot better since I was a girl—you'd have thought twice before so much as taking a pack horse in those days. Still, I suppose it must be all right if they're taking fancy big cars over there. Just as long as Daisy's mother and father say she can come.'

'Aunt Beth and Uncle Dave won't mind,' Eddie said. 'They can see her off, and we'll meet her when she arrives in Rotorua.'

'It's a long way for her to go on her own, though. Well, we'll see. I'll send a letter off to them today, and they can decide what they think about it.'

'And I'll write one to Daisy, then you can put it in with yours.' He already knew just what he would say in his letter.

Every objection that rushed into Daisy's mind at the suggestion of going to Rotorua for a holiday seemed to have been anticipated and answered in Eddie's letter. There was no need for her to worry about neglecting her studies, he said; a short break only meant she would return to school refreshed and ready to do better than ever. She would be away from Ruatane for less than a week, which was no time at all. Although if there was anything in her work that she was particularly anxious over, they could spend an hour or so working on it together. She was not to go thinking she would be a bother, he said, managing to convey a stern tone in his words. It would be no trouble at all to collect her when the motor car arrived, and Aunt Sarah would be happy to pay her fare and expenses.

He ended with the strongest argument of all: he wanted her to come, and would be badly disappointed if she said no—it would spoil the whole trip for him, he claimed. Daisy smiled, and set aside the last of her doubts.

Eddie had said he was sure Daisy's parents would be happy for her to go to Rotorua, which turned out to be quite correct. Granny's letter made it clear that Aunt Sarah would insist on paying Daisy's expenses, and any concern they might have had over letting her go on her own was removed when Daisy's Aunt Jane, who was married to one of Granny's older brothers, remarked after church the following Sunday that she would love to visit her daughter Esther, who lived in Rotorua, and whom she had not seen for more than two years.

'I've never seen her youngest one at all. And now they're moving in a couple of months, off to some place called Taihape.' Aunt Jane looked wistful as she spoke. 'That's way down towards Wellington, she says, so Lord only knows when we'll see her again.'

'Well, why don't you go over to Rotorua with Daisy?' her husband, Daisy's Uncle Harry, suggested. 'She could keep an eye on you, so I wouldn't have to worry about you getting up to any mischief on the way,' he added, with the glint in his eye that was generally to be seen when he and Aunt Jane were teasing each other.

Uncle Harry might have been joking about Aunt Jane getting into mischief, but he turned out to be perfectly serious in saying she could go to Rotorua. Their youngest daughter was still living at home, and could easily look after her father and brothers for a few weeks while Aunt Jane had a holiday.

That settled the matter. Letters back and forth were exchanged to arrange the details, with a telegram from Granny to confirm the arrangements a few days before the time for Daisy's departure.

The motor car journey would take all day, and the sun had not yet climbed above the valley's eastern hills when Uncle Harry and Aunt Jane arrived at the farm to collect Daisy. By the time her uncle's buggy rattled into town a thin, pale light was slipping through gaps in the cloud, adding no discernible warmth to the day. The air caught at Daisy's breath and turned it into wreaths of mist.

The motor car service to Rotorua had been running for several months now, ever since a man called Latham had moved to Ruatane. He had two large motor cars, and employed a local man, one of Bella's many cousins, whom he had taught to drive. Daisy's Uncle Bernard spoke highly of Mr Latham, who was apparently very reliable when it came to delivering various pieces of equipment that Uncle Bernard needed to order from Auckland.

Mr Latham's vehicle was already parked outside the Post Office, where he was collecting the mail to be taken to Rotorua. The motor car was called a Buick, and was apparently most up-to-date; it certainly looked very grand, with its shining metal, long, sweeping lines, and windows right around.

The driver finished loading the last of the mailbags, and opened the motor car doors to usher in his passengers before stowing away their baggage. Uncle Harry gave Daisy and Aunt Jane each a peck on the cheek, and slipped Aunt Jane what looked like a ten-shilling note, which quickly disappeared into her purse. Since the motor car trip cost two pounds each, Uncle Harry was spending quite a sum of money on Aunt Jane's holiday, but it was obvious that he did not begrudge it.

Daisy and her aunt shared the back seat with a large, comfortable-looking woman of about Aunt Jane's age who was going to visit her sister, and a sharp-eyed young woman who worked in the drapery store and said she was going to Rotorua to inquire about better-paying work there. In the front seat beside Mr Latham was a man in quite a smart suit, who greeted Daisy and her fellow passengers politely, but during the rest of the journey spoke only to the driver.

Aunt Jane's eyes were bright with the excitement of their trip. She bobbed her head as she talked of how much she looked forward to seeing Esther and her family again, her rapid movements dislodging several strands of hair from their pins. Her hair was a warm brown streaked with grey, with little more than a hint of the rich auburn she said it had been when she was Daisy's age.

'Esther says her little one is a real carrot top, his hair's much redder than hers ever was,' she said, tucking a loose lock back into place. 'But mine was just about the same colour as yours is. Your Uncle Harry reckoned that was the first thing he noticed about me,' she added with what was almost a giggle.

The man in the front seat had introduced himself as Mr Gale. On the rare occasions when her back seat companions fell silent, Daisy gathered from his conversation with the driver that he had come over from Rotorua a few days earlier, and was now returning there to catch the train back to wherever he lived.

'Business all right, is it?' Mr Latham asked at one point.

'Not too bad. Could be better. Still, there's always a demand for top quality,' Mr Gale said, patting the leather case that rested on the seat between the two men.

Despite the chill of the air outside, the interior of the motor car grew warm as they travelled, and Daisy became increasingly aware of a strong scent. At first she thought it must be a perfume worn by one of her female companions, but when a particularly severe jolt from a hole in the road sent Mr Gale's hat sliding to the floor she realised that the smell was emanating from his unnaturally glossy hair.

Around midday Mr Latham drew the motor car to a halt on a flat, sparsely-grassed patch of ground close to the road. They were about halfway into their journey, Mr Latham said, and this was the spot where he generally stopped to meet up with the driver coming in the other direction, making the trip from Rotorua to Ruatane.

They would stop for lunch here. After four hours squashed into the back seat between Aunt Jane and the young woman from the drapery, Miss Kirby, it was a relief for Daisy to stretch her legs; it was also a relief to breathe air that was not scented with whatever Mr Gale had put on his hair.

The ladies spread rugs on the driest section of grass and pooled the contents of their hampers, while the men chose to lean against the motor car to eat their own sandwiches.

'That'll be pomade,' Mrs Porter, the comfortable-looking woman, said when Aunt Jane quietly remarked on the smell coming from Mr Gale's hair. 'He sells that sort of thing—stuff the young chaps like to put on their hair, things for ladies, too. Creams and potions, colognes and suchlike. He comes over to Ruatane two or three times a year, I think. He goes around to all the barbers showing them his bits and pieces, then he takes a room at one of the hotels, so people can go along and see what's for sale. Nice stuff, he has, but it's a bit too dear, most of it.'

'I used one of his potions on my hair once,' Miss Kirby said. 'Turned it rough as wire—I had to put on half a jar of some cream he sells before I could get a comb through it. Came out a nice colour, though.' She looked somewhat wistful as she twisted a loose, mousy brown strand around her fingers.

'Well, I think it's a bit late for me to be bothering with that sort of thing, so I'll just keep my money in my purse,' Aunt Jane said.

'You and me both.' Mrs Porter patted a lock of Daisy's hair where it lay across her shoulder. 'And you've no need to go putting stuff on that lovely hair of yours, dear. Such a pretty colour! You're lucky you don't have freckles—you must be good about keeping the sun off your face.'

'Mr Gale's probably got a potion for freckles as well,' Aunt Jane said, smiling.

'Yes, he has,' Miss Kirby said. 'It doesn't work, though.'

Mr Latham's other motor car arrived while they were finishing off their lunch, sending up a small cloud of dust from the unseasonably dry road. Daisy had heard that it was not uncommon for a motor car to become thoroughly bogged down in winter mud, sometimes needing a carthorse or two to haul them out; putting up with a modest amount of dust was definitely preferable. She recognized the young man driving the motor car from seeing him at Bella's wedding; she caught his eye, and he smiled a greeting. The drivers exchanged a few words on the state of the roads and how the motor cars were running, with Mr Gale and the two male passengers from the other vehicle joining in as if they knew all about such matters.

Mr Latham came over to their group and tipped his hat. 'Almost ready, ladies? It's time we were getting on.'

Daisy and the others tidied away the remains of their picnic while Mr Latham gave the two motor cars a final inspection.

'We've still got a fair way to go if we're only halfway there,' Mrs Porter said. 'I'm going to be stiff as a board tomorrow, after sitting all this time.'

'Yes, me too,' Aunt Jane said. 'I must say it's very comfortable, though—much easier on the bottom than our old buggy.'

She shook crumbs off the rug she and Daisy had shared. 'We could have a bit of a sing-along to pass the time—I don't suppose those fellows will want to join in, but never mind about them.'

Aunt Jane had a pretty voice, though she said it was not as good as it had been when she was young.

'I used to sing at dances and concerts,' she told Daisy. 'That's how I came to meet your Uncle Harry—there was a dance in the valley when I was in Ruatane staying with my sister, and they got me along to help with the singing. Everyone was there, your Grandma and Grandpa, and your Granny with—'

For some reason Aunt Jane's smile faltered, though only briefly. 'Well, quite a crowd of them, anyway. Your uncle couldn't help but notice me, up in front of everyone singing away, and with that hair of mine. It turned out he liked the look of me.' She gave a conspiratorial grin. 'I liked the look of him, too, I don't mind telling you. It's not a bad way to meet a nice chap, singing is.'

'I'll bear that in mind,' Miss Kirby said. 'I'm still looking for one.' That made her companions laugh.

Mrs Porter slipped off to a sheltered spot in the bushes, while the men pretended not to notice as they sat in the motor car waiting for the ladies.

'I hope I didn't upset Mrs Porter, going on like that about nice chaps, with her being a widow,' Aunt Jane said in a low voice.

'Her?' Miss Kirby's smile narrowed her eyes and made her face look harder. 'She's no widow. I heard her husband ran off with a girl from a hotel a few years ago, before she moved to Ruatane. That's if he was her husband at all. I've heard a few stories about that, too.'

Aunt Jane's lips set into a tight line. 'Well, I wouldn't know anything about that, I'm sure,' she said. 'We all have our troubles, come to that—and some men are only out for all they can get. Best not to stick our noses in other people's business, don't you think?'

Miss Kirby appeared to be amused rather than abashed by Aunt Jane's pointed remarks, her smile holding firm as she strode over to the motor car and clambered inside.

Aunt Jane made no further comment on the subject, but when Daisy made to take her seat in the middle next to Miss Kirby, Aunt Jane said she would sit there herself, leaving Daisy to sit by the window. 'You'll get a better view from there,' she said.

The small shift in position made very little difference to what Daisy could see. No doubt her aunt hoped she had not understood all that talk of husbands running off, and whether or not Mrs Porter had been married at all; Daisy would certainly not disillusion her. Aunt Jane was quite right: it was no one else's business. And Mrs Porter seemed a nice lady; nicer than Miss Kirby, at any rate.

They made one last halt, to let the motor car's engine cool down after climbing a particularly steep hill. On a clear day there might have been a fine view from the top, but low cloud gave no more than glimpses of the area's lakes, lighter grey against patches of forest.

It was close to twilight by the time they reached the town. The streets were busy with carts and buggies; Daisy saw an occasional cyclist, and a motorised delivery vehicle that looked like a tall dray. The sun was dipping behind the tallest buildings when the motor car pulled up in front of a modest wooden structure, its front almost completely covered with painted signs advertising Mr Latham's transport service.

But Daisy had little attention to spare for such unimportant matters. She was too busy waving at the tall, red-haired young man leaning against a post beside the garage.

Chapter Eighteen

Daisy's weariness and stiffness at once seemed nothing at all. She fumbled at the door catch in her haste to get out of the motor car, and when Mr Latham opened it from the outside she only just remembered to send him a quick thank-you.

Eddie greeted her with a kiss on the cheek. 'Granny wanted to come and meet you, too, but Aunt Sarah said she'd better not, she's worried Granny might take a chill—the two of them were lying about in the hot baths all afternoon. I've got a motor car and driver just along the street.'

Aunt Jane's son-in-law was there to collect her and take her off to his home a little way out of the town.

'Be sure to give my love to your granny,' Aunt Jane said to Daisy. 'She's always been a special favourite of mine. Have a lovely holiday, dear.'

Daisy said her farewells to her aunt, Eddie gathered up her bags, and the two of them set off to the waiting vehicle.

Short as the distance was, within a few steps Daisy became fully aware of the pungent smell that had met her as soon as she emerged from Mr Latham's motor car. Eddie must have noticed her screwing up her nose, and guessed the question poised on her lips.

'Don't go looking at me like that, I didn't do it,' he said, grinning. 'The whole place smells of it, though—it's the sulphur dioxide from all the thermal activity. "Rotten egg smell", they say around here, but that's not what I'd call it. You more or less get used to it after a bit, then it hits you all over again. Still, at least there's no need to say excuse me if you do make a stink of your own, so don't worry about eating too much rich food.'

Within a few minutes of her arrival in Rotorua, Daisy was sitting in another motor car, this time with the whole back seat to herself. Eddie leaned around in the front seat to converse with her in between exchanging remarks with the driver. He already seemed quite well-acquainted with Mr Tucker, who had been retained by Aunt Sarah for the whole of their visit.

The hotel was not far away; the drive was so short that when Mr Tucker had delivered them to the front entrance Daisy wondered aloud whether it might not have been simpler to walk.

'That's all very well for you—I would've been the one carrying your bags,' Eddie pointed out. 'Come on, let's get inside. It's jolly cold out here.'

With the evening drawing in, it was indeed chilly. Daisy gave the hotel's exterior a quick glance, taking in a long, two-storeyed wooden building with a verandah along the upper storey and an iron roof with numerous chimneys jutting from it, then hurried indoors ahead of Eddie.

Granny and Aunt Sarah were waiting for them in a small parlour off to one side of the reception area, made cozy by a blazing fire. Amidst a flurry of hugs and greetings, exclamations of how nice it was to see her, and remarks over how tired she must be, Daisy found herself led up a broad staircase and along a corridor to the suite the family were occupying.

They had two bedrooms and their own sitting room, along with a bathroom to themselves. An extra bed had been provided by the hotel and placed in the dressing room that ran between the bedrooms, and this was to be Daisy's during her stay. The room was small, but it had its own window and more than enough space for her to stow her belongings.

There was time for her to have a bath before dinner, and Daisy made grateful use of the porcelain tub, feeling all the stiffness of the hours spent in the motor car soaking away. Afterwards she put on her good dress, made of fine, dark green wool with contrasting braid around the neckline and a belted sash tied low over her hips, and the four of them went downstairs to the hotel's dining room.

The meal was a fine one, with the sort of food Daisy knew was far more familiar to her Auckland family. As they worked their way through soup, a fish course, roast beef, and an elaborate meringue-topped dessert, their plans for the days ahead were discussed.

Granny and Aunt Sarah intended to spend every morning at the Bath House, where they could soak in tubs of water heated by the region's thermal activity and try out various treatments. The baths and massages sounded pleasant enough, but Aunt Sarah said she was yet to be convinced of the benefits of the mud baths that had been suggested to them. When it came to the electrical treatments on offer, Aunt Sarah was dubious and Granny said she was not at all keen.

'You might electrocute yourself, mixing electricity and water like that,' Eddie remarked, his tone not making the risk sound a particularly serious one.

'Well, I expect they wouldn't be allowed to do it if that was going to happen,' Granny said. 'I don't like the idea of it, though, having wires attached as if you were a light bulb.'

She turned her smile on Daisy. 'I'd certainly never hear the end of it from your grandma if she heard about me doing something like that.'

Daisy smiled back. Grandma had yet to move beyond her distrust of electricity, and still occasionally felt the need to warn Benjy and Daisy to stay clear of the electric wire at Uncle Richard's.

'I'm so glad you're here, Daisy,' Granny said, patting her arm. 'It'll be much nicer for Eddie now, too.'

From across the table Eddie caught her eye. He smiled, and nodded his head in agreement.

The Government Baths were housed in a building that looked as if it might have come out of a story book. Half-timbered walls of pale plaster were topped with steep roofs that bristled with ornate turrets. The long, verandah-edged building was dominated by a large central section that reared above the rest like a great tower.

'Doesn't it look grand?' Granny said when she noticed Daisy staring up at the building soaring over her. 'You could just about get lost in there if you didn't keep your wits about you.'

Eddie and Daisy went as far as the entrance, a lofty space with a huge wooden staircase, and with marble statues that Eddie said were based on figures from classical mythology. The whole facility had, he said, been set up to resemble the spas of Europe.

They arranged to meet Granny and Aunt Sarah back there in time for lunch, then went off to explore the park that surrounded the Bath House.

The gardens would no doubt be much prettier in spring or summer, with flowers in bloom, but even in early winter they made for a pleasant stroll. Daisy and Eddie wandered along the paths that led through grassed areas, stopping to admire some of the more attractive trees and shrubs. There was a croquet lawn, looking sad and neglected at this time of the year.

'I expect I could get hold of mallets and balls from somewhere, but we'd mess up the ground if we tramped around on it when it's soggy like that,' Eddie said; they left the lawn undisturbed.

The park even had a small geyser, spraying a fountain of hot water several feet into the air from within a fenced-off pond. They leaned over the railing, peering through the puffs of white steam created by the geyser to get a closer look. That afternoon they would see much more impressive thermal activity, Eddie said.

A mixture of genuine invalids and people simply feeling the need of being perked up came to the baths. Daisy and Eddie passed several visitors taking the air, some being pushed in wheeled chairs or with their unsteady steps guided by an able-bodied attendant, but the park was quiet, which made it a good place for conversation.

It was the first time since Daisy's arrival that the two of them had been alone, and the first time she could speak as freely as she wished. Even within the undoubtedly sympathetic hearing of her grandmother and aunt, Daisy felt the need to choose her words with some care.

At first speech seemed to pour from them both, with pauses only to draw breath and when they encountered other walkers. They discussed her schoolwork, with Daisy admitting her occasional frustration at the vagueness of advice from her teachers, Mr Ritchie's reluctance to venture beyond chemistry in his science lessons, and how little time either teacher could spare from their younger pupils to spend with Benjy and her. She shared funny incidents, too: windows broken by a wayward football; chemistry experiments that had resulted in smells similar to those of Rotorua, or small holes left in Mr Ritchie's trousers. Her recollection of the time spent at Aunt Rosie's, with all its noise and chaos and well-meant advice, had Eddie roaring with laughter; now that her visit there was safely in the past, Daisy found it easy to join in his amusement.

Beside one of the paths they found a statue of a soldier from the South African War, reminiscent of the memorial in Albert Park close to Aunt Sarah's house in Auckland. A wooden bench nearby seemed just the place to stop for a time; a rest for Daisy's feet, and the chance to sit quietly and let her thoughts settle.

This statue was of a local man, while the one in Albert Park represented the soldiers in general. Granny said that although the Auckland statue did not look much like Eddie's father, it still felt like a way for her to remember him. Being able to visit that statue was a special blessing, Granny had remarked once.

The Great War might have taken Daisy's own father, just as the South African War had taken Eddie's. Instead, he had come home to them, safe and sound. She had many blessings in her own life; not least among them the tall figure at her side, sitting close enough for her to wonder if the trace of warmth from that direction was real or just imagined.

Eddie turned from his own contemplation of the statue to meet her gaze, and his mouth curved into a familiar smile.

'You'll be all right with the schoolwork and everything,' he said. 'Come next year, I bet you'll be laughing about all the things that are getting you down now.'

He glanced at his watch. 'Just about time to meet up with Granny and Aunt Sarah. Let's head back now.'

They fell into step as they walked, and it felt quite natural for Daisy to slip her arm through his. The warmth that flowed through her was most definitely not just in her imagination.

Mr Tucker was waiting outside the hotel with his motor car by the time the family had finished lunch in the dining room, ready to take them to the thermal area called Whakarewarewa; "Whaka", he and other people at the hotel called it, perhaps daunted by the length of its full name.

Rotorua, although larger than Daisy's home town, was a small place compared to Auckland; the population was around three and a half thousand, the driver told them. They drove along a street lined with shops and offices, then left the town behind and went on a few miles into the countryside.

Tall clouds of steam told Daisy they were nearing their destination. The motor car drew to a halt; when she climbed out, she found that the distinctive smell of sulphur was stronger than ever here.

Guides, all of them local Maori women, took on the care of visitors to this area, with Daisy's small group having one to themselves. The necessity for a guide was soon clear; without their extensive knowledge of just where the safe places to walk were, it would be all too easy to stray from the paths and perhaps stumble through a thin crust of ash into a steaming crater while trying to get closer to some interesting spot.

Distraction was a frequent companion, with so much to catch the eye. Every few paces revealed another bubbling pool, its edges streaked with ashy soil in various hues; a quiet hollow where the ground steamed and tiny plants somehow clung to life; patch after patch where the ground was so hot that it seemed the very soil had melted into pools of boiling mud that spat themselves into the air and fell back again to the rhythm of a constant plop-plop.

'Keep to the path, dear.'

Daisy felt the guide's hand on her arm, and realised that she had taken half a step away from the marked route. She murmured her thanks as she returned to safety.

Guide Nina made frequent pauses, giving them ample time to take in their surroundings. She was a strikingly attractive young woman, with long, dark hair that fell in soft waves over her shoulders, warm brown eyes, and a clear, melodic voice even when she had to raise it to catch the notice of inattentive visitors.

Granny and Aunt Sarah made use of the occasional seats beside the paths, but Daisy wanted to have the closest possible view of every interesting spot the guide pointed out, while it was clear that Eddie was far too caught up in his fascination with their surroundings to take notice of such a trivial matter as tired feet.

'I saw steam coming out of the ground when I went to Ruapehu, and you get hot pools up north, but nothing like this,' Eddie said, peering at a pool of bubbling mud.

'What makes the ground melt like that just in some places and not others?' Daisy asked. 'Is it extra hot just there, even more than where the boiling water is?'

'No, the pools with clean water are where a spring comes up through hot rocks,' Eddie said. 'And the ground doesn't melt, it's not hot enough for that. You get mud pools where there's steam and gas coming up under rainwater ponds. The steam's quite acidic, and it breaks down minerals—mostly feldspar, I think—in the surface rocks and turns them into kaolin clay. The sulphur reacts with the clay and makes it that blackish-grey colour. Then it all mixes in with the rainwater, and the whole lot's at boiling temperature, so it bubbles away like that.'

'A real scientist, eh?' Guide Nina said, her eyes twinkling.

Eddie grinned back. 'Just stuff out of books. It wouldn't stop me falling in a hot pool if I was here on my own. Not like you, living here and knowing every inch of the place.' There was a village right in the thermal area, with its own hot pools and steam vents.

'Is it quite safe, living among all this steam and boiling water?' Aunt Sarah asked. 'Might you not be better settled in the town?'

'No, this is a good place,' Guide Nina said. 'You can have a hot bath whenever you like, and you don't need firewood to heat your house or cook the dinner. Of course you have to respect the dangers—our children learn that very young. There have always been people living here. They were relations of ours, and our families came to live among them after the great eruption.'

'When Mount Tarawera blew up?' Granny said. 'I remember that. I lived over on the coast then, in Ruatane—we only had ash on the paddocks spoiling the grass, that was nothing much. But it must have been a dreadful time for your people, with so many killed, and everyone losing their homes.'

'Yes, the old people say it was a hard time.' For a moment Guide Nina seemed to be looking into a great distance, as if seeing those long-ago days for herself. Granny had much the same expression; Daisy was sure she was thinking back to the time of the eruption, when Eddie's father was just a baby and Daisy's own father was yet to be born.

They walked on deeper into the heart of the thermal area, and a low rumble grew louder as they came to a plateau of rock that held what Eddie had told Daisy would be the highlight of their visit: the great geysers.

The two that the guide said were the largest were currently bubbling away, giving only a hint of what was to come. Quite a crowd of people had gathered here, each small group with its own guide.

Daisy and her companions had barely taken their seats when one of the geysers burst aloft, twice the height of a man. That one had been given the name Prince of Wales Feathers, after a royal visit to Whakarewarewa at the beginning of the century, Guide Nina told them; it had reminded the visitors of the feathers on the Prince of Wales' coat-of-arms. With some imagination, the plumes of steam did look rather like a cluster of huge, soft feathers.

'Now just wait a little,' Guide Nina said. 'When the Prince of Wales Feathers erupts, Pohutu is soon to follow.'

The first geyser was impressive; moments later when Pohutu joined in it took Daisy's breath away. A column of water shot upwards, perhaps a hundred feet high. Over and over the geyser burst from the ground, thundering and steaming and roaring. It dominated sight and hearing; the smell of sulphur seemed stronger than ever; light drifts of spray settled on her face. She could not have drawn her attention from Pohutu even if she had wished to.

Daisy was not sure how many minutes later it was when the geyser at last diminished and settled back into its small pool. She thought the ground was shaking beneath her; a moment later she realised it was her own exhilarated trembling. She was glad that the rest of her party decided to rest here for a time before exploring further. The guide was talking to Granny and Aunt Sarah, while Eddie had struck up a conversation with a man from another group, but Daisy was content to sit and watch the smaller geysers and the deceptively quiet vents belonging to the giants.

The previous evening Eddie had pulled out a notebook and drawn a diagram across two of its pages, showing how the geysers worked. Beneath the ground here was a large reservoir fed by rainwater, which was heated by molten rock and held in place by the narrowness of the geyser vents. Pressure built up inside the underground chamber until it grew strong enough to force a mixture of steam and water out through the vent, exploding as a great froth. This released pressure, until the reservoir filled and the whole process began again.

All that was going on under her feet. When they rose from the seats and moved on, Daisy was more aware than before of the places where the ground seemed warmer. Clouds of steam rising close to their marked route were a salutary reminder to keep to the paths, even if they had not had a vigilant guide.

'Do you get any fish in this stream?' Eddie asked when their path crossed a stretch of clear water making its way along a rocky bed.

'Yes, we do—even trout sometimes,' the guide said.

Eddie crouched down to dip his fingers in the water. 'It's quite hot just here. I suppose that means you can catch the fish already cooked.'

Guide Nina returned his smile. 'No, the fish are too clever for that. They know to keep to the cool water.'

They visited the Model Pa, which was a small, palisaded village set up to show how Maori had apparently lived before the arrival of Europeans in New Zealand. There were houses made from tree fern trunks and fronds, racks for drying food, and special buildings to store it. Then came their final activity before leaving Whakarewarewa: a short visit to the real village, which was still very much inhabited.

A bridge across the stream gave access to the village, and perched along its nearer edge was a line of boys. Many of them were clad only in short drawers, while the smallest boys had dispensed even with that.

These were the penny divers of Whakarewarewa, eager to show the tourists their skill in the water, and to earn a little money in the process.

'Throw a penny!' the call went up from the boys as soon as they spotted Daisy's group. 'Throw a penny!'

Eddie had come prepared. He pulled a handful of bright pennies from his jacket pocket and threw two or three at a time to the eager youngsters.

The boys were clearly very much at home in the water, diving in to follow the path of each coin and emerging a moment later clutching it in triumph. Daisy saw an occasional coin disappear into the mouth of its owner for safe-keeping, which gave her a shudder; she had always been told that she should never put a coin in her mouth, as you never knew whose pocket it had been in before. But with so much sulphur in the air, perhaps there was some in the water as well. Sulphur was a useful remedy against various skin diseases, as she knew from helping her Uncle Richard with taking stock of his medicines; it had also been widely used in inhalation stations during the influenza epidemic for its germ-killing properties, so it did not seem too much to expect that it might have some effect against the germs on a few pennies. And it was not as if the boys had any handy pockets to put a penny in while getting ready to dive for the next one.

Daisy watched for any children who might be missing out on the bounty, so that she could direct Eddie to send a coin their way, but she soon realised that there was no need; the boys were doing this for themselves, especially when it came to making sure the very youngest ones managed to get their own share.

Eddie held his empty hands aloft to show that all the pennies had been thrown, and they crossed the bridge into the village.

About two hundred people lived there, according to their guide, and from what Daisy could see at least half of those must be children. The houses that nestled close together were small, most looking to be no more than two rooms, and built of wood with iron roofs.

Around the houses were places where the ground steamed; warm pools; holes of boiling water. Here and there patches of sparse growth defied the heat; no doubt some of them concealed steaming holes. It must be interesting to live right among the thermal activity, Daisy reflected, but you would certainly have to keep your wits about you. And then there was the smell of sulphur, which faded from notice after a time, only to catch unexpectedly in the throat once again. Perhaps people stopped noticing it altogether if they lived in a place like Rotorua, but it was hard to imagine that might be the case.

Friendly smiles greeted them as they walked around the village. One lady showed them a flax kit of potatoes that she was about to lower into a boiling pool to cook. Not far away a square hole had been cut out of the ground for meat, which was covered with sacking and left to steam. In a separate area, several ladies were using the natural warm water to do a load of washing.

When they had walked around the village and returned to the bridge, Eddie said he would not mind exploring for a bit longer, and Daisy would have been happy to follow his lead. Aunt Sarah, however, said that it was all very interesting, but she felt she and Granny had walked as much as they wished to for one day, as well as having taken up quite enough of Guide Nina's time.

'I'll get you some postcards at one of those shops to remember it all by,' Eddie said to Daisy as they walked back to where their driver was waiting.

She smiled and thanked him, although she did not think she would forget a single thing about this holiday.

Much of that evening was spent discussing what they might do for the remaining two days of their stay. Granny and Aunt Sarah agreed that one last morning at the baths would be quite sufficient, which meant a longer outing would be possible on their final day, but for tomorrow there would not be time to go any great distance.

The man Eddie had been chatting with while they watched the geysers was a keen fisherman who had been impressed by a local trout hatchery, and had put the idea of a visit there into Eddie's head. Aunt Sarah showed no great enthusiasm for "going to see a lot of fish swimming about," even when Eddie added that there was a spring at the hatchery that was considered quite pretty.

'How about Mr Tucker takes Daisy and I out there while you and Granny are at the baths, then?' Eddie said. 'It's not all that far, we'd be back in time to collect you from the Bath House.'

It was a good solution, they all agreed, and Daisy added a request of her own.

'I'd like to see around the Bath House tomorrow, if the people in charge didn't mind,' she said. 'Especially some of those treatments Granny was talking about—they sound quite interesting.'

'Yes, Doctor Daisy has a professional interest,' Eddie said, grinning at her.

Daisy swatted his arm in pretended annoyance at his cheek, but she could not help answering his smile. She had barely thought about schoolwork or examinations for the whole afternoon, she realised.

'We can go in together tomorrow morning, then,' Aunt Sarah said. 'I'll speak to the relevant authorities, and I don't expect there'll be any difficulty.'

There was not the least difficulty the following morning, which was usually the case when Aunt Sarah wished for something to happen. After her aunt spoke to someone important, Daisy left Eddie to entertain himself in the grand reception area while she accompanied her aunt and grandmother through to where the treatments took place. They went off to the baths, and a briskly efficient nurse showed Daisy around.

'We keep the men separate from the ladies, of course,' she said, leading the way down a corridor. 'But I'll sneak you through to the men's side as well, I know some of the treatment rooms are empty today. There's plenty to see.'

There was indeed a good deal to see. Daisy was whisked from room to room, being shown such facilities as a special ultraviolet lamp that delivered the benefits of sunshine in an intensified form, and the air baths, where metal contraptions were fastened over injured or painful limbs and hot air applied.

One area was devoted to individual bathing pools. Her aunt and grandmother were probably there somewhere, but each tub was surrounded by partitions to give a measure of privacy. In the massage room, a lady who must have had very strong hands was working away at a pair of plump white shoulders; Daisy was abruptly reminded of watching her father knead bread dough, and had to disguise a laugh behind a small cough. The masseuse looked up from her work and smiled, then returned to working on the shoulders.

Most dramatic of all was the somewhat terrifying-looking electrical treatment. A patient would be made to sit in a full bath, while from a machine that rested on a trolley, all switches and dials, trailed electric cords that clipped to the bath's edge and snaked through the water.

'The expert fellows down in Wellington said we mustn't have a copper bath for this,' the attendant remarked. 'I'm not sure why—perhaps it's something to do with porcelain holding the heat better.'

Daisy had learned enough about electricity in her science lessons to know that it was more to do with conductivity and the danger of electric shocks, but she nodded politely and did not correct her guide.

There was not time to look around all the facilities; Daisy was unable to visit the mud baths, which she had rather hoped to see. But before leaving the treatment area she was handed a brochure that seemed meant as an advertisement. Painted illustrations on its cover showed people undergoing various treatments, all appearing happy and relaxed. A glance inside revealed text extolling the virtues of all that was on offer, and a photograph showed a man sitting in a bath tub, buried up to his neck in mud but looking surprisingly cheerful about it.

The treatments were certainly interesting, although Daisy had her doubts about how effective some of them might be. Perhaps she would ask her Uncle Richard's opinion when she got home to Ruatane.

She found Eddie comfortably ensconced in the reception area, finishing off a tray of tea and biscuits he had somehow managed to be offered by a sympathetic staff member. He was sharing his bounty with their driver, who had arrived a few minutes earlier.

'So you've found out all about what they do here, then? All right, let's go,' Eddie said.

Daisy once again had the back seat to herself, while Eddie sat alongside Mr Tucker, chatting alternately to the driver and to Daisy.

'How do you like riding in motor cars, now you've got used to it?' Eddie asked when they had been travelling for a few minutes.

'It seemed a long trip, coming all the way from Ruatane the other day—I expect it would have been a lot longer with horses, though. The motor car was very smart, but this one's even nicer,' Daisy said, bouncing up and down a little to try out the springs. 'It's very comfortable, and so clean, too.'

Every piece of metal in the motor car's interior shone as if freshly polished, and the leather upholstery felt supple under her fingers. Daisy noticed that Mr Tucker seemed to sit up even straighter at her praise of his vehicle.

'I'm trying to talk Aunt Sarah into getting a motor car one of these days,' Eddie said. 'She's not very keen yet, but I think she'll come around.'

'Wouldn't you miss going about in the carriage, though?' Daisy's aunt had a fine one, with a top that could be lowered in warm weather and a team of smart horses to draw it, the whole equipage kept in top order by

Walter Jenson, who was also in charge of looking after the gardens now that his father was largely housebound with rheumatism.

Eddie shrugged. 'I'd still get plenty of riding in, even without a carriage—I'm definitely not getting rid of Baron. And Walter never lets on about it, but the horses are a bit much for him these days, with that leg of his.'

A shrapnel wound had left Walter with a leg that dragged awkwardly. Eddie had once seen the scar, and had later given Daisy a vivid description of puckered flesh and wasted muscle. Walter had been lucky not to lose the leg altogether, Eddie said, but the maimed limb hampered his movements, and no doubt pained him at times.

'He must have a heck of a job just with the mounting and dismounting when he has to exercise the horses—I think he makes sure no one's watching him while he gets on and off. Of course I exercise Baron myself when I'm home, and I'd be happy enough to do the other horses as well for him sometimes, but he wouldn't like that, not when it's his job.'

'But he has a boy to help him with the work, doesn't he?' Daisy asked. 'It'd be too much for one man on his own, with all the garden as well.'

'Yes, there's a gardener's boy, he's good about digging over the beds and all that, but he's no horseman. It's not that easy to get a good stable boy these days, and Walter's particular about who he lets near the horses.'

Mr Tucker slowed the motor car while they drove past a lady on a bicycle. A horse-drawn baker's van had pulled up by the footpath; when the motor car sped up again the horse gave a snort and tossed its head.

'That's the other thing,' Eddie said, looking back as they passed the van. 'There's more and more motor traffic these days. It's still pretty quiet in places like this, but up in Auckland with the trams and motor lorries and a lot more motor cars, it's not really fair on the horses—not in the busy parts of the city, anyway.'

He swiveled on his seat to face Daisy. 'I might miss it a bit when we do get rid of the carriage. But you've got to do things like that sometimes. Everything can't just stay the same forever, eh?'

'I suppose not,' Daisy said.

Chapter Nineteen

The trout hatchery was some miles out of town, at a place called Fairy Springs. Mr Tucker parked the motor car off the road close to the entrance, and opened the door for Daisy before taking his place back behind the steering wheel.

'An hour or so should be long enough for us, if you want to go off somewhere else while we're here,' Eddie told the driver, but Mr Tucker pulled out a newspaper and said he would be quite happy to wait.

They went first to the hatchery's office, where a man who appeared to be in charge seemed gratified by the interest Eddie expressed in finding out about the work done there. The man, who introduced himself as Mr Hutton, offered to show them around. He pulled on his hat and led the way to the nearest path.

Looking at fish did not sound the most exciting of activities. Daisy had resigned herself to an outing that might be at best educational and at worst outright boring, worthwhile only for Eddie's company.

Mr Hutton walked on Eddie's left hand and Daisy trailed along on his other side, idly listening to their guide as he spoke of rearing young fish, harvesting eggs, and transporting their product around the country. It was a pleasant place for a walk, with the path running alongside a stream overhung with trees, and a welcome absence of any sulphur smell.

They rounded a bend in the path, and came to a wide pool formed out of a quiet section of the stream.

'Here we are.' Mr Hutton indicated the pool with a sweep of his hand, and Daisy looked more closely to see what was so special about this particular stretch of water. She saw pale shapes moving, swaying to and fro like plants stirred about in the current. The water was quite clear, though dark as tea left too long in the pot.

A shaft of sunlight pierced the overhanging branches to strike the water and illuminate the creatures crowding it. Daisy gave a gasp as she realised just what those shapes were.

'All those fish! There must be hundreds of them.'

'Rather more than that,' Mr Hutton said. 'Thousands just in this pool alone, and we have millions in total. They have to be reared in running water, and we've a fine, pure supply of it.'

He pulled a small bag from his pocket and handed it to Daisy.

'Here you are, Miss. See what they make of this.'

The bag contained what looked like breadcrumbs. Daisy took a handful and flung it over the water, which was at once alive with roiling trout,

211

squirming and twisting to get at the food, revealing the subtle markings along their sides.

These were juveniles, Mr Hutton explained; it was important to keep fish of different sizes separate, or they would eat each other. He grew more animated as he talked of the vast numbers they reared each year, and their hopes for increasing the numbers even further.

They walked past other pools, with fish of various sizes. The young trout were mainly fed on meat; liver was especially good for them, Mr Hutton remarked. In the wild they ate a good many insects, with grasshoppers a particular favourite. Daisy commented on how healthy the trout all looked, which elicited a satisfied smile from Mr Hutton.

This was a kind of farming, she realised, with its concerns around good breeding stock, animal health, and production levels. While she could not imagine fish ever being as interesting as the sort of animal that might run up to the fence to have its head rubbed, or bellow a greeting at the sight of a familiar figure, Mr Hutton's quiet pride in the hatchery's success was not so very different from her parents' satisfaction in a fine batch of new calves, or a particularly good milking season.

In a shed by one of the pools several men were working around a bench lined with bowls and containers. Daisy and Eddie watched as one of the men used a net attached to a long pole to scoop a plump trout out of the pond. Another man plucked it from the net, took hold of its tail in one hand and nudged its head between his arm and his side, leaving his other hand free.

While holding the trout over a wide metal bowl, he gave its body a deft twist, exposing an opening on its underside, then a careful squeeze. A stream of milky fluid filled with tiny eggs poured from the fish into the bowl, looking a little like runny sago pudding.

This was what Mr Hutton referred to as stripping the ova, which Daisy recognized as the Latin for eggs. The whole process could only take a short time, as the fish would suffocate if kept out of the water for too long. With the eggs duly extracted, the trout was placed back in the net and lowered into the pond. It gave a flick of its tail and swam off, apparently none the worse for the experience.

The eggs would be kept here, Mr Hutton told them, until the eye of the fish within formed, visible as a tiny black speck in each egg. They could then be safely transported; in answer to Daisy's questioning he described how the eggs were carefully packed in gauze, surrounded with moss and ice to keep them damp and cool. Eddie added a few questions of his own, mostly along the lines of asking advice on the best local angling spots in case he were ever to come back to Rotorua at a better time of year for fishing.

Their tour completed, Mr Hutton suggested Daisy and Eddie take a walking path that would lead them to the springs this area was named for, from where they could easily find their own way out of the hatchery. They thanked him and shook his hand, then set off in the direction he indicated.

A short stroll alongside the stream brought them to the springs, which bubbled into a rocky pool, the water very clear and well-populated with trout. The pool was overhung by acacia trees that must be beautiful when flowering; even at this time of year their feathery foliage made graceful patterns against the sky.

Eddie checked his watch, and said there was no need to hurry back to the motor car. After some searching they found a rock that was both dry and not overly bumpy, with just enough room for the two of them. It meant pressing close together, but that was no hardship.

The trout slid through the pool, weaving over and around each other like floating dancers. The branches overhead made shushing noises in the breeze, mingling with the chatter of the stream running along its rocky bed. Had the rock been a little less hard, Daisy felt she might have been content to sit there all day with that warm body close to hers.

'I feel like I'm an expert on trout now, after hearing all that,' Eddie remarked. 'And you must know all about the Bath House, getting a special tour.'

'It was really interesting,' Daisy said, more than willing to talk about people instead of fish. 'Some of it's just people wanting a sort of tonic—they like being fussed over as much as anything, I think. But they have quite a few men who were in the war, and they try different treatments for muscle wasting and chest complaints, that sort of thing. Even being able to ease the pain for some of them must make a big difference—just soaking in the hot baths can help with that—but it's wonderful if they can actually fix some of the damage. I'm going to look up some of Uncle Richard's books when I get home, especially the anatomy ones, and try and see how the treatments might work. And I can find out a lot more about it when I do physiology at university.'

She trailed off, aware that Eddie was smiling at her; aware, too, that her voice had been rising in pitch as she grew more animated. 'Why are you looking at me like that? Am I going on about it?'

'No, of course not. Well, maybe a bit, I suppose. But it's good—I like hearing you all excited about what you're going to do. A lot of people seem to just muddle along, doing whatever comes next without ever really thinking about it, but you know just what you want. And that's really good.'

Daisy pressed a little closer, basking in the warmth of his approval as well as that of his physical presence. 'What about you, then?' she asked. 'You know what you want, don't you?'

'Me? I've already got everything I want.' He gave a wry grin. 'Gosh, that makes me sound pretty pleased with myself, doesn't it? It's true, though—and I know I'm jolly lucky compared to most fellows, being able to do what I like instead of having to worry about what I'll do for a living.'

'But what if you wanted something different, and you couldn't do it because… oh, I don't know, just because it worked out that you had to do something else instead. Like when I couldn't go back to school because Papa was away in the army.'

Eddie shrugged. 'It's hard to think of anything. I've got to do that bit of work at the law firm this winter when I thought I might go skiing instead, but I can always do the skiing some other time. Anyway, it makes it worthwhile studying for all those law papers Aunt Sarah made me do.'

He frowned in thought, evidently giving the matter more serious consideration. 'I suppose whatever turns up you've just got to try and do the right thing. I mean, when your dad was away you didn't go making a fuss about having to give up school, you just got on with helping on the farm.

'You don't need to worry, you know,' he said, smiling once more. 'About doing the right thing and all that. You're going to be a doctor, and I can carry on just the way I am. So we're both all set.'

Eddie checked his watch. 'About time we were going, I think. Here, I'll give you a hand.' He helped Daisy upright from their perch, and they set off in search of the way out.

After collecting Granny and Aunt Sarah from the baths and then lunching together, they set out for the nearby village of Ohinemutu, which the hotel manager had that morning suggested as an interesting place for an outing.

They had not gone far before Eddie, after flashing a grin at Daisy, began expounding the virtues of the motor car: how pleasant it was to ride in; how little trouble it must be, compared to caring for horses; how much faster on good roads than a carriage.

'You're enjoying it, aren't you, Granny?' he asked.

'Yes, it's lovely and comfortable,' Granny said. 'So is the carriage, though, I always enjoy riding in that.'

Daisy hid a smile. Granny was so easy-going, and so ready to be pleased by whatever she was given; Eddie was unlikely to make much progress in persuading Aunt Sarah if he relied on any hint of dissatisfaction from her.

Eddie obviously came to much the same conclusion. He shifted the discussion to the growing busyness of Auckland's traffic, and how hard that could be on the horses. It was loyalty on Eddie's part, Daisy was sure, that made him steer clear of mentioning Walter's difficulties with exercising the horses; he would not want to dwell on any lack in his friend's ability to carry out his tasks while talking to Aunt Sarah, who was, after all, Walter's employer.

'I shouldn't like to lose the carriage altogether,' Aunt Sarah said. 'That would be too much of a wrench. There's something so very pleasant in driving around the Domain of a summer's afternoon in an open carriage.'

'No need to get rid of it,' Eddie said. 'You could mostly use the motor car—especially when you're going somewhere busy—and save the carriage for outings like that. Of course that wouldn't give the horses enough work, but the ones we've got now are getting on a bit, it'll be time to put them out to pasture before too much longer. Then you'd be better off just hiring horses from a livery stable when you were going to take the carriage out.'

'Hmm, I suppose that might be worth considering at some point in the future. Although Walter would have to learn to drive a motor car—and how to look after one, I imagine.'

'I think he might be quite keen on that—I've seen him looking at things in the newspaper about motor cars.'

'Really? Well, we shall see. I'll bear it all in mind when the time comes to make a decision on retiring the horses. I must say this motor car certainly is very comfortable.'

Daisy noticed her aunt shifting in place; although Aunt Sarah was far too dignified to actually bounce up and down, she was moving in a way that came surprisingly close to doing so.

Ohinemutu was a pleasant little Maori village on the lake shore. The main attraction for Daisy's party was its pretty church, St Faith's. It was an interesting combination of an English-looking exterior, with Tudor-style half-timbering and a tall steeple, and an interior richly decorated with Maori carvings and woven panels. The church grounds held a cemetery with ornate gravestones going back to the previous century.

There were yet more hot pools and patches of steaming ground here to catch the eye. A group of local children soaking in one wood-lined pool, watched over by an older girl who sat on the edge dangling her feet in the water, smiled and called out a greeting to Daisy and her companions.

They admired the fine meeting house belonging to the village, then took a footpath heading back towards the motor car and Mr Tucker. The path gave a good view over the lake, with an island clearly visible to one side. Eddie, who had been studying a map of the district the previous evening, said the island was called Mokoia.

A short way along their walk, half a dozen young boys appeared before them.

'You want to see a *haka*?' one of the boys asked.

On being told that Daisy's party would be very happy to see the traditional war dance, the little boys, the oldest of whom could not have been more than six years old, gave an energetic performance, with suitably fierce expressions and vigorous leaps. They ended the dance with a final great leap and a shout that would have done credit to boys twice their size, and Daisy felt they had fully earned the pennies and threepences Eddie handed them.

It had still not been decided just where they would go on the following day, their last in Rotorua. Mr Tucker suggested a drive that would take in five different lakes, an outing that he assured them was full of scenic beauties. Aunt Sarah expressed polite interest, but when they discussed the matter over a late afternoon tea back at their hotel no one seemed very enthusiastic at the idea of spending most of the day sitting in the motor car, no matter how comfortable it was.

'Especially when Daisy'll be stuck in the motor car all the way back to Ruatane just the next day,' Eddie said.

Two ladies sitting at a nearby table had overheard part of their conversation, and recommended what they called "the round trip", which meant a drive to a place called Waimangu, with good views of Mount Tarawera along the way, then a walk to Lake Rotomahana and a boat ride across the lake, which held hidden in its depths the ruins of the Pink and White Terraces that had been destroyed in Tarawera's great eruption.

'And then you visit the village that was buried in the ash,' one of the ladies said, wide-eyed with a sort of gleeful fear. She and her companion looked to be somewhere in their sixties, each with steel-grey curls pinned tightly in place, and alike enough to be sisters. 'It's quite a ghostly experience.'

'Oh, yes, I was all of a shiver afterwards,' the other one said, blinking rapidly. 'But really, it's a most interesting excursion.'

The ladies continued to press their recommendation until one of them recalled an engagement in another part of town that apparently required a change of dress. They fluttered off, leaving Daisy and her companions to a calmer discussion of the suggestion.

'I don't think it would be as long a drive as the five lakes outing, but it does sound as if we'd have to spend quite some time in the motor car,' Aunt Sarah said. 'I suppose it depends on just how interesting it would all be. What do you think, Amy?' she asked Granny.

'Oh, it's probably very interesting,' Granny said. 'I'm sure Daisy and Eddie would enjoy it—you would, too, Sarah. I'll be quite happy here on my own if you all go out there.'

Aunt Sarah frowned. 'But why ever should you want to stay here by yourself, darling? Is it the long drive?'

'No, it's not that. It's just... I remember it too well, back when the volcano erupted. When it was in the papers and everyone was talking about it, I remember thinking about those poor people trapped under all the ash, and being buried alive. I don't think I could enjoy going there and seeing where the village was.' Granny leaned across and patted Aunt Sarah on the hand. 'It's just me being silly, though. I don't want to spoil it for you young ones, don't take any notice of me.'

Aunt Sarah took hold of Granny's small hand and gave it a squeeze. 'You're not being silly at all—just your own dear self. And for our last day it must be something we'll all enjoy. I'm not sure I'd care for the round trip, anyway, the walk could be rather tiring.'

Daisy and Eddie joined in, assuring Granny that they did not at all mind not going to Mount Tarawera and the buried village; Daisy kept to herself the thought that parts of the outing did actually sound interesting. Eddie was right: she would be spending quite enough time in a motor car without that.

'What about going out on Lake Rotorua instead?' Eddie said. 'I'm sure I saw a sign up somewhere for a boat trip—I think there's one that takes the whole day.'

Eddie's suggestion was at once taken up by everyone. As well as having the advantage of meaning very little time in the motor car, the weather for the next day promised to be fine, making a day spent on the water particularly appealing. Eddie went off to the hotel's front desk to ask about booking the outing, and was back a short time later with the news that it was all in hand.

Next morning Mr Tucker drove them the short distance to the lake shore wharf. Their launch was tied up ready to depart, and Daisy's group joined the small knot of passengers shuffling their way towards the boat.

A light breeze ruffled Daisy's hair as she stepped aboard. The early sunlight came thin and watery through a veil of clouds, but with the promise of a fine day ahead. Eddie found seats sheltered by a canvas awning for Granny and Aunt Sarah, while he and Daisy chose to station themselves by the railing, where they would have the best view.

Daisy looked back at the land as the boat pulled away from the wharf. The town spread along the lake's edge, overlooked by the hospital buildings on Pukeroa Hill, and with Mount Ngongotaha further in the distance. On a point of land a short way along the shore to her right Daisy recognized Ohinemutu, with its pretty church on the lake bank framed by clouds of steam.

The launch cruised across the lake to Hamurana on its northern side, where they were to explore the springs for which the area was best-known.

They disembarked close to where a stream entered the lake, and walked alongside it for perhaps a few hundred yards. Sparkling water ran along a stream-bed tinted in so many shades of green, blue, yellow, and purple that it might have been lined with crushed gemstones. Bright green plants swayed on the current, glinting as the sunlight caught them.

Daisy had not yet tired of admiring the sight when they came to a widening in the stream where several flat-bottomed dinghies were tied up, ready to take the visitors out to view the spring from above. Some of the tourists were clearly nervous of clambering into the little dinghies, especially one rather large lady who clung to her husband's sleeve and swayed back and forth, making the boat rock alarmingly.

Fortunately she had chosen a different dinghy from that of Daisy and her party. Eddie stepped onto the boat first, and handed the rest of their little party aboard. Daisy could have climbed on quite easily without assistance, but she accepted the offered hand anyway, enjoying the feel of having her own held securely in his grip. Aunt Sarah managed the task of boarding with her usual stately gracefulness, while Granny was more nimble than several ladies who were probably younger than she was.

They had the dinghy to themselves apart from the man who was to row them and a cheerful Englishman called Pennington, who constantly exclaimed on the beauties of their surroundings with an enthusiasm that set his silvery moustache bouncing. His wife was not on the outing; she had instead chosen to spend the day at the baths. This was a sad loss, Mr Pennington said more than once, though by "loss" it was not clear whether he meant their being deprived of Mrs Pennington's company or the fact that she was missing the outing. His wife's absence certainly did not seem to put a damper on Mr Pennington's own enjoyment of the day.

The boatman stood in the stern, wielding a long pole. He pushed off, then propelled the boat along the stream and out into a broad pool, until they were directly over the spring.

Fairy Springs had been pretty; this place was awe-inspiring. Crystal-clear water rose from far below, making the pool shift and roil as if it were simmering. Lining the pool were rocks and sands in a myriad of colours whose brightness was not at all dimmed by the many feet of water above them.

Millions of gallons flowed from the spring each day, the boatman said. The water was thrust aloft with such force that when Mr Pennington took up the boatman's invitation to drop in a coin, rather than falling straight to the bottom the penny fluttered up and down in the current as if it were as flimsy as a leaf before finally sinking into the depths. Dropping in a coin was considered lucky, the boatman told them, so Eddie added a penny of his own, which seemed to take even longer to sink.

'Does that mean I'm extra-lucky?' Eddie asked; the boatman smiled, and said it probably did.

The water was exceptionally pure, they were told; Daisy dipped her hand in to gather some to taste, and found that it was also exceptionally cold. Trout flocked to the stream in summer, the boatman said, seeking relief from the warmer waters of the lake.

They bobbed about over the spring for some time, then returned to the stream bank for a picnic lunch before going back to the lake and the waiting launch.

The boat sailed on to the eastern edge of the lake, through a channel and into Lake Rotorua's smaller neighbour, Rotoiti. An inlet a mile or so from the channel led to their next destination: Okere Falls and its hydro-electric power station, which delivered electricity to the district.

A river had its source here, escaping the lake in a noisy tumble over rocks, and part of the mighty flow was diverted through the power station. Their guide explained the workings of the station with such enthusiasm and at such length that when he finally finished Daisy heard Aunt Sarah murmur to Granny that she almost felt she could now build a power station of her own if the fancy ever took her.

Steps had been carved nearby into the rock wall, winding their way downwards. Some of the more nervous tourists chose to remain at the top and study the view, but Daisy and the others followed the guide, to the accompaniment of thundering water and taking great care over patches made slippery by spray, down the narrow path and into an echoing cave.

The chief inhabitants of the cave these days were some large weta. Eddie pointed out one of the giant insects to Daisy, keeping his voice to a murmur; some in the party might have let out ear-splitting screams if they had seen the creatures. She knew that the weta were quite harmless if left unmolested, despite their formidable appearance.

219

This place had been a refuge in times of war with other tribes, their guide explained. Women and children would be hidden here, while the warriors lured their enemies to destruction. It must have been a dark, chilly refuge, Daisy thought as she gazed around the cavern. And it must have taken great courage even to reach it, as the steps were a fairly modern addition. In the days of those ancient wars, getting to the cave meant being lowered by rope down the rock face, dangling out over the water with the constant threat of being dashed against the rocks if the rope should fail.

The only danger to Daisy and her party was the risk of slipping on the steps, or perhaps taking a chill in the cave. But they left unscathed, climbed back up the steps, and boarded the launch for its return through the Ohau Channel and back into Lake Rotorua.

She stood beside Eddie, the two of them leaning against the railing as they watched the land slide past.

'I wouldn't mind if we had a bit longer here,' Eddie said. 'There's a lot we could see yet.'

'Mm, there is,' Daisy agreed. 'But I need to get home and catch up with my work—I feel like I've been lazy, having this lovely holiday.'

'And we've got to get back in time for the graduation ceremony. We can't have Aunt Sarah and Granny missing the ball, or I'd never hear the end of it,' Eddie said, grinning.

Daisy did her best to picture the grand ceremony with its parade of new graduates, followed by a glittering ball. 'I wish I could be there for that.'

'I wish you could, too. Then you could have a good laugh at me in my fancy hat and gown—at least I get to have one with a blue hood, not pink like the Arts graduates have to wear.'

The image of Eddie's shock of hair set off by a pink silk hood made Daisy laugh aloud.

He slid his hand along the railing until it nudged against hers. 'You'll have your own graduation in a few years, you know.'

'I wouldn't call it a few! It's going to take me seven years—and that's only if everything goes all right.'

'Well, however long it takes, I'll be at your graduation. I promise.'

He gave her hand a quick squeeze before turning his attention to the island they were steadily approaching.

Mokoia Island was to be their last stop on the excursion. It rose from the lake in a long mound a few hundred feet in height, emerald-green with the vegetation its rich soil supplied. It was a sort of volcanic dome, Eddie said, produced by molten lava coming through cracks in the lake bed long ages before.

It was also the setting for a romantic tale taken from ancient Maori history, which their guide related to them as the launch neared the island.

Long ago, a beautiful maiden called Hinemoa had lived on the shores of the lake. She was the daughter of a great chief, and because of her beauty and her high rank many young men wished to have her as wife.

Among these was Tutanekai, who lived on the island of Mokoia. He had fallen in love with Hinemoa when he saw her at tribal gatherings, but he had not dared declare his love. Although of good birth, he was not as highly ranked as Hinemoa, and he was sure her father would not accept him as a suitor. So he gazed longingly at her from afar, and although he sometimes thought she returned his longing looks, his love remained unspoken.

Unbeknown to Tutanekai, Hinemoa had indeed fallen in love with him. After many such encounters where they spoke only through their eyes, Tutanekai at last declared his love, and to his great joy found that it was returned.

Tutanekai asked Hinemoa to leave her home and come to dwell with him on Mokoia, and she agreed. He would play his flute, and she was to take one of the tribe's canoes and follow the sound across the lake to him.

But Hinemoa's people had guessed her intention. They hauled the heavy canoes high up on the banks, so that she was unable to launch one. Night after night, Tutanekai sat high on a hill playing his flute, and night after night Hinemoa heard the sound and wept, because she could not come to him.

At last she wondered if it might be possible to swim across to her lover. The thought of the wide water between them struck fear into her heart, but she determined to make the attempt. That night she strapped hollow gourds to her body to buoy her up, then slipped into the water and through the darkness followed the sound of Tutanekai's flute.

She swam to exhaustion, drifted for a time, and swam on, unable to see the land, and with only the music of the flute to guide her. At last she came to the island, and at her landing place found a hot pool, into which she eased her chilled body.

When Tutanekai's servant came to fetch water nearby, Hinemoa disguised her voice, pretending to be a man, and broke the gourd the servant had brought to carry the water. The servant went back to Tutanekai and reported that a stranger was in the pool, and Tutanekai strode down to find out who this insolent intruder might be. After some searching, for Hinemoa from shyness had hidden herself, he caught hold of her hand, and demanded to know who was there.

'It is I,' Hinemoa said. 'It is Hinemoa.'

She rose from the water, graceful as a lovely bird, and the joyful Tutanekai put his cloak around her and took her to his home and his heart. They became man and wife, and when Hinemoa's people came to the island searching for her, rather than the battle Tutanekai's family had expected they accepted the match amid great rejoicing.

Hinemoa and Tutanekai lived a long and happy life together, and their descendants, the guide told them, still lived in Rotorua to that very day.

He had timed his narration perfectly, finishing the tale just as the launch was tied up ready for the visitors to step onto the island and see the story's setting for themselves.

Houses were set among the trees just behind a stretch of sandy beach, close to fenced fields that, while currently lying fallow, were obviously cultivated. Daisy and her party exchanged nods and greetings with the locals, and followed their guide to a small pond, close to the lake but sheltered by low trees. This was Hinemoa's Pool, where she had rested after her swim and where Tutanekai had found her.

Daisy heard a low chorus of "ahhs" at the sight of this tangible memento of the romantic tale. She dipped her fingers into the water, which was indeed pleasantly warm, before joining Eddie and the others heading towards the boat again.

Eddie glanced back and forth between the island and the shore. 'It's not so very far, you know—not for a good swimmer, anyway, and I bet they could all swim like fish. I shouldn't think it gave her as much trouble as all that.'

'Shh, people will hear you,' Daisy said, giving him a nudge in the ribs with her elbow. There was still a certain amount of dabbing at eyes with lace-edged handkerchiefs going on around them. 'Don't go spoiling it when it's such a nice story. It even has a happy ending, not like a lot of those old ones.'

'No need to attack me,' Eddie said, putting on a wounded tone and rubbing at his side. Daisy narrowed her eyes at him, quite certain that her nudge had done no real damage; Eddie dropped the pretence and grinned. 'Well, maybe the water was extra-cold that night. And you're right, it's a nice story. It ends up better than Romeo and Juliet, anyway.'

It was to be their final evening in the dining room before leaving Rotorua, and Granny and Aunt Sarah wore the smartest of the gowns they had brought.

Aunt Sarah's was in dark red, a heavy silk shift with matching chiffon over it. The outer layer had a deep row of bronze-coloured beading along the hem, ensuring that the dress hung straight. Granny's gown was sapphire-blue, with several deep flounces below the fashionably dropped waistline. Embroidery in a slightly darker shade gave a subtle edging to the neckline and flounces. They would each wear a fur wrap, adding to their glamorous appearance.

Daisy only had one dress for evening wear, the green woollen frock that was currently her Sunday best, but Granny sat her before the room's dressing table with its large mirror and fussed over her hair, pinning half of it up while the remainder tumbled over her shoulders and down her back.

'Such pretty hair,' Granny said, twining a lock around her finger. 'It's always been a bit darker than Eddie's, and it's turned out a lovely auburn.' She settled another curl into place and slid a hairpin through it. 'I suppose you'll be wanting to put it up properly soon, if your mother says that's all right.'

'I hadn't really thought about it,' Daisy said, glancing at a long strand Granny had yet to pin. 'I'm just used to having it down.'

'Well, I suppose you've been too busy thinking about your exams and everything to go worrying about little things like that,' Granny said.

'Yes, you've far more rational concerns,' Aunt Sarah remarked. 'I'll confess that I recall when I was your age making rather a fuss over wanting my hair up and my hems down. I'm relieved to hear that you're so much more sensible at sixteen years old than I was.'

Daisy smiled back at her aunt. 'I'll probably leave it until I start at university, anyway—it might look a bit funny, putting my hair up when I'm in school uniform.' And when it came to hem length, there was little difference between her own mid-calf dresses and those of grown women. Even Grandma, who was not generally a great enthusiast for change, now wore frocks that ended several inches above her ankles; only a handful of older women like Aunt Susannah still kept theirs determinedly full-length.

'That does sound more suitable,' Aunt Sarah said. 'It'll be time enough to think about hairstyles when you come to stay with us next year.'

She opened her jewel case and examined its contents, although she and Granny had already chosen their jewels for the evening.

'And what about you, Amy?' Aunt Sarah asked Granny. 'Did you make a great fuss over putting your hair up and having longer dresses?'

Granny paused in the act of placing the latest pin; as Daisy watched in the mirror, she saw her grandmother's expression turn wistful.

'I do remember looking forward to all that—it seemed such an important thing back in those days. I must have only been a month or so older than Daisy is when I did start putting my hair up and everything. That was just before I got married.'

Daisy saw her aunt's hand grip the lid of the jewel case more tightly. Perhaps she was shaken at the thought of a girl little older than Daisy getting married; especially to a man who looked as stern as the grandfather Daisy knew only from old photographs. 'So you had matters even more serious than Daisy's to concern yourself with,' she said, her voice very gentle.

Granny gave a tiny shrug, and smiled. She slid the hairpin home and picked up another lock. 'You're quite right, Daisy, next year will be soon enough. There's no need to be in a hurry to grow up.' She quickly pinned the last section of hair, then took a step back to examine the results. 'There you are, darling. You look very smart.'

'You certainly do,' Aunt Sarah said. 'And may I add a finishing touch? This should be just the thing.'

Aunt Sarah's search of the jewel case had produced a brooch of pretty green stones set in gold. Granny helped Daisy pin it to the front of her dress, and the three of them admired the effect.

'Yes, that goes well with your dress,' Aunt Sarah said.

'It brings out the colour of your eyes, too,' Granny added.

Eddie, who took far less time to dress for dinner, had gone down ahead of them. When Daisy descended the sweeping staircase with her grandmother and aunt she found him in the hotel's lounge, chatting with two Englishmen who appeared to have only just arrived in town and who were now taking full advantage of Eddie's freshly gained knowledge of the area.

Eddie looked up from his conversation as Daisy reached the base of the stairs. He smiled, and made his excuses to the two men before coming over to join her.

'I was thinking I might have to go in to the dining room on my own if you'd taken much longer,' he said. 'You look nice, though—you all do,' he amended, his gaze taking in Granny and Aunt Sarah as well.

He glanced over at the dining room, which was steadily filling with guests. 'I'm ready for my dinner after all the running around we've done today. Shall we?'

Daisy took hold of the arm he held out to her, and the four of them went through to the table reserved for them.

While they waited for the first course, Granny and Aunt Sarah chatted about the graduation ball. The Governor-General would be there, travelling up from Wellington especially for the occasion, along with Lady Jellicoe and perhaps their daughter. There was much discussion over the gowns and jewels Lady Jellicoe and the Hon. Lucy might wear; Eddie caught Daisy's gaze and rolled his eyes.

She smiled back at him, though their words were giving her an even more magnificent mental image of the ball, with dancers whirling around the floor, the ladies like bright bouquets of flowers and the men smart in dress uniforms or evening suits, Eddie the most dashing of them all.

Conversation was interrupted by the arrival of their soup, and then shifted to a discussion of the journeys they were to make the next day, Daisy home to Ruatane and the others back to Auckland. Aunt Sarah was particularly interested in Daisy's experience of the long journey by motor car, as it was a trip she and the rest of the Auckland family might be making themselves in the not-so-distant future.

As the roads improved, and the railway pushed further into the Bay of Plenty, the coastal steamers that had for so long been Ruatane's only reliable link with the outside world were seeing dwindling demand. The boats were still busy with freight, but their passenger service had already ended for some of the ports, and talk in the district was that Ruatane's would cease later that year.

Daisy's Auckland family had always made the journey by coastal steamer. But when the passenger run ended, Eddie and the others would need to catch the train to Rotorua and then the motor car service on to Ruatane. Daisy told her aunt that aside from being somewhat cramped and stuffy compared to travelling by boat, especially on the more winding sections of the road, the journey by motor car was not overly trying.

'And the train's first-class carriage was quite acceptable,' Aunt Sarah said. 'It's not as if we have a great deal of choice in the matter, in any case.'

'Well, I suppose we could always try seeing if George could bring us part of the way on one of his trips,' Granny said.

Granny's youngest brother, Daisy's Uncle George, carried goods on his sailing ship between Ruatane and several of the smaller settlements along the coast, and sometimes went further afield; occasionally to Tauranga, and once or twice even as far as Auckland. Although he did not regularly take passengers, he did occasionally convey family members as a favour if he happened to be going somewhere that suited them. He was very proud of his boat, and when Daisy saw it at the wharf she was always careful to express polite admiration, but it had never been a particularly imposing craft, and despite Uncle George's loving care it undeniably showed its age.

Daisy could hear the uncertainty in Granny's voice, and she was not surprised when Aunt Sarah gave a decisive shake of the head.

'I rather think not,' she said. 'Eddie might be up for the adventure, but I'd prefer not to share my travels with sacks or animal hides, or whatever else he might be carrying.'

Granny smiled. 'Well, no, when you put it like that! I didn't really think it was such a good idea, not for you and I. But Eddie's always liked the boats, haven't you, dear?'

'It's more that I've always liked coming to the farm, and that was the only way to get there. No, the train's all right—and a motor car's really good to ride in,' Eddie said, sending a conspiratorial grin in Daisy's direction.

'Yes, I think you've made your point regarding the virtues of the motor car quite exhaustively now, Eddie,' Aunt Sarah said.

Granny and Eddie came along to see Daisy off next morning, leaving Aunt Sarah, who generally preferred a more leisurely start to the day, back at the hotel, from where they would collect her before going on to the train station for their own departure later that morning.

There was an edge of frost to the air, and the smell of sulphur seemed sharpened by the chill. Bella's cousin Noel was standing by the motor car when they arrived, rubbing at a mark on the chrome quite invisible to anyone else. He removed one of his leather gloves before shaking hands with them all, and they chatted briefly about the weather and the likely state of the road ('Not too bad,' in Noel's opinion), then left him to load Daisy's suitcase next to the mailbags while they moved a few paces away along the footpath.

'What a nice, polite young man he is,' Granny said. 'I remember him from the wedding—he was fetching his mother something to eat, she'd hurt her leg, I think. I'm glad it's someone we know. He seems as if he'll be a careful driver, too.'

'I bet he is—Mr Latham would have his hide if he got a scratch on that motor car,' Eddie said.

Granny smiled. 'Well, I was more thinking about Daisy than the motor car.'

'So was I, of course,' Eddie said, mock-outrage in his tone. He shared a grin with Daisy.

An elderly man with a clerical collar arrived a little after Daisy's group, and came over to greet them; in answer to Granny's polite inquiries he said he was going to Ruatane to visit his widowed sister, who was in poor health.

Several minutes later, when Noel had reached the stage of looking at his watch and tapping one foot, a cart pulled up a few yards behind them. Its driver climbed off and helped down his passengers; soon afterwards a woman bustled up to the motor car, leading a small girl by the hand and carrying a well-worn suitcase, which she passed to Noel.

While the other passengers climbed in, with the clergyman taking the front seat next to Noel, Granny hugged Daisy, and Eddie gave her a peck on the cheek.

'I'm glad there's a lady coming along, too,' Granny said. 'It'll be nicer for you, dear.'

Daisy murmured vague agreement; a few moments later she was not so sure. When she climbed into the back seat the woman was saying to the small girl,

'I hope you won't be sick every half hour like you were the last time.'

Daisy hoped so, too; if not, she hoped the child would give enough warning for Noel to stop the motor car. It was going to be a long day.

Chapter Twenty

It was a quiet time on the farm, with the cows dried off for winter, and Daisy enjoyed a peaceful few days at home with her parents before school started again. She did her best to describe the sights she had seen in Rotorua to her parents, who listened with equal quantities of interest and bemusement. Neither of them had had any closer acquaintance with thermal activity than seeing the distant plume of steam over White Island, and they clearly had no desire to match Daisy's experience of such things.

'I think we might've done a bit about geysers and all that at school,' her mother said.

'Did we? I can't have been taking much notice, then, I don't remember it.'

'That boiling mud sounds a funny sort of business,' Mama said. 'And hot pools all over the place can't be very safe. Having hot water right there when you need to do the washing would be quite nice, though.'

'Yes, I wouldn't mind that. It'd save a lot of hauling water, anyway,' her father said.

Benjy raised a brief show of interest in her travels when Daisy's family went down to Grandpa's, but she had time for only a bare summary before he managed to change the subject.

'Hey, I've had an idea for something we could try at school,' he said when Daisy paused for breath.

Daisy pursed her lips at him. 'We're not doing a play, Benjy. We can't go spending time on that sort of thing.'

'Eh? I wasn't thinking about a play. Though now you come to mention it …' He grinned, making it clear that he was teasing. 'No, I've been thinking about drill. I thought I might have a go at getting us out of it on Fridays.'

Daisy and Benjy's final class on Friday afternoons was Physical Training, or "drill", as the pupils generally called it, which the whole of the secondary department did at the same time. For Daisy and the other girls it largely consisted of waving about small dumb-bells in response to instructions called out by a teacher; Benjy and the boys spent much of the time marching up and down, and occasionally practised shooting on the school's small rifle range. At the end of the school week, when Daisy was eager to get home and see her parents, as well as press on with her homework, that last hour at school was at best boring and at worst annoying.

'That'd be really good. Do you think they'd let us off doing it, though?' Daisy asked.

Benjy shrugged. 'It can't hurt to ask. I'll make sure I go on about wanting to get home a bit earlier now we've got all this extra study for matriculation, that sort of thing. The worst they can do is say no.'

Nicky had left for his school in Auckland by the time Daisy and Benjy moved back into town for the new school term. Aunt Maudie commented several times during the first day or so that she hoped he had got back safely. Whenever she said it, Uncle Richard told her that he was sure the school would have let them know at once if there had been any difficulty. Aunt Maudie always agreed, but it did not stop her from being rather fidgety. Fortunately a letter soon arrived from Nicky, no doubt under instruction from his schoolmaster, setting his mother's mind at rest.

Daisy found a more receptive audience here regarding her own travels. Uncle Richard and Aunt Maudie were only too happy to be reminded of their honeymoon visit to Rotorua.

'Oh, we went there, too,' Aunt Maudie said when Daisy described the geysers and pools of Whakarewarewa. 'It was so interesting, I'd never seen anything like that.'

Uncle Richard showed interest in what Daisy had seen at the Bath House, though he looked quietly amused at her account of some of the more outlandish treatments. He and Aunt Maudie had not seen the Bath House, as it had not yet been built at the time of their visit, but they had spent a day on the lake, following a route similar to Daisy's. Aunt Maudie remembered that there was a romantic tale attached to the island, though she admitted to having forgotten the details.

'It was all very nice, anyway,' Aunt Maudie said. 'We had a lovely time, didn't we, Richard?'

'Yes, it was most pleasant, darling. A very interesting area to visit.'

Aunt Maudie looked positively soppy, and even Uncle Richard had a somewhat dreamy expression as they smiled at each other across the dining table.

The tender moment was interrupted when Lucy let her fork clatter onto her plate.

'*I've* never been to Rotorua,' she announced, quite unnecessarily.

'Well, of course you haven't,' Aunt Maudie said. 'We've only been the once, and that was before you were born.'

'I expect I'd like it very much, if Daisy did. Father, do you think we could go there one day?'

'Mm, I'd quite like to see it again myself,' Aunt Maudie said. 'But it's not easy for your father to take us all away like that, Lucy.'

'Well, we shall have to see,' Uncle Richard said. 'Perhaps we might follow in Daisy's steps eventually,' he added, with a smile in her direction.

If it had been anyone but Benjy trying to get the two of them out of that Friday afternoon drill lesson, Daisy would have held out little hope for success. The timetable was handed down from on high, and was not a matter for discussion, or something to be altered for the convenience of two pupils.

But the world was inclined to work a little differently for Benjy. On Monday, when Mr Grant dismissed the class for lunch, Benjy hung back until he and Daisy were alone in the room with their teacher.

Daisy had let herself be persuaded to come along, but she left the discussion to Benjy, confining herself to an occasional nod or murmur of agreement. He set about making his case, all wide-eyed earnestness and every word weighted with sincerity. He stressed that he and Daisy needed that extra hour for study. As things were, they arrived home late and worn out every Friday, getting them off to a bad start on weekends, much of which were, in any case, taken up with helping at home—work they were, of course, only too happy to help their families with, but it did not leave much time for homework. He even managed to hint that there might be an element of danger in making the journey back to the valley so late in the day, when the light was low.

'I'm impressed by your eagerness to get on with your study,' Mr Grant remarked, the twinkle in his eye suggesting that he was not wholly convinced. 'Perhaps I should consider giving the two of you more homework, since you're so keen.'

Daisy did her best to mimic Benjy's expression of mild enthusiasm at the suggestion, but Mr Grant smiled and said there was no need for that.

'I'm fully aware that you're both working hard. And I must say you make your case with impressive gravity, Benjy. If you decide not to take up the teaching profession, perhaps you should consider a career in the law,' he added, smiling more broadly. 'And yes, you may be excused from drill on Friday afternoons. Try not to lord the fact over your less fortunate schoolfellows.'

Mr Grant waved aside their fervent thanks, and shooed them outside as he set to gathering up a bundle of papers.

'As if I'd want to be a lawyer,' Benjy said when they were out of their teacher's earshot. 'It'd probably be just about as bad as being a teacher.'

'Well, just in case you change your mind about that, shall I tell Uncle Richard you'd like to start learning Latin?' Daisy asked, her expression mock-serious.

'Not likely!' Benjy pulled a face, then grinned. 'That's good about getting out of P. T., eh?'

'I'll say,' Daisy agreed fervently.

Grandpa was particularly impressed at Benjy's success.

'That was pretty smart of you, boy, talking your teacher into getting let off early like that,' he said when he came to collect them the following Friday. Fortunately he had already visited Aunt Maudie a few days before and heard the news from her, so knew to arrive an hour earlier. 'Of course I always did say you took after your ma.'

It certainly made it simpler for whoever had the job of taking them home that week, which at this time of year with no milking to worry about was generally Grandpa or Daisy's father. They could now be reasonably sure of getting home before dark, even on the gloomiest days.

School otherwise went on much the same. A run of bad weather meant their classrooms took on a persistent smell of damp, only partially alleviated when draughts crept through gaps around the windows.

The winter months of 1923 brought more illness than in the previous few years, with an epidemic of influenza that was much more widespread than the usual seasonal attacks. Deaths were regularly reported in the newspapers, and even in isolated Ruatane several people had to take to their sick beds. But while a few pupils were missing from school during the outbreak, the illness seemed mostly confined to the frail and elderly. Not like those dreadful few weeks in 1918, when the war was scarcely over and a new, invisible enemy was creeping right into people's homes, launching its attacks most savagely on the young and fit. No wonder the very mention of influenza frightened people so.

An influenza epidemic on top of the ordinary winter ailments meant extra work for Uncle Richard, and although he never complained of it in Daisy's hearing, there were many evenings when she could see weariness in him as he sat in the parlour with the family.

Daisy glanced over at her uncle one evening as he leafed through that day's newspaper, and noticed his attention caught by an item. She was just close enough to be able to make out the headline, which in large type declared: "Influenza Outbreak: Precautions Necessary."

'Really, they shouldn't print such things,' Uncle Richard said; apparently more to himself than anyone else, but Aunt Maudie looked up from her stitching.

'What's that, Richard?'

'Nonsense like this.' He slapped the newspaper down on the arm of his chair. 'It purports to be giving useful information on avoiding sickness, but it's a barely disguised advertisement for some potion—a so-called medicine. I call it disgraceful, exploiting the fears of the public in the interests of profit.'

'Well, I'm sure you're right, dear, but you really shouldn't read those things if they aggravate you. You're running around looking after people all day—and half the night, too, sometimes—you should have a bit of peace and quiet of an evening.'

'I've half a mind to write to the editor,' he said, glancing down at the offending article. But he caught Aunt Maudie's anxious frown turned on him, and left the newspaper where it lay. 'You're quite right, my dear. The readers of such items would hardly be likely to pay much notice, in any case.'

He sat further back in his armchair, and as Aunt Maudie began telling him about the visits she had made that morning, Daisy saw her uncle's eyes close.

It was not uncommon during that winter term for Uncle Richard to come home late from visiting a patient, to a dinner kept warm for him by Aunt Maudie. If it was one of the evenings set aside for their Latin studies, and if his return was not so very late that everyone except Aunt Maudie had gone to bed, he was always prepared to go over Daisy's work with her.

'As long as you're not too tired, that is,' he generally added. 'I don't want to keep you up late when you've school in the morning.'

Daisy would assure him that she was not at all tired, while wishing she could say much the same to him with regard to staying up late with another demanding day before him. But telling her uncle that he looked badly in need of sleep would be disrespectful, and claiming to be too tired when all she had done was sit in school would sound ungrateful, as well as being dishonest. She was always careful to have her work completed ready for him to check, and her books and pencils close to hand, so that she would not keep him waiting a moment longer than necessary.

Timmy tended to begin yawning, and remind Aunt Maudie that it was close to his bedtime, on nights when his father was out late and they were due for a Latin lesson. Neither of his parents forced the issue; Aunt Maudie was easily convinced that he needed his sleep, and Uncle Richard almost certainly lacked the energy on those late nights to cope with an unwilling pupil.

Weary though he must be, Daisy's uncle was invariably patient, and generous with the time he spent on explanations, during her classes with him. She thanked him after each lesson; simple thanks seemed unsatisfactory, but were all she had to offer.

*

Fortunately Uncle Richard did not have to be out late every evening, or he might have been taken ill himself. Sometimes he even managed to have a quiet afternoon with no patients at all, reading or catching up with his paperwork; especially after the influenza outbreak subsided.

During her first year at high school Daisy's uncle had made it clear that she was welcome to share his desk on such occasions. She did not often ask to do so that winter, not wanting to rob him of his rare solitude; only when she had particular need of the quiet space.

On one such afternoon, a biting wind was keeping them all indoors after school and Timmy had persuaded Benjy into playing a card game; a supposedly quiet activity that, on Timmy's part at least, involved slapping down cards accompanied by hoots of triumph or shouted protests. An occasional 'Not so loud, Timmy,' from Aunt Maudie had only a brief effect; Lucy's complaints had none at all.

Flora somehow managed to ignore it all and carry on with her piano practice, but Daisy found it difficult to concentrate on the French translation she needed to finish. After one particularly rowdy outburst, she gathered up her books and slipped out of the room.

Her uncle was working at a bench by the window, making the most of the daylight. He greeted her with a smile, and cleared a generous section of his desk for her before returning to his task.

Now that she had the peace and quiet to keep her thoughts in order, Daisy soon finished. She closed her exercise book and looked over at her uncle, who was still caught up in his work.

The wooden case standing open on one end of the bench was a familiar sight to Daisy, though it was normally kept on a shelf, but this was the first time she had seen her uncle using the microscope the case usually contained. Uncle Richard had brought it out from England years before Daisy was born, and although its brass showed signs of wear it was a fine instrument, obviously well cared for.

He straightened up from leaning over the microscope and noticed Daisy's attention on him.

'I've been attempting to diagnose a troublesome ailment,' he said, indicating the bench and its contents. 'When the symptoms are inconclusive, a microscopic examination sometimes helps.'

'Is it influenza?' Daisy asked.

He shook his head. 'No, I think we're over the worst of that now. I haven't seen any new instances recently, at any rate. But I suspect I may have a case of tuberculosis here—perhaps you're more used to hearing it referred to as consumption.'

He would not let slip the patient's name, of course; Uncle Richard was always careful to keep the details of people's illnesses private. And consumption was common enough, as a rumoured ailment if not always an actual one, for there to be little risk that Daisy might guess who it could be, even if the patient were someone she knew.

Her uncle appeared about to tidy things away. Daisy briefly pondered whether the request hovering on her lips might be too bold, then decided to ask anyway.

'Could I please have a look?'

She saw surprise flit over his face, quickly followed by what might have been gentle amusement. 'I don't see why not. The material on the slide is quite sterile, so I won't be putting you at any risk of infection.'

He moved aside to make room for Daisy to stand at the microscope. 'Is the slide in focus for you?'

'I think so.' She squinted slightly, but her field of view still seemed to consist almost entirely of greyish-blue blobs.

'Now, do you see any small rod-shaped items? They'll be darker than the rest of the slide.'

Daisy cautiously twiddled a knob to sharpen the image a little more. Scattered among the blobs, she now noticed, were several longer shapes coloured a distinctive bright red. 'Yes, I see them! One... two... five, I think.'

'Your eyes are sharper than mine, then. I only noted three, but I think they're clear enough for a cautious diagnosis, although I'll send a sample off to the Health Department's laboratory for confirmation.'

Daisy looked up from the microscope and let her eyes adjust to the full-sized world around her. 'So those little rods are from consumption— tuberculosis, I mean. It makes them easier to see, being that red colour.'

'Yes, they're tubercule bacilli. Their colour's the result of a staining process. Would you like to see how I go about making a slide?'

Daisy made it clear that she most certainly would, and settled in to watch carefully.

'I won't go through the entire process in its full detail,' Uncle Richard said. 'But I can demonstrate the basic steps for you.'

He showed her a specimen jar holding a thick, gelatinous mass. This was a sputum sample that he had first heated with some caustic soda to break up the lumps, then left to settle.

'Yesterday I removed a small amount from this jar and spread it across a clean slide to form a film,' Uncle Richard said. 'When it had dried out, I passed it over the flame of a spirit burner, which fixes the film as well as rendering the organisms harmless. Then it was necessary to stain it, so the tubercule bacilli would be visible.'

The staining process was a complicated business, requiring three different substances and a thorough rinsing after each step. First came a five-minute immersion in a stain called carbol fuchsin that had been heated till it steamed. The slide was then dipped in acid for a minute or so, removing most of the red colour; then the final substance was used, methylene blue. This stained everything on the slide except the tuberculosis bacteria, which retained the bright red that Daisy had already seen under the microscope.

'Tuberculosis is rather more demanding than some other bacilli,' her uncle remarked as he put away the various bottles in a cupboard that looked to hold at least a dozen others. 'There's a waxy layer within the cell walls that makes them resist easy staining. A pair of German doctors were the first to describe this particular process.'

'Do you have to use different stains for every sort of disease until you find the right one?' Daisy asked, her heart sinking a little at the thought.

'Oh, it's not quite that bad, or nothing would ever be diagnosed! Generally one suspects a particular complaint before beginning, and there's a useful method called Gram staining that eliminates many organisms with the one test. But yes, it can take several attempts, using different procedures. That's more the business of medical specialists known as pathologists than an ordinary doctor such as myself, though—I confine myself to a few common conditions, and where necessary have the laboratory check further. Speaking of which, I must get this ready to be sent off tomorrow.'

He placed a sealed glass tube containing part of the sputum sample into a small box lined with cotton wool. A piece of paper was wrapped around the tube; probably with the patient's details, although Daisy was careful not to look.

'It still must be a lot to remember, though.' The lists of chemical compounds they had to learn off by heart had seemed daunting in her early days of secondary school, but anything she had achieved in her studies was dwarfed by the task of keeping track of all the necessary combinations and procedures for using that cupboard of chemicals.

'Well, the most familiar of them become second nature after a time. And I haven't had to rely on memory alone since the days when I was studying for examinations—I've ample texts to consult when in doubt.'

That was all very well, Daisy thought to herself, but even knowing which books to look in would take a good deal of study. No wonder it took so many years to become a doctor.

Uncle Richard attached an address label to the package and set it on a corner of his desk.

'They have more powerful microscopes than mine at the Government Laboratory, so will get a more accurate count. Especially if they first culture the bacteria—I sometimes do that myself, though not with suspected tuberculosis.'

When Daisy expressed an interest in the culturing process, her uncle showed her a lidded glass container called a petri dish, into which a jelly-like substance called agar would be poured and allowed to set, then used as a medium for microscopic organisms that had been carefully introduced via a loop of sterilized wire to grow and multiply. A sample of the colony could then be removed, again using sterilized wire, and placed under the microscope for study.

'It all takes time, of course,' Uncle Richard said. 'And having to send things to and from the laboratory adds further delays. If we had a hospital here in Ruatane it might perhaps have its own laboratory with up-to-date equipment, which would be a fine thing. I'd like to think the town will gain that distinction eventually, as the population increases. In the meantime, I do my best with what's at hand—although with a disease like tuberculosis the options may be limited.'

'You can't really cure it, can you?' She would not ask any questions that might seem an attempt to find out who the patient was, but her uncle seemed willing enough to engage in a general discussion of the disease.

'That's typically the case, unfortunately, though there can be some success in managing the disease, at least for a time. It's sometimes recommended to send a patient to a sanatorium, and those institutions can do fine work with good food, fresh air and sunlight, but I prefer to see sufferers cared for at home wherever possible, with due instruction given on the precautions necessary to prevent infection. Separation from home and family can itself harm well-being, after all. I've heard of a certain amount of success from an operation known as artificial pneumothorax, which involves temporarily collapsing the diseased lung by injecting gas into the chest. It allows the lung to rest, which might give the opportunity for it to heal itself. Of course a procedure like that must be performed by a surgeon under hospital conditions.'

Uncle Richard put away the specimen slide, then took a large book from a shelf and turned to a section about halfway through.

'Here's a clearer illustration of the tubercule bacilli,' he said, placing the book on his desk for Daisy to look at. 'And would you like to see some other slides under the microscope before I put it away? I've a collection that contains some interesting ones.'

'I'd like that very much, thank you, if you're not too busy.'

'No, I've the rest of the day to myself, unless I happen to be called out to a patient. I'd be delighted to share my collection with an interested observer. I haven't had the slides out for some time, but I'm fairly sure I know where they are.'

While he rummaged in a cupboard, Daisy studied the drawing, which showed rods that resembled those she had seen under the microscope. Above that was a larger illustration, revealing how the rods were gathered into cavities within the lungs.

She turned several pages, and found drawings of a range of other bacteria in a variety of conformations: thin and whip-like; clusters of blobs with what looked like tiny tails; bizarre shapes that could have been miniature sea-monsters. Each coloured plate was protected by a sheet of thin tissue, and the descriptions alongside had names like "Eudorina elegans", "Volvox globator", and "Spirillum undula". The beauty of the illustrations made an odd contrast with the damage those organisms could wreak.

'Yes, here they are.' Uncle Richard lifted a flat wooden box from the cupboard, placed it on the bench by the microscope, and opened it to reveal rows of glass slides held snugly in individual slots against a lining of fuzzy green cloth.

There were dozens of slides, all arranged in categories. He took several from each section and set them out for Daisy.

The collection included small insects and many-legged creatures, some surprisingly beautiful algae, and parts of the flowering sections of several plants. One slide even held a juvenile fish. There were samples taken from the organs of larger animals, sliced thinly enough to make them almost transparent. Some of the slides were similar to pictures she had seen in the book of microscopic images, but these real-life objects illuminated by the late-afternoon sunlight had a glow that the flat illustrations could not match.

The play of light and colour reminded Daisy of Lucy's enraptured descriptions of the paintings she had seen in Auckland's art gallery. Surely no painting could be lovelier than the images under the microscope; images that revealed a new dimension to the world, hidden from the naked eye.

Daisy would cheerfully have spent the rest of the day going through the slide collection, but when she looked up from the last of those her uncle had set out for her she realised that the light was dimming; she also noticed that her eyes were growing weary.

She straightened up, stretching out her shoulder muscles, and glanced across the room to see Benjy standing in the doorway.

'Dinner'll be ready soon, I thought I'd better let you know in case you need to wash your hands or something,' he said.

'Goodness, is it so late already?' Uncle Richard said, looking up at the wall clock. 'I'd rather lost track of the time.'

'And I haven't helped get dinner on. Sorry, Benjy,' Daisy said, though her small pang of guilt was eclipsed by the awareness of what she had learned in the last hour or so.

'That's all right, I just had to peel a few extra spuds. I might eat some of yours to make up for it,' Benjy said, smiling. 'I popped my head around the door a while ago, but the two of you looked that wrapped up in whatever you were doing, I didn't like to disturb you.'

'Yes, we've been very busy with our investigations,' Uncle Richard said. 'The afternoon has flown by.'

'Anyway, I told Maudie you had your heads together working on something or other, and she said to leave you to it. But she says you'd better get a move on now, she'll be taking the roast out of the range in a couple of minutes.'

Benjy went back the way he had come, and Daisy set about packing away the slides while her uncle got the microscope ready to go back into its box.

Before returning each slide to its slot she held it up to the window for a moment; even without the magnification that would have rendered the details visible, the effect was like tiny gems in shades ranging from pale pink through to deep violet. Thanks to her uncle, Daisy now understood something of the staining process that had created these images.

The final slide had been stained with blue; a muted shade across most of the glass rectangle, but cut through with skeletal lines of a dark bluish-purple. The striking colour, along with all the discussion on diagnosing and treating disease, brought up a memory for Daisy, and with it a question.

'Uncle Richard?'

He looked up from fiddling with one of the many little hooks that were required to make the microscope case secure.

'What is it, dear?'

'I was wondering…' She paused to choose her words with care. 'Back during the influenza—the really bad one after the war, I mean—I remember… well, people sometimes turned black with it.'

He nodded slowly. 'Yes, that's quite correct—or at least a dark purple hue that we call heliotrope. It was a distressing sight for those watching over the sufferers, especially when it became apparent that if the discoloration continued to darken, and delirium persisted for longer than a few days, there was little hope of recovery.'

Her uncle's memories of those times could not have been comfortable ones, making Daisy cautious of pursuing the discussion, but the question had been quietly nagging at her for years. Uncle Richard was the only person she knew who would be able to give her authoritative answers; she

238

also dared hope he might understand that it was a genuine desire for knowledge driving her, not idle curiosity.

'Why did it happen?' she asked. 'What made them turn that colour?'

'It's a phenomenon known as cyanosis, from the Greek for blue. If pneumonia follows upon influenza, the infection attacks the lungs, bursting many of the small blood vessels there. The air spaces fill with blood and other fluids, and the lung tissue becomes consolidated, making it incapable of properly aerating the bloodstream. When the blood is deprived of sufficient oxygen, the skin colour changes from a healthy pink into dark purple or blue.'

'And that means the person's going to die?'

'Well, cyanosis on its own doesn't mean that rapid death is inevitable. The body does its best to fight back against the infection, and sometimes the patient's system manages to gain the upper hand. But with the influenza of nineteen-eighteen being so severe, pneumonia was far more common a consequence than it usually is, and in a particularly virulent form. The cyanosis was sometimes of a deep inkiness that I'd not observed before, suggesting that the lungs were beyond recovery. When death did follow, the body quite rapidly grew darker still. I certainly saw a few that I'd describe as black. It was a dreadful time.'

His voice had dropped to little more than a murmur on the last few words, and the silence that followed might have grown awkward if Daisy had allowed it to persist. 'I see,' she said. 'Thank you for explaining it all.'

'You're most welcome, dear, although I'd suggest that you don't speak of this widely. I'm sure you wouldn't want to bring up distressing memories for anyone who lost a loved one during that time.'

'Oh, no, I wouldn't do that.' It was easy to be sincere in her assurance. Not betraying her uncle's confidence would be reason enough to keep the knowledge to herself; the risk of upsetting anyone made her all the more determined. Perhaps Uncle Richard was thinking of Kate. It was not a matter Daisy would feel able to raise at home about her mother's little sister; still less would she mention such a thing to Grandma.

Before Kate's death the only human dead body Daisy had ever seen was that of her great-grandmother, who had died when Daisy was nine. There had been nothing frightening or distressing about seeing Great-grandma, who had looked as if she had fallen into a peaceful sleep. What a comfort it was that she had not suffered, everyone had agreed, just slipping away at the end of a long life.

It was hard enough for the family to lose someone as young as Kate, who had been barely a year older than Daisy was now; Grandma and Grandpa's last memory of their daughter must be of her body ready for burial with her skin the colour of a fresh bruise.

No, it was not a subject Daisy would raise with her mother or grandmother. The only other person she had ever discussed it with was Eddie, and even with him it was not a matter to be dwelt upon. Sometimes when they were speaking of those days during the epidemic, when in the course of his visits to the homes of influenza sufferers he had seen for himself a body darkened in death, he would abruptly feel the need to turn the conversation, making Daisy realise that they had veered close to matters of which he would rather not speak. She never pressed the subject when she could see it made him uncomfortable; such things were not for idle conversation.

Daisy had always been taught to try to say the right thing; she had realised for herself that knowing when to say nothing at all was just as important. Perhaps that was even more the case for doctors.

Uncle Richard fastened the last hook on the microscope case, and Daisy passed the box of slides over to him.

'Those were really interesting, thank you.'

'I'm glad you enjoyed them. You'll have many opportunities to explore the microscopic world when you begin your medical studies—and no doubt with far more up-to-date slides than in my modest collection—but a small head start on such matters can only be useful.'

Chapter Twenty-One

There was certainly no talk of anything closely related to living organisms during school lessons, where science classes continued to be set solidly in a routine of chemistry with an occasional venture into physics. That made the glimpses Daisy's uncle gave her into his work all the more valuable. He might mention the symptoms of an illness and how he treated it, or how a particular medicine was believed to work. His explanations of the way different substances interacted gave Daisy fresh insight into the practical application of all that chemistry, and with it a greater admiration for the subject.

'There's an interesting item here on a new treatment for diabetes, using a substance called insulin,' Uncle Richard said one afternoon, indicating one of his medical journals. 'It's not exactly bedtime reading, but you're most welcome to look at it if you'd like.'

Bedtime reading was not worth attempting during the week, no matter the material. If Daisy left the bedroom lamp on, Lucy took it as an invitation for chatter; even with the light out she sometimes did the same, but at least in the dark Daisy could feign sleep, and Lucy would soon give up.

Fortunately the weekends gave the chance for a little extra reading when Daisy had caught up with her schoolwork. She readily accepted his offer, and from then on her uncle lent her his journals whenever one happened to contain an item he thought she might find of interest (and, Daisy suspected, when he thought the article was simple enough for her to understand). Although it often took some effort to find her way through the unfamiliar terms, the journals were frequently a good deal more engrossing than her textbooks.

On those weekend evenings at home on the farm, Daisy did her schoolwork at one end of the kitchen table while her father kneaded the bread and her mother shaped the dough into loaves, the room softly lit by the lamp's warm glow and the sound of her parents' voices a soothing accompaniment to her study.

Late in winter came calving time, and Daisy enjoyed the familiar task of helping to feed the new arrivals, guiding the questing little muzzles into a bucket of milk. They had a good proportion of heifers that year, which her parents were pleased about; they would not be able to keep all the calves, and when it came to selling them heifers would fetch a much better price than bull-calves.

Grandpa had a healthy batch of them, too, as Daisy saw for herself when she and her parents went over to his farm one Saturday. They arrived well before lunchtime, to give Grandpa plenty of time to show them the new calves, but he had not yet finished when they heard Grandma calling from the house, telling them to get a move on before the food got cold.

As was often the case at Grandma's table, multiple conversations took place at once. Grandma imparted the latest news of various family members; commented on what a long while it seemed until the holidays, when they could have Benjy and Daisy back home for a decent stretch of time; checked that everyone had enough to eat, especially Benjy.

Aunt Maisie joined in whenever Grandma paused for breath, at one point asking Daisy how she was getting on at school. Daisy managed a quick 'All right, thank you,' before Aunt Maisie was distracted by a sudden need to fetch more carrots from a pot keeping warm on the range. It did not matter; Daisy knew the question came more from politeness than from any real desire to hear the answer.

Her parents were still discussing the new calves with Grandpa, somehow managing to keep up the thread of their conversation despite Grandma's frequent interruptions. Uncle Joe was occasionally part of their discussion; when he seemed about to speak, the others were careful to hold back so that he could make his husky voice heard.

They talked of the qualities seen in the new calves, which ones might have been passed on from sire or dam, and how that might influence their breeding decisions for the following season. Between Daisy's mother and grandfather they knew large parts of the different bloodlines by heart, and those two in particular never seemed to tire of the subject. They had an especially lively discussion on the importance of a proper escutcheon, the shield-like pattern of hair growing in different directions on the back end of a cow, and how strongly its quality was linked to how productive the cow would turn out to be.

Daisy and Benjy shared tolerant smiles across the mountain of roast potatoes on Benjy's plate. Such conversations had been a part of Daisy's life as far back as she could remember, and were comforting in their familiarity. By next winter she would be away at university; this might be the last time she would sit at this table and hear those animated discussions on conformation, vigour and productivity.

'I wouldn't mind seeing how Mick and Danny's cows have done,' Grandpa said. 'The last couple should've calved by now. I might go over there next week, in case they're worried about any of them.'

Uncle Joe gave a snort. 'I don't know, Pa, I think it's another sort of calf Danny's worried about.'

He shot a cautious look in his mother's direction, and got a hard stare in return from Grandma, but Daisy was fairly sure she saw the other adults hiding smiles. She studiously pretended not to have noticed the remark, though she was quite aware that Uncle Joe was talking about the baby Bella was carrying.

She had not seen Bella for a month or so, but her state had been obvious by then, although no one referred to the matter within Daisy's hearing. She gathered that Bella had stopped going out, but was having plenty of visitors, Daisy's mother among them.

'I'll go with you, then,' Grandma said to Grandpa. 'Maisie and I can do some extra baking to take over, in case they're getting short of biscuits. I want to see how Bella's keeping, too.'

'That's a good idea,' Grandpa said. 'We'd better keep an eye on both sorts of calf, eh?'

It was Grandpa's turn for a stern look from Grandma, but he grinned and patted her hand, and Daisy heard what sounded like a muffled giggle from her own mother. Grandma darted a glance at the youngest two; Daisy did her best to look interested in nothing beyond the food on her plate, while Benjy's expression of blissful innocence would have fooled an observer a good deal less partial than Grandma.

A few weeks before the end of term, Mr Grant told Daisy and Benjy that he had asked the headmaster to send away for the matriculation examination's application forms.

'We certainly don't want to leave it too late,' their teacher said. 'I imagine there'll be some sort of fee your parents will have to pay, but I shouldn't think it'll be onerous.'

A little over a week later, Mr Grant asked the two of them to stay behind after the final class of the day.

'He must've got the forms already,' Benjy murmured to Daisy as they waited for their fellow pupils to leave the room.

Daisy saw what must be the application forms, along with what looked to be a covering note on special letterhead, on the teacher's desk. Mr Grant picked up the forms, but rather than handing them over at once he fiddled with the sheets of paper, replaced them on his desk, then took them up again.

'Your application forms have arrived,' he said. 'The school will need to organise some paperwork as well before the examinations, but you needn't concern yourselves with that. In the meantime, take these forms home to your parents as soon as you can. They need to be sent in by the beginning of October, along with the application fees. Regarding that...'

Mr Grant paused and cleared his throat before continuing. 'Yes, regarding those fees—there's a rather unexpected issue with them. The usual charge is two guineas per candidate, but that's for centres with at least ten pupils put forward. With fewer than ten, I'm afraid the regulations require a total payment of twenty guineas, even in a case like yours with only the two of you sitting the examinations. I'm sorry to be the bearer of bad news.'

Benjy was the first to recover the power of speech. He even managed to sound fairly calm as he thanked Mr Grant and took the application forms. Daisy murmured what she hoped sounded like polite thanks, and followed Benjy from the classroom.

'Twenty guineas!' Benjy said as soon as they were safely out of earshot. 'I never thought of it costing anything like that.'

It was a vast amount; enough to buy a decent riding horse, or two or three good house cows, or a perfectly sound gig and the harness to go with it. Daisy would not have felt comfortable asking her parents for two guineas; expecting them to come up with many times that amount would be quite ridiculous.

Benjy glanced at her expression, and appeared to guess her thoughts. 'Don't worry, I'll ask Pa to pay for both of us. He wouldn't expect your ma and pa to.'

They were walking along the road now. Benjy looked over his shoulder, but few people were about, and there was little risk of being overheard. 'I'm not much looking forward to asking him, though,' he said, pulling a face.

Grandpa was quite well-known as a successful breeder of pedigree Jersey cows, as well as being important in the world of dairy factories and co-operatives, but twenty guineas was twenty guineas.

'Such a lot of money. Do you think...' Daisy trailed off, unwilling to voice her fear.

'What, that he might say no?' Benjy shook his head. 'I shouldn't think so, not after letting me go to high school all these years, and buying uniforms and everything. He won't even go on about it, Pa never does. Still... I don't know, it makes me feel pretty selfish. I mean, there's Joe and the others working away on the farms. I sit around inside all week, and now I'm putting my hand out for money again.'

Daisy thought of her own parents, always busy, whether with milking, tending the horses, building fences or planting crops. 'I know,' she said. 'People say things like we might go wearing ourselves out with all the study we have to do, but all the others have been working hard since they were still at primary school. And then they have to run around after us, fetching us home on the weekends.'

The two of them were walking along so slowly that Daisy's feet were almost dragging; she picked up her pace a little, to avoid scuffing her shoes. 'Sometimes it feels like we're always asking for things.'

Benjy heaved a sigh. 'Well, I've got to ask for something big this time.'

Benjy was right, of course: Grandpa said he would pay the twenty guineas, though Benjy reported that he had gone rather quiet on first hearing the news. Grandma had been sure there must have been some sort of mistake over the amount, but Grandpa showed her the form, which allowed for no doubt.

Daisy was aware of discussions on the subject between her parents. She was not meant to overhear, and the conversations stopped abruptly when they noticed she was within earshot, but not before she had caught remarks about possibly being able to scrape together a pound or two to give Grandpa when the next cream cheque arrived. Daisy pretended not to have noticed, and went about her business.

The winter term was almost over when Grandpa picked up Daisy and Benjy one Friday afternoon. He had just collected the mail from the Post Office, and he handed Daisy the letters addressed to her parents; 'There's one for you in there, too,' Grandpa said.

Daisy gave the other two envelopes the barest of glances. One looked as if it might be an account from the general store; the other was addressed in elegant handwriting to "Mr and Mrs D. Stewart". Of far more interest was the one addressed to her, which she at once recognized as being from Eddie. She put the other items of mail into her schoolbag, and opened her letter.

It was quite short, which did not surprise her, given how soon Eddie would be there for the holidays and able to share all his news in person. He told Daisy he had bought something for her, which he would bring down rather than posting. He also mentioned that her parents would be hearing from Aunt Sarah by the same post.

Daisy retrieved the letter addressed to her parents and studied it more closely. Yes, that handwriting did seem familiar; perhaps from letters Granny received when she was staying on the farm. The style had just the blend of decisiveness and cool elegance Daisy would have expected from Aunt Sarah. The envelope, too, had a weight and texture that suggested quality; it was also identical to the one that had contained Eddie's letter.

Staring at the envelope, no matter how intently, failed to give any clue to its possible contents; neither did Daisy have any success in guessing what Eddie's gift for her might be. She put both letters away and wished, not for the first time, that Grandpa's cart did not travel quite so slowly.

*

'A letter from your Aunt Sarah?' Daisy's mother said. 'Are you sure, Daisy? She doesn't usually write to us, just sends her love in your granny's letters.'

'Well, Eddie said she was sending one to you.'

Her mother's lips twitched in a half-smile. 'Then it must be right, if Eddie said so.'

Daisy placed the mail on the table; her father took the one that looked like an account, and slid the other over to Mama.

'You can open this one,' he said.

'I shouldn't think it'll bite, Davie,' Mama said; Papa did not look completely convinced.

She tore open the envelope and removed a sheet of paper.

' "Dear Beth and David",' Mama read out. ' "It has come to my attention that a fee will be charged for Daisy's matriculation examinations. As I am sure you will recall, quite some time ago I took upon myself the privilege of bearing any costs associated with Daisy's education. Accordingly, you will find enclosed a cheque to cover the said fee." '

She looked up from the letter and met Papa's gaze, her eyes suddenly bright. 'The rest of it's just "my regards" and all that—she sends her love to you, Daisy. But there must be...'

Mama scrabbled through the envelope and pulled out a piece of paper. It was indeed a cheque, made out for the sum of twenty-one pounds, which was the same as twenty guineas.

The three of them admired the cheque, then Daisy's mother put it in an old cake tin where they kept accounts and receipts.

'We'll take it down to your Grandpa tomorrow,' she said. 'I can hardly wait to see his face.'

The pleased relief on Grandpa's face was indeed worth seeing.

'I could've managed all right,' he said, holding the cheque between his fingertips as he studied it. 'Still, it's a fair sum, and there's always something needs fixing up on one farm or the other. I'm still going to pay half of it, though—I'm not having Sarah paying the lot.'

'I don't think she'd mind, Pa,' Daisy's mother said.

'That's not the point, though. It's very good of her, but I can't have her paying for Benjy's share as well.'

'But it would cost the same if it was just me sitting the exams.' Daisy was reluctant to push herself into a conversation on so grown-up a subject as money, but her grandfather appeared to have overlooked this important point. 'It's the same whether it's one person or two.'

Grandpa smiled at her. 'You don't miss much, eh? I suppose you're right as far as the numbers go, but it's the principle of the thing, love. Benjy's my son—and you're my granddaughter, come to that. It's only right I should pay a share.' His smile turned into a grin. 'Mind you, I'm glad you and Benjy are the only ones set on this matriculation business. I hope the other grandchildren don't all go getting the same idea.'

Grandma let out something close to a snort. 'I shouldn't think that's too likely.'

'No, I expect you're right—and a good thing, too,' Grandpa said, still smiling.

Grandma, Grandpa and Aunt Maisie went as far as the garden gate to see Daisy's family on their way, while Benjy came along with them to where the horse was tethered.

'I'll write to Sarah tonight,' Daisy's mother said to Papa as they waited for Benjy and him to harness the horse to the gig. 'I should get on and thank her straight away, and I can let her know about Pa wanting to pay half the money. Daisy, you can write a thank-you note to go in with the letter.'

'That's a good idea,' Daisy said. She would be sure to use her very best penmanship for her note, as well as the pretty stationery that had been a gift from Granny.

'It's very good of them both, you know. Benjy, I hope you've thanked Pa properly.'

'Of course I have,' Benjy said, looking up from fastening a buckle. 'He sort of brushed it off, though, as though it wasn't worth making a fuss over.'

Grandpa had reacted in much the same way to Daisy, first of all when she had spoken to him soon after they received the news about the examination fees, and again today when she had chosen a relatively quiet moment to thank him once more. While he had spoken kindly on both occasions, and told her it was nothing to worry herself about, he was clearly a good deal happier about it all today.

'Your pa looks that cheerful, you wouldn't think he's having to shell out ten guineas,' Daisy's father remarked, echoing something of her own thoughts.

Benjy gave the horse's neck a rub, and stepped back out of the gig's way. 'Well,' he said, 'I suppose once you've got your head around the idea of paying twenty guineas, ten doesn't seem too bad at all.'

Chapter Twenty-Two

The end of August brought the school holidays, and the arrival of Granny and Eddie. As had been rumoured for months, the coastal steamers' passenger service to Ruatane had come to an end, and for the first time their visitors had journeyed by train and motor car. It meant the trip had taken two days, with an overnight stay in Rotorua before travelling on to Ruatane in one of Mr Latham's motor cars.

Daisy went into town with her father on the spring cart, and after a quick trip to the general store they were well in time to meet Mr Latham's passengers. Eddie helped Granny climb up to sit next to Daisy's father on the driving board, then sat beside Daisy in amongst the baggage.

'The motor car was lovely and comfortable,' Granny said as the spring cart bounced along the track. 'The whole trip was much nicer than on the boat—at this time of year, anyway, when you get the spring storms.'

Granny had, by her own account, never been a good sailor; unlike Eddie, who claimed to enjoy the sea in all weathers.

'I was worried it might be a bit of a crush for Eddie,' she added. 'He said he had lots of room in the front for his legs, though.'

'Yes, there's nothing wrong with motor cars,' Eddie said. 'I'd had enough of it by the end, mind you, and it might get too hot in the summer. I suppose he could put the top down, we'd get the breeze then.'

'We'd get the dust, too,' Granny said, smiling ruefully. 'Hours and hours of it. I must say the boats used to be quite nice in the summer—in the calm weather, anyway.'

She reached over to squeeze Daisy's father's hand where it rested on the reins. 'It's a shame Auckland's so far away. But it's worth the trip to be able to see you all, no matter how long it takes.'

Eddie nudged at a sack of flour to make a little more room for his elbow, and stretched out his legs until they almost reached right across the bed of the cart. His face was already pink from a stiff breeze, his smart shoes had acquired a coating of road dust, and he was smiling as he gazed at the sky and at the paddocks they were passing.

'Of course it is,' he said, turning his attention from his surroundings to his companions, until his smile rested on Daisy. 'It's always worth coming down here.'

It might be school holidays, but Daisy was very aware that the matriculation examinations were only three months away now. She managed to devote some time each evening to her studies, with Eddie helping her decide where to concentrate her efforts. Occasional vague remarks from their teachers suggesting that the headmaster might send away for a description of what was likely to be in the examinations had yet to come to anything, making Daisy even more grateful for Eddie's solid advice, based on his own experience.

As well as his advice, he had brought something more tangible with him. The mysterious item he had mentioned having bought for Daisy turned out to be a University of New Zealand Calendar, a book packed with information on courses and regulations and, of more immediate interest, with details on the matriculation examinations, including what material might be covered in the various subjects. This section on matriculation was, Eddie told her, how he had discovered the fee of twenty guineas.

'I remembered back when I sat it Aunt Sarah had to pay something,' Eddie said. 'So I looked it up in the calendar to see how much it cost, and I found out about them charging all that in little places where there aren't many people doing matric. Of course I told Aunt Sarah, and she got straight on to it.'

Daisy squeezed his hand in gratitude, and was rewarded with a smile.

She insisted on working every evening, but on fine days she allowed Eddie to persuade her to be out and about with him for much of the time. At this season the paths into the bush were too muddy to be appealing, but there were ample opportunities for walks without venturing beneath the trees. They roamed the farm, checking the new calves and helping tend the horses; strolled along the creek bank; climbed a hill behind the farmhouse until they were high enough to see far along the length of the valley.

After lunch one day the two of them rode down the valley to Grandpa's farm, planning to spend the afternoon with Benjy until it was time to go back for milking. Grandma, who was used to the boundless appetite of boys, had glasses of milk and a laden plate of biscuits on the table almost before they had closed the kitchen door.

'Let's take it out to the verandah,' Benjy suggested.

'Yes, that's a good idea,' Grandma said. 'You need to get some fresh air while you've got the chance, after being stuck in that school all the time.'

The three of them settled onto the verandah steps with the plate within easy reach. Lunch was still a recent memory, but the biscuits were nice, and Daisy enjoyed her own small share.

The examinations were on Benjy's mind, too, and he was eager for any advice Eddie could give on preparing for them.

'Don't let on to Ma that we're talking about the exams, though,' he said, brushing biscuit crumbs from his trouser leg. 'She's not even keen on me doing a lot of homework on the weekends during term time—she says I should be having a rest from schoolwork when I'm home.'

He cast a glance at the front door, obviously wondering if his mother had approached the verandah without being heard, unlikely though that was; Grandma was not noted for moving silently.

'She thinks we've got too much work now, just at high school, and if I'm not careful she might go getting ideas about the university and what that'll be like. I don't think she'd change her mind now about letting me go—Pa would help me talk her around again, anyway. But she gets worried I might be wearing myself out. You know what she's like.'

Benjy said it with a rueful smile, and without the merest trace of irritation. Grandma had indeed always been inclined to fuss over him, and the family's frightening experience of influenza had made her even more so.

Eddie assured them both that he would not say a word to Grandma about their topic of conversation.

'Let's have a look at this while I'm here,' he said, pulling out Daisy's university calendar. Though not a large volume, it would not fit in Daisy's pockets; Eddie's jacket had much larger ones. 'It's good you're thinking about the exams already—you don't want to leave your swotting till the last minute.'

'I don't know how we'll ever manage to remember it all, though,' Daisy said.

The last half of a coconut-topped biscuit disappeared down Eddie's throat. 'Don't try learning everything off by heart, or you'll drive yourself silly. With science there's a few things you can just about guarantee are going to be in the exam, it's worth learning those, and when you're swotting up on maths you'll want to go over the basic rules for geometry and algebra.'

'Hang on, I want to write some of this down,' Benjy said. 'Ma doesn't seem to be taking any notice of what we're doing.' He risked a dash along the passage to his room, and returned with a notebook and pencil.

'I'd better not get any of the textbooks out here, just in case. Now, what do you reckon will definitely be in the exams?'

Eddie flicked through the calendar and rattled off advice, which Benjy scribbled down as quickly as he could manage, muttering an echo of Eddie's words as the pencil scratched away.

'Boyle's Law... states of matter... hold on a minute... oxidation and reduction...'

Daisy had similar lists in her exercise books at home, with references to the pages of the calendar, thanks to the time spent with Eddie. She was relieved that it all sounded quite familiar, although she fully intended to compare her own notes with Benjy's when she next had the chance, just to make sure she had not missed anything vital.

Eddie ran through science and mathematics, and passed briefly over history, which he considered would mainly consist of dates and names of the various kings. French, he said, would mostly be translation, with a few questions on grammar.

'The English exams are pretty easy,' Eddie said. 'It's just questions on grammar and punctuation, that sort of thing, and writing an essay. Make sure the essay's long enough, and be careful about your spelling—I remember my teacher saying that counted for a lot.'

Benjy slid along the top step until he could lean his back against the verandah railing. 'It doesn't sound too bad, I suppose—well, except for the maths and science, anyway.'

'No need to worry,' Eddie said. 'I'm sure you'll do just fine.' His words seemed addressed to Benjy, but his smile was on Daisy as he spoke.

Grandma chose that moment to call down the passage, asking Benjy if he had a warm enough vest on under his clothes. Benjy slipped the notebook into his pocket before assuring her that he did. The afternoon was wearing on, and it would soon become chilly; rather than risk her grandmother getting the notion of asking about Daisy's own underwear, she rose to her feet and said it was time for her and Eddie to leave.

Eddie's last few days on the farm went by in a rush, while Daisy made sure to extract all the advice he could offer regarding the examinations.

'Keep an eye on the clock when you're in the exams, that's quite important,' he said on the day before he was to leave. 'You need to work out how much time you should spend on each question, depending on how many marks it's worth. Oh, and make sure you show your work in maths. I bet you already know that, but you don't want to go forgetting when the time comes.'

His gaze turned serious. 'I know how clever you are and how hard you work, Daisy, and I know what's in those exams. Just don't go getting too nervous, all right? You can do it. I'm quite sure of that.'

The following morning Daisy and her father took Eddie into town to catch the motor car with Mr Latham. By the time she saw him next, the matriculation examinations would be over, with nothing more to be done but wait anxiously for the results.

Eddie left on his own, as he had commitments at the university and Granny had decided to stay on for a few more days. She had been vague in Daisy's hearing as to her reasons, but Daisy's careful (and inconspicuous) attention to the frequent references made to Bella in conversation between her mother and grandmother had led her to realise that Granny was hoping to be still in Ruatane when the baby was born. She caught occasional remarks along the lines of 'She certainly looks ready,' 'Danny's very good about getting her to put her feet up of an afternoon', or 'It really could be any time now.'

Bella might have looked ready, but it appeared that her baby was in no rush. Granny stayed on for over a week, and might have remained even longer had she not had a pressing reason to return to Auckland.

Eddie would turn twenty-one in October, which was not far off now. While he had not appeared overly excited about this himself when talking to Daisy, Aunt Sarah was determined to celebrate his coming-of-age in suitable style; 'She wants to make a big fuss over it,' was how Eddie had put it, in a tone of amused tolerance. By the time Granny left, she had received several letters from Aunt Sarah that Daisy gathered were encouraging her to hurry home.

'Sarah says she wants me there so we can decide on the menu and the flowers and everything,' Granny said. 'Not that she really needs any help with that sort of thing,' she added, smiling fondly. 'But it's nice to be asked.'

After the impossibility of attending Eddie's graduation ceremony in May, missing the celebrations for his twenty-first birthday was a fresh disappointment for Daisy. But she was careful not to spoil her grandmother's cheerful anticipation by giving any suggestion of complaint or moping; instead expressing a keen interest in the details.

Granny was more than ready to tell Daisy all she could possibly wish to know about what was planned.

'We're going to have a dinner party—I think there'll be a dozen sitting down to table. Then there'll be a few more people arriving after dinner, and we'll have music in the drawing-room—your Aunt Sarah said she's arranged a string quartet. The maids will move the furniture against the walls and roll up all the carpets, so there'll be room for dancing, just a few couples at a time. I'm sure it'll all be lovely.'

It was eight years since the one visit Daisy had ever made to her aunt's house in Auckland, but she had clear memories of those grand rooms, although she had never seen them full of guests. She closed her eyes and pictured the brilliantly polished dining table laden with serving dishes and shining cutlery; the sideboards with their heavy silver candlesticks; broad bowls crammed with flowers; the maids in their starched white aprons slipping in and out of the room with course after elaborate course.

The drawing room would be brightly lit, and full of laughter and lively conversation. Daisy tried to imagine the elegant music and the dancers gliding around the floor, the ladies in lovely dresses. No doubt it would be very different from the dance at Uncle Danny and Bella's wedding, with sheep-clipped grass rather than gleaming floorboards; no doubt, just as on that occasion, Eddie would be the most handsome man present.

Aunt Sarah also wanted Granny there to help with choosing their birthday gift for Eddie. They were to give him a watch, Granny told Daisy. He already had a pocket watch that they had given him when he was still at high school, its silver case somewhat battered, but a timepiece perfectly adequate for everyday use. The new watch, though, was to be a special one, to mark such an auspicious birthday.

'It's going to be a gold watch, one he can wear on his arm,' Granny said. 'The young men seem to like that sort these days—ever since the war, really—and we want him to have a watch he'll like, not an old-fashioned one. Your Aunt Sarah's been looking at quite a lot of them, and she says she's got it down to three to choose from, so I'll help her decide when I get back. Then we'll have Eddie's initials engraved on it in time for his birthday.'

Before he left the farm Eddie had mentioned to Daisy that he suspected their aunt and grandmother might be planning to give him a watch, and that he had dropped a hint or two as to the sort he most admired.

'If they're going to buy me one anyway, it might as well be a decent one,' he commented.

But Granny seemed to think it a great confidence she was sharing, and Daisy did not disillusion her by making even the slightest reference to Eddie's remarks.

Her own gift for Eddie, which also happened to involve his initials, had to be a modest one, though she put all the skill and care she was capable of into it. An ordinary cotton handkerchief would not be sufficient for a twenty-first birthday gift, but, thanks to the quality of the garments in Aunt Maudie's basket of cast-offs, Daisy had been able to make one out of a large square of silk cut from the most intact portion of a discarded petticoat. In one corner she stitched "E. M. S." in silver-grey thread, holding the cloth taut in an embroidery hoop borrowed from her aunt and making the letters in an elegant curved script drawn out for her by Lucy.

She finished the handkerchief just in time for Granny to take it back to Auckland with her, carefully wrapped in tissue paper and with a square of calico folded around it for protection. Granny would keep it safely in her chest of drawers until Eddie's birthday.

*

Barely a week after Granny's departure, Daisy and Benjy were met at the door of Uncle Richard's house after school one afternoon by Lucy, whose face showed that she was bursting with news.

'Bella has a little boy,' she said, clearly delighted at being the first bearer of such important tidings.

Aunt Maudie appeared from the kitchen, her hands dusty with flour. 'That's right. Danny came around to tell us this morning, and I popped in to see them this afternoon, just for a minute or two.'

'Are they all right?' Daisy asked.

'Yes, Bella's very well, and he's a lovely baby. She's tired, though, she won't be wanting a lot of visitors just yet. I expect you'll be able to go and see her next week.' Aunt Maudie smiled more broadly. 'I shouldn't think they'll be able to keep your grandpa away for long, though. Not with it being a boy.'

Daisy and her parents went down to her grandfather's farm in the spring cart the following Saturday afternoon. A piece of metal holding one of the cart's sides in place had snapped when her father was driving home from the creamery, and he wanted to see if Grandpa had anything suitable for a replacement, rather than having to buy a new part in town.

They had scarcely entered the house before Grandpa began regaling them on the wonders of the new baby, who was to be called Ernest.

'He's a fine size, all right. And clever, I'll bet, the way he's taking notice of things already. Danny was talking about getting him outside to show him the cows, but Bella didn't seem too keen on that just yet.'

Grandpa could still be heard talking about little Ernie when he and Daisy's father went off to look through Grandpa's large collection of useful bits and pieces for all sorts of farm machinery.

'I thought Pa would've had enough grandchildren by now not to make such a fuss over another one,' Mama remarked to Grandma. She shut the door behind the two men and came over to join Grandma at the kitchen table. 'You've got ten of them now, after all.'

Grandma rolled her eyes. 'Your own grandfather was just the same when Arfie was born.'

She meant Daisy's great-grandfather, and Arfie was Uncle Bill and Aunt Lily's oldest, named after Great-grandpa, and by all accounts a special favourite with him.

'This one's the first Kelly grandchild, and it's a boy, so he'll carry on the name when we're gone,' Grandma said. 'Men are like that, even the sensible ones like your Pa—you should've seen how silly he was when Joey was born. I suppose it's natural enough, a man wanting a son, then thinking the same way about grandsons.'

She glanced across the table at Daisy, who was helping Aunt Maisie set out cups and saucers.

'Ernie's a fine little chap, all right. But your father loves them all just the same as each other. It doesn't really make any difference whether they're boys or girls.'

Daisy's mother settled her cup more snugly on its saucer. 'No, of course it doesn't,' she said. 'Not these days, anyway. Girls can even be doctors now.'

That was definitely a smile hovering on Mama's lips; Daisy rather thought she saw an answering one from Grandma.

It would not have been polite for Daisy to tell Bella that all small babies looked much alike to her. But Ernie was plump and healthy, and when Daisy was holding him she felt a small surge of pride when Bella said the baby was smiling at her, despite being unable to see any sign of a smile herself. While Uncle Danny seemed in no rush to agree when Bella claimed that the baby almost never cried, it was obvious that both parents were immensely proud.

Daisy was not surprised when she heard that her Auckland family would not be attending little Ernie's christening, which took place two weeks after his birth. Granny would not have wanted to make the journey again so soon after her last visit, and everyone in Aunt Sarah's household was no doubt caught up in the preparations for Eddie's birthday.

There was quite a gathering of family members even so; far more than would comfortably have fitted in Bella's small parlour. Fortunately they had a lovely spring day for the occasion, so that the guests could spill outside and on to the verandah. Grandpa was still taking every opportunity to tell everyone what a fine new grandson he had, though he grinned a little shamefacedly when Grandma caught him at it. But on this particular day it was perfectly natural for people to fuss over the new baby, who seemed remarkably unconcerned as he was passed from one set of arms to another.

Daisy had to make do with hearing about Eddie's birthday celebrations from a distance. Her grandmother had promised to tell them all about it, and Granny was as good as her word. She described the food at their dinner party, with an astonishing five courses; the armloads of flowers carried inside to decorate the dining room and drawing room; the pretty gowns worn by their lady guests. After dinner a group of musicians had played for the dancers, and even the guests who had been present for dinner had somehow managed to do justice to a generous supper.

The whole affair had gone on till past midnight, a time repeated with some astonishment in Daisy's home.

'Fancy staying up that late,' her mother said, studying that part of the letter as if she doubted the evidence of her own eyes. 'And such a crowd of people in the house! Think of all the cleaning up afterwards.'

Daisy's father had paid a brief visit to the house in Auckland during the war, on his way to the army camp, so had a better idea of the running of Aunt Sarah's household. 'I suppose they left that to the maids and all. Still, I bet none of them felt much like getting up in the morning.'

'It's a good thing they don't have to milk cows, then.' Mama shook her head, her expression somewhere between amusement and mild disapproval. 'I don't know, I'm sure it was all very grand, but it does seem a lot of fuss just for a birthday.'

Eddie would have agreed with her, no doubt, having said much the same to Daisy before he left. A note from him addressed to Daisy was tucked into the same envelope as Granny's letter, and Daisy read it at the kitchen table while her parents moved on to discussing what needed doing on the farm, which was clearly a matter of much more interest to them than the latest news from Auckland.

Eddie's letter disposed of his party in a few brief sentences. The food had been good, the dancing "all right". He seemed pleased with his gold watch; Aunt Sarah had bought just the sort he had been hinting he might like, of a brand called Longines that came from Switzerland.

It was clear that for Eddie the highlight of his birthday celebrations had been a weekend camping trip he took with two of his friends from university. They had gone hiking in the hills west of Auckland, and pitched their tent in the bush close to one of the west coast beaches.

The sea along that coast was far more wild than in places like Ruatane on the eastern side of the country, and Eddie admitted that he would have been wary of swimming there even if the water had not been too cold. But he and his companions had had a fine time roaming along sand sculpted into ridges by the wind, and clambering up a large, vaguely lion-shaped rock lashed by salt spray.

When they tired of being attacked by sand-laden wind, they had explored the bush, making use of roughly cut paths when the route suited them, or pushing their way through thick growth to explore what looked an interesting direction. On one occasion this had led to a slither down the slick, muddy side of a gully for Eddie, whose spirits had clearly not been at all dampened by the experience; Daisy thought she detected a hint of pride over just how thoroughly coated in mud he had managed to get.

Afterwards he had given himself a rough wash in a stream, and had changed into fresh clothes before their return to town, as he might otherwise not have been allowed on the train. The muddy trousers, he reported, had been declared not worth washing, and barely fit for rags, thanks to the sharp twigs and occasional rocks on his slide down the gully.

Granny had mentioned, no doubt in her usual mild way, that it was a good thing Eddie had not taken his smart new watch on the outing; 'As if I would have!' Eddie wrote, his pen-strokes more vigorous on those words. Daisy could hear his voice in her head, which made her smile.

He had not taken the handkerchief she had made for him, either; it was much too nice for that, he said. Eddie managed to make it sound almost as grand a gift as his new watch when he told her he had worn the handkerchief at his party, and would save it for best.

She folded the note and took it through to her room, to be stowed away with other letters he had sent her over the years.

Chapter Twenty-Three

Granny's description of the party, along with Eddie's more meagre version, was the closest Daisy was likely to get to such a grand occasion while living in Ruatane, and the modest family gathering for baby Ernie's christening would probably be the last celebration of any kind until Christmas. For now, the rapidly approaching matriculation examinations were occupying most of her waking thoughts.

Their application forms and the necessary twenty guineas had been sent off well in time, along with special certificates signed by the headmaster stating that Daisy and Benjy had each satisfactorily carried out a course of practical work in science.

This was a special requirement for the science section of the examinations, as they had discovered when studying the forms. Daisy had her doubts over just how thoroughly they could be said to have covered the subject to matriculation level, given the scant attention paid to some areas of science as well as the many experiments they had simply repeated from their fifth form during this last year. But Benjy brushed aside any such qualms.

'I bet no one ever checks up on that stuff, anyway,' he said. 'Eddie more or less said so, didn't he?'

Daisy was perfectly willing to be reassured; Eddie had indeed said that he had heard something along those lines when talking to lecturers and other people he knew at the university.

Spring was always one of the busiest times of year on the farms, with ploughing and then planting out the potato crop in addition to all the usual work of milking and tending to the animals. Aunt Maudie had taken on driving Benjy and Daisy home every Friday; thanks to Benjy's success at getting the two of them excused from the Friday afternoon drill lesson, she was able to get out to the valley and back before dark without having to rush uncomfortably.

The examinations were to take place in early December, which was now only a matter of weeks away, and Daisy and Benjy were studying harder than ever, including on Friday and Saturday nights. Benjy even managed to convince Grandma that the work would do him no great harm, though he did report various worried mutterings from her, and frequent urgings to come through to the parlour of an evening instead of staying in the kitchen by himself.

'I just keep saying I'll be there in five minutes, and that keeps her happy for a bit,' Benjy said.

During the week, when they were staying in town, the two of them studied together, testing each other from the textbooks' lists of questions or from the notes in their exercise books. They worked out a plan of study, doing two or three different subjects a night.

Uncle Richard suggested that it might be best to abandon Daisy's Latin lessons so that she could devote more time to preparing for the examinations. Somewhat reluctantly, she agreed. It was all very well wanting to avoid being too far behind everyone else when it came to taking Latin at university; she would not even be going there unless she passed her matriculation.

'Of course there's no reason not to continue with your Latin studies, Timmy,' Uncle Richard said.

Timmy's initial response was outrage at what he claimed was the unfairness of Daisy's "getting out of having to do Latin". Faced with the inarguable fact that Daisy was only dropping her Latin lessons to spend even more time on other subjects, Timmy went off to his own lesson, dragging his feet so dramatically that he rucked up an edge of the hall rug.

By the following evening he had come up with the claim that he needed to practise his batting every afternoon before the cricket season got fully underway, which meant he would not be able to start his homework till after dinner, and could not possibly fit in Latin on top of that.

His father managed to hold firm against Timmy's excuses and generally woebegone demeanour for almost two weeks before announcing that perhaps they had all had enough of Latin lessons for the time being.

'We'll have the whole of next year to bring you up to a proper standard in the subject before you go off to join Nicky,' Uncle Richard said, the hint of a smile in his eyes. 'I can assure you that I'll be proof against all arguments when February arrives, Timmy, so I suggest you enjoy your freedom for now.'

The daylight hours were longer, with summer so close, and Timmy did indeed make the most of them, usually playing outside until his mother called him in to clean himself up before dinner. On the warmer afternoons Daisy and Benjy often took their books out to the verandah, from where they had a clear view of Timmy with his cricket bat. He showed some impressive agility as he leapt and twisted to connect bat and ball, coping with awkward bounces off the side of the house.

Daisy and Benjy were both willing enough to express admiration when Timmy asked if they had noticed a particularly impressive shot, but they resolutely refused all his pleas to join in the game.

'We've got to study, Timmy. Sorry, but you'll just have to manage on your own.' Daisy had to make much the same remark so often that after a time the words emerged almost without conscious thought.

'Unless you can talk Lucy or Flora into it,' Benjy sometimes added; purely for the pleasure, as he privately told Daisy, of seeing the look on Timmy's face.

'*They're* no use,' Timmy grumbled.

Daisy and Benjy had grown quite skilled at studying against a background of thuds and crunches, punctuated by loud groans or whoops of delight, depending on the success or otherwise of Timmy's latest attempt with the bat.

'List the forms of carbon,' Daisy asked Benjy one afternoon.

'Crystalline and amorphous,' he answered promptly. 'Crystalline carbon occurs in two forms, diamond and graphite. Amorphous carbon may be found as charcoal, coal or... what's that last one? No, don't tell me... lampblack, that's it. It's a product of the imperfect combustion of oil and coal.'

'That's right,' Daisy said. 'It's when there's not enough oxygen to—'

'Never mind that,' Benjy interrupted. 'We just need to know the definition, not what it means. All right, I'll ask you one.' He ran his finger down a list of topics. 'Give the properties of nitrogen.'

'A colourless, tasteless, odourless gas. If it's mixed with oxygen and subjected to electric sparks, oxides of nitrogen are produced. A mixture of hydrogen and nitrogen treated the same way forms ammonia.'

Benjy checked the textbook, frowning. 'It doesn't say that here.'

'Doesn't it? Let me see.' She scanned the section he pointed to, and smiled. 'It's the same really, Benjy. It just mentions odourless before tasteless, and it doesn't say that bit about ammonia. I think Uncle Richard told me about that—ammonia's quite interesting, because it's good for killing germs.'

'Well, I expect you're right, but I think I'll stick to what's in the book.'

The difference in their approaches had become apparent in their first days of revising together. Daisy enjoyed seeing the patterns of structure or properties that linked the different classes of elements and compounds they had studied, but Benjy could not be budged from the bare lists of names and numbers. It was the same with the various axioms and scientific laws, where Benjy was content to rely on his excellent memory to learn them off by heart while Daisy liked to understand as much as she could of the reasoning behind them. For him, subjects like science and mathematics were no more than a somewhat irritating means towards his end of attending university; vague though he still appeared to be about just what he would do once he was there.

Fortunately this did not stop the two of them working amicably together. In response to Daisy's next question, Benjy quoted Boyle's Law word-for-word as it appeared in the textbook. They agreed that was enough chemistry for the day, and moved on to practising their irregular verbs for French.

Aunt Maudie, prompted, Daisy suspected, by a quiet suggestion from Uncle Richard, said Daisy and Benjy were quite busy enough studying for their examinations, and would not allow them to help with getting dinner on.

It was kindly meant, no doubt, and they did make good use of the extra time, but it also led to a certain amount of friction with Lucy, who clearly felt herself to be ill-used. Meal preparations now involved loud clattering of utensils or slamming down of dishes, audible from the verandah or parlour, and halted only by an exasperated, 'Be careful with that, Lucy,' from Aunt Maudie. Later in the evening there would be pointed remarks over the washing-up as to the large number of potatoes that had needed peeling, or carrots to chop, or cleaning up to be done.

'It might be just as easy to help as listen to all that,' Benjy murmured to Daisy one afternoon, and she quietly agreed.

Uncle Richard always asked over dinner how their study was going, his manner making it clear that he was genuinely interested. He also did his best to help with any topics that might be puzzling them, although he freely admitted to having forgotten a good deal relating to subjects he had not made use of since university.

'This matriculation business does seem to have been going on for an awfully long time,' Lucy said one evening when her father had just made an attempt to explain the difference between a stable equilibrium and a neutral one, and had promised to hunt out one of his own old textbooks to check his explanation. 'You two must be sick of it all.'

Benjy swallowed a mouthful before answering. 'Not much use being sick of it. We just have to get on with it.'

'But we don't seem to have heard about anything but exams for months and months now.'

'I think that's a slight exaggeration, my dear,' Uncle Richard said. 'But these examinations are a significant event for Benjy and Daisy, and we must all do our best to support them.'

'Of course we must,' Aunt Maudie said. 'It's not so very long now, anyway.'

Lucy sniffed. 'I certainly hope not. You poor things, it must be ever so boring,' she added with lofty condescension.

Daisy alternated between a wish just as fervent as Lucy's that it might all be over and done with, and a nagging sense that there was yet more study she and Benjy could do if there were only a little more time. But the final few days passed, December began, and on the first Tuesday of the month Daisy and Benjy entered the school grounds to sit the first of the examinations.

Directed by Mr Grant, they made their way behind one of the primary school classrooms to what was little more than a storage space (fortunately one with a window) that had been emptied of its stacked chairs and piles of textbooks to make room for them. A man called Mr Webb, who as well as having a menswear store on Ruatane's main street was chairman of the school committee, had offered to be supervisor, and when Daisy and Benjy came in he was already installed beside a trestle table under the window. Two desks had been set up for them, pushed against opposite walls to be as far apart as the small room allowed.

They exchanged a quiet 'Good luck,' took their seats, and waited for the instruction to turn over the examination paper.

By the end of the following week, most of the hours that had not directly involved examinations were little more than a blur in Daisy's memory. They must have eaten and drunk, and washed themselves; undressed and gone to bed at night, and risen and dressed again in the morning. She had a vague recollection of having done such things, but it paled against sharp-edged images of the hours she and Benjy had spent in that little room.

From time to time the muffled voice of a teacher crept through the wall from the neighbouring classroom, and when the classes were let outside for morning or afternoon breaks she might hear the laughter of their more carefree schoolfellows in the playground, but within the room the only sound was the scratch of pen against paper, scribbling ever more rapidly as the hands of the clock drew closer to the moment when Mr Webb would announce that it was time to stop writing, and Daisy would lift her hand and realise just how badly her wrist was aching.

French and history each had a single examination; the only two of their subjects to do so. Neither brought any nasty surprises, with the required verbs and their forms familiar ones and the translation fairly straightforward. In history, where the university calendar had informed them the questions would range over the period from 55BC to 1485AD, Daisy found the names and dates of the various kings and battles in that long period between Julius Caesar's invasion of Britain and the Wars of the Roses coming readily to mind.

English had two examinations, each of them three hours long. Daisy and Benjy compared notes when walking back to Uncle Richard's afterwards, and on both occasions agreed that it had gone fairly well. Benjy said he had spent longer than he had intended while writing about

262

an imaginary visit to a play, as the subject had caught his imagination, but had realised in time and brought his essay to a proper conclusion, as well as completing the large number of questions devoted to sentence structure, punctuation, and general grammar.

When completing their matriculation applications they had chosen the Physical Science option, Mr Ritchie's emphasis on chemistry making this the obvious choice. Daisy had no intention of taking the supposedly easier (and aimed at girls) option of Home Science, and since they had done nothing in the way of botany or physiology it would have been foolish to select Natural Science.

Daisy had spent more time studying for this subject than any of their others, since it appeared to be the most relevant to her future medical studies, working on her own as well as with Benjy. Those hours and hours rewarded her when the questions in the examination papers were reassuringly familiar. She could picture the periodic table in her mind; recall the lists of elements and compounds in their textbooks; almost smell the results of various chemistry experiments over the years. There was even a question about pendulums, which she answered at some length and with a labelled diagram thanks to her clear memories of the special lesson on pendulums they had had with the school inspector.

She so thoroughly lost herself in the questions that when Mr Webb said, 'Pens down, please,' it took a moment for her to remember where she was. She left the room after the second of their two science examinations feeling cautiously confident, only to find that Benjy's mood was quite different.

'I think I got my sulphates and sulphites mixed up,' he said, his satchel dragging on the floor as they trudged down the corridor. 'And then I went blank on nitric acid—I couldn't remember which bit had a two after it and where the three went. I hope I didn't mess the whole thing up.'

They were to have another examination that afternoon, and the thought of two hours' worth of algebra would not have been helping to lift Benjy's spirits.

'I'm sure it won't matter if you only got a couple of little things like that wrong.' Daisy was careful to say nothing of her own more encouraging experience; that would only make Benjy feel worse.

'No, but what if I messed the whole thing up?'

It was unusual to see him so glum. 'You won't have done that, Benjy. Not with all the work we've done, and you're so good at remembering things. Anyway, I bet you've done really well in French and English, so that'll help make up for it.'

Benjy shrugged. 'Maybe. Those ones weren't too bad, anyway.' He made an attempt at a smile, with only limited success. 'You know, it got so bad once or twice in there, when I was struggling with those formulas and all that, I wondered if I might've been better off doing agricultural science for matric, with all the stuff I've heard from Pa about farming over the years.'

'That would only work if you'd taken any notice of him,' Daisy said, and was rewarded with a snort of laughter from Benjy.

'Ah well, there's no use worrying about it now,' he said, sounding much more like his usual self.

'No, there's not,' Daisy agreed.

They settled into a quiet corner of the school grounds and took out their packed lunches.

While she chewed her sandwiches, Daisy mulled over the salutary experience of their latest examination. It seemed to her that it revealed the limitations of blindly memorising bare lists of facts. If you had no idea what any of it meant, forgetting one little item on the list could leave you hopelessly lost. Rather like finding your way along a complicated and unfamiliar route by counting crossroads, with no real idea of your destination; which might be all very well until you missed a turning.

But this was something to remember for her own future use, not to make Benjy feel bad. They finished lunch and tidied away the remnants, then took the opportunity for a short stroll around the school grounds as a change from the hours of sitting still.

The bell rang, signalling the end of the lunch break. It was time to go back to that small room and find out what the next two hours had in store for them.

It had never seemed quite so far from the school to Uncle Richard's house than on those days when Daisy and Benjy had examinations in both morning and afternoon. Just trudging along the footpath took all Daisy's energy, leaving nothing over for speech. Benjy was in a similar state, making for a silent journey.

On the first such occasion, Aunt Maudie said the two of them looked as if they had not slept for a week.

'Get out of those uniforms and then have a nice sit-down,' she said as soon as Benjy had closed the door behind them. 'I don't want to see you getting any of those books out tonight, either.'

'I'd just as soon not,' Benjy said, letting his satchel slip from his grasp to land on the floor with a soft thump. 'I don't know, though, we probably should go over a couple of things.'

Reluctant though she was to argue with her aunt, and tempting as the thought of ignoring their textbooks for an evening was, Daisy echoed Benjy's statement with as much vigour as she could muster. But when

Uncle Richard came in from his study, he agreed with Aunt Maudie.

'Perhaps after dinner you could spend five minutes or so looking through your notes on tomorrow's subject,' he said. 'And then I suggest you retire for the evening rather earlier than usual. I'd say that at this stage a good night's sleep would be more useful than anything.'

As her uncle almost certainly knew a great deal more about examinations than anyone else among Daisy's acquaintance, it was easy to let herself be persuaded; all the more so when she really was so very tired. After changing out of their school clothes, she and Benjy settled into the parlour's most comfortable armchairs.

Daisy had briefly wondered if Lucy might bridle at the special attention being given to Benjy and herself, but you could never tell with Lucy. Rather than showing the least sign of jealousy, she appeared genuinely sympathetic; almost overpoweringly so. She took it upon herself to fuss over Daisy and Benjy, scurrying back and forth from the kitchen with glasses of milk and plates of her mother's nicest biscuits, and enlisting Flora to help with setting up side tables within easy reach and arranging footstools.

'I could stand a bit more of this,' Benjy said in a low voice when Lucy had darted from the room in search of fresh biscuits.

Daisy sank a little deeper into the armchair, resting her head against the cushion thoughtfully arranged by Lucy. 'I could, too.'

'Better make the most of it,' Benjy said, wriggling his sock-clad feet on the footstool. 'I shouldn't think it'll last long.'

Two English and two science examinations were bad enough, but having to sit three in mathematics bordered on an outrage in Benjy's opinion.

'It feels like we've been swotting for the maths ones just about *forever*,' he grumbled while they were studying one afternoon, irritably scratching lines through a quadratic equation that had refused to reveal its unknown quantity. 'I don't know why we have to have more of them than anything else. I wouldn't mind if we had three English ones instead.'

By the time they faced the third mathematics examination, Daisy was in full agreement. One had been entirely devoted to arithmetic, with question after question on fractions and decimals, square roots and percentages, and measuring the areas of various different shapes. The second was algebra, with factors and graphs and equations of varying complexity to solve.

This final one was in geometry, and it did have the large redeeming quality of being the last of all their examinations for matriculation.

Daisy and Benjy entered the little storeroom for the last time, and alongside the usual pens and pencils set out the drawing instruments they had been told to bring along for this examination. Benjy had a cloth bag with his set squares and other tools, which he emptied onto his desk in a clatter of wood and metal. They had been purchased for him by Grandpa after Mr Ritchie sent away for them on his behalf.

Daisy pulled from her satchel the wooden box containing her own drawing instruments. Benjy's were serviceable; hers had a certain beauty. She placed the items in a neat line along the edge of the desk: the compasses, with one pointed end and a place to screw in a pencil on the other side, and the semi-circular protractor, both in polished brass; the set squares of a reddish-brown wood she had been told was mahogany; the folding ruler, mahogany with fine brass hinges. The box and its contents had arrived from Auckland in her first year at high school, paid for no doubt by Aunt Sarah, but chosen by Eddie, who had gone to a particular shop in Auckland that specialized in such things.

She closed the box and pushed it to the far side of the desk, then ran her fingers lightly over the protractor, feeling the contrast between the smooth brass and the markings etched along its edge. Just for a moment, she closed her eyes so that she could picture Eddie, smiling at her with his face full of confidence. 'You'll be all right,' he had said. 'I know you can do it.'

The anxious knot within her had subsided to a mere fluttering. Daisy opened her eyes and waited for the instruction to turn over the examination paper.

After having every waking moment crammed full for so long, when the examinations were over Daisy found herself at something of a loose end until term finished. She and Benjy muddled along through their final few days at school, reading poems during Mr Grant's classes and helping clean the benches in Mr Ritchie's. On their final day they joined in with packing away books and washing blackboards, then piled up the desks and chairs in Mr Grant's classroom.

By the doorway of what had been their form room all through their four years of high school, they shook hands with Mr Grant for what might be the final time.

'Please accept my very best wishes,' Mr Grant said. 'You in your medical career, Daisy—and Benjy, in whatever direction life takes you. I expect great things of you both.'

They joined the knot of pupils moving through the school gates and out along the road. Farewells were called back and forth as their companions scattered, singly or in small groups, heading towards their own homes. Some of them would be back next year; others, like Daisy and Benjy, were leaving school behind them.

Timmy had run on ahead, and none of their other schoolmates lived very close to Uncle Richard's, so Daisy and Benjy had the final section of the walk to themselves as they made their way along the road, through the gate, past the neat garden beds and up to the house. Aunt Maudie was to take them out to the valley, and the gig was out of its shed and ready, the horse harnessed and cropping grass by the front fence.

They had done most of their packing the previous evening, so all that was left was to change out of their uniforms and add them to their suitcases.

When she emerged from the girls' bedroom, Daisy found the whole of Uncle Richard's household assembled in the parlour, Aunt Maudie checking her hat in the mirror over the mantel while the others stood ready to say their farewells.

Timmy shook Benjy's hand, but squirmed away from Daisy's attempt to kiss him goodbye; he did, however, snatch up her suitcase and announce he would carry it outside for her, which she decided to take as his own way of showing fondness. Flora and Lucy both embraced her, Lucy even shedding tears, although she would no doubt see them again within days.

Aunt Maudie patted her hat in place and turned from the mirror.

'I'm sure we'll all miss having you two here,' she said, watching as Daisy extricated herself from Lucy's firm grasp.

'We certainly will,' Uncle Richard said. 'You've both been welcome additions to the household—and I'll feel the loss of my partner in medical inquiry.' He turned a warm smile on Daisy.

Daisy and Benjy squeezed onto the seat of the gig beside Aunt Maudie, and twisted around to wave at the others, who lined the verandah to see them off.

'Of course you'd be welcome to come and stay with us again any time,' Aunt Maudie said, her words set against the clip-clop of the horse's hooves as it settled into a steady trot. 'And perhaps you'll see Nicky sometimes when you're up in Auckland,' she added, brightening visibly.

'Yes, we might be able to,' Daisy said.

Benjy slipped her a grin. 'I'll make sure we do,' he said.

Aunt Maudie took Benjy as far as his garden gate. Grandma appeared in the kitchen doorway as he came up the path.

'Come in for a cup of tea,' she called, but Aunt Maudie shook her head.

'Not today, Ma,' she called back. 'I want to get home before it's too late.'

'Wait a minute, then, I've got a couple of things for you.' Grandma disappeared inside, and Daisy stepped down from the gig to keep a steadying hand on the horse's bridle until Benjy ran back down the path with what proved to be a box containing carrots and lettuces.

He stowed the box under the seat, Daisy climbed back up, and Aunt Maudie gave the reins a shake.

'I'd better not mention I've got plenty of lettuces in the vegetable plot,' she said to Daisy. 'Your grandma won't let anyone get away without some baking or something from the garden, though. It's easier just to take it than argue,' she added, smiling.

A short time later they were pulling up in front of Daisy's home, and her mother was hurrying up from the direction of the cowshed to meet them, a few streaks of brown across the heavy calico apron she wore only for milking.

'I'm glad I caught you, Maudie—we did an extra batch of bread last night, and I saved a nice loaf for you. I put by a few eggs, too, in case you don't have enough at home.'

'My goodness, I've done well today, what with you and Ma,' Aunt Maudie said, eyes twinkling.

'It's all in a basket on the bench, Daisy. You run and get it, I'm too dirty for the kitchen.'

Daisy returned a few moments later with the basket to find the two of them deep in conversation, her mother loosely holding the bridle while the horse took full advantage of the opportunity to snatch a few mouthfuls of grass. Aunt Maudie paused from telling Daisy's mother how much she was looking forward to having Nicky home for the long holidays, took the basket from Daisy, and lifted the cloth to peep at its contents.

'Mm, that bread looks lovely,' she said. 'It'll make a change from shop bread. And I could do with the extra eggs, my hens have been lazy just lately.'

'You won't have Daisy and Benjy to feed on the weekdays any more, though,' Mama said, wiping her hands on a comparatively clean patch of apron before giving Daisy's shoulders a squeeze.

'No, but I'm sure Nicky will have a good appetite—even more than usual, I mean. He'll be looking forward to proper meals again after all this time.'

She stowed the basket under the seat and took up the reins. 'I'd better get a move on. If the girls go forgetting to start the meat cooking, goodness knows what time we'll end up having dinner.'

'Thanks for bringing me home today, Aunt Maudie,' Daisy said. 'And thank you for having me to stay all this time. I could never have gone to high school at all without you and Uncle Richard.'

'It's been no trouble at all, darling. We really will miss you, you know. Make sure you come and see us over the summer, before you and Benjy go off to Auckland.'

'It's so nice to have you back,' Mama said when they had waved Aunt Maudie off, her gig sending up small trails of dust in its wake. 'I've made some of those coconut biscuits you especially like, we can have them with our cuppa. And I thought we might have one of those chocolate puddings tonight.'

Daisy slipped an arm around her mother's waist, carefully avoiding the brown smears on her apron.

'It's lovely to be home—and not to have any exams to study for! I'll be able to help you and Papa instead of being stuck in my books all the time.'

'Yes, you must be glad to have finished all that business.' Mama glanced over her shoulder down towards the cowshed. 'Your father must've just about finished by now, but I might pop back down and do the last one or two with him.'

Daisy gazed around herself, taking in the hills to either side, the bush and the paddocks, and their own little cottage facing out towards the sea. Four years of going back and forth from the valley to her uncle's house every week; four years of trailing to and from the little high school; four years of poems and French verbs and struggling to do chemistry experiments in their sparsely equipped science room. Four years of homework and study, all leading up to those all-important examinations. She had done her best; now there was nothing to do but wait to find out whether or not her best was good enough.

She released her mother from her embrace, and picked up her suitcase. 'That's a good idea, Mama. I'll put the kettle on,' she said.

Chapter Twenty-Four

It still felt strange to have no schoolwork to do, but Daisy had no difficulty finding plenty to keep herself occupied; during the daytime, at any rate. She helped with milking and other work around the farm, and with getting the meals on and clearing up after them.

The imminent arrival of the Auckland family members brought an extra burst of activity. Along with Granny and Eddie, Aunt Sarah would be paying her annual visit to the farm; a visit which Daisy's mother always seemed to feel required the house to be not merely neat and tidy, but as close as possible to pristine.

'Anyone would think the King and Queen were coming to visit—bringing half a dozen dukes and duchesses with them, as well,' Papa teased as under her direction he unhooked the parlour curtains.

'Daisy, take those outside and give them a good shake. You can do the bedroom ones next, Davie. I just want the place looking nice, that's all. Sarah must be used to having everything just so.'

Her father took down the other curtains, and Daisy duly carried armloads of calico out the front door and stood at the top of the steps to shake out any dust. Afterwards she draped the curtains over the verandah rail; there was no point taking them back inside until all the other work that was likely to generate extra dust had been finished. They took the mattresses outside for a thorough airing, Daisy and her mother carrying one between them while her father easily hoisted the others.

All the mats were rolled up and taken out to the clothesline to have the dust beaten out of them. Daisy was in the midst of hanging several over the line when her father appeared around the side of the house, carrying a bucket of water with a scrubbing brush in it.

'That's the trouble with taking the curtains down, now it turns out the windows need cleaning,' he said, setting down the bucket to help Daisy with the mats. 'Your ma's doing them on the inside, but I don't want her trying to get up a ladder for the outsides.'

He picked up the heaviest of the mats and tossed them over the line, while Daisy arranged the lighter ones.

'Thanks, Papa,' she said. 'I'll make a start on these, then I'll go in and help Mama with the windows when I get sick of beating rugs.'

Her father took up his bucket once more. 'I think your ma would have me painting the house on top of everything else, if there was time for that before they all turn up from Auckland,' he said, grinning at Daisy. 'It's a good thing they're coming next week.'

*

Their modest cottage could never be made to look remotely like Aunt Sarah's grand house in Auckland, but by the time they had finished their flurry of activity the whole house smelt of soap and polish. The garden was not neglected, either, with trimming and dead-heading in the flowerbeds and all the vegetable beds weeded.

'Doesn't the garden look lovely?' Granny said as soon as the buggy, borrowed from Grandpa for the occasion, had drawn up to the garden gate. 'What a show the roses are putting on this year.' And when she was ushered into the kitchen ahead of everyone else, she lost no time in saying how smart the house was.

'You always keep everything so nice, Beth,' she said to Daisy's mother. 'I hope you didn't go to any extra work for us.'

'Oh, it's no trouble really,' Mama said, but she was clearly gratified by Granny's praise. Eddie and Aunt Sarah made polite comments of vague agreement, but Granny was the only one of the three with any real idea of what was involved in getting the house into such a state.

'Don't let on to anyone else, but she got me to do most of it,' Papa said, making everyone laugh.

'Well, I'm sure you were a big help,' Granny said, patting Papa on the arm. 'You were always a good boy.'

On the way out to the farm, Granny and Aunt Sarah had both asked Daisy how the examinations had gone.

'Fairly well, I think. I'm not really sure,' Daisy said, doing her best to sound neither overly confident nor as anxious as she secretly was.

She appreciated their well-meant assurances that she was certain to have passed, but she privately felt that if it were at all possible she would sooner forget about examinations until the results arrived, which would probably be weeks away yet.

It was different with Eddie, of course. He waited for their first opportunity of some privacy, which was after dinner on the evening of their arrival. He then extracted from her a brief account of her examinations in the various subjects, along with a more frank admission as to how she felt she might have done, and confirmed that the results were likely to come out in the third week of January.

'Sounds like they went all right for you—no nasty surprises in the questions, either,' he said. 'It's over and done now, anyway. Best not to chew it all over.'

271

Eddie was as good as his word, saying no more about the examinations, and shifting the course of the conversation whenever anyone else raised the subject.

Granny and Aunt Sarah lost no time in visiting the other family members up and down the valley, either walking or borrowing the family's gig. They went to Grandma's first of all, where it seemed they were regaled at some length over how hard Benjy had been studying for the examinations, and how well he was sure to have done; Granny's report on this visit was one of the occasions when Eddie felt the need to turn the discussion into a fresh direction.

Aunt Sarah was particularly eager to go up to Uncle Bill's farm, as she wanted to see Aunt Lily, who was some sort of cousin to her, so they went there next. They had an enjoyable visit, according to Granny, with Aunt Lily playing several pieces on the piano. Emma had been keen for them to see her little boy, Dougie, who had just turned seven and was doing very well at school, according to his mother and grandmother.

'It was lovely to see them again,' Granny said. 'And Dougie's such a nice boy, ever so polite. But it does make me sad to see your Uncle Alf like that. I don't think he'll ever get any better, not after all this time since the war.'

'I'm surprised you saw him at all,' Daisy's father said. 'He usually makes himself pretty scarce if anyone comes around.'

'Well, it was only for a minute when we first got there. He said hello, then he slipped off somewhere before we'd even sat down.'

'I'm not sure he said as much as that,' Aunt Sarah remarked. 'I certainly didn't make out any words.'

Granny sighed. 'No, you're probably right. It's such a shame, when I think of what he was like as a boy.'

They went next door to visit Granny's older brothers, Daisy's Uncle John and Uncle Harry, and their families, but it was decided that they would leave seeing Aunt Maudie and the others who lived outside the valley until Christmas, which was now only days away.

Daisy's grandmother and aunt would, no doubt, have been happy to take her with them if she had asked, but she was more than content to stay home with Eddie; and not just because the relations would probably all ask in a well-meaning way about the examinations.

Staying home meant being in company with Eddie through most of their waking hours. They helped with milking; collected eggs from the fowl run; fed and groomed the horses. It was a busyness very different from the months and months of study, much too enjoyable to seem like work. After dinner the two of them sat off to one side of the parlour, leaving the grown-ups to talk; or (in Papa's case) to doze quietly if they all sat up longer than Daisy's parents usually did.

Daisy had grown used to somewhat later hours from spending so much time in her uncle's house, but after a day full of activity and spent mostly in the open air the evenings brought a pleasant languor that was quite unlike the tightness in her temples and dull ache behind her eyes that hours of study tended to bring on.

When the others lit candles from the lamp and went off to their various rooms, Daisy made up her own bed, which had to be out here in the parlour while Aunt Sarah was staying with them. She retrieved sheets and blankets from where she had left them folded and out of sight behind the sofa that morning, and tucked them into place. The sofa was not quite long enough, as well as being rather lumpy, but that did not prevent her from drifting off into a delicious sleep within minutes of putting out the lamp.

Christmas came the week after Eddie's arrival. The church was packed for the service that morning, and when the congregation emerged into sunshine people milled about or wandered from group to group, wishing each other a happy Christmas and catching up with acquaintances who might live at some distance, to be met only on special occasions such as today.

After the service, Daisy and her family went to Grandma's for Christmas lunch. With all of Grandma and Grandpa's children and grandchildren present, as well as Granny, Eddie and Aunt Sarah, they made a crowd of twenty-seven. The large dining table in Grandma's kitchen, which had benches down each side, sat ten fairly comfortably; today twelve adults managed to squeeze around it, along with baby Ernie and Aunt Rosie's youngest, Ian, who were both small enough to be held on laps.

Grandpa and Benjy had set up a long trestle table outdoors, shaded by trees, for everyone else. Daisy had the distinct impression that Lucy was on the point of working herself into a state of indignation at having to sit with the little ones, unwise as that would have been in Grandma's house, but any complaints from her were forestalled when she realised that Aunt Maisie, Uncle Joe and Uncle Mick were to eat outside with them; especially when Aunt Maisie took charge of Aunt Rosie's other children, who were much the youngest of the group.

Their plates were loaded with roast lamb, new potatoes, boiled carrots, peas and beans. It was a warm day, and by the time Daisy had ploughed through the meat and vegetables, followed by a generous helping of steaming hot Christmas pudding swimming in thick cream, she might have been in danger of nodding off where she sat, had she not gone somewhat beyond comfortably full.

When even Nicky, who according to Aunt Maudie had hollow legs, said he could not fit in another bite, Daisy and the other girls gathered up the empty plates and carried them through to the kitchen.

It took several trips back and forth, during which time she noticed Eddie and Benjy organising the younger boys into some sort of game while Uncle Joe and Uncle Mick fiddled about stuffing tobacco into their pipes and coaxing them into life.

Uncle Joe succeeded first; he drew on the pipe, eyes half-closed in pleasure, then hurriedly pulled it out of his mouth to let a cough escape. Daisy had heard him claim that smoking eased his chest, though she had seen no sign of it; quite the reverse, if anything. But he said that a doctor in the convalescent hospital where he had been a patient after being invalided out of the war had recommended it, and a hospital doctor must know more than a farm girl who thought she might be able to go to medical school.

The men who had been among those pressed around the dining table were shooed from the kitchen for the cleaning up to begin. They went willingly enough, probably glad to escape the hot kitchen (not to mention any risk of being asked to help). They ambled off down the kitchen steps and joined Uncle Joe and Uncle Mick at the outdoor table, while inside dishes were stacked on the bench and the basin was filled with the first of what would be several loads of hot, soapy water.

Daisy counted eleven women and girls in the kitchen, but in spite of so many bodies having to move back and forth past each other in somewhat cramped conditions, the work went smoothly. Grandma assigned tasks to everybody, with Aunt Sarah only allowed to stack the dried dishes while the others took turns washing and drying. The heaviest task, carrying the dirty water outside, was left to Daisy and her younger aunts.

Four-year-old Katie had insisted that she wanted to play outside, but in her struggle to keep up with the older children she fell over almost at once. Her high-pitched screams brought Aunt Rosie running out to snatch her up and comfort her, although it appeared that Katie was mostly upset at the thought that her pretty dress might have been torn. The dress turned out to be quite undamaged, and Katie herself had sustained nothing worse than a slightly skinned knee, which was duly fussed over when Aunt Rosie had carried her inside and sat her at the kitchen table. She was soon happily working her way through a plate of biscuits that Aunt Maisie loaded up for her.

There was a cheerful buzz of conversation in the kitchen, punctuated with excited whoops from the garden; a glance through the window told

Daisy this happened when someone was tagged in a chasing game, or a tossed ball was successfully caught. Most of the uncles were still sitting at the table, but Uncle Bernard had joined Eddie, Benjy and the smaller boys in an open area of the back garden. He was striding about, shouting encouragement to the players when not busy tossing little Ian in the air, making the child squeal with delight.

'Nicky and Timmy wanted to bring their cricket things,' Aunt Maudie said when the thud of a ball against the side of the house made them all look up. 'We said they could make do with a football, though. Richard said it was all very well risking his own windows, but Pa's were another matter.'

'Quite right, too,' Grandma said. 'That'd be a jolly nuisance.'

'And I was worried they might hurt one of the little ones, so I made sure they only brought a squashy sort of ball,' Aunt Maudie said. 'Nicky's used to playing with boys his own age at school, and Timmy's shot up these last few months.'

'You wouldn't think they'd want to run around in this heat,' Aunt Maisie remarked.

'No, but they don't seem to notice it,' Aunt Maudie said, peering out the window. 'Well, at least they'll wear themselves out, then we should all get a decent sleep tonight.'

Aunt Rosie crossed the room to get a view through the window. 'Especially if those big boys wear themselves out, too,' she said, grinning rather foolishly.

For some reason this remark threw Aunt Maudie, as well as Daisy's mother, into a fit of giggling, which set Aunt Rosie off as well.

'What's got into you girls?' Grandma asked, looking over from the washbasin.

'Nothing, Ma.' For a moment or two Aunt Maudie looked no older than Lucy as, with a visible struggle, she schooled herself into calmness. 'Just checking up on the boys.'

'Well, mind you don't drop one of my good plates with your nonsense.'

The work took four loads of hot water, each heated on the range, used until it turned the colour of gravy, then tipped out close to the hedge in a corner of the backyard. At last the final dish was dried and put away, the benches wiped down, and the tea towels hung up to dry. Grandma looked around the room to see that everything was done to her satisfaction, then went through the back door to the porch.

'Come around to the verandah, you lot,' she called, her voice easily cutting through the mix of chatter and laughter. 'We're going to have our cup of tea out there.'

Aunt Rosie hoisted Katie onto her hip. Cups and saucers were loaded onto trays, along with lemonade for the younger ones and slices of Christmas cake. Daisy was entrusted with one of the heavy trays, which took careful balancing as she went down the passage towards the front door. Long familiarity with her grandmother's house meant she knew which floorboard was inclined to sag underfoot, and the particular spot where an edge of the narrow strip of carpet had curled up, ready to catch an unwary foot.

The men had already made their way around the outside of the house, ambling along in the wake of small boys who had not yet run out of energy to dash about. Uncle Bernard had Ian on his shoulders, while Ian's older brothers were taking turns at being swung around by Eddie.

Daisy placed the tray on a small table, and found a spot for herself on one of the verandah steps, as the chairs would all be needed for the ladies, while the remaining food and drink was set out.

At the promise of cake, the ball was abandoned to roll into a rosebush while the boys lined up to be issued a slice each. They soon had crumbs (and, in the case of the smallest boys, smears of icing) all over themselves, but no one seemed concerned; their mothers had taken the sensible precaution of having them change out of their Sunday best clothes after church.

The little boys barely seemed to have noticed the heat, but Eddie had joined the men in removing his jacket, and his face had taken on a decidedly pink tinge. He took a plate with a slab of Christmas cake, and sank onto the step just below Daisy's.

At first they were both too preoccupied with the generous helpings Grandma had served them to be able to talk. Even when both slices of cake had disappeared, it did not seem worth the bother of raising their voices sufficiently to be heard over everyone else.

Daisy leaned back against the nearest wall, listening to snatches of conversation and watching the little ones as they resumed their games. Eddie rolled up his shirt sleeves and resisted all blandishments from the younger boys as they called to him and Benjy to join in.

'I can't keep up with you fellows. Anyway, I'll catch fire if I spend any more time in the sun,' he said, pointing to his flame-coloured hair as if in evidence of the danger.

There was not a breath of wind, but the verandah supplied welcome shade. Daisy sipped at her lemonade, content to sit on quietly, surrounded by her family and with Eddie's shoulder nudging against her knee.

Even Aunt Rosie's boys finally tired of running about, and found a spot to sprawl in the shade of the hedge. Katie had migrated to her father's lap and was singing bits and pieces of nursery rhymes to Ian, who was snuggled up to Aunt Rosie.

Bella looked up, alert at once to a sound only she had noticed, and went off to fetch baby Ernie, who had been sleeping on Grandpa and Grandma's big bed through all the noise and bustle. She returned to the verandah with Ernie in her arms.

The little boy had obviously woken in a cheerful mood. He gazed around at the sea of smiling faces, chortling and waving his chubby fists. Ernie already had a fine head of light brown hair, currently sleep-ruffled into tufts. Bella flattened the crest of hair on top of his head with a soft kiss, and passed him to Grandma's outstretched arms.

Ernie spent the next half hour or so being passed around from one lap to the next, laughing delightedly at each new perch. Even Aunt Sarah was prevailed upon to hold him for a few moments, and although she did not indulge in the high-pitched baby talk that the other ladies used to coax fresh giggles from Ernie, she remarked to Bella that he seemed a healthy little fellow, and certainly a cheerful one.

'He's just like the other Ernie was at the same age, isn't he?' Grandma said to Granny; of course she meant her little brother, who had died in the war and who this Ernie was named after.

'I think his hair might've been a bit fairer, but yes, this one does make me think of him,' Granny, who must be the only other person present who could remember Uncle Ernie at the same age, agreed.

Grandma's eyes seemed to have become a little misty. 'He was a dear wee fellow. Remember how I used to love looking after him when he was just a little chap? I was always asking Ma if I could take Ernie on outings, wasn't I?'

Daisy detected a hesitation before her other grandmother answered, and when her response did come it gave Daisy the impression of being a careful one.

'You were a lovely sister to him, and he was lucky to have you.' She patted Grandma's hand, smiling. 'You've always been good with little ones, Lizzie. No wonder you turned out such a wonderful mother.'

The composition of the various groups that had formed after lunch stayed much the same. The younger boys had soon had enough of sitting quietly, and after increasingly plaintive pleading managed to persuade Eddie and Benjy to join them in kicking around the ball, although their efforts were noticeably less vigorous than earlier in the day.

The men now clustered below the verandah in the shade of several plum trees. Daisy's adult male relations comprised farmers, a harness maker, and a doctor, and were perhaps an oddly assorted bunch, but they managed to find a shared interest in such topics as the weather, sports, and the local magistrate's recent delivery of a Studebaker motor car, which was rumoured to have cost him over six hundred pounds.

The women were still cooing over little Ernie, although Aunt Rosie was mostly concerned with a rather wriggly Ian. It was lovely to have a new baby in the family for Christmas, they said, kissing and fussing over Ernie, who remained a cheerful recipient of the attention.

Daisy joined Lucy and Flora in wandering among what were referred to as Grandma's flowerbeds, although it was Aunt Maisie who tended them. Grandma had said they could pick whatever they liked, and Lucy took her at her word, pressing Daisy and Flora into service helping her gather fat bunches of cornflowers and long sprays of sweet peas, as well as the snapped-off heads of several pale cream lilies. The three of them then sat on the verandah steps, where Lucy devoted herself to trying out different combinations of flowers according to shape and colour. Daisy would have been content to watch the boys playing, had she not been called upon every few moments to give her opinion on Lucy's latest bouquet.

Granny was taking a turn at holding Ernie, and Daisy was sitting close enough to hear her say quietly to Bella, 'I think he might be a bit damp, dear.'

Bella apologized profusely, and took some convincing that Granny's pretty dress of pale blue silk was not in the least damaged by a tiny patch of dampness that would easily be sponged out.

'That was the last clean nappy I brought,' Bella said, pulling a face. 'We'd better head home before he gets in a state.'

'Probably time we got a move on, anyway,' Uncle Danny said, studying the angle of the sun over the western hills. 'Mick and I'll need to make a start on the milking or we'll be doing it by moonlight.'

This marked the beginning of a general exodus of the family members who had to travel any distance. Abandoned jackets (and in some cases shoes) were gathered up, as were small boys who insisted they wanted to carry on playing. Nicky and Timmy were unwilling to part with Eddie until he gave a promise of paying them a visit before he went back to Auckland.

Lucy wrapped some of her bunches of flowers in a damp cloth to take home with her, and arranged the remainder in a vase in the parlour. There were exchanges of kisses and hugs, amidst a squirming of small boys reluctant to submit to such treatment, then the families in their three buggies set off down the track.

'You've no need to rush off yet, not with you being so close,' Grandma said to Daisy's mother. 'There's time for another cup of tea before you go, anyway.'

As Daisy's family only had to go next door, her parents agreed that there was no great hurry. Aunt Maisie went off to make a fresh pot; Granny went with her, and was back soon afterwards with a visible patch on the front of her gown where she must have sponged it down. The day was still warm enough for the signs of dampness to fade within minutes.

The garden was now a good deal quieter. There was room on the verandah chairs for all the adults, while Daisy, Eddie and Benjy shared the steps.

'Show Uncle Frank and Aunt Lizzie your nice watch, Eddie,' Granny suggested.

Eddie was careful not to take his smart new watch out on the farm, but this morning's outing to church had been a good excuse for him to wear it. He had prudently removed the watch and put it in his jacket pocket while running around with the younger boys; he now retrieved his jacket from the back of Granny's chair and took out the watch. The silk handkerchief Daisy had embroidered for him was in the same pocket; he refolded and replaced it, casting a quick smile in her direction as he did so.

He had shown Daisy his watch on the day of his arrival, but this was the first time anyone from Grandpa's household had seen it. The watch was solid enough to look suitable for a man to wear, while having an elegance of line, and even a sort of delicacy in the hands, which were in a filigree of fine metal. Its face was white enamel, with black numerals, and with a smaller dial set into it that showed the seconds. The case was gold, satiny smooth along the back and with a pattern like fine rope-work incised around the edge.

Daisy looked on as the watch was passed from hand to hand and duly admired. Benjy was particularly taken by it, and readily accepted Eddie's suggestion that he try on the watch. He tilted it to and fro to see the effect of sunlight against the shining metal and glass, then removed it from his wrist with obvious reluctance.

'It's a really nice one,' he said. 'Here, have a look, Ma.'

Grandma ran her fingers along the watch's leather strap. 'Yes, it's very smart. It wouldn't do for you, though, Frank,' she said, passing the watch to Grandpa. 'Not hanging on your wrist like that, getting caught on things. You need one you can keep in a pocket, out of the way. I suppose it's all right for the sort of work you do, Eddie,' she added, her slight frown making it clear that she had very little idea of whatever it might be that Eddie did to fill his days.

Eddie grinned at her. 'That's right, Aunt Lizzie, it suits me just fine, mucking about with books and all that.'

'And he leaves it at home when he's out chasing beetles,' Aunt Sarah said, making everyone laugh.

When the fresh pot of tea had been drunk, more cake eaten, and Eddie's watch securely fastened back onto his own wrist, it was time to go home. Daisy's mother drove the gig, Granny and Aunt Sarah sharing the seat with her, while Daisy's father rode ahead and Daisy and Eddie brought up the rear on two of the farm's other horses. Everyone from Grandpa's household came to the garden gate to see them off. Daisy waved to Benjy and the others, then turned to pay proper attention to the track.

Once or twice in the course of their visit she had been sure someone or other was on the verge of asking her or Benjy how the examinations had gone; thanks to Eddie's deft efforts at turning the conversation onto another path, she had passed the entire afternoon without having to say a word on the subject.

Chapter Twenty-Five

Amidst all the well-wishing on New Year's Day, Daisy was struck by the realisation that it was no longer "next year" she was looking forward to. It was 1924 now; this was the year she would be starting at university. As long as she had passed her matriculation, of course; but Eddie was right: it was best not to waste time and energy on such thoughts.

Aunt Sarah certainly spoke of Daisy's coming to Auckland as a settled matter.

'You must be sure to come up well before term begins,' she said one day. 'We'll want to have a proper amount of time for shopping—now you're leaving school uniforms behind, we'll need to make sure you have an appropriate wardrobe.'

'Never mind clothes, she'll need to organise her textbooks and stationery and everything,' Eddie put in.

'Of course she will, Eddie, but I plan to leave that in your capable hands,' Aunt Sarah said, smiling.

Aunt Sarah said that before she went back to Auckland she wanted to make it clear to Benjy's parents that she would be perfectly happy to have Benjy staying with her while he was at university, so soon after new year she went next door with Granny for a visit one afternoon, while Daisy and Eddie were getting the cows in for milking.

Aunt Sarah looked rather amused when she and Granny returned.

'I appear to have invited Benjy's parents to stay as well,' she said. 'Or at least to be my visitors while they see him settled in, which I imagine may take some time.'

Daisy's mother stared in astonishment. 'What, go all the way to Auckland? Ma's never been away from Ruatane in her life!' She recovered herself, and smiled. 'Well, if anything could ever have got Ma away from home it'd be checking up to see that Benjy's all right.'

'You might have trouble getting rid of them once they've moved in, Sarah,' Daisy father said, grinning. 'Aunt Lizzie won't want to let Benjy out of her sight.'

'No, Pa can't be away from the farm for too long, so I shouldn't think they'll stay more than a week or so,' Mama said. 'Anyway, they'll know Benjy will be quite all right with you and Aunt Amy.' She frowned as a fresh thought struck her. 'But will you even have room for everyone?'

'Oh, I expect we'll manage,' Aunt Sarah said. 'I'll rather enjoy having a houseful. It may mean Eddie having to sleep in the stables with the horses, but that wouldn't present any difficulty.'

Of course no one took her remark seriously, although Eddie pretended to look worried.

'Well, I'm glad Daisy doesn't want us trailing up there with her,' Mama said.

'Benjy mightn't want it either,' her father pointed out. 'He won't get any say in it, though.'

'No, I suppose not. You really don't mind about us not coming with you, do you, Daisy? I mean, you're going up there with your Granny, it's not as if you'll be on your own—and you've been there before, anyway, when you were little. So you won't be nervous or anything, will you?'

Daisy assured her that she would not be in the least nervous. She would miss her parents, of course, but that would just be one of the many new things to get used to. Asking her mother to leave the valley for any length of time, especially to brave the bustle and noise of Auckland, was even harder to imagine than having Grandma cope with such unfamiliar surroundings.

'It'll be nice having Benjy with us,' Granny said. 'It's very good that he'll be able to go to university like Daisy, with him being so keen. I must admit I wondered if he'd be allowed to, when it meant leaving Ruatane.'

'Benjy's always been good at getting his own way with Ma,' Daisy's mother said. 'But I was the same, Aunt Amy, I didn't think she'd ever agree to letting him go away like that. I don't know how he's managed it.'

Daisy kept her own thoughts quiet. She did know, and from the most reliable source: Benjy himself. Right from their earliest days at high school, he had spoken at home about the possibility of his one day going to university; at first in only the vaguest terms, but gradually and ever so delicately as more and more of a matter already settled. Benjy's stated aim had been to end by having Grandma think it had been her own idea; if he had not quite managed that, he had certainly come close.

As was her usual practice, Aunt Sarah departed for her own home early in January. She left amid vague talk of matters that needed her attention, and meetings that might be taking place soon. Daisy did not doubt that this was more or less true, but she was equally certain that her aunt must look forward to a return to her own comfortable house.

Her annual trip to the farm might be a pleasant novelty for a few days, and she always cheerfully took on whatever tasks she could persuade Daisy's mother into letting her do. Shelling peas was a common one, as it required neither skill nor great physical effort, and Aunt Sarah claimed she enjoyed it.

'It's really rather relaxing, the way it allows one's mind to wander,' she remarked one day. 'Perhaps I'd make a passable kitchen maid in time.'

She let out a laugh at the notion. 'Shelling peas suits my capabilities better than embroidery ever did, in any case. I've never had the patience to be good at that sort of thing.'

Being miles of dusty roads away from a town that itself held few of Auckland's opportunities for entertainment, helping in the kitchen, and sharing a tiny bedroom with Granny would no doubt turn from novelty to trial if Aunt Sarah were to extend her stay beyond a week or two. So she duly said her farewells, reiterated to Daisy that they would go shopping as soon as she arrived, and set off for Rotorua in one of Mr Latham's motor cars, on the first stage of her journey home.

Her aunt's departure also added to Daisy's comfort, as she could return to her own bed instead of making do with the lumpy sofa. Sharing the bed with Granny was no real hardship; as well as being so small, her grandmother was a considerate bedmate, lying very still and keeping to her own side.

When Daisy looked back on that summer, she remembered it as a golden time, with bright days that were somehow never too hot; when rain fell only at night, and only often enough to be welcome. There was ample grass for the cows, who responded by producing generous quantities of rich, creamy milk. The tall grass ripened into a hay crop so abundant that there would not be the least fear of running low on winter feed.

She and Eddie spent most of the daylight hours outdoors together. Even during the annual haymaking, when the men from up and down the valley went around each farm to gather in the crop, Granny said there was no need for Daisy to stay home, as she was there to help Mama with meals, so they were barely apart all day long.

While the haymaking was on, Daisy went out with her father and Eddie each morning. She scrambled onto dray loads of hay to be borne over to the nearest stack, slithering down out of the men's way before they began piling up the latest load, as carefree as if she were still a child. She took off her shoes and stockings and paddled in the creek, joined by Eddie when the workers paused for a rest. By the time haymaking was finished, her arms were quite brown from the sun.

At home on their own farm, when they were not busy helping with the work the glorious weather meant there were ample opportunities for walks in the bush, or up a hill to admire the view; or to go paddling in the creek, with their boots, socks and stockings left on the bank while they scrambled over rocks and waded through deeper spots, luxuriating in the sensation of cool water flowing over bare flesh.

Daisy woke each morning to a delicious sense of anticipation for the day ahead. No doubt it would be sunny again, and no doubt Eddie would suggest yet another walk. When they were out on the farm together he talked of outings they could go on in Auckland, as well as telling her (at times in great detail) about the creatures he hoped to study, rattling off Latin names and the places where such species might be found, and recounting discussions he had had with academic staff at the university.

Of course it was quite deliberate, Eddie's constant urging of fresh activity. He was doing it to keep her from dwelling on her examination results. Their imminent arrival could never be completely driven from her mind, but thanks to Eddie it remained barely in her consciousness for much of the time. This special effort on his part was not something they spoke of; Daisy was sure he must know how much she appreciated it, without her having to say a word.

In early January Daisy remarked that perhaps she should be thinking about taking up her Latin studies again; busy though he was keeping them both, Eddie actively discouraged any such suggestion.

'There'll be plenty of time for that later,' he said the second time Daisy raised the subject. 'We can always get out my old textbooks and go over them when you come up to Auckland.'

Despite a lingering fear that she would be behind her fellow Latin students, Daisy let herself be persuaded. Going back to her studies would probably make her brood over her examination results, which was no doubt a large part of Eddie's reason for discouraging it. And if she did fail, any further study would simply have been a waste of time...

But thoughts of failure were not to be permitted, especially when Eddie was going to such an effort to keep her from brooding. So Daisy's books remained undisturbed, and her days continued to be full of quiet pleasures.

It was hard to remember when she had last had a real holiday, with no pressure of schoolwork to dull any enjoyment; certainly not since she had started high school, and even before that, the war had been casting a cloud over them all. No wonder Grandma remarked on how bright and cheerful Daisy seemed these days.

'You were getting quite a frown on you for a while there,' she said. 'It's good to see you back to your old self.'

Beyond the simple happiness of looking forward to another carefree day spent in Eddie's company was something else; a feeling that seemed a large part of why Daisy so often found herself smiling for no apparent reason, but which was impossible to put her finger on. She was happy in the moment, of course, and when she let herself think about the year ahead there was the adventure of studying at university to look forward to.

But what was that other feeling just beyond her reach, retreating further the more she tried to pin it down? The sense of something on the verge of coming into existence; wholly new, and yet somehow already a part of her. When she was out roaming on the farm with Eddie, the elusive feeling danced on the edge of Daisy's awareness, sometimes giving the fleeting sensation that her world was encased in glass of an impossible fineness and clarity, suffusing her surroundings with a sharpened brightness beyond even that given by this glorious, golden summer.

The sensation was as fragile as such glass would be if it existed, shattering at a touch; to be exulted in, not dissected. Whatever the mysterious something might be, it warmed Daisy to her centre, and lent an extra lightness to her step as she and Eddie wandered the farm.

Perhaps her mother felt something of it, too; though if she did, it was as an unsettling influence rather than one that filled her with pleasant anticipation. She sometimes seemed jittery, and inclined to begin a sentence then let it trail off; she had also got into the habit of asking Daisy where she and Eddie were going, and how long they would be away, whenever they were about to set off outdoors. This was not something Daisy had experienced; or at least not since she had been small enough to be at risk of falling into the creek if left unsupervised by someone older.

'Do you want me to stay and help with something?' Daisy sometimes asked after such questioning, but her mother always said no, there was no need; Daisy should go off and enjoy herself.

'Just don't be too long,' she generally added, without being specific over what she meant by "too long".

It was a strange time for her mother to begin worrying over how long Daisy might be out; it was not as if she had any homework these days to make her have to hurry back to the house. Perhaps Mama was still a little worn out from the extra work of Christmas, and the small strain of having Aunt Sarah to stay.

Benjy occasionally rode over to spend an hour or so with Daisy and Eddie. January was more than half through when from the top of a hill they saw him coming up the track one morning, riding an elderly horse that had done good service in past years taking Kate and then Benjy to school, but which these days even Benjy could not persuade into a trot. By the time he drew up to the garden gate, Daisy and Eddie were there to meet him.

'It'd be just about as quick to walk,' Benjy said as he slid from the gelding's back. 'Still, the old fellow likes an outing every now and again.'

They helped him take off the horse's tack, then left it to graze along the fence line, knowing there was no risk that old Laddie might roam any distance, before setting off by common consent to investigate a cluster of fruit trees at the bottom of the garden.

'Wasn't Grandpa going into town this morning?' Daisy asked as the three of them ambled along. 'I thought you might've gone with him.'

'I was going to,' Benjy said. 'Then he said something about him and Joe might drop in at the dairy factory to see the manager. I didn't fancy standing around for hours listening to them talking about the price of butterfat and all that, so I thought I'd come over here instead.'

'Well, I'm glad we're more interesting than the butterfat price,' Eddie said with a grin.

One of the plum trees always had a huge crop soon after Christmas. Most of its fruit had already been gathered, and turned into jars of deep red jam that now lined a shelf in the kitchen, but enough plums remained to reward a search, especially for searchers not put off by bird-pecked fruit. They picked the lower limbs clean, then looked upwards speculatively.

Eddie, they agreed, was too heavy for the spindly branches. If Daisy had been a few years younger, she might have tucked her dress into her drawers and got him to give her a boost, but she did not suggest it today. Instead, Benjy clambered up a few branches and handed down fruit to the others, until they each had brimming handfuls. Benjy scrambled to the ground, and the three of them sat with their backs to the tree trunk, munching on the deliciously tart fruit and gradually creating a circle of plum stones around themselves.

As well as the company of people his own age, visiting Daisy's farm gave Benjy the opportunity to discuss Auckland without the risk of Grandma's overhearing; 'And getting the wind up about me going away,' as he put it. In the intervals when their mouths were not fully occupied with devouring plums, he prompted Eddie to talk about the city and its possibilities; expressing polite interest when Eddie veered onto rugby or other sports, but listening intently when he spoke of garden parties and dances, and most avidly of all to talk of visits to the theatre.

'Gee, it sounds good,' Benjy said after Eddie's vivid description of a musical performance he had attended in the spring, a drama set in ancient Egypt and with elaborate sets and costumes. 'I'd love to see something like that.'

'You'll be able to soon enough,' Eddie said. 'Winter's when they generally put most of them on.'

'I hope so.' Benjy pulled a face. 'I wish we knew how we'd done in the exams one way or the other—I'm that sick of waiting, I'd almost rather know I'd failed than keep hanging on.'

Daisy looked over at Eddie, whose expression told her that he was on

286

the verge of changing the subject, as he had so many times over this summer. She caught his eye, and sent an unspoken message not to bother. The arrival of their results must now be so imminent that there no longer seemed much point in hiding from the matter.

Eddie gave an almost imperceptible nod to show his understanding. 'Shouldn't be long now till they come out, anyway,' he said. 'You'll both have done all right,' he added before popping another plum into his mouth.

Daisy knew there was no risk of Eddie making a thoughtless remark along the lines of, 'You could always have another go at the exams.' Back when he sat his own examinations at high school that would, no doubt, have been the case, but they all understood that things were very different for Daisy and Benjy.

If it turned out that she had not passed matriculation, she could not possibly expect yet another year of people running around after her, taking her to and from town every week, and paying out large sums of money for her to sit examinations she was not clever enough to pass. There would be no second chance. Failure would mean the end of any grand dreams of becoming a doctor.

Benjy's dreams might be vaguer than hers, but they depended as completely on passing those examinations.

'No, it shouldn't be long now,' he said around a plum. 'Then I'll find out whether I'm going to be milking cows all my life.' He spat out the plum stone, which travelled several feet in a tall arc. 'I suppose I could always take Bernard up on his offer,' he added with a mock-earnestness that made Daisy laugh.

'Eh? What are you on about?' Eddie asked.

Between them, Daisy and Benjy recounted Uncle Bernard's comments on how a 'smart lad' like Benjy should be out earning money rather than bothering with school, let alone university, and his offer to 'find you something to do myself'.

'You did a good job of sounding grateful,' Daisy remarked.

'I had a beggar of a time not laughing,' Benjy said. 'I know he meant well, but I shouldn't think I'd be any better at saddlery than I would at farming.'

'Well, at least you've got that to fall back on if you decide you can't be bothered with university,' Eddie said. He ducked his head as Benjy lobbed a plum at him.

Daisy did not usually pay much attention to the mail over the summer, when Eddie was there in person rather than writing letters to her. But as the time grew ever closer when they could expect the examination results, she quietly wished the mail could be collected from the Post Office more often than once a week, as it generally was when they went into town for shopping. Often Grandpa picked up theirs with his own if he went in on a different day, but then she had to wait until he saw her father at the factory, or her mother and Granny went to call on Grandma.

Just a few days after Benjy's last visit, Daisy and her family were sitting down to lunch when they heard the sound of hooves on the track, soon followed by the click of the gate's latch. Daisy opened the kitchen door to find her grandfather walking up the path.

It was an odd time of day for a visit, but Grandpa had a particular reason, which soon became clear.

'I picked up the mail this morning,' he said when he had come inside and greeted everyone. 'There was one each for Daisy and Benjy—it turned out it was about the exams. Here you go, love.'

Grandpa held out an envelope, and Daisy took hold of it with hands that had begun to shake.

She was vaguely aware of talk going on around her. Mama asked if Grandpa would like to sit down and have a cup of tea with them; Grandpa thanked her, but said he'd better get home, as Grandma was keeping lunch waiting for him. He would have left bringing the mail till later, he said, if Benjy had not pressed the point that Daisy would be waiting anxiously for her results. Benjy had wanted to bring the letter himself, but Grandma had heard him cough once or twice that morning, and had decided he was to stay indoors.

'Benjy's done all right in his,' she heard Grandpa say. Of course she should say how pleased she was to hear that, and send her congratulations with Grandpa, as she heard the others doing. But the power to speak had deserted her.

The envelope sat heavy on her palm. She turned it over and tried to slip a finger under the glued flap, but her hands were trembling too badly for her to manage the delicate task.

'Come on, Daisy, open it so we can hear how you did.'

That was her father's voice. Daisy looked up to find a circle of faces turned on her, various shades of encouragement on each.

Along with the encouragement, Eddie's face bore a slight frown of concern. 'Do you want to go off and open it on your own?'

It was exactly what she wished she could have done, but it did not seem right to keep everyone waiting; not when they had all helped her reach this moment.

'No, it's all right,' she said. 'It's just... I can't seem to do it. The glue's sticking too hard, and I don't want to rip the whole thing.'

Eddie took the letter from her unresisting hold, picked up an unused knife from his side plate, and deftly slit the envelope open.

'There you go,' he said, handing it back to her.

Daisy let his eyes, with their steadying gaze, hold hers for a moment. Then she took a deep breath, pulled out a typed sheet, and carefully unfolded it.

What seemed a sea of text met her; words and numbers jumbled together and as meaningless as if they were in a foreign language, until she realised they were the names of subjects with marks written below each one. She stared at the page, willing it to make sense, until her eyes were caught by a large letter "M" at the end of a row of numbers.

'I've passed.' The words dropped into a room that had fallen silent. 'I've got my matriculation.'

Daisy's father engulfed her in a bear hug that lifted her right off her feet. Eddie stood back while Mama, Grandpa and Granny all kissed her and congratulated her, then when they were all standing about saying how well she had done, and joking about which side of the family she might have got her cleverness from, he gave her a kiss on the cheek.

A broad grin spread over his face. He took hold of her hand and squeezed.

'I knew you could do it,' he said quietly.

His hand was warm on hers, and Daisy felt her mouth curve into an answering smile. She had passed. In just a few weeks, she would be on her way to Auckland and to university.

Chapter Twenty-Six

Daisy had felt herself happy before; now, without even the faintest anxiety over examination results to cloud her thoughts, in the following days she sometimes found herself light-headed from the mixture of present joy and new adventures ahead of her. The weather continued to be golden, and she and Eddie still spent all their daylight hours together.

They went over to see Benjy soon after the results arrived, for mutual congratulations and a comparing of marks.

Daisy's were all solidly in the sixties and seventies, with science and English her two best; Benjy's had far more variation. He had barely scraped through in mathematics and science, and joked that he had obviously done exactly the right amount of study, with no wasted effort. At the other end of the scale, he had scored an impressive eighty-seven percent in English, which was even better than Eddie had managed in his own matriculation examination.

'Not bad for a couple of farm kids, eh?' Benjy said. He walked them to the garden gate, where they might have chatted a little longer had Grandma not called from the kitchen doorway, telling Benjy not to stand around outside in case it made the cough (which seemed undetectable to anyone but her) worse. Benjy rolled his eyes, grinned at them, and went obligingly back to the house.

Daisy would be going up to Auckland with Granny, a trip that had been arranged some time before. One of Mr Latham's motor cars was to take them to Rotorua, from where they would catch the train north. They would be leaving around the middle of February, giving Daisy a fortnight or so in Auckland before the university term began, for shopping and other preparations.

Eddie had put off making his own arrangements, unlike in other years when he had always been prompt in setting a firm date for his return. He had not said why, beyond vague comments that there was no need to be in a rush, but Daisy was quite certain it was because he had wanted to be there when her results arrived, however those results might have turned out.

Now that was over and done, he needed to set about organising his journey. It was too late for him to get to Auckland in time for the annual sailing regatta, but friends of Aunt Sarah's who had a grand yacht had invited him on a sailing weekend heading to an island north of the city, and if he left fairly promptly he would be able to set off with them. Eddie claimed to have no great skill as a sailor, and said his main usefulness was pulling on ropes and doing any heavy lifting required, but he enjoyed getting out on the water.

He and Daisy had at first both assumed he would travel by motor car and train, but a chance remark by Granny changed his mind. After visiting her brother Thomas at the Bank of New Zealand one day, she mentioned that Uncle Thomas had said their youngest brother, Daisy's Uncle George, would be taking his boat to Tauranga soon. Messages back and forth soon established that Uncle George would be quite happy to take Eddie along for the voyage, and from there he would be able to catch one of the regular steamer trips to Auckland.

'Tommy says it's a bit rough-and-ready on the boat,' Granny said. 'I expect there won't be a proper cabin, or anything like that. But you won't mind, will you, dear?'

'No, of course not,' Eddie said. 'I can sleep on the deck, if it comes to that. Anyway, if this weather keeps up, going by boat'll be better than stuck in a motor car all that way.' He grinned as he added, 'And if Uncle George decides to trust me with any of the work, that'll be good practice for going up to Kawau Island with Mr Wells.'

He would be leaving the following week, but that still gave them several more days together, and the chance to discuss the best use of Daisy's time before her own departure.

It would do no harm, they agreed, for Daisy to look over her science notes, and perhaps to brush up on her Latin.

'There's no need to overdo it, though,' Eddie said. 'You'll manage all right when you get to university. And I'll be around to give you a hand if you need it—I expect you won't, though. You'll pick it all up just fine.'

Daisy was a good deal less sure about that, and the knowledge that Eddie would be close at hand was a comforting one; especially when it came to Latin. That was the one further subject she must pass to be able to go on to Medical School, and she had never formally studied it.

When she was staying on the farm, Daisy's grandmother always spent a good deal of time baking. She did not like to get in Mrs Jenson's way up in Auckland, she said, and it was a treat for her, not really work at all. Granny was a good cook, and Daisy noticed in the days after her examination results arrived that her grandmother was baking the cakes and biscuits that were Daisy's particular favourites.

The special treat one day was a chocolate cake, its layers sandwiched together by a creamy filling and the whole topped with thickly spread icing. Eddie and Daisy licked the bowls out before the cake went into the range, and the uncooked mixture gave promise of something special. When the cake made its appearance at afternoon tea, it proved to be rich, moist, and utterly delicious.

It was so very nice that everyone had a second slice; large slices at that.

'Goodness, we've almost eaten the whole thing at a sitting,' Granny said. 'You boys might as well finish it up.' She divided the modest amount of cake remaining into two equal portions, and passed one each to Daisy's father and Eddie.

In between giving due attention to the cake, Daisy and Eddie discussed what was still to be done before she began her studies.

'I'll pop over to the university when I get home,' Eddie said after swallowing down a mouthful. 'I can pick up the enrolment forms and lists of textbooks and things, so we'll be organised to get your books and stationery and all as soon as you come up—when you're not out buying shoes and dresses with Aunt Sarah, anyway,' he added, smiling at her. 'You've pretty well decided just what courses you're going to do, haven't you?'

'More or less,' Daisy said. 'I'm not exactly sure which science ones I should take, though. There's quite a few of them, I don't think I could fit everything in.' They had pored over the university calendar together, but had got no further than agreeing that most of the subjects looked interesting, and might well be useful. 'I'd quite like to check with Uncle Richard about it—he said a while ago that he'd help me pick which ones I should do.'

'Yes, that's a good idea,' Eddie said. 'We could ride in tomorrow if you like.'

Daisy's mother had appeared to be fully involved in a conversation about Uncle Harry and Aunt Jane's latest grandchild, but she must also have been giving part of her attention to Eddie and Daisy's discussion. Before Daisy had the chance to answer Eddie, her mother cut in.

'No, you can't do that,' she said. 'It's too far for you to go on your own.'

Eddie let out a bark of laughter. 'What, do you think we'd get lost or something? It's not as far as all that, we'll be all right.'

'I said you're not to go!'

The sharp note in her voice was an unfamiliar one, and Eddie looked as startled as Daisy felt. Her father and Granny, too, turned quizzical expressions on Mama.

Mystifying as her mother's reaction was, it had come out of Daisy's musing aloud, and she felt it incumbent upon herself to soothe matters.

'It's all right, Mama, Eddie and I can probably work out what courses I should take. I don't really need to talk to Uncle Richard.'

Her mother appeared shaken by her own outburst. She glanced away for a moment, as if gathering her thoughts.

'No, I expect you should talk to him,' she said when she had recovered herself. 'Your Uncle Richard must know all about that, and I wouldn't want you to end up studying the wrong things—not after all the hard work you've done.'

She took a sip from her teacup, which trembled a little in her hand, then carefully replaced it on its saucer.

'We'll all go in together,' she said. 'Aunt Amy, you'd like to see Maudie and the girls again before you leave, wouldn't you?'

'Yes, that would be lovely,' Granny said. 'I've a letter to post to Sarah, too, I'd like to get that away so she'll hear about Daisy doing so well in her exams. And I can let her know when to expect Eddie back home.'

'All right, then, we'll go in tomorrow,' Daisy's mother said. 'We'll take the cart, so we can get the stores as well as Daisy asking Richard about all that university business.'

She glanced at their plates. 'You've made short work of that cake, but we've time for another cuppa before milking. I'll get a fresh pot on.'

'Would you like me to make it, dear?' Granny asked. 'You seem a bit tired today.'

'No, I'm all right, thank you. It's so hot, that's all.' She rose from her chair and made for the tea caddy, which sat on a corner of the bench.

Daisy took the teapot outside and emptied the leaves under a rosebush, then came back into the kitchen and carried the pot over to the bench.

Her mother took it from her with a murmured thanks, a smile warming her eyes and making her look much more like her usual self. She opened a cake tin and put a few biscuits on a plate, which she placed in front of Eddie.

'There you are, just in case you've still got some room after all that cake.' She patted Eddie's arm. 'It's very good the way you're helping Daisy with all this, Eddie.'

'Oh, she doesn't really need any help from me—she just has to put up with me going on about it.'

Eddie made light of it all, but Daisy saw a hint of relief in his eyes; whatever had upset her mother seemed, for the moment at least, to have passed.

The following morning, Daisy's father dropped the four of them off at Uncle Richard's front gate before heading towards the general store, armed with a shopping list from Mama and entrusted with Granny's letter to Aunt Sarah.

After all the help her uncle had given her over the years, Daisy had been anxious for him to know of her examination success as soon as possible. To her relief, her grandfather had decided to call on Uncle

Richard soon after the results arrived, so the family already knew Daisy's good news.

Nicky and Timmy ran around from the back garden to meet them. They led them into the house, where Aunt Maudie and the girls greeted them warmly, with kisses and congratulations for Daisy over passing her examinations.

Uncle Richard was busy with a patient, Aunt Maudie said, but she did not expect him to be much longer. In the meantime, they all settled around pretty little cane tables on the verandah.

While Daisy and her mother and grandmother sat chatting with Aunt Maudie and the girls, Nicky and Timmy took possession of Eddie, discussing motor cars and sports results, with Nicky taking every opportunity to show his familiarity with Auckland landmarks, and to drop the names of Old Boys from his school into the conversation.

'I'll be going to Nicky's school next year,' Timmy said at one point. The eager note in his voice probably caught his mother's attention; Aunt Maudie glanced over at the boys with a wistful expression, but she said nothing to dampen Timmy's enthusiasm.

When Eddie happened to mention that he was travelling part of the way to Auckland on Uncle George's boat, it was Nicky's turn to show bright-eyed eagerness.

'Eddie's going as far as Tauranga on Uncle George's boat, Mother! I could go with them instead of on the train, couldn't I?'

'Well, we'd have to ask your father,' Aunt Maudie said. 'And we'd have to ask Uncle George, come to that—he mightn't have enough room.'

'Father won't mind. Neither will Uncle George,' Nicky said, in the tone of one who could not imagine being unwelcome in any circumstances.

'We've already arranged about the motor car, and I think your father was going to book the train this week. But I must say I'd rather you didn't have to go all that way on your own again, not till you're a little bit older.'

Nicky was sensible enough not to let his mother see him rolling his eyes over her careful solicitousness. Daisy had heard from her own mother that Aunt Maudie had hoped it might be possible for Nicky to travel with Granny and herself, but they were leaving too late for that, as the university term started later than his school's did.

'You wouldn't mind Nicky tagging along with you, would you, Eddie?' Aunt Maudie asked.

Eddie assured her that he would not mind in the least, and Granny suggested they drop in to see Uncle Thomas at the bank, and ask him to send a message to his brother.

A door closed on the other side of the house, and Daisy saw an elderly gentleman, who she thought might be the minister at one of the town's smaller churches, making his way down the path. Aunt Maudie at once sent Flora off to make a fresh pot of tea, and a few minutes later Uncle Richard appeared on the verandah.

'Father, I can go on the boat to Auckland with Eddie, can't I?' Nicky at once accosted him. 'Uncle George is sure to say he'll take me.'

Uncle Richard managed to put off Nicky's demands while he greeted his visitors and added his own congratulations for Daisy. With a rather clearer explanation of the proposed journey from Aunt Maudie and Eddie, he soon said that Nicky could go on the boat, too, as long as Uncle George agreed.

Aunt Maudie also mentioned that Daisy had come to ask his opinion on her university courses.

'You three sit over here, so you can have a proper talk about all that,' she said, setting out tea things for Uncle Richard at a table off to one end of the verandah. 'I want Aunt Amy to tell us about the latest fashions in Auckland before she goes.'

Daisy and Eddie took up their own cups and plates and joined Uncle Richard. Nicky and Timmy perched on the verandah rail close to their father's chair, eager to be part of the masculine (despite including Daisy) discussion, but their enthusiasm faded when it became clear what the sole topic of that discussion would be.

'No point thinking about schoolwork until I have to,' was how Nicky summed up matters before he and Timmy went off to the backyard and their makeshift game of cricket.

Over tea and biscuits, Daisy explained that she needed some advice over her science courses, and reminded her uncle that towards the end of her fifth form year he had mentioned helping her decide which subjects would be most useful for her to take during her year in Auckland. Eddie took the university calendar from his jacket pocket, opened it to the right section and passed it to Uncle Richard.

Her uncle looked through the pages on the various science subjects, with Eddie offering input on the courses he had done himself, regarding their detailed content and how much study each one might demand.

'Yes, that all looks much as I'd expected.' Uncle Richard closed the book and placed it on the arm of his chair, then turned to Daisy.

'I know from my correspondence with other medical men that much of your first year at medical school will be devoted to science generally, rather than specifically medical studies,' he said. 'They assume their students have had a basic grounding at high school, and of course you've passed your science examination at matriculation level, Daisy, which is a fine start. But I do feel that advancing your knowledge of science would benefit you—if nothing else, it will put you on a more equal footing with fellow students who've attended more prestigious high schools.'

'Yes, I'd really like that,' Daisy said. 'I know our school's not as good as the big city ones.'

'Which makes your achievements all the more impressive, my dear.'

'I'll say,' Eddie put in, adding to the warm glow Daisy felt at her uncle's praise.

'You'll be taking Latin, of course, as it's required for your medical preliminary,' Uncle Richard said. 'As well as that, I suggest you take physics, chemistry, botany and zoology.'

'Do you think I'll really need all those?' Daisy asked.

'Well, they'll be of varied worth to you in future years—I can't say I've made notable use of physics since qualifying, for instance. But they're all subjects that will be covered at medical school, so it would be advantageous for you to be well prepared.'

'Yes, I see. I just hope I can manage to do them all properly, though.'

'Of course you will,' Eddie said. 'You won't have any trouble with them.'

'I'm in complete agreement with Eddie,' her uncle said. 'You've a way of picking things up quickly, and I'm quite sure both that and your diligence will stand you in good stead.'

Daisy felt herself blush to the roots of her hair as she murmured her thanks for such generous praise.

The three of them discussed what preparations Daisy should make before she began her formal study of Latin, with Eddie mentioning that he planned to go over the various grammatical structures with her before term started. Uncle Richard agreed this would be wise, and recommended that Daisy also practise translating a few short passages from material with which she was already fairly familiar, just to get back into the way of it.

Her father arrived with the now-laden cart, and there was a certain amount of standing about, with various members of Daisy's family saying they must get going, then someone thinking of one more thing to say.

When they did at last make serious moves to leave, Daisy grasped a moment of relative quiet to exchange a few more words with her uncle.

'Thank you for helping me decide about the subjects, Uncle Richard,' she said. 'And for all the other things, too,' she added, the words coming out in a rush. 'Helping me with Latin, and telling me about being a doctor, and finding out about the medical school and... and everything.'

She trailed off, wishing it did not sound so feeble. Uncle Richard had spent hours and hours helping her during the years she had spent in this house; perhaps just as importantly, he had taken seriously her ambition to become a doctor, when she would not in the least have blamed him for laughing out loud at her audacity. To have the encouragement of a man like her uncle had gone a long way towards making her believe it really might be possible.

To put all that into a few words was beyond her; but perhaps that sense of inadequacy showed in her face when she held out her hand to be shaken. He took it in his own, smiling at her.

'It's been my pleasure, Daisy. And the best thanks you could possibly give me is to have all the success I believe you capable of.'

Chapter Twenty-Seven

Eddie's departure grew closer, but this year the knowledge brought Daisy none of its usual weight of impending disappointment. Before the month was out, she would be following in his wake.

And still the elusive feeling lingered; the sense of holding her breath while waiting for something quite new yet oddly familiar; present, but not quite perceptible. Something that made her smile without knowing why she did so.

The only thing that came even close to clouding that magical summer was her mother's occasional odd mood. There were no further outbursts, but sometimes Daisy would sense attention on herself, and find her mother watching her thoughtfully; almost broodingly.

Such moods seemed fleeting, and the next moment Mama would be her warm self again, smiling at Daisy and perhaps bestowing a quick kiss on her forehead. She was, if anything, even more affectionate than usual, to Eddie as well as to Daisy, often ruffling his hair or giving his arm a pat as she passed his chair.

'You used to do that when I was little,' Eddie remarked one day when he and Daisy returned from visiting Benjy, to both be greeted with a kiss from Mama. 'It seemed like every time I came inside you'd say, "Have you got a kiss for your aunt?" ' he added, smiling at the old memory.

'Well, in a way you'll always be little to me—you and Daisy both—no matter how grown-up you get,' Mama said. 'That's just how mothers are.'

Granny said there was no need for her to see Eddie off at the wharf, as she would be back in Auckland so soon. On the day of his departure, she said her goodbyes to him after morning tea before setting off across the paddocks to the farm next door, where she planned to spend a few hours visiting her brothers and their families. She would be having lunch with them, and probably afternoon tea as well.

Uncle George had said they would be setting sail in the afternoon, to take advantage of the high tide over Ruatane's notoriously challenging river bar. That gave Daisy and Eddie time for one more long walk on the farm before lunch and the journey into town.

Mama did not ask where they were going, saying only to keep an eye on the time so as not to be late for lunch. When they were a short way up the hill behind the farmhouse, Daisy looked over her shoulder and saw her mother standing in the doorway, watching them. She waved to Daisy, then turned and went back inside, closing the door behind her.

They climbed higher, then paused to admire the view along the coast, as well as far out to sea where White Island had its usual greyish-white sheet of steam and ash, a sign of its constant volcanic activity. The island's cloud was the only one to be seen on a sky of pale sapphire, set against a blue-green ocean with the sunlight striking sparks off it.

A soft breath of breeze off the sea stopped the day from being too hot for pleasant walking. They followed a ridge line, each gain in height delivering a wider view of the coast to each side of their valley, till bay after bay was visible, fading off into a soft blue haze of distance.

They chatted idly as they walked, discussing the view, Eddie's upcoming voyage and what pleasant weather he would have for it, the bookshops he planned to take her to in Auckland. From time to time they fell into a companionable silence, the loudest sound the swish of booted feet through grass.

Pasture gave way to bush near the top of the hill, with scrub and low trees pressing against an old fence, the wood of its rails long worn to silver-grey. They briefly considered climbing the fence to explore the bush, but soon decided it would not be worth the effort of pushing their way through the rough scrub of this pathless section.

Instead, they crossed the ridge and made their way down the other side, their route describing a long loop back towards the house.

'I suppose I'd better get on and finish packing when we get back,' Eddie remarked.

'Haven't you done it yet? You haven't left yourself much time.'

'Well, it's nearly all done. I just have to chuck in a shirt and a few pairs of socks, I think.'

'Don't you dare go chucking anything,' Daisy said, mock-affronted. 'I'll have you know I ironed that shirt myself the other day, I don't want you creasing it.'

'Hmm, should I check you didn't burn any holes in it?' Eddie asked, stepping nimbly aside to avoid the slap she aimed at his arm. 'No, don't worry, I'll treat it as if it was made of tissue paper.'

Their meandering path led them close to the farm's old cottage. By unspoken agreement, they ambled over and climbed the few steps to the verandah, with the front door opening off it.

The rooms in this building were all somewhat smaller than their equivalents in the newer house, but the layout was recognizably much the same, with four rooms in the main section and a closed-in half of the verandah to make an extra bedroom. The house had not been lived in for years, but the wooden building was still reasonably sound, and good, dry storage was always to be valued.

Daisy's father had fitted hooks and shelves to make best use of the space. A set of shelves was loaded with short lengths of finished timber for which he had not found an immediate use but which were too good to burn; sacks that had held grain or chaff were tidily stacked along one wall, to be used at some later stage for potatoes. One room was filled with various pieces of tack that were not used often enough to find a place in one of the main sheds. The scent of old leather, and of the oil regularly rubbed into the more valuable pieces to keep them in fine condition, was a powerful presence in the cramped space.

The windows were small, and their panes of glass coated with dust. Even with the brightness of the day, only a soft light penetrated; in duller weather the rooms would have been thoroughly gloomy. Traces of the sacking that had once served as curtains still clung to the window frames in places, though most of it had long since crumbled away to become part of the dust on the windows and floor.

There was also a large quantity of dust in the air, no doubt stirred up by their feet as they wandered through the rooms. A tickle in Daisy's throat turned into a cough, and going back outside for fresh air seemed more inviting than further idle exploration.

An old plum tree stood in front of the house, its limbs twisted and covered with lichen. Its fruit was usually left for the birds, as it was easy to gather all the fruit they could possibly want from trees nearer the new house, but Daisy and Eddie managed to gather a handful each from the lower branches. They carried their bounty back to the verandah, and settled themselves at the top of the steps, carefully avoiding any rotten-looking boards. Now they had shade and breeze, a pleasant view, and something to eat.

The plums were the last of that season's crop from the old tree; small and somewhat wizened, but intensely sweet. Talk ceased while they dealt with the plums, carefully spitting out each stone to disappear into the rough grass in front of the verandah.

Daisy's legs were nudged up against Eddie's at the narrow head of the steps. She disposed of the last of her plum stones, then shifted her position slightly to lean against a verandah post so that she would not be digging her knees too firmly into his thighs.

Daisy had been born in this very house. Eddie had lived here, too, when he was small, in the days before Granny had gone to live in Auckland, taking him with her. The narrow little room formed from the closed-in section of verandah had been Eddie's in those days; years before that, it had been shared by their fathers.

She could not remember a time before Eddie. Their lives had been intertwined for almost the whole of hers; more deeply into their shared past, they were linked by the two boys who had been brothers before they became Eddie's and Daisy's fathers. Her sudden awareness of the weight of their shared history sent a small shiver through her, despite the warmth of the day.

A climbing rose had long ago been planted by Granny against one side of the house. These days the only care it received was occasionally being hacked back when it threatened to overwhelm the building. The plant had rounded the corner of the house, and now thick, trailing stems twisted and scrambled along the verandah rail, reaching close to the steps.

Every summer it bore pretty white blooms, but by now its short season was all but over. A few blousy flowers clung on, along with one perfect little bud close to Daisy's arm.

'Look, there's still a nice one left,' she said, brushing the bud with her fingers.

Eddie leaned forward for a better look. 'Mm. It'd be a shame to waste it, out here where there's no one to see. I know just the place for it.'

He took a pocketknife from his jacket, reached past Daisy and cut a stem several inches long with the bud at its tip, then carefully nipped off the thorns. 'There, that should be safe enough. Hold still a minute, I don't want to go poking you in the eye.'

Daisy held her head steady while Eddie tucked the rosebud into her hair just above one ear.

'It doesn't look silly, does it?' she asked.

'No, it suits you. It looks really nice.'

His face was close to hers as he examined the effect of the rose, his mouth curved into a soft smile. Instead of pulling away, he leaned even closer until his lips touched hers as softly as if a feather had brushed against them.

Eddie must have kissed her dozens of times over the years; perhaps hundreds of times. But not like this. Not a kiss that made her heart swell in her chest and left her short of breath; that sent warmth flooding through her as if the sun had swooped a little lower in the sky to turn its face full upon her.

He drew back, mouth open and eyes full of a dawning awareness that must match Daisy's own. For a moment she felt him waver on the verge of kissing her again; instead he resumed his seat next to her and faced straight ahead, hands on his knees.

Daisy followed his gaze, staring out towards the sea at the end of the valley. Her hand crept over to nudge against his fingers, and he lifted his own hand to cover hers, squeezing it in a gentle caress. Eddie's hands were warm, the skin dry and lightly calloused after a summer of outdoor tasks. Daisy grew aware of an almost imperceptible thrumming, like a line pulled taut in a stiff breeze. They sat pressed so close that she could not tell if it came from her or from Eddie; perhaps it was both of them.

And now it was elusive no longer, that sense of something new yet familiar; breathlessly anticipated yet already a part of her. Now it was clear and bright as polished crystal; warm as a soft flame; wholly unmistakable. It was Eddie. It had always been Eddie.

This new knowledge was still too tremulous—too fragile—to be put into words, even to Eddie. Silence held them as they sat on the old steps, hands firmly clasped, staring out at a world painted by sunlight in shades of sapphire and emerald.

The sun's position had not perceptibly changed, so it could not have been so very much later when Eddie spoke at last.

'I suppose we'd better head back to the house soon,' he said.

'Yes, we should,' Daisy agreed.

Several more minutes passed, with no movement beyond a slightly firmer grip on Daisy's hand. At last Eddie gave himself a small shake and set his feet more firmly on the next step down.

'We really had better get on, or they'll be out looking for us—it must be just about lunchtime now.' He rose, helping Daisy upright as he did so.

They set off, hands still tightly clasped, and for most of the short walk back neither of them felt any need to speak.

They were almost in view of the house when Eddie came to a halt, their entwined hands meaning Daisy stopped at the same time. He turned to face her.

'I'm glad you're coming to Auckland soon,' he said.

'So am I.'

Much the same words had already been shared many times over the summer, but now they bore a whole new significance. Daisy felt her mouth curving into a smile that matched Eddie's; a moment later he darted forward and snatched another kiss. It was over almost before Daisy realised; if it had not been quite so brief, she might have wrapped her arms around his neck and held him in place.

'Uncle George'll be sailing without me at this rate,' Eddie said. 'Let's get a move on.' He gave her hand a tug, and they marched off at a quicker pace.

The house came into view, and they were still holding hands. The thought of being observed struck Daisy with a sudden shyness. She slipped her hand out of Eddie's grip and cast a glance at the house. Perhaps that was a face at the kitchen window, or perhaps it was only her imagination.

They were met by the scent of well-cooked mutton when almost at the back door.

'Mm, that smells good,' Eddie said. 'Do you know what's for lunch?'

'Chops, I think. And apple sponge for pudding.'

'I hope there's plenty. I've worked up a good appetite, all that walking and… and everything.'

His smile was such a lovely mix of foolish and cheerful and just a little bit shy that Daisy could not help but burst out laughing. Of course this set Eddie off, too, and the two of them had barely recovered their composure by the time they walked into the kitchen.

'You two sound cheerful,' Daisy's father said. 'What's the joke?'

'Oh, nothing much,' Eddie said. 'Just Daisy being silly.'

Even the poke in the ribs Daisy gave him for his impertinence did not dim Eddie's smile. She smothered a giggle, and helped dish up the meal.

After lunch, Eddie headed off to his room to finish his packing and Papa went outside to get the gig ready; Mama was not coming into town with them, so they would not need to take the cart or borrow Grandpa's buggy.

Daisy and her mother washed the dishes while they waited for the men. Mama did not comment on the rosebud tucked behind Daisy's ear, although Daisy had seen her eyes dart to it as soon as she and Eddie entered the kitchen. She was rather quieter than usual, and seemed a little tired. Once or twice when Daisy thought she was on the point of speaking, she looked away into the distance and said nothing. But Daisy did not at all mind the silence, blithely wrapped as she was in her memories.

Eddie was soon back with his suitcase, pointedly assuring Daisy that he had taken great care over folding his clothes. Mama wiped her hands on her apron before offering him a paper-wrapped parcel, tied up with string fastened in a neat bow.

'I've made you some sandwiches, just in case you get hungry on the boat,' she said. 'There's a few biscuits in there, too—those coconut ones you especially like.'

'Thanks, Aunt Beth, that'll be really good,' Eddie said. 'I don't know what they do for food on the boat, but I bet this is better.'

She smiled at him, although she looked more pensive than cheerful. 'Have you got a kiss for your aunt, then?'

Eddie placed the parcel on his suitcase and bent down to kiss Mama on the cheek. She wrapped her arms around his neck, keeping him in his awkward leaning posture for several moments before she released her hold to let him stand upright again.

'You know I've always been very fond of you, Eddie,' she said, patting his arm.

Eddie's expression was a mixture of affectionate and quizzical, matching Daisy's own feelings. 'I know you are. I can tell by how good your cooking is,' he said; no doubt a deliberate lightening of the mood.

She laughed—just a little—and turned back to the bench.

'I'll do the last of these dishes, Daisy,' she said. 'Your father will be around in a minute, you'd better get changed. Oh, and put that pretty rose into some water first—you won't want to wear it into town, it'd only wilt.'

Chapter Twenty-Eight

Daisy climbed onto the gig next to her father, Eddie sat down on her other side, and they set off down the track, with her mother standing by the gate to wave them out of sight.

The gig's seat was a snug fit for three, especially when two of them were as solidly built as Eddie and Daisy's father, but it was no hardship to be pressed close to the two men she loved most in the world. While her father was preoccupied with the reins, she lowered her hand on the other side till it was just below the level of the seat. A moment later she felt it nudged, then stroked, then firmly held.

Their hands remained clasped until the gig reached the outskirts of Ruatane and other people appeared, working in gardens or walking along beside the road. For the remainder of the drive, Daisy kept her hands folded on her lap.

Uncle George's boat was moored at the far end of the wharf from the tethering area where they left the horse and gig. It was a small hive of activity, with men darting about loading cargo, pulling on ropes, and making all manner of adjustments to various hooks and pulleys that were no doubt essential to keeping the boat afloat; or at least to allowing it to sail at a useful pace. A knot of men working at speed in such close quarters seemed a recipe for chaos, but no one appeared to be getting in anyone else's way; they worked so smoothly, in fact, that it gave Daisy the impression of skillful performers taking part in a particularly lively dance.

She saw Uncle George himself at the centre of things, standing on a raised section of the deck surveying the activity and shouting an occasional instruction. He soon spotted them, called out a greeting in his booming voice that must carry well even in high winds, and leapt nimbly from the boat to the wharf.

Uncle George was not particularly tall, but he was broad across the shoulders. He tended to stand with his feet wide apart as if braced for any movement; no doubt from spending so much of his time on a swaying deck. A curly brown beard covered the lower half of his face, split by a wide mouth that generally seemed to be smiling. The skin on the visible part of his face had been tanned to a deep reddish-brown from his years of being out in all weathers, so that at first glance he appeared a similar shade to his crew, most of whom were Maori.

He engulfed Daisy in a bear hug, pressing her against a jacket that smelled of tobacco smoke and more than a hint of fish, then shook Daisy's father and Eddie by the hand.

'You've turned up in plenty of time to give us a hand loading, eh, boy?' he said, slapping Eddie on the shoulder. 'No, you'd best keep out of it for now, or you'll be getting underfoot—don't you worry, I'll have you working once we're underway. Let's get this stowed, then.'

He took hold of Eddie's suitcase and swung it in an arc towards the boat. 'Eh, Tama!' he yelled when the case was already in flight.

One of the young men, presumably Tama, looked up from nudging a sack of potatoes into place, sprang onto a hatch, and caught the suitcase, all within the space of a moment or two. He called out something that must have been in Maori, Uncle George responded in the same language, and the two of them threw back their heads in laughter, looking surprisingly alike as they did so.

Uncle George seemed happy to let his crew get on with things while he talked with Daisy's small group. They stood about for several minutes, discussing crop yields and butterfat prices, the recent weather, and the freight Uncle George expected to load in Tauranga for the return voyage. Occasionally he turned aside to shout an instruction to one of the crew in what seemed to be English with Maori words scattered through it, then returned to the conversation closer at hand, usually (although not always) remembering to lower his volume.

Eddie was in the midst of doing his best to answer Uncle George's questions on Auckland's likely demand for potatoes in the coming months when their conversation was interrupted by new arrivals: the whole of Uncle Richard's family had come along to see Nicky off, which meant that more greetings, kisses and shaking of hands ensued. Nicky, with Timmy close at his older brother's heels, was eager to go aboard at once and explore.

'Yes, you can have a good look around as soon as these fellows have finished loading,' Uncle George said, gesturing at his crew. 'I'll give the whole lot of you a guided tour,' he added, his tone leaving no doubt that he considered a tour of his boat to be quite a treat.

Nicky reluctantly accepted that he would have to wait to board until Uncle George gave permission. In the meantime, he stood by the edge of the wharf pointing out various features of the boat to an admiring Timmy while Uncle George looked on with amused tolerance.

'Good at climbing, are you, lad?' he asked when Nicky paused for breath.

'Yes, I am,' Nicky answered promptly. 'I can get up the really big trees on Grandpa's farm.'

'I'll bear that in mind,' Uncle George said, pretending to look thoughtful. 'I might need someone up the top of the mast if we hit any storms.'

Excitement lit Nicky's eyes, while at the same time something more like horror crossed Aunt Maudie's face. A moment later Uncle George's roaring laugh made it clear that he was not serious.

'We'll leave that sort of thing to the chaps who know what they're doing, eh? I don't want to be fishing you out of the water, boy.'

The others all joined in the laughter, although Aunt Maudie's seemed somewhat forced. While Nicky resumed his description of the boat to an attentive Timmy, pointing out the masts with an emphasis probably intended to give the impression that he would be perfectly capable of scrambling up either of them, his mother came over to Eddie's side.

'You'll keep an eye on Nicky, won't you?' she asked in a low voice.

Eddie assured her that he would, and Aunt Maudie rewarded him with a warm smile.

'It's such a weight off my mind, knowing you'll be there as well,' she said. 'Nicky's a good boy, of course, but you know how excitable boys get at that age.'

The boat would not be sailing for at least another hour, but Daisy's father glanced at the sun's angle and said that they needed to get a move on to be home in time for milking. Daisy did not particularly mind having to leave early; with so many others around, there was little chance of any further conversation with Eddie.

Eddie shook hands with Daisy's father, and leaned close to kiss Daisy goodbye. His lips brushed against her face; just a peck on the cheek, but quite enough to send a quiver through her. It astonished Daisy that no one around them appeared to have noticed anything out of the ordinary.

'I'll see you soon,' she said while her mouth was still close to his ear.

'I can't wait.' He spoke so quietly that his words came as a whisper of breath tickling her skin.

There was ample room on the gig's seat with only Daisy and her father to share it, but Daisy chose to sit close by his side. As they left the town behind them, she slipped her arm through his and leaned her head on his shoulder.

He looked over, saw her happy expression turned on him, and smiled back at her.

'It's good to see you so cheerful,' he said. 'You used to make a bit of a fuss sometimes when Eddie went off back to Auckland.'

'That was only when I was little. Anyway, I'll be off myself soon.'

'So you will,' he said, giving the reins a flick to encourage the horse to a smarter pace. 'I don't know how you managed to go growing up so fast— one minute you're my little girl, next thing I know you've gone and turned into a real young lady.'

Daisy squeezed his arm tightly. 'I'll always be your little girl, Papa. But that doesn't mean I can't be a grown-up at the same time.'

Daisy's mother was at the back door to greet them when Daisy and her father came along the path.

'You've timed that well,' she said. 'The kettle's boiling, and I've just got a batch of scones out of the range.'

The tea had been poured by the time Daisy had changed out of her town clothes and returned to the kitchen. Her father was telling her mother about seeing Uncle Richard's family at the wharf; Mama asked if they were all well, but otherwise said little.

Daisy slipped a freshly sliced scone into her mouth, soft and warm and dripping with melted butter. She closed her eyes to enjoy the sensation, and at once saw in memory Eddie's face close to hers, whispering of how much he was looking forward to seeing her again.

'Did Eddie get off all right?' Mama's voice startled Daisy into opening her eyes, but it was Papa she was asking.

'They were still standing around when we cleared out,' he said. 'They're probably sailing about now—he's got good weather for it, anyway.'

He finished his cup of tea and polished off a third scone. 'Better get on with this milking, I suppose. You want to start getting the cows in, Daisy?'

Mama broke in before Daisy could answer. 'You go on ahead, Davie, we'll come down later. Let's have another cup of tea and we can have a talk, just us two,' she said, turning to Daisy. 'We mightn't get many more chances, with you going away so soon.' She let her hand rest on Daisy's shoulder, rubbing it gently.

'I'd like that, too,' Daisy said, placing her hand over her mother's.

Papa went off on his own, and Daisy emptied the dregs from their cups outside the back door before rejoining her mother at the kitchen table. Mama poured fresh tea for them both, then sat turning her cup round and round in its saucer as she waited for it to cool.

Despite saying she wanted to talk, Mama did not for the moment seem to have anything to say. Daisy took a cautious sip of her own hot tea and began to fill the silence, at first with idle remarks about what a lovely day it was, then with talk of her imminent journey to Auckland. She would go shopping for her textbooks and other study needs as one of her first outings; Eddie was to find out exactly what she would need as soon as he got home. Eddie had been telling her about what to expect in the subjects he had studied himself; Eddie would take her across the road from Aunt Sarah's to the university on her first day. Her words were full of Eddie, she realised; and how could they not be, when he so filled her thoughts?

Her mother had noticed it, too. She stirred her tea and gave Daisy an oddly wistful smile.

'Eddie this, Eddie that,' she said. 'You've always been the same. Do you know, that was your first word? "Eddie", you came out with one day—before you'd said Mama or Papa or anything.'

Her first word. Her very language had begun with Eddie. He had been a part of her life from the time before her memories began. Only this morning had she discovered just how deep the link between them was.

That new knowledge was a joy bubbling within her, and the urge to share something of this joy with her mother was a strong one. Daisy was still searching for the right words to describe these glorious new feelings when her mother spoke again.

Mama was sitting very upright, hands folded and placed on the edge of the table.

'When your father asked me to marry him,' she began, startling Daisy with what seemed an abrupt shift of topic. She gave a little laugh. 'Well, he didn't exactly *ask* me. "I'm going to marry you, Beth," he said.' Her attempt at mimicking Papa's much deeper voice made Daisy giggle.

'Then I said, "Well, of course we're going to get married," and that gave your papa a bit of a start. "When did you decide that?" he said. And I said...' She paused, her eyes distant as she recalled the words of long ago. 'I said I hadn't ever exactly decided, I just knew. I'd always known.'

'Always known,' Daisy echoed. 'Yes. Oh, yes.' Her mother knew. She understood. It had been the same for Papa and her as it was now for Daisy and Eddie. Just the same.

'Well, next thing we had to ask your grandma and grandpa about us getting married,' her mother went on. 'I remember your grandma was a bit worried, just at first, because your father and I are cousins. But then she said it would be all right. It didn't really matter, because we're only second cousins. That's not close enough to worry, you see. Not like...' Her voice caught, and she swallowed audibly before continuing. 'Not like you and Eddie.'

A shimmer of memory rose into Daisy's awareness: of the time soon after the war ended, when the influenza epidemic had first begun to shake her sense of the world as unassailably strong and solid. Now the crystal brightness enclosing her shivered as a myriad tiny cracks formed. 'We're first cousins,' she whispered; a fact always known that had suddenly taken on a newly ominous significance. Outrage flared within her: she had heard of first cousins marrying, so it could not be against the law. Some people tut-tutted that it was not quite proper, but why should she care for that?

Her mother must have seen the protest on her lips.

309

'It's more than that,' she said, her voice very gentle. 'I mean, if you work it all out...' Again she had to pause before continuing. 'You're first cousins because your fathers were brothers, but Eddie's father and I were cousins, too. So that must make you more than just first cousins. It's more like... well, it's almost as if you're brother and sister.'

The cracks ran deeper, then joined and spread until the world collapsed into a million shards that dissolved into nothingness. Daisy sat very still, the room's only sound that of her own breathing, until her mother spoke again.

'You don't need to help with the milking today,' she said. 'Your father and I can manage.'

Daisy looked down at her lap, and saw that her mother had placed a hand over hers.

'Yes, I'd rather stay up here,' she said, distantly surprised at how ordinary her voice sounded. 'I might get my clothes and things sorted out for going away.'

'That's a good idea. Your granny won't be back for a while yet, so you can have a bit of time to yourself.'

Mama rose from her chair, slipped an arm around Daisy's shoulders and planted a soft kiss on her cheek.

'I'm sorry, Daisy,' she murmured.

Daisy managed a nod. She sat very still, staring down at her lap, and listened to her mother's footsteps, followed by the sound of the closing door.

Mr Latham's motor car pulled away from its space in front of the Post Office. Daisy's parents faded into the distance, and Ruatane itself dwindled then disappeared, the final sight of it obscured by the clouds of dust that soon rose around the motor car.

The dust meant there was nothing to see on either side, and Daisy's view to the front was taken up by Mr Latham's head, topped with a flat cap. A man from the Post Office was riding in the front with him, the two men talking away quite animatedly about motor cars and paying little attention to the passengers behind them.

Daisy and Granny had the back seat to themselves, but even with the ample space that provided, it was not long before the motor car was uncomfortably warm and airless. This February weather was far too hot; the listlessness that had made everything seem such an effort in the last two weeks must be the fault of that. She would rather blame it on the weather than on the knowledge that lay flat and heavy within her. The heat of summer would pass.

The cloth of her navy blue dress already felt limp and clammy. She would have preferred not to have chosen such a heavy fabric for the trip, but this was the darkest dress she owned, and Granny had advised her to wear a deep colour to avoid spoiling anything pale with the grime of travel. Especially on the train, Granny said. There were cinders flying everywhere, and they could mark clothes badly. You had to be careful, too, she said, to avoid getting any in your eyes, as that was quite painful.

Daisy felt a hand brush against her arm, and looked across to see her grandmother smiling at her.

'We're all so pleased you're coming to stay with us,' Granny said. 'Especially Eddie, of course—you two have always been such friends, it'll be lovely for you to spend lots of time together. He's been looking forward to you coming to Auckland ever so much.'

There were no cinders here, but Daisy's eyes had begun to sting. They had been red and swollen much of the time recently, and now something was irritating them afresh. Perhaps some of the dust from the road had crept into the motor car. Yes, that must be it.

She was not crying. It didn't count as crying even if your eyes were brimming, as long as you did not allow a single tear to spill over. Daisy stared straight in front of her, to where Mr Latham's well-pomaded hair and his large cap filled her field of view, and allowed herself a cautious blink.

'I'm looking forward to it, too,' she said, in a voice so gratifyingly steady that it might have belonged to someone else. 'I'm very lucky to be able to study at the university, and I'm going to work really hard. The most important thing for me to do is to try and be the very best doctor I possibly can.'

Author's Note

Dr Geoffrey Rice's *Black November: The 1918 Influenza Pandemic in New Zealand* was an invaluable resource in the creation of this book.

The tale of Hinemoa and Tutanekai is a familiar and much-loved one in New Zealand. There are several versions, differing in details but with a common central story. I have used the version found in Sir George Grey's *Polynesian Mythology and ancient traditional history of the New Zealand race, as furnished by their priests and chiefs*, first published in 1855.

Made in the USA
Middletown, DE
24 January 2017